Tales in Hindsight

Stories of 20/20

KL Watkins

Tales in Hindsight

This book is a work of fiction. Names, characters, businesses, organizations, places, events, and incidents are the product of the author's wild imagination and are used fictitiously. Any resemblance to actual persons, living or dead, events or locales is entirely coincidental.

Copyright © 2022 by RawEdits, Ink.

All rights reserved.

Published in the United States by RawEdits, Ink., Washington

Book design by RawEdits, Ink.

Cover art and internal images by KA

Hat symbol and rabbit are personal signatures of the author, KL Watkins.

First Edition

Tales in Hindsight

Special thanks to my friends and family and their immense amount of patience, and to everyone who volunteered their creative input. This book would not exist without you.

Tales in Hindsight

For the muses.

May they continue to whisper.

May we continue to listen.

STORY CONTENTS

In the Beginning……………………………………………..1

Dragon Empress………………………………………….. 24

Tree House…………………………………………………. 36

Under the Moon…………………………………………….78

Titan in the Walls…………………………………………..92

Legend of Manethíera……………………………………106

F.O.O.L……………………………………………………..120

Pirate of Ulíe………………………………………………138

Glory……………………………………………………….. 156

Grace………………………………………………………. 174

Cerb Mare………………………………………………… 198

Cloud Hunter…………………………………………….. 210

First Rule…………………………………………………..224

Last Call……………………………………………………247

Tales in Hindsight

Stories of 20/20

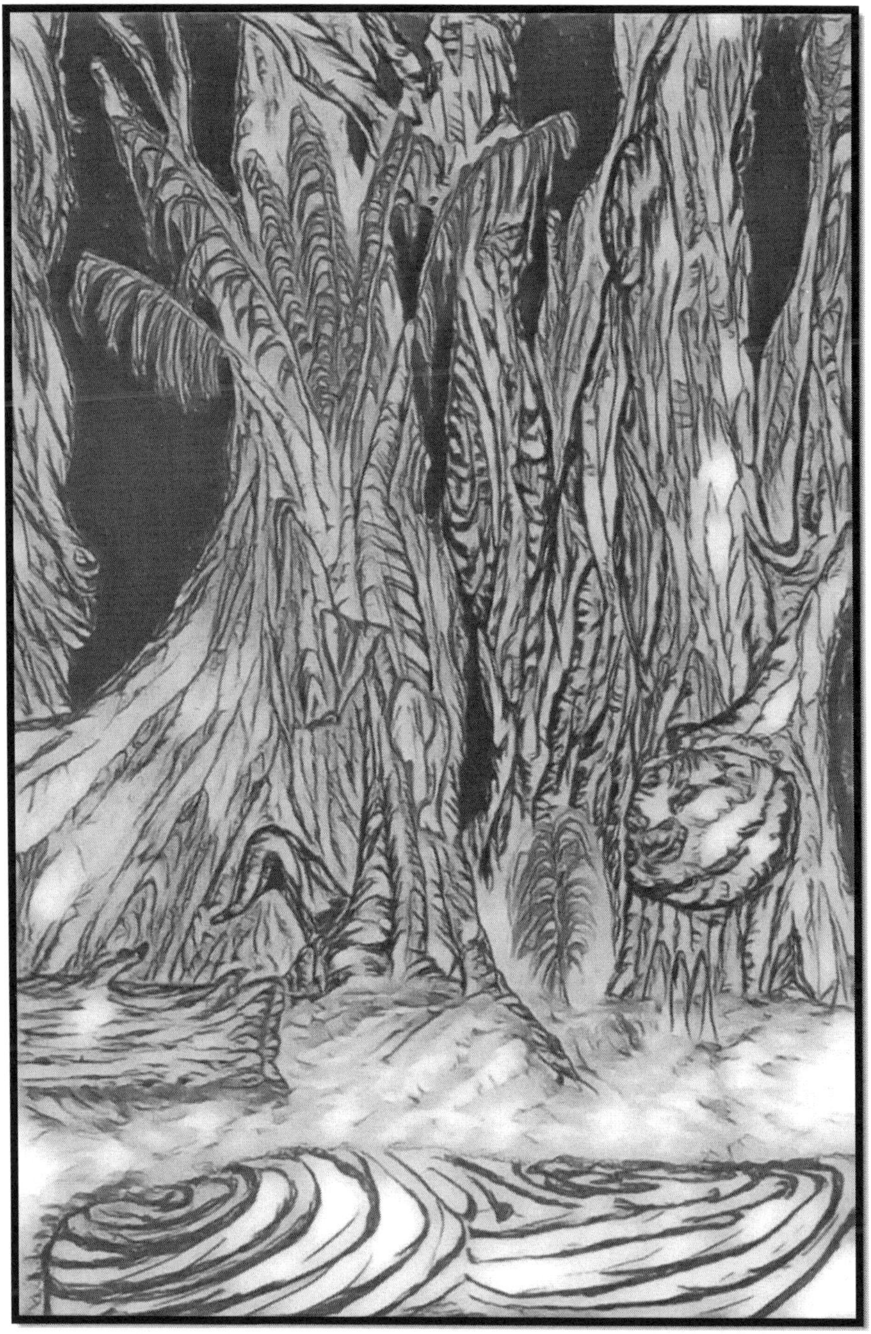

Tales in Hindsight

✨ In the Beginning ✨

All is quiet and all is dark.

Deep in a forgotten forest, in a lost hollow filled with more shadows than light, more roots than leaves, more amnesia than memory, Time stands still. If there is a sun that tracks across the sky—if such things as *sky* and *sun* exist at all—it makes no difference to the hollow. The canopy of gnarled, skeletal limbs of forgotten trees is too dense and too tightly interlocked to allow such events as day or night to leak through. The hollow is cast only in gloom and has been for a long, long time. Countless Ages have come and gone—or ever were—the hollow has forgotten the World. And the World, the hollow, in turn.

It is dark. And it is quiet.

Nothing changes.

Nothing stirs.

Almost nothing lives here save the trees without their leaves, and barely at that. And one, single soul dwelling deep under the ground where the damp, jet black soil is deepest. So quiet and so still, the great beast slumbers. Unmoved by Time, untouched by sun or fresh air that it has forgotten what they are. It moves not a muscle; it has no need. It does not eat; it does not drink. In a brumation so complete, its belly has grown cold. The only desire it has left is for silence.

Silence and sleep.

It is dark under the soil, so much more so than the hollow above. Dark and dank. Locked in the perpetual damp of the Earth, the cold is all its scaley hide recalls of touch. The sharp musk of the decay, malodorous and sweet, is the only smell to fill its nose. The giant's world is small and wrapped in a delicate bouquet of rot. Motionless for eons, alone for longer, the beast remembers nothing. Nothing but the cold, the dark, and the damp. It does not wonder; it does not dream. The old beast simply waits. For what, it does not ponder. Until the beginning—or perhaps the end—is ushered in one day by the smallest and slightest of creatures.

A single bird. One that might have passed the hollow right over, as countless others have, in need of rest from a journey impossibly far flitters down through a tiny hole in the canopy. Finding a perch upon a lone skeletal finger of a low hanging branch, that single little sparrow fills its tiny breast full of air and begins to sing.

Buried deep underground, the old beast knows nothing of the little sparrow's journey. Not where it came from nor what it looks like. Only that, for such an insignificant little thing, to burst forth such trilling notes in a place that knows only silence: pandemonium. Its dainty twittering pierces the dense soil, penetrating all the way down to ears that have not heard a sound in eons. The beast wakes. Wakes but does not stir, no matter how much this tiny disrupter may try, lighting from branch to branch, throwing its voice here and there.

Nuisance—the beast's first thought after an eternity without one. The old monster lets out a long, irritable sigh. Its belly ignites, setting loose a thin stream of hot vapor to leak up through the ground. The first sign of its existence in far too long, and Time—once again—takes notice. Change, at last, comes to the hollow.

Slowly, at first. More birds arrive. The small chirps of a single sparrow are soon overtaken by thrilling voices of warblers and raspy calls of ravens. There are sharp cries, croaks, and other ear-pinching trills of many day birds. Throaty, haunting hoots and silence shattering screeches of night birds then echo beneath the stars. Cycles return to the ancient hollow. Gentle chirpings of young soon add to the ever-present, unending choir of the adults. The noise never stops. Nor are the sounds held at bay by dirt or rock. The old beast, deep under the surface, hears them all.

More creatures begin to arrive, invited into the hollow by the songs of the birds. Creatures of all sorts. Ones that walk on four legs, others that crawl on hundreds; some that slither, sliding on their bellies along the ground; a few that leap, bounding over long spans. The hollow is forgotten no longer but found. As is the old beast, with the intrusion of small vermin that dig through the soil, their inquisitive whiskers tapping at the giant's entombed body. All the scuttering and the scraping; the thunderous running, the wayward howling; the grunts and the snorts and the cries of death—such noise! The beast moans. Wisps of its vapor wafting up from the Earth's surface becomes a regular sight, and its agitation sends deep rumbles throughout the hollow.

The old, tired beast can sleep no longer.

Its body begins to feel more than the squeeze of the damp soil, more than the tiny creatures crawling through it. Awake now, after lying so still for so long, the beast begins to ache. Yet, though its muscles yearn for movement so loathed, the old giant stubbornly keeps to its burrow in hopes that the invasion above might abandon the hollow. That is, until a whole new sound arrives. One the old monster knows will never leave.

This sound, too, starts small but is one to which all the newly colonized woodland creatures also fall silent to and listen—a hush the old beast might have otherwise reveled. Far away, and far too close for the beast's comfort, comes a simple, dull chop struck repeatedly. A rolling, thunderous crash soon follows as a tree is brought crashing to the ground. Birds flee skyward in an explosion of screams and frantic fluttering. All creatures scatter. Deep below the surface, an ancient beast lets out a mighty groan that reverberates far beyond the reaches of the hollow. The chopping continues, undeterred.

Then comes more.

Electrical whirring takes over. Trees smash to the ground as consistent as thunder in a lightning storm. A tempest, and it is coming closer. The ancient hollow is to be discovered by the only creature that can undo even the oldest of legends: Man. This is not the beginning at all. For the beast, it is the end.

It can withstand the hollow no longer.

A snort, heated from the fire ignited and churning in its stomach, sends a geyser of steaming vapor spewing up through the soil and into the air. What creatures that remain quit the hollow with haste. Brays of fright are swallowed by the sudden shuddering and quaking of earth, rocks, and roots. The center of the hollow ruptures. A great upheaval equal to the sheer enormity of its size, the beast—after Ages untold—bursts forth from its tomb. Enormous trees twisted by Time's absence snap like dry twigs. The hollow is ripped asunder.

All black, this beast. A devastating corruption caused by its long endured self-internment. Sun light let in by the destruction of the tightly woven canopy, is not only swallowed by the deep ebony of its scales but brings the beast pain as well. The old beast turns away. Keeping to the shade of the forest as best a monster of such size can, it seeks a new den. Someplace deeper into the forest, perhaps. Somewhere far from Man and his machines. A place where it may dig a new sepulcher in which to escape the growing noise. But the forest outside the hollow is alive and prosperous. So much green! Trees are younger and not as large as the ones it knew. Grown more tightly together, for a beast so large, the going is arduous. Thin, wiry branches grab at the long, curved spines along the monster's back and tangle between the horns on its head. The old beast's irritation grows.

To the South, the old legend makes its way, squeezing its bulk through the tight-knit flora and over ground dense with foliage. The air is cool and fresh and all but absent the sickly-sweet aroma of rot. It is intoxicating. So much so that when a lungful turns sour, noxious, and wholly unpleasant, the beast is brought to a sudden halt.

It comes to the forest's abrupt end. The clearing beyond stretches as far as it does wide, with the horizon in the distance, and is anything but empty. Towering higher than the largest tree, monolithic structures of iron and steel stained black and pumping out great plumes of grey smoke have been built on nearly every available patch of ground. There is hardly a blade of grass to be seen. And such noise! The high-pitched clash of glass breaking, the blaring of sirens, sharp and ear-splitting. Guttural blasts, bangs, crashes, and booms, issue from everywhere and nowhere at the same time. Sprinkled throughout it all, the constant peppering of voices: shouting, yelling, talking. Overhead, a cluster of mechanical things sail across the sky, propelled by spinning blades droning as loud as a bee—if that bee had been the size of the old beast itself.

The entire place reeks. The stink of Man and his machines and oil. The very air feels greasy. The ground is harder and blacker than stone, far more brittle, and reaching right to the edge of the young forest. How long has the beast been asleep, for Man to have invented Himself so far? With the heat in the monster's belly boiling up its long throat, the beast turns away from the city of iron and glass. There will be no suitable den for it to find here.

To the East, the massive, lithe beast roams, making its way down and out of the forest altogether. Beckoned by the alluring scent of warm waters and warmer sands, the old beast climbs the rise of a large dune covered in tall grass. At the crest, again, it is forced to stop, crushing the wispy, yellow blades under its massive bulk. Below is a long stretch of coastline. The wide beach of soft, white sand sloping gently into the rolling surf is crawling with Man. A flash of fury sparks red in the beast's eyes.

Such a bland creature, they must be compelled to surround themselves in a vast array of horded color. Their strange, upright bodies are wrapped in cloth of every hue, and they mar the pristine beach with even more as they then lay on or under colorful fabric to avoid a vibrant yellow sun still young. And their behavior—the yelling, the laughing, the shoving, and caressing—pains old ears that yearn for silence.

These, too, smell of grease. And oil. A slick sort, chemical even, perfumed with other scents that they seem eager to apply to their skin. Man's machines are here, too. Whirring motors propel all sorts of floating contraptions across the water's surface or up into the air. Yet, even with their power, none of the pesky little busybodies stray far from shore. The beast will find no room here.

To the North the old monster wanders, crossing a vast wasteland of red sand and rock. Everything is hot and parched—a devastating place for such a creature. Deep chasms promise respite in cool darkness but offer only stone of which a beast of his ilk can make no use. The open desert guarantees corruption far worse than the hardened black tar of rot the old monster's scales have already so greatly suffered. Yet, even here, where few creatures survive, where plants seem non-existent (nothing green, anyway), the old beast finds Man.

Scattered, scant, and frail as tumbleweeds, they still yell and holler at one another as they endure the desolate expanse. They have no machines, but they do have animals. Strange creatures. Curiously tall on four lanky limbs. Necks like snakes, and backs rolling with two small hills encumbered with Man's things, they passively go along led by the ropes attached to their noses. Grunting, snorting, and bellowing from time to time, the creatures are as noisy as the men leading them. The old beast avoids both by a wide berth.

Out of the desert and into the mountains the old beast climbs. Higher and higher, to a place where magick once dwelled—if the old beast could remember what magick was. Above the lakes and rivers and seas; far from vast plains of grass and acres of leafy trees; higher than the clouds, to where the air thins. Over rock and stone of a craggy mountain, to the base of a grand peak the black-scaled beast makes its way, to a wide, deep cirque mere spans below the summit. At the edge of the sheltered, bowl-shaped depression, the old monster halts.

Snow is falling. Winter is in full swing here, but it is not the snow that stops the old beast in its tracks. At the base of a sharp arête- connecting the peak's two largest horns several structures stand inside a fence encircling most of the secreted valley. Even here is Man's settlement. Puffy, white smoke billows from a square, brick column jutting up from the sharply angled roof of a large dwelling.

Animals are kept here, too. Dozens of them. Small things, as fluffy and white as the smoke pouring from the chimney, they munch contently on a layer of green sprinkled across the snow. Many have offspring, as does Man. Such noise! The bleating of the lambs, the laughing and screaming from Man's kin, all pierce the dense bone of the beast's skull. Grinding, chugging, and whirring of machines chew up the land—it's all so noisy! The red, electric fury sparked at the beach, now fans into rage. The beast opens its mouth wide. From its gaping maw it sets loose a great roar.

Is there nowhere for a beast to go? Is there nowhere not crawling with *Man*?

The old monster veers to skirt the settlement, ignoring the discord of barking dogs and Man's calls, wholly different than before, echoing off the rampart. Racing up the broken, sharp face of the mountain's peak, the beast slips over the ribbed edge of the arête and escapes the excited frenzy.

To the West, the tired old beast flees, down to where the land flattens once more. To where stone and cold gives way to lush grass and a warm breeze; to where the land ends at the rolling surf of the Nine Seas; to where Man is nowhere to be seen. Though the beast may be old, it is no fool. The soil is rich, the ocean vast and brimming with Life, the ancient monster knows Man will discover this place. He will find it, till it, sow within it his dreams. Upon it he will raise both kith and kin and bring about progress. Ships already dot the horizon. Massive ones still far from shore. At the edge of a loamy beach, the monster does not hesitate and departs solid ground for the cool rush of deep waters.

Man does indeed ride the waves. The very idea sends the beast's belly to churn with the fires of bitterness and hostility. It keeps its distance from the vessels, yet the pulsating melody of chugging engines drum into its giant body. The water around the beast begins to boil as it searches for a place remote enough where, *surely*, silence still exists, and Man does not. Deep into the heart of the Nine Seas, where the waters are deepest and a most pristine shade of cobalt blue—with not a ship in sight—the old beast, tired and spent, lumbers onto a rocky shore at the base of a single island towering above the surf.

There is not a sound save the crash of the waves upon the boulder-ridden beach. Briny winds free of soot and smoke caress an old monster's long, scaley snout. No smell of oil nor metal comes with it. A promise of warmer breezes compels the beast to climb the sharp rise of a stony cliff as black as its own scales. The rumbling purr of the sea fades. To the beast's old ears, at last, blessed silence. A wave of relief washes over the tired monster not unlike the wash of the sea against the beach below. Like the waves, that preemptive relief also recedes, just as predictably. Rising over the cliff's edge, the ancient creature is met first with the sight of great trees. Broad in both leaf and height and, crawling all about their roots, Man.

Even here, beyond means or measure, a village thrives. One built of wood and stone instead of iron or glass, but by no means quiet nor simple. The structures are squat but wide, with swooping rooftops supported by thick, ornamentally carved columns. Many structures stand on stilts, but a few sit square on packed earth, and all are decorated with flags and ribbons of every color whipping wildly in the sea breeze. Man's machines are here too. Motors, pumps, saws, and mills make light of Man's work, but bare feet, goats, and dogs provide transportation.

This means nothing to the old beast. Nothing at all.

Oh, how they start to scream when suddenly faced with a monster towering above their settlement, sending them to scatter in every direction. Such noise! The tired, old beast can contain his wrath no longer.

Anger flashes in its eyes, red and electric. The rage boiling in its belly sparks and its mouth opens wide exposing rows upon rows of cone teeth dagger sharp. The fed-up old monster unleashes a power of such antiquity that no name for it exists. A ferocity, so destructive, as to level the village in moments. The beast spares none, nor does it care for the few who manage to flee. A thriving metropolis is reduced to splintered, smoldering ruins. The island falls quiet.

Silence, at last.

※ ※ ※

Tales are funny things. They have lives of their own and, like all living things, they have ways of getting around. And get around they do, often much quicker than those who recount them. Tales can span Time in a way that no other living creature can. Never to age, only to fade should they cease to be spun, tales seek to be heard. Such is how far-fetched accounts of a mythical creature should happen to reach the ears of a most unlikely individual. An adventurer, not wholly unlike the beast she seeks though not nearly as aged. A young explorer, seasoned in ways no other can remotely lay claim, least of all those in a village at the edge of the Nine Seas through which she makes her way, one sunny, hot, boisterous afternoon.

The village is not so old. Those who lent hand in its construction still live, though aged and too frail to aid in its continuing growth. Keeping, instead, to the warm fires in taverns and inns and home hearths, they are always ready with a story or two in exchange for a meal or the company of one apparently young, bright-eyed, and curious traveller. There is a sense of freshness still about the village. The exteriors of the buildings with their low swooping rooftops are not so weathered. Flags and ribbons whipping in the air are vibrant with color and the cloth not so tattered or worn by the wind or sun.

The open-air market is a lively atmosphere not yet bogged down by routine or boredom. The vendors still shout with voices full of exuberance to make a sale. Any sale. To them, the young adventurer appears less experienced than she is. A fresh face, even if partially hidden under the over-sized hood of her long, rough-spun, wheat-colored cloak that she always wears, the hood pulled over her head whenever she is in public. How enticing her large, bulging satchel must be as she makes her way through the venue crowding the main street. Jewelers, crafters, and tailors all shouting at her the loudest—all of which she passes by. Her eyes are set for a much bigger game of far more value.

She has come far. Further and for much longer than most could fathom. Almost a story herself, Time moves differently for the young adventurer. The people she encounters, those who pass her on the street or along the roads she has walked, or at meals with whom she has shared, are as brief and blurred as the raindrops that make up a storm. They last longer only when they have a tale of interest to offer. And she has heard her share of tales; she has followed them, in fact. Tales are how she now finds herself squeezing through the noisy market of a healthy village spreading over a grassy plain at the edge of the Nine Seas.

The docks are not so crowded, but they are busy. Sailors, bargemen, helmsmen, linesmen, cabin boys, deckhands, and crew, constantly dart here and there shoring up ropes to anchor boats or relieving their knots to make them ready to sail. Merchandise is loaded and unloaded, hauled in and out of the market, along with passengers, animals, and news.

There are no engines in the village. The mechanical disease that spread across the land, without explanation or remedy, sparred not one motor or mechanized instrument. Life, however, refused to die, and neither did the demand for goods that came from shipping routes. The long-lost art of harnessing wind and work once again became new and propelled Man forward. Ships of wood could still float, and idle hands could still muscle ores, as the ship moored at the end of one dock in particular—to which the young, seasoned traveller makes her way—can attest.

A tale is what brings her here. The last in a string of many is what compels her to a certain ship ready to set sail. A tale told to her only nights before, from the mouth of an old woman as frail as the yellow daffodils perky in the cup next to her and wrapped in a black and red checkered blanket. She told a tale of when she had been young and spry, when she escaped an island deep in the heart of the Nine Seas, from the monstrous beast that had destroyed her entire village in a single breath. The young traveller listened to her tale, discrediting the details not even slightly and, after which, wasted no time seeking out and paying a tight-lipped, dispirited looking captain for passage of unique interest. In the end, it took all her coin—a bargain as far as the traveller was concerned.

Escorted aboard the ship at the end of the dock by a young lad, a compass and a rolled piece of parchment sticking out of his coat pocket and a dream of legendary prestige in his mind, the curious traveller faces the expanse of the sea laid out before her. A royal carpet of sparkling blue, she can almost see the island still days away. It is a vastly different view than when she had first set out on this path, so long ago.

There had been a forest when she began her quest, and the first tale she encountered was already old by the time she found it. A tale about a monstrous beast that rose from out of the Earth in a dark hollow deep within a forest of giant, ancient trees. The tale came from a tree harvester who had heard it from another who heard it from someone else. Already filtered through so many mouths, passed down through many generations of tree harvesters, that the tale she heard had been littered with inconsistencies, fantasies, and more than a pinch of doubt. Nevertheless, the adventurer had listened about the day the ground shook and the machines started to seize. She heard about the steam that spewed out of the Earth in a cloud, so big, that it could be seen leagues away.

It was said that the team of tree harvesters at the time—all long passed before the adventurer arrived—had already decided to quit the forest when violent eruption drew them back in. Deeper than any had ventured before, they discovered an ancient hollow too old to harvest tucked deep within densely knotted trees as tough as stone. Nothing bigger than a deer could slip through. A few harvesters did also and found the heart of the hollow freshly destroyed. It was as though the Earth herself had birthed a monster of her own making—or so the story goes.

When those original few returned, a hot tale filling their mouths, they found all the machines in the nearby villages and towns grinding to a halt. So pitted with a sudden onset of rust and corruption that no manner of labor could get them started again. With no reasonable explanation as to what had caused the rapid mechanical decay, the tales spun by the tree harvesters began to circulate fervently.

Tales of a beast and mechanical corruption took the adventurer South, to a city made of iron and glass at the edge of a forest. A dead city. One with more stories than people to tell them. A mechanical metropolis full of wonder and industry reduced to nothing more than a mausoleum of rust and ruin. Few inhabitants remained, working futilely on the seized machines. Of course, they had their guesses as to what caused the unforgiving decay—of no interest to the young adventurer. Then they had their stories, and that interested her greatly.

Those tales, too, were old, though not quite as aged as those that had led her to the iron city. Passed down from grandparents who had heard about the day the ground rumbled when they had been children themselves. They told of the day when commerce and fortune abruptly ended, when the city slowly succumbed to rot. She listened the stories of how most fled, not in search of a place where mechanical things still worked, but from the wild rumors of a monstrous beast spotted at the edge of the forest. A creature as black as the night, with eyes like liquid rubies and steam venting from its nostrils that many believed had come to torment and devour them.

Preposterous, of course, for such a creature to reduce itself so low as to eat Man. The young adventurer knew better even then, but the tales had their merit and so she had listened and so allowed them to carry her East, to a simple town of humble farmers near a coast with a perfect sandbar beach. Under a warm, clear sky, amid playful breezes rich with the scent of salt and decay, she had found more tales of this illusive creature and the destruction seemingly left in its wake.

None she spoke to had been alive to witness the event; this tale, too, was one already handed down. It had appeared one day as a great shadow that fell over the crest of the dunes flanking a once popular beach. A story of a brilliant red flash, like lightning, that arched over the dunes, that sent the people to scatter and their machines to die and rust. Their people abandoned the beach. Not only was sand no place to grow crops, herds, or children, they feared the monster that was rumored to surely eat them should the people return to their hedonistic ways. They left the beach to the beast, but the beast never returned, of that the traveller was sure. Like her, it had fled.

From there, her sensitive ears caught murmurs that trickled from the North. Across a hot, red-sand desert, her pursuit was kept alive by tales whispered from the hushed mouths of wandering nomads forever leading their grumpy camels. They did not speak much and only hinted at the monstrous serpent that their grandfathers' fathers claimed to have seen slink across the barren landscape, dragging a massive dust storm in its wake. Their stories drove the traveller up into the mountains, to settlement established generations ago in a hanging valley of a high cirque. There, in a large brick and wood home surrounded by sheep and carcasses of old, dead machines, she listened to a tale not quite so old spun by a woman of considerable age who spoke about the day of her birth.

It had been a quiet morning, the old woman told, shattered by the sudden alarm of dogs barking that drove her pregnant mother outside. Across the sheep pasture covered in snow, at the edge of the cirque, she said her mother had been met with a terrible sight: a great beast of enormous size. A serpent like no other, black as the void with red fire blazing in its ruby eyes. The terrifying monster had let out a thunderous roar that shook the dishes from their shelves, scattered all the family's sheep to the opposite lip of the valley, and caused her mother's water to break along with every machine on the homestead. Even machines brought in later were reduced to rusted scrap within days. It was as though the land itself had been corrupted.

The old woman claimed her mother's last sights of the creature had been it fleeing over the arête. So, to the West, the young adventurer followed the creature's tale. To the quaint yet bustling village by the sea that is now slowly disappearing behind the gentle wake of the ship sailing at full mast. Her face to the wind, her hood secure over her head, the young adventurer breathes deep the salty air. This is as close as she has ever come to catching the legend that she has chased over more than land, but Time as well. She is close, she can feel it.

The vessel's crew keep mostly to themselves. Too busy with ropes and booms keeping great, white sails full of wind to pay their lone passenger little more than curious glances. What they must think of her. Sailors have their own tales, too. They mutter them often, especially when they think her out of earshot. If only they knew just how acute her miraculous ears are, or when she notices their whisperings grow more fearful, the further they diverge from their habitual shipping route.

No one in their right mind goes this deep into the Nine Seas, they say, that it is a dangerous place. They speak of a monstrous sea serpent that passed through here once not so long ago; that is when, they say, the end began. Wreckages of old iron ships still partially afloat and pitted with rust, their hulls cracked and slowly leaking, gives their superstitions credence. Still, they sail on.

Leagues beyond their usual route, and days past the last sighting of a ruined ship from older times, an island appears in the distance. A large island, perched atop a dramatic cliff towering above the waves crashing over a half-sunken beach of rocks and boulders. An island densely packed with broad-leafed trees, vines, and silence. No birds ride the air or greet them with squawking. No islanders crowd the beach to welcome the two-man dingy and its young passenger rowing to shore, launched from the ship anchored in deeper water.

The closer they get, the more the young explorer can see how twisted the trees are. Their trunks look as though they have been split, root to crown, then tangled tightly about themselves into gnarled, warped versions of what they used to be. Though they stand at such odd, curved angles, their interwoven branches encumbered by large, spade-shaped leaves create a canopy as thick as the trees are tall, effectively blocking all light from reaching the forest floor.

"Why come here, Miss?" asks one of the two men, pulling back the ore in his hands as the wooden hull of the little boat slides up the pebbly bank. "This island—" he shakes his head and sucks on his lower lip. "—is bad place. *Haunted* place."

"Home to an evil spirit, they say," the young adventurer kindly picks up. "That blew in one day on the back of a tempest. A punishment sent by the Gods whom the people had angered; I've heard the tales."

The bald man, skin baked to a permanent deep brown, shakes his head, his eyes bright with as much astonishment as alarm. "Then, why go?"

The young adventurer hops the lip of the dingy. Her boots land with a shallow splash to the sturdy stone making the lip of the beach. She pays the man a final glance. "For that evil spirit, is why I am here." With smile and a firm tug to the strap of her satchel hung securely from one shoulder and across her body, she makes her way up the beach to the path leading to the green land higher still.

Nothing grows on the cliffside and the switchback path up the craggy, black stone is surprisingly clear and wide. An easy climb, and the sound of crashing waves and the more subtle splashing of oars fade away below. The dingy and its ship will come back for her, but not for many months when the ship's voyage returns from lands on the other side of the Nine Seas—she has plenty of time to explore. An endeavor that suddenly feels exceedingly monumental as she steps off the path at the top of the cliff and faces desolation.

A city once thrived here. Built from wood and exceptional craftsmanship, ruined shambles are all is left of either. The land has already reclaimed much of the once colorful island metropolis. Splintered beams and sun-bleached rooves alike are wrapped in thick, sickly green and brown, barbed vines. Grass as tall as her knees grows in bunches through the gaps between the felled debris.

All is quiet.

Where are the birds? Where are the deer, the rabbits, the crickets? Surely, there must be insects, yet the air holds only silence. It is not yet too late to recall the dingy, let it take her far from the island and leave it forgotten. But she has come too far, for far too long, to quit now. Despite her worries, and the enveloping silence sticking to her skin as thick as the humidity, she picks her way to the edge of the vandalized village to the abandoned rice fields that grow wild on its outskirts. Dozens of squared plots make for a veritable emerald mote separating a lost city of Man from the lush jungle all but consuming the island.

The hushed stride of the adventurer's boots through the grass and over damp soil is obnoxiously loud to her sensitive ears in this blanketing shroud of dead calm. Crossing into the shade-swallowed jungle is worse. Trees clustered too tightly stops the movement of air. Only leaves at the top of the canopy rattle. Closer to the ground, the air is strangled and muggy. Her skin aches with perspiration that has nowhere to go. Thorns, vines, and gnarled low-hanging limbs grab at her cloak and her bag constantly threatening to rip both away. Bulbous roots and hidden stones catch her feet. Progress is slow and the impounding quiet makes her heart yearn for company.

Squat, bell-shaped temples carved out of stone start to peek through the dense foliage the deeper into the jungle she goes. Remnants of a civilization far older than that of the destroyed city. This island is old, and Man has obviously lived here long before the chaos that rode in one day to chase them out.

Where is that beast now?

Might she not find what she seeks?

Could it have moved on already?

Without Man, and their tales of the beast, what hope has she to follow? Is it possible that she has come so far to have it just slip through her fingers?

Determination pushes her through the thick growth as much as her legs do. Arms up to protect her face from the branches and crisscrossing vines closing in tighter and tighter, she does not see the bright light of the sun until she is falling into it. The bramble suddenly giving way, the young adventurer tumbles into an unexpected clearing. Sand cushions her knees, and her hands sink into the likes of a beach... in the middle of an island jungle? A cool breeze cleanses her face of the hot, stagnate air trapped in the oversized hood still in place over her head. She breathes deeply to wash away the confining, oppressive, silent damp of the surrounding forest.

The clearing is not particularly large. Compared to the claustrophobic squeeze of the twisted growth everywhere else, however, the little glade is sprawling. Pale yellow sand soft enough to lie down on and dream encircles a pool of crystalline water of topaz blue. A temptation that, for a tiresome traveller sticky with sweat after such a lonesome journey, is too enticing. She finds it easy to relieve her shoulder of her satchel, setting it down on the sand at the jungle's edge. Her gaze on the water, she strides down the beach to the pool.

Kneeling at the edge, she sinks her hands into the water and is surprised to find it so cool. Bringing some to her lips, she drinks. Cold, fresh water runs down her throat and hits her stomach, instantly beating back the heat and quenching a desperate thirst. More water to cleanse her face, the explorer breathes deep once more. Her muscles unclench. For the first time in longer than she can rightly recall, the adventurer is alone. With no eyes to pry, her hands rise to her hood. What would be the harm? After all, there is no one else here to see her uncovered.

Her fingers on the rough hem of the hood, a sight in the pool causes her to pause. A stone's throw from the bank opposite her, two glowing orbs seem to hover just below the surface. Fish, she wonders, but the spheroidal shapes do not move, and she has never known a fish so brightly red. A sort of plant, perhaps, growing off the submerged bank. But then, they are gone, only to return in a blink. *Eyes.* A cold wave of understanding washes over the young adventurer, and mortal chill runs up her spine when the burning red orbs rise and vanish from the water without ever leaving it.

Crouched on the sand, her gaze lifts to the shadowy depths of the jungle ahead, to the pair of bright coals glowing hot and hovering much higher in the trees than the adventurer is tall. With barely time to fully grasp the terrifying spectacle, a cloud of matte-black smoke billows up through the tops of the trees. No, not smoke, the adventurer's jaw drops agape, but an enormous, sinuous body rises above the canopy. Blacker than ink, coils upon coils fill the sky, all but blotting out the sun, while the orbs remain floating in the trees, locked onto the adventurer crouched on the other side of the glade.

Finally, the monster lifts its head. Not until the gigantic, horned skull breaks free of the canopy does the adventurer realize she is on her feet. Only when the beast's muzzle cracks open and issues a gravelly snarl, is she aware that she is slowly backing away. Before she can stop herself, to remind herself why she is here in the first place, a stick snaps under the heel of her boot. The sound echoes across the glade.

The beast draws its lips back into a terrible grin, exposing a dragon's maw of long, cone-shaped teeth, dagger-sharp. "*Noisy,*" it growls, and the traveller hears.

Anger ignites in its eyes with a red flash of crackling light—it is the adventurer's only warning. The beast's cavernous jaws drop open. Her boots dig into the sand as she flees a beam of hot, white light, as bright as the sun, that flies from the monster's mouth. An ear-splitting screech of the monster's weapon fills the glade—the very weapon responsible for the destruction of the island's village.

She found it. After all this time, she found the beast of legend; the very creature that fell from a pink sky so very long ago leaving it blue. But that is another tale. For now, the traveller runs.

The loose sand makes her slow and the screeching, white-hot light bares down too quick for her to outrun. She dives into the tangle of jungle, behind an old fallen tree just in time as the beam sweeps overhead and winks out. The top half of a tall tree an arm's reach away is reduced to ash, leaving nothing to fall on her. Her ears buzzing, the adventurer dares a peek over the log.

She spots first her satchel—right where she should not have left it in the first place—at the charred edge of the jungle and remarkably unscathed. A hole as tall as she has burned through the thick, warped trees, and the lip of sand before it is as hard and slick and dull as unrefined glass. The sharp, acrid smell of green, wet wood turned to cinders stings the insides of her nose, and the thick, ashy smoke makes her eyes water.

On the other side of the pool, opposite the damage, the beast which caused it collapses to the sand. The beast is a monstrosity. A giant, serpentine body cruelly treated and twisted by Time unmeasured, it is a corrupted version of the glorious creature it once was. Its head is crowned with a pair of spiraled horns as grotesquely curled as the trees. Long, curved spines jut out along its spine from head to tail. And its eyes: polished rubies the size of the traveller's head that smolder with animosity. Only a part of its body fits in the glade, sliding across the sand and making a go for the traveller's abandoned satchel. For the beast's sake, as well as her own, she cannot allow the bag's contents to be damaged.

Now or never, she jumps from her hiding spot for the exposure of the sand. Fast as a whip snake, the beast lunges, jaws open wide. Horrific white fire smashes the log where she had been hiding to splinters, turning whatever is left instantly into ash. The young explorer runs. Her back growing hot as the beast swings its terrible electric beam after her. *Too close*—the adventurer drops to her hip and slides. The crackling beam sweeps overhead missing her by the length of a hand. She wastes no time.

On her feet, she sprints back the way she came, fiercely working her hands and fingers through old patterns she learned long ago huddled around a campfire with companions she has never forgotten. The old beast means to kill her, but she has not come unprepared, and the beast—as fearsome as it is—is old and slow. Its body is too big for the glade and turning around is difficult. For the moment, the back of the serpent's giant head is to her. Taking aim, the young adventurer throws a single burst of her own light that is not white at all, but gold.

Magick.

An old practice wielded by skilled hands still new with its use despite how long ago she learned it. The streak is no bigger than a throwing knife and flies across the pool of liquid topaz to strike the beast with precision, slicing a shallow sliver through dull black scales low on the serpent's body. A hint of pink flesh shows through.

The beast stops. Its large head swings down to regard the damage she has inflicted, and the old monster snarls a thunderous growl the shakes the glade. The beast draws its massive, square muzzle up and back. Its red eyes spark crimson lightning as they lock on the adventurer once more. Its jaws open wide, but this time the youthful explorer is ready. She bolts as the hot, electric white fire explodes from the giant's maw.

Quick along the sand to the jungle's edge, to a sturdy tree she leaps. Her feet hit the trunk and run upward a few strides before pushing off into a back flip over the crackling white beam that passes underneath. The tree is cut in half. Most of it burning away instantly as she lands on the sand and sprints back the way she came, to the bank opposite her unguarded satchel. The ear-splitting shriek of the beam goes quiet as the old beast pursues her as fast as the small glade allows. The young adventurer tosses two more shards of dazzling gold, grazing the monster's belly and neck, to make sure that it does.

Directly across the pool, the beast locks her in its sights, its mouth already agape. When the beast fires, not only does the young adventurer expect the attack, but she charges to meet it. She leaps directly into the beam's path, drawing a panel of transparent gold across her body no different than a soldier would a shield. Magick collides. Blasting, chaotic white hits the immovable shield of gold and is reflected to the beast that sent it. The explosion is so hot that steam fills the clearing. Mixing with the acrid smoke of burnt vegetation, vision of both girl and monster are clouded. The old beast's jaws snap shut.

Wet sand is there to catch the adventurer's boots. Her shield evaporates and she tosses another shard of gold. This one flies to the base of the beast's head. Wrapping around it once, the shard darts back to the sand at her feet, yanking the beast's neck down with it. The great serpent falls with earth quaking force. If birds did reside in the enveloping forest, they would have taken flight with the resounding crash. The young explorer holds her ground.

"Noisy thing," grumbles the beast in a voice so low that its pursuer can feel it in her boots as well as in her wonderous ears. "Uncaring destructor."

"Noisy? *Me?*" the adventurer retorts, pointing one long finger at her own chest before sweeping it to gesture at the surrounding jungle. "I am not the one who caused all this damage." She kneels before the giant's great, blackened head, her voice turning soft yet firm. "I found you by following tales of the destruction that *you* left behind. Seems to me, the noisy one here is *you*."

To this, the beast gives a noticeable start, but it does not lift its enormous head from the sand even though her magick shards that brought it down have dissipated. Its eyes—darkened to obsidian now, with only small sparks of yellow flickering within—track the damage to the jungle before settling, once more, on its young, uninvited guest.

"You mean to vanquish me then?" the beast growls. "Well, get on with it, mighty hunter. Bring me the peace of eternal silence."

"I did not come to end you," she ripostes. "In fact, I have tracked you through the Ages to bring you a gift."

Her satchel is damp and coated in sand but undamaged. She leaves the beast to retrieve it. The beast does not move. Nor does it when she returns. From the bag, the young adventurer removes a large shell that curls in on itself on one side. Out of rolled folds of the shell, she extracts a thin, glass vial half full of a brilliant white substance.

"This is scale from your own kind—the last of it. May remember who and what you are."

Unafraid, she lifts the beast's muzzle and pours the whole of the vial's contents into its mouth.

The change is subtle at first, but instantaneous: the beast's eyes clear. No longer bright with fire or rage, they soften to the color of rich soil flecked with bright bits of blue, green, and gold. Life returns to a thing so ancient. Memory returns. The beast is not a raging monster at all. Once upon a Time, it had been a *dragon*.

"What are you called?" the old dragon asks, its deep voice more of a hum now than a thunderous rumble.

The young traveller takes hold the hem of her hood and pushes it back. Long, thick, red-brown hair cascades down her back. Freed after so long, her large, pointy ears rise to their full height and twitch, glistening with fine fur of the same color. Her eyes are a similar earth brown as those of the dragon, and they sparkle with delight.

"I am Ophelia."

"You are not of Man," replies the dragon in surprise that, at last, lifts his head from the sand. "*Wildling.*"

She nods. "The last of my kind."

"Or the first," the dragon rumbles, deep and warm.

Feeling stronger, the dragon lifts his head higher. Sun light strikes his face and bathe the crown of his skull. His twisted horns straighten and shorten. They remain spiraled, but not grotesquely so. The spines along his back are beginning to fade. Soon, they, too, will be gone.

"A wildling who wields magick."

"An old magick," Ophelia returns with a pleasant smile.

"Very old," agrees the dragon. "And quite new. Is it your wish to learn more?"

"What is your wish?" she asks instead, climbing to the top of a tree cut to a flat stump—a good place to sit. "Now that you know yourself, is silence still what you desire?"

With a snarl, the old dragon turns his head. His scales, blackened by loneliness, despair, and dead soil, are brightening to the sparkling white they once were. "I wish now for company. There is much I can teach one who is willing. Will you sit with me?" asks the dragon, pulling his coils in more comfortably around him. "Will you listen to my tales?"

The ship which brought her will not return for many months more—not that Ophelia ever planned on leaving this island on it anyway—she has nothing but time. On the flat top of a fresh stump, cold now of the fire that had cut it, she sits, her legs drawn up and crossed. With his spines all but receded, his color more opalescent with little black remaining, and an audience willing to lend an attentive ear, the dragon spins tales of his own. Starting where all good tales do. In the beginning...

Tales in Hindsight

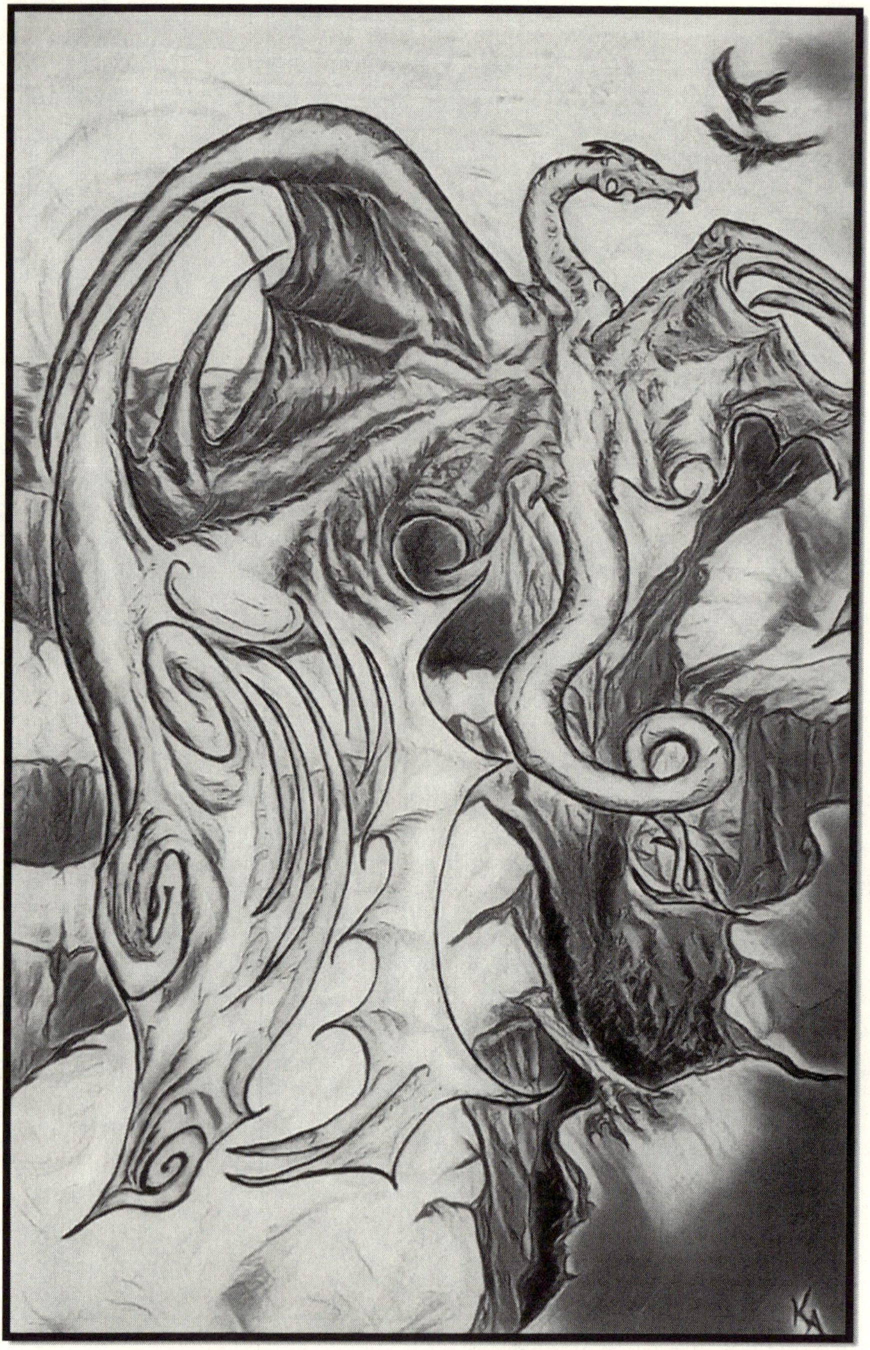

JANUARY

✦ The Dragon Empress ✦

It is the banging of hammers.

That is the sound which draws the huntress and her clan out from the trees to the wide stretch of open ground flanking the sheer drop off cliffside. The sky is still mostly purple and pinks but won't be for much longer. A great sun is on the verge of cresting the western horizon—it was not always so. Glorious and orange though darkened with age, it is an old sun. Its rise will banish the deep tones of night for a muted, shadowless glow of a clear day. And in that magical moment between the dark and the dawn, when all night creatures have settled in to sleep and those that live for light a mere breath from waking in turn, when all should be quiet and still, the sounds of labor can be heard. Axes chopping, saws sawing, and hammers slamming nails home echo up and down a vast plain of short grass at the edge of a cliff; it is the unmistakable sound of labor.

For the huntress and her clan, such clamor can only mean one thing: men. And she finds them, half of a league from the sharp drop-off where solid ground gives way to open air and a maddening mazework of stone cliffs, ravines, and slot canyons that crack the Earth as far south as the eye can see. Scores of men. All hard at work constructing several great catapults fit to take down a giant; they give away their intentions entirely. A dragon has been spotted in the area. That very rumor is what brings the huntress and her clan to this place, also. Where there is a dragon, there is coin—and reputation—to be made or lost; dragons have grown scarce these days.

With a dull burst of burnt ochre, the great sun breaks the dark line of the west—was not always so. Light spills over the men on the field sending each to scurry like cockroaches. Dropping their tools, they rush to either load each catapult, stand ready at the release levers, or huddle in the spaces in between and out of the way.

"This is a large group," speaks the huntress's second, his approach to her side silent as a breeze. "Larger than most. Either they' are desperate or—"

"They are backed by coin," she finishes for him.

He snorts his contempt. "I hope it's the former," he nods to the squadrons of armored men maneuvering into place spears long enough to be flagpoles. "For their sake."

A good man, her second, and her most trusted. His shaggy dark hair, bright eyes, and olive skin that casts him as both dark and light: he can blend into any crowd in any region. Only the gold strips of plated armor inlaid in his dark green trousers set him apart from the commoners. As with all the men in her clan he goes bare-chested. Unlike the others, his forearms are encased, from elbow to hand, in gauntlets of polished gold. A special design of articulating plates allows his wrists to move unhindered and protect his hands while leaving his fingers free. Level-headed, but somewhat of a showoff, he has been by her side since the beginning. She has only ever called him by one name: True.

"If not," he says through an easy grin, feeling her stare. His gaze drifts across the twenty or more catapults of various styles littering the field, all made from and armed with the trees this army chopped down under the cover of night. "I will gladly take my payment from *their* hides."

The threat makes her smile. He will do no such thing, not while she is around, but the sentiment is one she understands and his charm she admires.

The world slowly brightens as more of the great orange orb emerges from the horizon. Soft light glints dimly off the soldiers' armor, but not off that the huntress wears. The gold and silver articulating plates that cover her seductive frame from neck to toes, and the finned helmet upon her head, glow as warmly as a fire on a cold, dreary day. She is a sight to behold and the shuffling work on the field stalls. Many heads turn: she has been spotted, and not by only the army.

Two men stand apart, closer to the tree line. They turn to take in the sight that has captured the attention of the men on the field. One of them is obviously part of the army ambling about their tasks. With his armor of a heavy, silver steel, polished and scuff-free—unlike the rest outfitted in less attractive, brutish iron—this man is of much higher rank. His plump companion is dressed in a long, plain robe of fine brown fabric, expertly woven, and leather sandals on his feet. Their secretive parlay comes to a halt when their eyes, too, fall on the gang emerged from the trees led by one relatively small woman in full-bodied armor fit to perfection—she knows the sight she makes.

"What brings you out to such flat ground, so early this day?" she asks first, as is her right.

"It is no concern of yours," comes an irritated snap from the man wearing armor. A proud man, bare faced and bald headed, with deep creases around his eyes and on his forehead. "Good Lady," he adds in afterthought. He attempts a bow, but his chest piece is too long and crowds the range of motion around his hips. "There are many thieves about, sire." These words he directs to the man next to him with only a slight twist of his head, unwilling to take his eyes off the woman.

The second man clearly has never experienced a single physical battle of any sort in his life. Doughy and soft and expanding at the middle, his robe hangs over his round frame with little form below an impressive stomach. The dome of his head is bald and smooth while a ring of dull brown hair, cropped short, encircles the rest of his head down to the nape of his neck. He has all the appearance of a humble monk, but the huntress is not fooled. This man reeks of coin.

"This is a business matter," the man in robe regards her for the first time. "One already hired out, I'm afraid."

"Is that so?" she returns, understanding the man's intent full well. They have both judged her correctly and where one is threatened, the other has just proposed an opportunity, should certain circumstances arise. "What sort of business is that, to involve catapults and an army dressed for war?" she asks but already knows the answer.

"Dragonscale," speaks the robed man, as blunt and rich as his attire.

As she expected, and so allows a glimpse of false surprise to show on her face. "Dragonscale," she repeats sourly, portraying the ridiculousness of the very idea.

"Yes," replies the man who is most certainly not a monk.

"How much?"

"Half a single vial's worth, at least."

She laughs incredulously. "Half a vial's worth of dragonscale that you expect it to be collected at *dawn?*"

"Yes!" shouts the armored man. He has had enough, and his bellow once more draws the attention of his men on the field. "At *dawn!* I will get that vial of dragonscale and anything else this man wants from the dragon *my* men are about to take down."

The soft rumble of laughter from her own men echoes faintly behind her. She gives no response outside a mirthless chuckle of her own before turning her face to the man with whom she is interested in speaking to.

"I can get you the vial you need. At sundown. And for double the rate you've already offered."

The armored man begins to protest, but the robed man, with one hand on his purse, dismisses him with a wave from the other. "Dragonscale is what I want, and dragonscale is what I will pay three times the previous arrangement for. I don't care who delivers it or how it's procured."

The challenge is set, and the woman from the forest nods.

"The bargain began with *me*," roars the man in bulky armor. "And it will be completed by *me*."

"How, exactly, do you expect to catch a dragon at dawn?" the huntress addresses the blowhard a final time.

In the time it takes for him to ferret out an appropriate reply, one is given for him, far in the distance. A haunting bellow rides the air straight from the rising orb in the west. Life on the flat expanse is brought to an eager halt. Anticipation has all eyes transfixed on the sky in the direction of the call though the beast who issued it is still obscured in the orange-yellow glow of the sun.

The armored man raises one steel-sleeved arm, one finger pointing toward the sound. "*That* is a dragon, is it not?" He speaks as though the resonating cry of a dragon on approach is proof enough of his already coveted success before swinging the same finger to point at the face of the woman who dares to challenge it. "*You* and your men will *not* interfere. Keep back and watch what a real army can do."

The robed man says nothing, but his eyes are set in agreement. The huntress concedes and takes a few steps back, her rabble giggling and conversing quietly amongst themselves. Sitting in the grass, they are relaxed. Several content themselves with tying up long strips of cloth with branches and sticks; they know their time is coming. The huntress alone remains standing. Her hands resting on her hips, she looks out across the field. The army of men in cumbrous iron armor like metal fishbowls, scurry like fry in a pond under the sudden the dark shape of a giant predator.

The appeal of hunting dragons at dawn is apparent, materializing as a dark horizontal slash across the lowest edge of a burnt-orange sun on the rise. Still plagued by night's chill, the dragon is flying low and closing fast. Cool mornings such as this lack the thermals needed to lift a creature so massive higher into the sky, to where the air thins, and the dragon can suspend itself under its own power. Above the clouds, a dragon will spend most of its life in safety. But, when they return to the ground to nest, even a slight morning chill will keep a dragon close to the ground until one, or both, warms up. A low flying dragon is an easy target—for fools and the foolhardy. The huntress is neither.

Under the shouted commands of their ill-fitted armored leader, the catapults are cranked back and locked into ready positions. The dragon, black as coal, is close enough for a guttural growl to roll across the land like distant thunder. *"Fire!"* their leader shouts, and the order is repeated down the line to the first armament in the dragon's path just as the beast comes within range. Then, working back the way the order came, the catapults are released, one by one.

Spears fly first, driving the gargantuan beast lower and so shortening the range of motion for its impressively long wings. Harpoons with ropes attached are launched next, but too late. The broad, curved heads of the harpoons bounce harmlessly off scaly hide, and the ropes catch nothing. The nets are the last and on point, but the dragon has been pestered enough. It whips its barbed tail suddenly to one side, smashing the stoutly built catapults to splinters.

The dragon turns. It wheels around in a wide arc to face the pestering swarm of armored men it would have otherwise been content to fly harmlessly over. A hollow rush of air being drawn into lungs, each the size of a small hut, is the beast's only warning. The dragon stretches out, its wings reaching high. With a powerful downstroke, its neck long and low, a stream of liquid fire is expelled from the creature's nose, covering man and catapult alike in a sticky substance that ignites. Everything is engulfed in flames.

The huntress knows that a dragon's fire can even burn on the surface of water; that nothing can extinguish those flames until the sticky substance burns away. Blazing bits of debris bounce off the dragon's tough hide to rain down on the men lucky enough to escape the initial blast. Many are lost. With a final gale kicked back from the dragon's massive wings, the fire fans out and the beast dives over the edge of the cliff and out of sight.

The thing about dragons is that they tend to nest where the flight path to leave it is along a flat draw with enough space to pump their wings and stoke the boiling inferno in their bellies that keeps them aloft in frigid skies. Any discharge will keep the beast low to the ground, if not land, until their stomachs make more. This dragon is old, and it is spent. Slipping over the edge without hesitation into the tight, confining mazework of jagged cliffs and deep ravines is evidence that the creature has long established routes here. The huntress smiles.

A single step forward is all the signal her clan needs. They are on their feet and moving with no time, and not a single movement, to waste. The man in robes watches, amused yet with an air of boredom and impatience growing on his face. The leader of the decimated army remains indignant. He does not want to look at her, but the huntress notices his fragile sideways glance.

"Let us show you how this is done," she says with a smile bright in confidence without a touch of warmth.

For such a petite woman, she commands the attention of all who have survived the terror that she coolly pursues with elegant grace. Her group is the best at what they do. They have hunted together for a long time and ravines are nothing new; dragons crave confinement. Giving orders is not necessary. Dividing themselves, half of her team use much smaller grappling hooks than those employed by the army to swing across the deep canyon, to the next isolated plateau. The other half stay on the mainland and take off at a run, moving parallel to the plateau the others have swung to, heavy bundles of coiled rope hanging from their shoulders.

Dragon wrangling is an art. It is the finesse of it that attracts the beasts in the first place. Voices drive dragons away. So, for the few calls her team needs to coordinate, whistles are issued instead, and long-established patterns periodically fill the canyons with the sounds of birds. More grappling hooks are thrown across the ravine, the ends of which are attached to the coils of rope her hunters remove from their shoulders and lay on the ground, the attached sticks and branches poking out in every direction.

The huntress makes for the cliff's edge where her second stands at the ready, the end of a rope anchored high on the flat plateau on the other side of the canyon in his hand. She does not think twice about taking the rope, nor does she question the security of its attachment, the huntress simply steps off the edge. A short, fast drop and the rope pulls taught. She swings over clouds pooling above the darkness below and around the bladed edge of the towering island of rock before pitching upward to where another of her clan is there to catch and pull her up safely.

The stretch of ground her team has chosen is a good one. Long and relatively flat, the plateau is not wholly unlike the deck of a ship. On one side, the canyon is a wide-open maw with plenty of space to accommodate a creature as massive as a dragon. On the other, between the plateau and the mainland, the ravine is straighter but much narrower. Pinching so close near to where the huntress stands that the dragon will be forced to rise. Beyond that, a vast labyrinth of wide, crooked, and twisting canyons offers plenty of avenues a dragon can get lost in. But first, it will have to clear the narrow slot.

She listens to the whistles carried on the breeze, short and snappy. Then, they go silent: the guidelines are set. Blinds are simple devices and could never hold a dragon, but when dropped correctly they will drive one onward and prevent it from landing. She dares not wait long, her chances of luring it back diminish with each breath.

Calm and steady, a wise huntress always checks the setup before she springs the trap. The cracks in the rock, the lines in the cliff face on either side, and across the complex system of expansive voids; she looks over it all. Especially a withered trunk of a once gigantic tree that catches her eye. Felled long ago, before the ground cracked and canyons formed, it spans a narrow bottleneck to an adjacent plateau.

She turns away. The huntress is ready.

Facing the direction in which the dragon fled, and the descending line of her clan perfectly positioned, she raises her hands to cup them around her mouth. The huntress calls two long, drawn out notes, *"Sol-aye!"* Her voice rings out, bouncing her song off the sheer, black stone face of the canyon walls. Then, her call echoes back, but it is not hers at all. A deep roar answers, reverberating through the rock as much as the air—the huntress can feel it in her feet. The dragon has heard her.

"Sol-aye!" This time the mirrored call comes from a clanmate, furthest down the line: the beast has been spotted. Now, to make it rise. The huntress makes her call once more and the response is almost immediate: the dragon is being drawn to her now. Whistles ring out, the furthest guideline is pulled, and the first curtain of sticks tied along a

length of rope drops with the dragon's passing, closing off any retreat. The huntress has only moments now, and no second chances.

One by one, her clan is on the move. As the blinds drop, they race the cliff's edge, marking the progress of the beast flying still out of sight below. They are closing their distance to her fast. Why does the beast not rise?

The closest of her clan pulls their line and begin to run; the huntress is out of time and the dragon is out of space, yet it will not break cover. *But it must*, she thinks, her eyes locked on the darkness below. The canyon will grow too narrow for the beast. *Yet, its roost is this way.* Such a massive creature, jet black from tip of beak to tip of tail, and old... and sighted only recently? The way it slipped so assuredly over the edge into the hidden mazework of slot canyons and ravines, that the huntress, at once, makes a calculated judgement. She digs in her toes and, with all her strength, sprints for the fallen tree bridging the chasm to the neighboring clifftop. The sound of True calling the only name he has used for her reaches her ears as she races for the next edge. Explanations now are impossible; she must make this count.

The gap here appears too narrow for a dragon of this size. *But maybe*, she thinks as she makes for the chasm. *Maybe it is only narrow close to the surface.* Then, solid ground disappears from beneath her feet. The huntress plummets into inky darkness. Fog envelops her. Light fades. Wind roars in her ears as it slips unimpeded over the slick curves of her helm and plated armor not wholly unlike that of a dragon's scaley hide. She can almost hear the creature's breath. She feels its heartbeat pulsating with excitement. The sky vanishes, but the huntress has no mind for it as the shadows of the chasm abruptly turn solid black.

* * * * *

The giant sun is near its apex when the huntress's clan returns to the charred remnants of the army's lost battlefield. The glow cast by the orange orb may be warm and casts few shadows, but it darkens the faces of somber men, nonetheless. One group is without their leader and the steel-suited commander of the bedraggled army is as smug and sour as ever in the face of a victory he did not earn. "Where is your huntress?"

True is the only one with a calm and relaxed demeanor. "She will be here," he answers serenely, his eyes pinned to the south.

The commander puffs, the robed man sighs, and all the soldiers remaining turn their defeated gazes to the blackened ground. The forest clan, too, seems to wither under the weight of quiet unknown. True knows better. He, more than any other, knows who she is. He will wait.

A dry chuckle, meaningless and guff, at last escapes the commander's throat as the sun passes its zenith. His mouth opens as if to speak when his words are choked off by a deep, yearning call emanating from somewhere under the orb's dim radiance. All who can, look, as the dark silhouette materializes far in the distance of the pale, blue-gray sky. Raven black and increasing in size with every down stroke of its massive wings, there is nothing speedy about the dragon's return to the field. Hope blooms, and the hard faces of battered men softened with child-like curiosity. Ignoring the looks of shock and aww, and the utter disbelief of an ego-tarnished commander, True simply waits, a peaceful grin on his face.

Flying in slow and low, the dragon comes to hover over the field. The beat of its wings drives gale-force winds to keep it steady. Anyone standing is pushed to their knees, and those on their knees cower to the ashen ground, their arms covering their heads. Fully warmed now, the dragon bobs steadily, letting its hind legs stretch toward the Earth. With a final deep, rich call that resonates deep into the bones of all present, the creature's enormous leathery wings lift it skyward where it may soar for days.

"This one will not return," comes a strong, feminine voice. All heads turn to find the petite woman covered head to toe in sleek, silver and gold metallic plates. Under the ruddy glow of a dying sun, she shines radiantly. "It will find a new roost and your army will have to find new work."

"Empress," True speaks first, bowing his head over a bent knee.

She tips her head to him in mutual respect then turns to address the man dressed in rich brown robes that now appear pathetically dull. On his knees, his eyes are on the thin, glass vial in her hand, full of fine, feathery strands of glittering white.

"Dragonscale," speaks the Empress of Dragons. "One vial, full."

The man who looks like a monk takes the vial with trembling fingers; he has never seen so much at one time.

"It's not so difficult," speaks the Empress, recognizing the look of astonishment. "If you bothered to understand them, instead of kill them."

The robed man says nothing but unhooks his fat purse and hands it over knowing full well that, had he brought more coin, he would have paid it just as readily. The commander looks much smaller in his bulky armor and his mouth is clamped shut watching her toss the heavy purse to her clan with little concern. Each of her people in turn dip into the bag and hurl a single coin each to the broken men of the ruined army who pounce upon the scraps like starved dogs—like herself, her clan hardly needs the money. With her people in tow, the Empress retreats into the trees knowing full well that none who have witnessed this day shall soon forget it. Then she wonders how many more will be joining her.

Tales in Hindsight

Tales in Hindsight

FEBRUARY

✧ Tree House ✧

Is this right? **Dutch wonders, staring at the words on the work order.**
Sure, the boss is prone to sloppy handwriting sometimes; more than once he has had to ask for clarification on the old man's scribbled gibberish. Except, this time, the black ink scrolled in a man's blocky hand is clean and legible. Tree House. So clean, so neat. Hell, Dutch has half a mind to consider if Gina, the old man's secretary, wrote it herself. But those bold, solid lines… It is obvious that the relaxed hand at work had belonged to a man, and old Charlie's calloused mitt has been the only man's hand to have written so much as a single word on any work order.

Has Dutch ever seen the man relaxed enough to pull off such a feat of penmanship? Back in the day, maybe. Back when Dutch had still been a young, prepubescent buck on summer break from school and working for his Pop in hopes of earning enough cash for a bus ticket to any place hell and gone from this town (look how great that plan turned out.) *Old* Charlie had been just plain *Charlie* back then, and Dutch had a different name, too. Dolores had still been alive, and TerAvest Landscaping had been a thriving new business—not to mention the only in town. *Just* Charlie, along with two close friends (and Dolores, of course) had been the sole employees. Charlie *had* been relaxed back then, even smiled on occasion. A bittersweet thought. When it quickly sours, Dutch returns his attention to the invoice in his hand.

In the top right corner, where the date of hire is usually stamped, Dutch finds none. Just a blank field. His eyes drift close and an irritated hiss escapes between his clenched teeth. Really, he shouldn't be surprised. Back in the day, sometimes relaxed and wholly plain Charlie also had the bad habit of not stamping dates on open work orders. Gina, initially hired on as an accountant, had put a stop to that. No one is quite sure when Gina climbed the ranks to secretary except that, at some point, no invoice moved in or out of that office without passing her scrutiny first. If anyone had known when that official transition occurred, that would have been Dolores and she has taken the answer to that bit of trivia to the grave. One decade later—and one funeral too damn late—Dutch finally got that bus ticket he had wanted. Another decade more and Dutch is back, eyes darkened, and soul tarnished, but with strong hands aching to be useful once again.

Returning to the comforting embrace of familiarity had been an easy decision. Adjusting to the slow life of this seaside town, however, has proven to be more difficult. He had hoped to find joy, but now Dutch is willing to settle on losing the nightmares. Old Charlie hasn't exactly made the transition a smooth one, either. That tough, potbellied, bald-headed hound dog can have a good mean streak when provoked. He did not like it when Dutch left, and him with four green hires fresh out of high school looking to earn a little cash for a bus ticket to somewhere other than here. Tender-skinned fingers and weak backs to boot. Delegating Anthony to hand him an invoice that pre-dates the Gina Era and sending him out to a property on the furthest reaches of city limits—where clearly no one lives—is nothing more than the old man's revenge.

Turning off his truck, Dutch reads over the invoice again.

TerAvest Landscaping

SUBJECT: Tree House   DATE:

SERVICE REQUEST: Weed and vine removal. Tree trimming/removal. Lot leveling and general cleaning. Project to be completed by any means necessary.

CLIENT: County Commissioner
Payment upon completion.

Even the hand-written address at the very bottom is perfectly legible. Right on top is the circular, red seal for TerAvest Landscaping, freshly stamped—one of Gina's procedures to mark a new job as 'opened' to be signed with her initials when completed. That seal was all Dutch had seen at first, when Anthony shoved the paper into his hands and relayed Charlie's orders to *"get this one handled."* He had already fought with the old man the night before and, not in the mood to deal with him again so soon, Dutch had settled for his habituated glance to the bottom of the paper and punched the address into the truck's GPS. A forty-five-minute drive then brought Dutch to the last exit on the outskirts of town for a nondescript dirt road off the highway—Branch Street, how fitting—and steered the truck along a rut-filled road under a thick canopy of the trees, so tall, that all but blocked any view beyond. He had parked right where the little red pin on the GPS indicated his destination should be—smack in the middle of a green field spanning for miles—and turned the key to kill the ignition before looking at the invoice again.

Dutch grew up in this town, knows it like the back of his hand. He only used the damn GPS to log the miles for work purposes—also a new practice for TerAvest Landscaping instilled by Gina when old Charlie acquired company trucks (along with a ball-and-chain loan to get them) and their use had to be carefully documented. Had Dutch not been so stone headed and bothered to properly read the invoice in the first place, he would have shoved it right back into old Charlie's wrinkled, bear paw of a hand and wouldn't have left the office at all. Dutch chuckles: if he wasn't hell and gone from all things civilized, he'd almost be grateful.

Progress seems to have reached even this sleepy, seaside town. All thanks to the county's procurement of hectares of fresh ground along the city's outskirts, ready to be broken for development. Sure, most of the buildings shine with new paint and the iron mill has been refurbished and is running better than ever, but much of wholesomeness he remembers feeling as a kid has been lost. Now there hangs a sense of commercialization over it all, and the town absolutely pulses with anticipation of an influx of new money.

Yes, progress has touched everything. Except here. Here, along a forgotten dirt road, an ancient contract stands open and—as far as Dutch can ascertain—has yet to be started, let alone completed. Behind the truck, to the right of the bumper, a flimsy, orange, plastic stake pokes up from the soil four feet from the road. It's one of Charlie's, a relic from the days when the old man used them to mark properties of active clients before the implementation of the stamp and initial method currently in place. Hell, Dolores could have staked that marker herself and, if the wall of growth beyond the stake is anything to judge, her eyes may have been the last to see this place.

"It's payback," Dutch nods and speaks to no one except his own ears. "That's what it is. The old man hates me."

This can't possibly still be an active client. Can it?

With no good excuse *not* to—and certainly in no hurry to return to the office and the snide laughter surely awaiting him there—Dutch opens the door and slides out of the truck, leaving his phone and the metal box with the workorder clamped to the top on the bench seat.

What he mistook for a dense hedge towering over his six-foot two-inch frame, obscuring anything that may lay behind it, upon closer inspection he finds to be a wrought iron fence instead. So encumbered with vines as big around as his thumb, limbs of stunted trees with thick strands of old man's bread hanging in clumps pushing through from the other side, it is not until his face is inches away does Dutch spot the bars all but consumed by the thick bramble. No wonder he never knew about this place; it hardly looks like a *place* at all.

He strolls along the impenetrable barrier. His eyes so engrossed in the lush tangle of green, bemused by the sheer density and looking without much effort for a passage through, that when good habits cause him to look back, he finds the truck has shrunk in the distance. *This is ridiculous*, he thinks, slowing his pace to a lackluster stroll. This could go on for miles. Hell, would he even be able to tell when the fence ends? An exasperated snort out his nose, Dutch turns back and is immediately startled. A gaping black hole ripped right through the dense jungle of vines stares back, opened wide like a cavernous, gaping maw of a gigantic monster. Dutch's feet turn to cement.

He can see how he missed something so alarmingly obvious: the gap in the barrier is off set. Tucked back at an angle, hidden from the road, the opening had been invisible until he walked past it. A deep breath calms the pounding in his chest.

"An illusion."

The shroud of thick tangle curves over a splendidly twisted, black barred gate standing slightly ajar. The space beyond is as black as the void. Though the gate is open, when Dutch lays a hand on one of the bars, he can tell that the gate is solidly grounded. Its hinges might be rusted beyond repair. Maybe the tangled growth or the sheer weight of it crushing down on every side have caused the gate to seize. No matter how Dutch tries to muscle it, the gate doesn't budge, but thanks in part to working a long-standing trade as a landscaper, he is still blessed with a physique not much changed from his athletic, teenage years. Slim and strong, his frame just squeezes through the opening when he turns sideways, with hardly a smudge on his grey tee-shirt or the flannel hanging open, unbuttoned, over top.

The dark canopy is comprised of the lush limbs of elm and cherry trees tightly woven together. In full green but no longer in bloom, what space there is between their branches is thick with spiderwebs, as is the narrow path leading through. Many are very much face-level and an image of his ballcap still sitting on the hood of his own truck back at the office, where he had swatted it down in irritation, pops into his mind. Now he wishes he had grabbed that instead of storming off as he had. Thankfully, the dense growth proves to be surprisingly shallow. Five or six strides of his long legs relieves Dutch of the cold, inhospitable shadow and back into the brilliant sunshine of a warm morning growing late under clear, blue skies. The rest of what he finds is not so inviting. From a gloomy tangle, he is popped straight into the strangle-hold of wild growth blanketing the vast, open stretch of a treeless estate.

Dutch blinks once—twice—yet the visage remains. The sweet aroma of cherry blossoms fills his nose making his head light and pleasantly dizzy. He breathes deep before remembering that there are no blossoms to smell, yet the sweet perfume does not abate. The sprawling, rolling yard is covered in woody-stemmed long grass, as tall as his thighs in places, and all of it gone to seed and browning. Here and there, however, Dutch spots signs that this was not always so. There are gaps and noticeable curves in places where he can almost see rectangular garden beds lined up in a row. Instead of herbs or vegetables, dandelions and dead nettle run rampant.

Nestled close to the thick tangle of trees and blackberry bushes against the estate's western edge stands a house. *A house? Hardly*, Dutch scoffs to himself. To call that structure a *house* would be akin to calling the ocean a lake, even if it is chock-full of scum, algae, and a host of other molds and mildew marring the surface. Mansion is a more appropriate word, and one that appears as ancient as it does monumental.

How has he never known about this place? How many summers did he spend riding bikes and venturing deeper into the woods than he or his friends should have, and not one glimpse of a gargantuan house hidden amongst the trees? Of course, there had been rumors of a witch who lived somewhere nearby, but what neighborhood full of kids doesn't? Hell, Dutch told a few himself! But none of the stories ever made mention of a house, and a colossal one such as this would certainly have made boyhood news. This—Dutch shakes his head—this is like finding a secret estate belonging to the Rockefellers (one they clearly forgot about) and him with all the legally binding permission to wander about as he pleases. It's enough to make a man wonder.

There must be a lot of money tied up in a place like this. If the county hired old Charlie to clean it up, then he likely stood to make a financial killing, even years ago. So, why is the old work order still open and the property, well, like *this*? Could the place still be occupied? Dutch shakes his head again. Impossible. No one could live here; this place has not been touched in decades. A faint path of two narrow lines hints to where a regularly used driveway once connected the road to the house, yet no car or truck has come or gone in years.

His gaze sweeps over the house. A cold, windless chill tickles the back of his neck. He hears nothing. No birds, no crickets, only the whispering hush of air. Dutch might as well be the last living thing on Earth. He should go back to the truck. He should start the engine, drive back to town, shove the workorder back into Anthony's hands, and drive the hell back out of this town where he never should have returned. But he can't. A determined sigh dispels the icy tickle prickling his skin; the day is too perfect to listen to fears and Dutch is not leaving until he gets a closer look. Hell, he has nothing left to lose, and so follows the faint path through the tall grass heading for the house.

※ ※ ※

On a couch, in a room too cavernous for a sole occupant, a woman lies asleep wrapped in her warmest flannel blanket. Enveloped in a fuzzy field of vibrant red and black squares, she is locked in a deep sleep blissfully unaware that she has lost her place in the book that has fallen closed on her lap. The book is not the type she is accustomed to. The type she tends to stay away from, in fact, but it happened to show up one day, leaning against the solitary tree standing twisted and tall in the solarium. The book, like the tree, are oddities that shouldn't be, but exist nowhere else. She had tried not to be taken in by its cover. Resisted cracking open the jacket for a tempting peek inside, but the sharp claws of intrigue already had her in its grip. Even then, she made it wait.

For days, she left it on the table an arm's reach from the single couch in a room that could have held dozens comfortably. And what a table. Unlike the woman or the book, the table is the one piece of furniture that belongs in the room, and there will never be another like it. Once a burl of fantastic size, its top was sanded flat generations ago and polished to provide enough space for a large family to sit around without even an accidental elbow touch. Below the smooth surface, the rest of the burl tapers down to several strong, curled tendrils holding it steady. Other than some minor yet necessary shaping to make the surface usable, the ancient piece of wood is untouched.

Throughout the base are visages of all manner of beasts intricately intertwined as to seem a part of the wood itself. Several birds, squirrels, and one rounded backend of a beaver, its paddle tail just cresting into view on one side, were all once living, breathing things—or so the story goes—that had become trapped and forever locked in this state. It is a story the sleeping woman has heard since she was small. A large portion of the base is a single feature: a claw nearly the length of the woman's arm, wickedly curved but coming to a harmless point. A dragon's claw, her mother used to tease, of some reckless beast that held on too long.

Such stories used to be so easy to believe. They made the choice to remain behind an easy one. Look at her now. Alone on a lone couch in a great room that once hosted elaborate masquerade balls but has not had more than a single occupant for longer than she can rightly tell. At some point, those stories turned to poison. Fairytales became make-believe only meant to confuse and coerce and distract from the work needing to be done. There must always be one to keep the House going, and when there is only one, chores stack up; she simply lost the time for such stories. Soon, she lost Time, altogether.

Sadly, the table is proving itself to be more resilient than she. Days passed after the others left. Months, and longer. The woman felt herself growing slower, weaker; she grew tired. The House turned monstrous as her living space within its walls grew smaller. Once the grounds became too much for her to handle, she stopped going outside. She forgot about the seasons; inside the surrounding grove they never changed. Day and night meant nothing; inside the house, conditions never changed. That was when the cracks started to show. One may keep the House standing, but one hardly fills it when there used to be so many. Now, the walls have grown cold, and the massive roof is getting heavier. The House has become little more than an empty shell. Should it all come crumbling down, will the table still stand? The woman has wondered, more than once.

Damage has never shown in the great room before. Then again, she rarely leaves her little apartment behind the kitchen these days. When the last time she had, she could not recall if she tried. No more than she could explain why she did this time only to find the wondrous glass panes making up the bubbled-out wall of the solarium, faded and murky with grime and the western wall cracked. A fissure had opened the wall from the floor to very near the ceiling. She had turned away from the sight, choking back hot tears when her gaze fell onto the grand table, still polished and solid and, on it, the book of tales she had refused to acknowledge since she found it however long ago. Discovered anew for the second time, its bright cover as colorful as her dreams overtook memories too painful to recall.

It felt good to pick the book up: solid and smooth in her hands and brimming with potential. The way the spine cracked when she opened it, so fresh and new, as though her hands had been the first to have done so. The smell of the paper trapped inside beaconed her fingers to turn the first page, then the next.

A book like this did not belong in her little apartment. The very thought repulsed her. So, finding her flannel blanket already on the couch, sitting down and wrapping it around her shoulders had been as easy as slipping into a hot bath. Her feet abandoned the floor and her woes over the neglect slowing consuming the House faded to distant recesses in her mind. Tucked into the corner of the couch, the woman who had sworn off such fanciful tales obeyed the pull of the those contained in the book. She sank into the cushions as did her mind into the wonderous worlds held in ink and type just waiting—*craving*—for her to decipher them.

A fire in the oversized hearth would have been nice though one had not been lit there for years now. Wrapped in her blanket, the faint aroma of smoke seeded deep into the fibers from the countless fires that once did warm the House, she had almost believed the hearth held one more. She could almost hear the crackling of the wood as she sank into the first story. The room seemed to brighten as the world outside turned dark. The stars came out and she with no desire to see them. The crystal scales of the extravagant chandelier hanging above her glittered with light from a fire that she did not light. The moon may have come out, she never noticed. Her mind drifted, leaving the place she had sworn to maintain for a world where dragons roamed, where warriors chased them in hunt for a prize desperately coveted.

She had not felt her eyelids grow heavy. She never noticed the warm lure of sleep pull them down. Snug in the embrace of the couch and blanket, sleep snuck up on her. For the first time in what could have been years, could have been eons, the great room, and the solarium with its single, standing tree, had company over the course of the night.

❈ ❈ ❈

The grass, though tall, hardly impedes his stride as Dutch cuts across the wilds of an otherwise grand lawn separating the castle of a house from the woods. With every step the house grows. The whole thing damn near fills the skyline. Dutch must tilt his head up slightly to take in the sharp angles of the multiple, dramatic pitches that gives the roof the appearance of a distant mountain range. A curious design. The architecture is like nothing he has seen before. More stone than wood here, more wood than stone there; the house belongs in a story of its own. One that would take a lifetime to tell.

Ribbed pillars of white stone hold up a great slab of dark marble that not only cloaks an absurdly large entrance and doorway but is the only part of the roof that is flat, save for a slight downward angle. Shade is all the fills the space underneath that could hold a dozen elephants stacked two high. Scattered over the chaotic field of pitches and eves, slender, vertical pipes poke out of the roof. Vents, Dutch figures. There is only one chimney, and it is unmistakable. Practically large enough to be a smokestack for some gothic industrial plant, it is built like a campanile with the sharp angles and steeply descending sides of a medieval church, and host to several smaller steeples surrounding its base. All that's missing is the bell at the top.

The mastery in architecture is a wonder all its own, it is also dilapidated. The whole mansion, in fact, looks... wrong. Where there are no obvious signs of there ever having been a fire in its past, the impression that there had been—and a bad one, at that—lingers. Two-thirds of the otherwise expertly crafted brick, wood, and glass appears to wilt. It sags with a relenting breath of abandonment. Despite the warmth of a perfect day, gooseflesh breaks out along the skin of his arms. A structure like that, he thinks, would most certainly be condemned by the city no matter how grand—and suddenly the work order makes sense. But that was years ago, long before Dutch quit this town the first time. So, why is it still open? The money alone to tame an estate like this—Dutch is hard pressed to picture old Charlie turning away from such profit. His brow creases, one eyebrow cocked at the peculiarity of it all. That the city, or the county for that matter, hasn't pushed harder to get it done is just as idiosyncratic. All of it leads him to one conclusion, the only one that made any sense at all: The house is still occupied.

Looking down the length of the mansion, back the way he had come, the southernmost third of the house does not look so despairing. The exterior is filthy but sturdier—nothing a good wash and a fresh coat of paint couldn't cure. A fantastic bubble of bulging glass and iron framing caps off that end of the house. The exterior is caked with grime, but every pane is intact, and some are even clear at their centers.

Several strides before the solarium, Dutch notices a door he had not before. A white door, plain and simple, that looks more fitting for a back porch of a country farmhouse than the long, wilting, eastern face of a foreboding, gothic monstrosity built for giants. The round copper knob he imagines would fit nicely in his hand. He can almost smell the warm, yeasty aroma of freshly baked bread just pulled from a hot oven, or the savory, salty goodness of a beef stew that has been simmering for hours. A moment lost in fantasy before wondering how long it has been since he last ate.

He takes in the whole of the property, and the grounds that are clearly too much for a single caretaker to handle, once more. With no signs of tools or equipment—or vehicles, for that matter—there is no evidence that a caretaker even exists. But an empty lot this size could not survive alone; there must be an occupant living here. The window at the top of the cozy little country door is small but clear, and the short curtain covering it on the inside is pristine white. Out of curiosity or compulsion—he can't decide which—Dutch is compelled to approach. The copper knob is worn smooth and tarnished from a lifetime of use. There is no sign of a deadbolt or any sort of latch, yet Dutch gets the distinct feeling that, should his hand take to the knob, he would find it locked.

Should he knock? Would someone answer? No one can possibly live here, and yet the urge to touch the door is overwhelming. He lifts his hand to… do something. *This is crazy*, he thinks, his hand hovering between knocking and just grabbing the knob. An agonizing decision, though he can hardly say why. Then, the decision is made for him.

❀ ❀ ❀

There had been a shadow outside, she is sure of it. Though she cannot say that she *saw* anything, Ara had been asleep, but something bigger than the usual bird had moved across the glass walls of the solarium. She *felt* it. It is what woke her. Ignoring the cramp in her neck that sleeping on the couch often brings the following morning, Ara is quick to her feet. The book, forgotten in her lap, slaps hard against the wood floor with the silence of the blanket immediately to follow. She blinks the heavy drag of sleep from her eyes and listens. Quietly she stands, waiting for any sign of, well, anything.

It is bright inside the house today; it isn't always so. Empty as usual, but there is a fine, electric current in the air. A certain heaviness hangs over the room, a hush, as though the house itself holds its breath in hopes of not being discovered by uninvited, prying eyes.

The glass panels making up the solarium are bare and unobstructed save for the mildew creeping in along the edges she pretends to not see. Though made of the finest glass money could buy, providing a clear view they do not. The egress of geometric patterns and designs recessed in multiple layers with the thickest part at the center of each pane, and any visage—either in or out—is blurry and warped even on the brightest of days. Designed to catch light, not to showcase, they turn any view into a smear of color and shadow. Though the smudged image of the encroaching grass and trees is the same, with hardly a leaf out of place, she is sure *something* passed by.

Have the vultures from the city returned to circle her once more, looking for signs to start landing and take test nibbles? They haven't been by to harass her into selling in, well, she cannot be certain how long—Time has lost track of her, she can feel it. Besides, city officials on the snoop are never this quiet. There had been no sound of an engine nor car door, no smell of exhaust. There are no voices, no rustling of paper, no careless footfalls—is the House finally starting to play tricks on her? How long *has* it been since last she saw another living soul? Could the others have come back for her at last? Impossible. They wouldn't be coming in from the outside.

Her answer comes with hardly a stir in the descended quiet. A shadow, for sure this time, darkens the light behind the white lace curtain covering the rectangular window high up on the only door left to the outside world. Finally, with something tangible to focus on, she crosses the room before realizing that she has taken a single step. The copper knob is cool in the grip of her flushed hand. She twists hard and yanks back even harder, and the man she finds standing there, just a short reach away, appears just as startled as she.

He is tall. Six feet if he's an inch; her eyes come level with his chest. Broad shouldered and tapered waist, he is well-toned and fit almost to the point of wiry, with taut muscles to rival athletic men in their early twenties. His long face, however, is aged with more experience than some fresh, young buck. His brown eyes are bright and sharp and burdened with some sort of unshakable sadness. His sharply inclined nose is livened by a playful thin goatee encircling the thin lips of his mouth. His angular jaw hangs slightly agape in boyish befuddlement at finding himself face to face with someone he, too, had not expected to find. Ara's surprise evaporates and, instantly, she becomes wary.

The jeans he wears are faded but the fabric is unblemished and made to withstand rigorous outdoor labor. His loose-fitting denim shirt is clean and hangs open exposing the white tee-shirt underneath. If his clothes weren't warning enough, his boots give him away dead to rights. How *stupid* of her. To think the county had stopped sending their hounds to sniff out if she still held her ground or not. She has grown soft. Slow. Complacent. As if the grounds weren't proof enough of that already. Only seconds have passed since pulling the door open on this dashing smuggler and her wariness is burned away. Now, she hates him.

Well, he's seen her. Seen that she does still stand in the way of progress. Ready to slam the door in his face, he suddenly smiles. A grin of such charisma and charm that her grip on the door's edge goes slack.

"Hi." His voice is clean and crisp with all the sweet, smoky warmth of toasted honey. All she needs to do is to swing her arm and that voice, that grin, will be gone, but she can't. When she doesn't answer, instead of fading, his smile only grows wider, warmer, with a gentle glee that brightens his dark eyes—eyes that have not yet strayed from hers, yet.

"Do you live here?" he asks.

Dumb question, and she allows the thought to show readily on her face.

The corner of eyes squint. "Dumb question. Right." His charm is as thick and sweet as a dark rum and just as intoxicating. The fact that she has not immediately chased him from her property is worrisome, and yet the door remains open.

"Look, I'm—"

"Trespassing," she interrupts, the spell finally broken.

"She speaks."

She blinks. Heat rushes to her cheeks and her heart is beating faster; if he is from the county, they have sent their best. But this is not the first scoundrel she's encountered, and not likely the last; she will not be so easily seduced. Quickly she regains her composure in hopes of keeping that blush from showing.

A dismissive cough and he finally breaking his gaze to absently survey all the house's interior that he can readily from his place outside the door. "Do you live here alone?"

That does it. She needs no further proof and the invisible string holding her back finally snaps. "Did you bring an actual workorder to clear me out this time, or did you drive hell and far simply to traipse about my property looking to make a name for yourself?"

Maybe it was the sound of her own voice, so strong and firm after not having heard it in so long, that gives her a molten rush of courage. Maybe it was the flash of concern, brief but genuine, that crossed his face under his brow slightly furrowed that sparks a surge of rage. Either way, this scoundrel has overstayed his unwelcomed visit. If there is one thing she knows about scoundrels, it is that the longer they are allowed to work their magic, the harder it becomes to cast them out.

"Hear some stories, did ya?" she goes on, watching the bigger man shrink back, little by little, away from the door. "Grew curious from the rumors? Feeling lost and confused about your own life that you thought a stroll through the House of Legend, where a family has suffered far more than you can imagine, who sought this final refuge only to be ostracized, that it might bring you some desired clarity? Or are you here simply to do someone else's dirty work and line your pockets with thirty pieces of silver?"

"What?" he manages to mutter. "Thirty...? Silver? You mean like Judas? I'm not—" he fumbles for words. "I mean, I didn't—"

He is right where she wants him: on the ropes and ready to run with her poised to strike. He goes silent. Shaking off the mocked hurt screwing up his face, he lifts his empty palms in surrender. "Look, this got really rocky, really fast, but I think I can clear all this up. I do have a workorder. It's in the tru—"

"So, you *are* with the county?"

"No. I mean, well, not exactly."

"Well, which is it?" She is practically yelling now, and she doesn't care. "Either you do, or you do not. Either way, now you've been here. You have seen with your own eyes that this house is *not* vacant, that these grounds are *not* abandoned, and the county *cannot* have it to build more of its precious outlet malls that you people so desperately want. *I* did not hire you, *you* were not invited, and you can take that message back to your bosses and tell them that they are welcome to try again in another decade."

He has backed into the tall grass in face of her advancing, verbal barrage, and she could not be more pleased. Without taking her eyes off him, she retreats to the reclusion of the House and slams the door before another word can be said.

※ ※ ※

The storm raging in that woman's hazel eyes is blessedly cut off by the slam of the plain white door. Dutch stands, for a moment, paralyzed. An entirely different sort of silence washes over the estate, a heavier, more purposeful one. The door does not open again, nor does the curtain move. Everything is exactly as it was, and Dutch half wonders if that exchange happened at all. Of course, it had. Not even in his wildest dreams could he invent such a woman. *Let alone one who lives* here *alone*. His gaze sweeps across the field of over-grown wild and the mansion sagging under its own weight and woe: none of it makes sense. Nor does a bit of it sit well with Dutch. He might lift a hand, to rap his knuckles on the door, but he has no desire to meet that rage again, or the business end of a shotgun for that matter.

His feet do start moving but away from the house, back the way he came through the tall grass and into the dark passage of the surrounding thicket—not that there is much of a difference. The pleasantly brilliant day turns gloomy. Clouds have rolled in; shadows are in bloom. A chill leaches away warmth left by the sun. Emerging on the other side of the gate and onto the road, the spreading grey has even reached the truck, turning it more of an ash color than the off-white it should be. The drive back to town is going to be a long one. Especially long when the driver-side door handle doesn't budge. Dutch tries again and again to no avail before his hands drop to his pockets. They're empty.

"Are you kidding?"

Through the window, he can see the metal box with the workorder pinned to the top—the very thing that has brought him all the way out here to begin with—on the otherwise empty bench seat inside the locked truck. On top of that are his keys. Why would he put them *there*? His cell phone, too, sits uselessly in one of the two cup holders slung low under the radio.

"You're *not* kidding," Dutch bemuses to himself. *At least it's not raining*, he thinks, running his hand through his hair. Yet, no sooner does the thought come and go, the darkened sky above cracks with a bright flash and rolling thunder rumbles down into his bones. Raindrops began to pelt his face.

"You have *got* to be kidding!" he shouts.

In seconds he is soaked.

❀ ❀ ❀

The sudden onset of an unexpected storm is a welcomed distraction. Holding her place against the door, using it to keep herself up, the thrumming of the rain beats through the fog enveloping her thoughts. She hasn't moved since, once more, entombing herself in the thick, oozing quiet steadily invading the House. The first person she has met, face to face, in she doesn't know how long has just run away from her snarling. Who could blame him? Who could blame *her*? Outsiders have been trying to take this place away from her family for longer than she has dwelled within it. Take it, burn it, level it to make way for progress. And they will never stop. Well, they can't have it, not while she still breathes. Even if the others *have* left her behind. Even if she is the last who will ever be…

Being outside was terrible. The state of the grounds had been a shock. How long has she kept herself trapped inside? No wonder that the country tried again; this is the worst state the property has ever been. When did the work become too much for one? How long ago did she give up trying?

Maintaining the grounds is not the only chore to have slipped through her fingers, but it is the most obvious and the first she could not reclaim, no matter how she tried. At some point, the manual labor simply grew tiresome. Her body had started to ache in ways it hadn't before. Her mind ached more. The omnipresent quiet of the place, when it had been anything but for generations, bored a hole right through her. She started to rest more. The more she rested, the weaker she grew. Attempting to heal herself, she moved into the little apartment tucked behind a wall in the kitchen, and that was when cracks began to show inside.

Maintenance to the House was always a chore she knew was coming, but one she had deluded herself into thinking could wait until the others returned. Or rather, she had not believed that they would be gone for so long. She did her best to immediately tend the damage only to find, instead, the encroaching rot just under the surface. Decay—*inside the House*—is not only a travesty but a duty she had *never* anticipated. Yet, there she was, staring at the work she could not possibly do herself. Through trial and error, she managed to make simple repairs inside while the unruly growth outside continued unchecked. Any attempt she made to tame the yard only resulted in more corrosion inside.

In effort to alleviate the workload, she began shutting up parts of the House. Room by room, wing by wing, she reduced her living space down to only her little apartment, the kitchen, and the great room with its solarium. The plan seemed to work, at first. With the House shut down to only the vital parts needed to keep it alive, she had been able to trim nearly half the grounds to a presentable level, and that was when the fissure opened high up on the north wall in the great room. It had been a devastating blow. Her confidence that she alone could keep the House alive until someone came back for her crumbled.

The fissure was more than spackle could fix. Soon after, the glass of the solarium began to fog, grime started to collect in the corners. The House, for the first time, felt old and cold. Dusty. Abandoned. A decaying carcass with her trapped inside. So, when she found herself caught in the gaze of a handsome stranger the county had sent to extract from her what she swore to protect, she had wondered—just once and only for a moment—if letting it all go would be so bad, and it had been that very thought that hit her with such a terrible shock.

Pressed against the door, her eyes drift close against the truth: she had been tempted. It is all too clear now, how much control she has lost. How much longer will she be able to fend off the vipers? That man is surely well on his way to report all he found—they will only try harder now, until they break her.

How could she have entertained the thought of letting them have it, this sacred place? As ancient as it is, it is also *hers*. And her grip is slipping.

The embrace of the loneliness is a cold, damp shroud numbing her to the core and obscuring the delicate sound of hesitant rapping at the door holding straight her back. *It is nothing more than the rain*, she wants to believe, but when the knocking comes a second time, and louder, surer, her heart knows better. *Don't answer*, whispers fear. *You know who it will be*, but she is already turning around. *He will make you leave*, the darkness warns as her steady hand grasps the knob. There is no whisper when she twists the knob and is gone entirely when she swings the door open wide.

There he is stands, her gentleman caller, filling her doorway a second time and soaked as a rat that fell off a ship and into the ocean. His angular face is tipped downward and water drips off the point of his nose. His dark eyes may be steady and clear, but he looks about as happy—and surprised—as she.

"You're not going to believe me," he begins, the sour taste of humility etched on his face. He turns his head, looking southward, his lips pressed together the way lips do when they are forced to speak the truth despite its ridiculousness. "I seem to have left my keys in my truck. And it's locked."

"I'm sure you have someone to call."

One corner of his mouth pulls back in a grimace that only manages to make his face more appealing. If she is not careful, this scene might cause her to remember what smiling is like.

"I do," he says, his gaze swinging back to her, unperturbed by her cold demeanor. "The thing is…"

"Your means to do so are also inside your locked truck," she finishes for him.

He does not move, but he does look relieved. "Yes."

It's a tactic, comes fear's final warning, echoing between her ears and making her yearn for the coolness of her apartment. If it is, she considers quickly, then all the better to get him off her property as soon as possible. The only way to do that is to let him in. But only this once. And only for as long as he needs to be gone.

For the first time in all the years she has resided in the House, her feet shuffle aside to allow an outsider to enter. The ease of doing so is downright frightening.

❈ ❈ ❈

After first coughing up something wet from deep within his lungs, old Charlie lifts the receiver of an even older push-button phone, ringing off the hook, on Gina's desk. Where in hell is that woman? It's not his job to answer the damned phone. Hell, it never was.

"Hello. TerAvest Landscaping, hello," he answers dryly despite the phlegm he can already feel gathering anew. There is a voice on the other end of the line, scratchy, muffled, and a million miles away to old Charlie's old hearing. He presses the cold, hard plastic receiver firmly to his old ear, struggling to make out the words coming through. "What's that you say, now? You need a *rush* job?" He tries to mimic the words he thinks he hears—little good it is doing.

The fuzz smooths out and, when the voice comes through a little louder, old Charlie's face brightens with recognition easily shaving off a few years' worth of age—if only someone were around to see it.

"Oh, Dutch, my boy!" his old voice rings with refreshed clarity. "Can hardly hear ya, son. What job, now? Green *grouse*, you say? You mean the golf club? Nah, son, Anthony finished that just this last Tuesday. They won't be needin—"

More static and then the voice comes through more firmly. Shouting, in fact, and still old Charlie strains to grasp it. Something about that certain set of words Dutch keeps saying, over and over, that old Charlie feels he should know. "Tea... *mouse?* Three? Ta—? *Tree? Tree...* house? Tree House!" Recollection hits on his last try with the stinging snap of a twisted-up wet towel. A surge of electric alarm shoots up his tired, old spine forcing it straighter. Hot, searing pain shoots up a back weakened by age and sorrow, and—for the first time—old Charlie ignores it.

"Did... did you say *Tree House?* Dutch, listen to me, boy." Charlie grunts to clear his throat and steady his nerves. "I know things haven't been what you expected since you got back, and I don't know how you got your hands on that work order—yes, technically it is still active but— What's that?" Charlie presses the receiver tighter to his ear. "Your keys? Oh! I hear you loud and clear, my boy. I'll send Anthony with a spare set. But, Dutch, listen. Do not go in that house. Don't step foot onto the property. I'll explain everything when you get back, just... Stay by the truck, okay, Dutch. Dutch?" But the voice on the other end is gone, there only static. When that cuts out too, Charlie is left holding a muted phone to his ear with no way of knowing how much of his warning managed to get through.

He finds Anthony in the garage, leaning against one of the many hip-high, metal tool stations, gabbing with the rest of the lot that makes up TerAvest's labor force. Charlie makes straight for him, spare keys clasped in a meaty hand. He can't be sure which of them sees him coming first, but Anthony is quickest to regain his more professional posture. Just in time, too, to catch the keys Charlie hurls instead of letting them hit him in the face like Charlie had wanted.

"*You,*" the old man growls, shoving the end of a blunt finger in a not-so-weak poke to the young man's chest. "You sent him to *Moore* House. What in blazes is wrong with you?"

An icy current fills the garage, overtaking everyone in it and smothering their gaiety into silence. All eyes, other than Anthony's, are suddenly only interested in the cracks in the concrete floor and not one bit interested in meeting the gaze of an irate boss.

Understanding dawns and old Charlie roars. "You *all* knew? And you just *let* him go?"

"We didn't think he would actually—"

"Moron," Charlie's voice cuts Anthony's off as cold and sharp as a hatchet cleaves bone. "Dutch wasn't around when all that nonsense took place. He knows nothing about that house, and I have worked tirelessly to keep it that way. Now, he's there and locked out of his truck. Go fetch him," says old Charlie, lifting a meaty paw and extending a single finger in the vague direction of that damned house. "Or find yourself another job."

Sparing no time to waste, Anthony drops the keys twice in his hustle to a truck of his own.

❀   ❀   ❀

"Charlie? I didn't get that last bit, Charlie. Hello?" But a scratchy dial tone is the only response Dutch gets. "I swear that old man's hearing gets worse every day," he says to the curvy, metallic handle of the old-style receiver before placing it back onto its antique, hand-crafted, brass, four-pronged cradle—and here he thought that push-button phone that old Charlie refuses to part with was old. Who has a *rotary* phone anymore? One straight out of the Victorian era, no less. Dutch is surprised the thing works at all.

The call silenced, Dutch looks to his host, which he has not done since crossing the threshold of the white farm door into the house and offered use of a phone that belongs in a museum. She is standing close by, but not too close, with her hip against the butcher-block top of the island separating the kitchen from the short expanse to the door. Sitting on the countertop near her hip are two steaming mugs hot with tea she made while he used one relic to talk to another. The loose knit, pale bule sweater and black slacks draping over her frame hides the shape of her. Though the fabric looks soft and of high quality, the muted colors make her look like a drab moth, an out-of-place blemish in the magnificent kitchen surrounding her.

What a kitchen! *Distinguished* is a good word. *Gothic* would be an even better one to describe the style had the cabinets not be such an inviting shade of deep green, with every door and corner accented in vibrant yellow. Silver knobs adorn the glass-faced doors that leave nothing to the imagination as to what's inside, and all the cups, glasses, plates, and bowls within are white with crisp lines that scream modern. Exaggerated swooping lines along the top and bottom edges of both cabinets and doors, that curl up to elongated points at the corners reminds Dutch of the vampire movies he used to watch as a kid. With a vaulted ceiling and deep corners so thick with shadow, he would not be surprised should someone suddenly materialize from one. Startled? Sure, but not surprised. Not one bit of it matches the plainness of his hostess.

"Well," Dutch starts awkwardly. "You sure do have interesting taste in style."

Not moving from her place at the edge of the island, she shrugs. "The kitchen is whatever it needs to be."

"Is that so?" Dutch asks, unsure of exactly what she means. Is she suggesting that the kitchen designed itself?

"How does it accomplish that?" he asks with his best playful smile.

His hostess is not amused. In fact, the stoniness of her face gives Dutch the impression that she is not kidding. How can that be?

"How is it that you have come to find yourself in this kitchen, at all?" she asks instead. Much calmer now than she had been what seems like hours ago, she is no less defensive. Arms folded low over her ribcage but not crossed, her jaw relaxed—she's almost approachable. She has an appealing face. Easy on the eyes but also one that could be lost in a crowd, and Dutch suddenly no longer cares about the room. He can't look away from her and how she stands so perfectly still, watching him in return. Hell, he's practically forgotten all about Charlie.

"Are you not afraid of this place?"

The question hits Dutch like a mist of lemon water and he remembers where he is. "Afraid? Why would I be afraid of a house? Especially one I didn't know existed until this morning?"

"But you're from here?"

Dutch shrugs, eyebrows as well as shoulders. "I grew up here, ya, but I've been gone for a long time." Her gaze is direct, she really is listening to him. The feeling brings as much solace as it does apprehension, and Dutch is forced to drop his gaze to the steaming mug that she slides toward him. He leans over it, breathing deep the aromatics of cinnamon, cloves, and something else vibrant and earthy that he can't put his finger on.

"The funny thing is," he chuckles dryly. "This place looks *ancient*."

The woman nods causing locks of her long, wavy, dark hair to drape one shoulder. "This place is very old."

Dutch nods with her. "And yet, I've never heard of it. Not even when I was a kid. It's like this place just—" he twirls one hand in the air. "—appeared today."

"And yet, you have a workorder," she counters as smooth as silk. "An old one."

He must admit, she's got him there. He takes a sip of the tea.

"Perhaps," she shrugs, her arms dropping to hang in front of her, hands softly clasped. "Back *then* was not the right time for *you*."

If the world can stop—no matter how unimaginatively brief—for Dutch, in that moment, it does. His heart continues to hammer away in his chest but all else slows to a barely perceivable crawl. Right down to the particles of dust in the air. Reined to a twinkling halt, the tiny specs hover in the pleasantly dim light that sets his hostess's face aglow. A mature face, yet one with a peculiar ageless quality, simple and elegant; Dutch no longer hears the storm raging outside. Baggy clothes may disguise her shape, but the line of her shoulders is straight, and she stands without a slouch. Her hands, weathered and dry, strong, with nails cut short, are not the sort of hands that shy away from hard work. Yet, despite all the strength and poise and effortless grace, she—like the house—seems damaged by despair. The mere thought of the workorder in the truck fills Dutch with the compulsion to tear it to shreds.

"Why did you leave?"

Her question breaks the spell. The moment is gone, but not lost. Permanently captured in Dutch's mind, it will be there for him to look back on later and see it for what it really was. For now, time rolls on and the rain continues to pour outside. The heat of the tea fights back a settling chill. She had asked him a question, one that threatens to open doors to memories he would rather forget. Things he is not ready to have another person hear about, especially her. A good shake of his head closes that door firmly but does not lock it.

"I went looking for something," he answers true.

"What were you looking for?"

"I don't know." Dutch drinks more of the tea. "Wonder, I suppose. Meaning." Another sip. The flavor of the tea is one he feels he should know.

"And you didn't find it."

"Who says I didn't?"

"Well, you're here, are you not?" She takes her first sip from her own mug. "If you had found it, you wouldn't have come back."

The tea is, at once, too spicy and Dutch is not sure how much more of it he can drink. He glances at his wrist before he can remember he stopped wearing a watch long ago. How long has it been since he called Charlie? Anthony could be pulling up to the locked company truck any moment.

"It is time for you to go?" asks his hostess.

Dutch opens his mouth to answer but closes it promptly: No answer will be the right one. "Well, you wouldn't want some stranger just waltzing in here uninvited, now, would you?" He tries to put comfort into his grin, but the overwhelming compulsion to leave keeps warmth from his face.

Pulling his hands away from the mug, he thanks her for the hospitality and dry place to wait and rises from his seat. Three long strides bring him to the white door. Outside, the storm has stopped, having dissolved to a fine mist. Dutch turns back to fill his eyes with the sight of her, standing in the open doorway, one last time. Her arms are back up and crossed at her chest.

"Good luck," she says, a ghost of a grin playing at her lips. "I hope you find what you are looking for."

Whatever trepidation that made him rush for the door washes away. In the gentle light of her salubrious grin, Dutch sees a different woman than the one who answered the first time and is suddenly struck with worry that he may never see her again. Not knowing what else to do, he extends his hand.

"My name is Dutch."

Looking down at his hand, her grin faulters but it does not disappear. Just as Dutch is convinced that she won't take it, that she is about to retreat inside and away from him forever, she takes a full, deep breath, and a tentative hand reaches back.

"Ara."

It's a false name, Dutch can hear the dull ring of it the instant it falls from her lips. He would know, it's not like he gave her his real name either. She could give thousands of names and they would all sound just as sweet.

He is walking before he realizes that he's turned. His boots are crossing into the shade before the feel of the tall grass brushing against the legs of his pants is gone. He looks back over his shoulder in hopes of catching one last sight of her only to find the dark, tangled hedge separating him from the estate. Instead of being inside, he is steps from the road. In the distance, much too far to be of any importance, a faint rhythmic chugging of a truck engine rides a lazy breeze. The way back to his truck, and the town further still, are near at hand, yet all Dutch can think about is the sweet perfume of cherry blossoms in full bloom.

❀ ❀ ❀

No passing shadow rousts her from sleep this time; inside her little apartment, there are no windows. Like most days in recent memory, Ara had not planned on leaving her apartment, but the room's omnipresent light bouncing off the steeply angled ceiling—the underside of the grand staircase inaccessible to her now—is burning her eyes.

The room always did have a queer, natural light, reminiscent of a Time before the House was a house. Normally, it gave her rest, cleared her thoughts, washed out the hurt that she has no right to feel (she agreed to this after all). Equipped with everything she needs the little apartment makes forever feel not quite so long. Except this day. This day, Ara is awake, her head buzzing with nervous energy and her body aching to move. The idea of rest suddenly seems tedious and the pocket door separating the apartment from the kitchen slides open too easily with the softest touch.

The curious light, an odd shade of blue, spills across the stone floor skirting the kitchen and, with it, she can see dust. This is not the first time she has noticed dust slowly accumulating in the House, but it is for the kitchen. She had rested comfortably in the thought that at least one room has remained so resilient and unaffected by the crushing weight of Time's absence, that is, until the arrival of her unexpected guest. She had been preparing tea that she had not planned to make, for the visitor she had not intended to host, when she noticed fine particles drifting through the air. Had he noticed, or had he been too busy shouting into the handset of her telephone? Now she can see a fine layer collecting along the edges of the cabinet doors. How long had she been in repose, in the little room under the stairs?

Dust is a bad sign. Dust in the kitchen, the heart of the House: disastrous. That, along with the arrival of a stranger—one allowed to come inside, no less—sent Ara spiraling into crimson void of melancholy. She had retreated into the security of her apartment the moment her guest was out of sight. Contained in the quiet, drowning in the room's strange light, Time could simply pass over her and maybe all would simply be forgotten. She might have succumbed to the room entirely had a compulsion she cannot describe not make her crave the world outside.

Her black and red checkered blanket is draped over one of the two chairs tucked against the kitchen island. She wraps it around her shoulders. The copper knob of the white door is cool to the touch and leaches warmth from her fingers, but twists smoothly releasing its latch. Morning air, still crisp, rushes her face and tickles her bare feet below the hem of the long, simple white dress she wears. She pulls the blanket around her a little tighter.

The sky, yellow and pink with the sun of a new day on the rise over the eastern horizon (as it should), is all but clear. Early still, the muted light helps her to ignore the grass and weed choked estate. Better not to think about it, she resolved long ago. She can't even say where the tools are anymore. One day, the wild will be at her doorstep. Will the House even *be* a house then? What will become of her? The blanket is not as warm as it used to be. Still intact, it is growing old and threadbare, she is careful not to pull it too tight.

"Hi."

The sudden voice is alarming and yanks her gaze to the direction of the old gate lost somewhere in the trees. Terrifyingly close, and strolling closer still with easy determination, is her stranger.

That's three times now he has come to her door. This time, there are three small, black cartons in his hands. In each, flowers like yellow stars stand proudly, defiantly from the tops of long, emerald stems. Not only has he returned, but he also brings flowers. Quickly, before he gets too close, she suppresses the surprise she feels slipping the tight reins of her control. The blanket has loosened and slips off her shoulders. Crossing her arms locks it down. *He returns with charm, nothing more*, she reminds herself. Despite that disarming grin on his strong, intelligent face, Ara holds firm her ground at the edge of the door.

❀ ❀ ❀

"Ara, right?" Dutch proclaims once he's close enough to not have to shout.

Where she does smile back, it is more out of greeting and holds very little warmth. She also crosses her arms over that black and red checkered blanket awfully tight.

"And you are Hutch."

"It's Dutch, actually," he replies with a wink. "But close."

"Right," she replies, drawing out the word slow and stretched as to imply that she is in on some secret joke lost on him. At least she's not throwing him out immediately. "And those?" she tips her head to the items in his hands.

"Daffodils."

"I can see that."

"I've never been particularly fond of cut flowers," says Dutch, coming to a stop within an arm's reach from her. "And these little beauties come back every year. I thought—"

A spark of lightning flashes in her eyes and the hairs on his arms stand on end.

"Thought *what?*" She does not shout, but the gravity in her voice is enough to send his heart plummeting to his stomach. "You thought I'd like to *plant* them? *Where?*" An arm whips out from under black and red checkered folds in sweeping gesture over the grounds and sending half the blanket to the ground.

Dutch is frozen solid, abashed. The words he had been so sure about a breath before are stolen, burned, and fly away like ash.

"Are these meant to make me feel bad, or just to rub my failure in my face? What good are flowers in this place? Don't you think that if I were capable of the upkeep needed that I wouldn't have a field of them already? Is this your plan, to use shame to finally drive me from my home? No more stories, no more tales, no more wonder, just silence and ghosts and one hell of a profit margin?"

The flowers suddenly feel too heavy and horribly cheap in his hands. The venom of her words strikes deep, but it is the glassy shell of tears held back in her eyes that cuts him to the bone. Her rant has drawn her away from the threshold of her door. Her bare feet are wet with the last night's dew and smudged black with damp soil. She has closed the distance between them to within inches without either being aware of it. Looking down slightly to meet the hot gaze from this frightened, overwhelmed woman, Dutch feels the small, helplessness of a child.

"Is that why you're here?" Her eyes blink rapidly, beating back tears. "To remind me of all I cannot handle on my own, or is it to bribe me away with some empty promise of a better life?"

Dutch tries to speak, but nothing he can say will make this situation better. Her tears are ready to fall, and he cannot bear the thought that a word from him might be that last push to send them over the edge.

"Tell your vultures, they can have my property when they remove my cold, dead body from it."

I'm not here to take anything from you, are the words Dutch desperately wants to say—draws the breath for, in fact—only to have them shot down by the slam of the plain, white door in his face. Again.

A robin sails over his head to the surrounding trees that keep back the dawn already lifting from the horizon. It is not dark, but it is not very bright either and a passing breeze rustling through the tall grass fills the air with dry crackling: the only sound. The growth may be wild, but old it is not; surely all that is needed are the right tools. He turns to the hard face of the white door and knows damn well that he's not about to knock.

❀ ❀ ❀

Ara does not cry; she will not. To give in now will only invite doubt and that will be the end of the House. The others have all left, but they all might still come back. Unless she admits defeat, then they will certainly not. One sad tear and all her hard work, generations of toil and sacrifice, will spoil, the House will collapse, and everything will fade into grey nothingness. No, the House cannot fall, and neither shall one, single tear.

Alone in the great room, her back to the door, Ara stares at the fissure that has opened the western wall, floor to ceiling. Cracks as faint as spiderwebs have already started to stretch across the ceiling, reaching for the glass panes of the solarium. This is not how the House should look. *And he had brought her flowers.* Shame, heavy and cold, weights her shoulders and sets her jaw to clench. That *need* that had dispelled her slumber and shooed her from her apartment settles in her legs and arms as an ache, a desire to move, to stretch, to do the work that she has run from for too long. For now, there is nothing she can do about the fissure in the wall, nor the grounds gone wild. Dust, however, wipes up easily with a clean, damp cloth and some soap. So, Ara gets started.

Ambiance inside the house never changes much. Always just enough light to comfortably see by, she contently moves from wall to wall to floor, and all the corners in between, wiping all the dust she encounters. Only the soreness in her arms, legs, and back stand as testament to the amount of time she spends in effort to rid the kitchen, hall, and great room of dust until Ara can work no more. Finally, too tired to think of dinner and too exhausted to bathe, she retires to the cool, replenishing hue of her little apartment to recoup the energy she's lost. It is all she needs for now.

There is no telling how much Time has passed when she wakes, sluggish from missed meals but otherwise recharged. How many days that have come and gone, or how many dawns and dusks she's missed, are equally unknowable. The House is silent as a tomb save for the mice that she recently started to hear scurry through the walls—a thing a healthy House would never have allowed.

The light has still not changed much, but the dust has: it is everywhere. She might as well have not cleaned in years—again. Her heart hammers in her throat; it is all too much to bear. In the same clothes she has been wearing for a day, maybe longer, Ara runs from the House knowing full well that the outside is not much better. But there is a promise of air, cool and fresh, and birds singing hidden in the leaves of trees that gently rattle in a friendly breeze, and all of it hits her the instant she flings wide the door. Caught in the riptide of a calm morning, Ara is pulled from the house at a sprint until the sight of the grounds suddenly sets her feet to anchor.

It is not so early in the morning as initial impressions suggested. The sun is high, and the sky is a brilliant, bright blue. The air is not crisp at all but warm and Ara breathes it deep. Her chilled body warms, loosening the talons of anxiety and sorrow squeezing her chest. The grass at her feet has been cut short. No woody stalks of wild grass reach halfway up her legs, no weeds cluster in unsightly patches, there aren't even any leaves or trimmings left to decay into the ground. Nearly a full quarter of the estate is tamed into a flat, lush carpet of soft, cool green refreshingly damp under her bare feet.

Ara blinks.

On her left, even the grass is cleared away exposing sharply defined squares of deep brown soil contained in ankle-high walls made of the stones she had collected herself as a child. In one far corner of the first garden bed, bright yellow flowers stand tall and cheerful, the black plastic containers they had come in have been discarded to the ground. A second freshly unearthed bed is next and is still empty. A few strides more along the new edge of trimmed grass, smack in the middle of a third bed yet to be completely restored, stands Dutch.

She knows that isn't his real name, no more or less than hers is Ara, but the large pickax he's left impaled in the dirt of the third garden bed is real enough, as is the churned soil and displaced flora covering his boots. Who is this man? Ara wonders, and not for the first time. How long has he been standing there, watching her, silently leaning against the sharply angled pickax, and waving a gloved hand when their gazes meet?

He doesn't speak, just waits patiently for her to decide whether she will approach him or retreat to the confining familiarity of the house; she has every right to be wary. He is wearing a ballcap today, a blue one that makes his well-worn jeans look white. Above the bill is a ring of dampness. His white shirt may cling to his chest, back, and shoulders, but his face shows little fatigue, especially when his smile brightens as Ara's feet casually close the distance between them.

"I did knock," he says, then shrugs. "That was a couple of days ago. I was starting to get worried. One day more and I'd have been ready to do more than knock."

Ara looks for the threat she wants to hear, ferrets for the scheme lurking behind his words, and feels strangely dismayed when she finds none. His eyes are dark but soft and weighted with more than a little sadness. Had he really been worried? Would he have kicked in the door just to check on her? Why would he do either? Ara has no answer.

"I brought my own tools, didn't think you'd mind," he says gesturing to the rakes, shovels, hoes, and various smaller items littering the ground. "I wasn't about to go rummagin' around looking for yours." He almost says more—his lips purse a bit—but his breath stalls. Then, like an old friend who already knows all her secrets, he winks. "You were right about the flowers," Dutch says instead, standing tall and taking up the pickax. "Turns out, so am I. They look nice there, don't they?"

Ara doesn't answer—she doesn't need to. So perky and delightfully yellow in the fresh garden bed big enough to hold dozens of them: they do look pretty.

"So, you planted them," she responds though it is a struggle to do so. "Why keep going?"

Dutch strikes the ground twice before answering. "They're small flowers." He swings again. "Hard to see in all this. Besides," another pause, another swing. "Flowers can only do so much alone. The more space I clear—" His swing sends dirt flying. Small clumps hit her dress. Ara doesn't care. "—means room for whatever else you want." Dutch pauses to swing again. "Tamed ground will work for you, instead of against you. That's what my Pop always said, anyway."

"I'm not paying you for this."

The words are out of Ara's mouth before she realizes. Dutch stops his work. The pickax suspended above his head, the next swing forgotten and nearly falls to the ground. The glare he shoots her with from under the bill of his hat is more searing than an iron heated red hot. Regret burns on her cheeks while ice sinks to the bottom of her stomach and Ara fights to keep both from showing on her face. Dutch, however, makes no such effort to conceal the dull shock of contempt from his. "Well, I'm glad we're on the same page about something."

He turns away and returns to swinging the pickax, with a little more force this time but back to it he does go. Who *is* this man? Ara stares at him a moment longer.

"I'll bring you some water." She does not wait for a reply for it was not a question. A full twist on her toes and Ara returns to the House. A breathless *'thank you'* that she tries not to hear reaches her ears just fine. Inside, dust has accumulated everywhere. Well, this simply will not do.

❀ ❀ ❀

And so it goes, day after day, with Dutch sometimes beginning his work before Ara woke, sometimes after. Of course, he never had any real way of knowing when she was awake or not, or if she slept at all, until she steps foot outside and that she does daily since their last encounter in the garden. Where she would never linger for long nor make any move to pick up a tool or pull a weed, she never failed to bring him water or meals and always right when he needed either. What she did inside for hours, alone, remained a mystery.

Ara hardly says a word, but for Dutch, that in no way implied her as cold. Always polite and never brash, her patience with whatever dumb question of his or awkward attempt at conversation showed no bounds. All of it Ara accepts with warm, watchful eyes and a relaxed mouth and Dutch finds himself, daily, wanting to tell her everything. Every secret, every twist and turn in his life; every treacherous deed, every humble act, every effort in seeking redemption; the story of his journey in constant search for... something he can still not name—he wants her to hear it all, even if for no other reason than her reaction, but all of it he holds back.

The estate, this house, Ara, *everything* seems so magically strange here. Always fed, but Dutch never smells food cooking, nor does he hear any of the usual clamor that often accompanies meal preparation: the opening or closing of cabinet doors, the clash and clang of pots and pans. *Had there been a refrigerator?* He had been inside only once, and barely a single room at that, yet Dutch somehow thinks not. No stores, no pantry that he could account and, as the days passed, he witnessed no groceries being delivered, and Ara certainly did not leave. Yet his meals continued to arrive as fresh as if the vegetables had come straight from the garden and prepared by expert hands all the while without sign of another soul on the property, anywhere. Where did it all come from? How she came to be here, all alone like this, Dutch wonders most of all.

Questions he could ask, nearly does at times, but that image of her face, of her attempts at concealing that silent, seething anger, the sadness, and a slim glimmer of forgotten hope swirling together inside a woman on the brink of desperation chokes Dutch into silence every time.

How many days pass? Dutch lost count at some point. He cannot say when she started to work with him in the yard, only that it came as a shock one day when he happened to look up, and there she was, wearing overalls, with gloves on her hands and her hair contained in a bright blue handkerchief. He found her digging in the dirt of the first garden bed, carefully avoiding the daffodils already there, several of his smaller hand tools scattered around her knees. When had she snatched them from the pile that he moved with him as he worked? Then again, he *had* been leaving his tools there at night, so she could have moved them at any time.

A quiet worker, Dutch grew accustomed to seeing her where she was not a moment ago or absent entirely when he was sure she hadn't moved. No tells, no warning, she would either be there, or she would not, silently sowing seeds in the beds he's cleared without bringing attention to herself. Still, she regularly retreated into the house for long periods of time announced only by the subtle click of the white door opening or closing. So, when a nagging feeling to look for her stops his work, Dutch finds the door wide open, and filling the space is Ara, clean and with her hands empty. A twist of her head, bidding him to follow, she disappears into the house. The idea of taking a break inside, to sit on a chair instead of on the ground is an offer too tantalizing to pass up—as would any break he might spend in Ara's company.

Walking in this time is easy, and the smell, or rather the lack of one, hits him first. The distinct odor of mildew and dust he realizes he had smelled before only due to the absence of their scent now, and suddenly he understands what Ara had been doing, inside all those days.

Every surface shines with a certain fresh gleam usually reserved for things brand new when they had been matte and muted before. There is a glow inside the house, warm and welcoming, that had not been there. For Dutch, it's like finally coming home after a lifetime of arduous travel and finding supper on the table. He can almost smell the savory broth and the vegetables and cutlets of beef that have long been simmering. The sweet, earthy aroma of hot corn bread fresh out of the oven is downright palpable. The sharp spice of steaming cider is more than he could hope for, yet when his nose draws him into the kitchen, he finds all he expects set and served on the island. A waiting meal, for one.

"How did you come to be here, all by yourself?" He hadn't planned on asking. Told himself not to, in fact. Deliciously full, and warmed by the cider both physically and mentally, Dutch is relaxed. Too relaxed. Hell, that question was bound to leak out sooner or later.

Ara does not seem to mind, and she does not hesitate. "Someone has to stay."

"So, the others just left?" Dutch tests the waters carefully, watching her upturned face and eyes looking impossibly far. "Where did they go?"

"To the stars," she says with longing in her voice and a fragile smile playing with her mouth. She could not say another word, just sit there with that look, and Dutch would be happy to just watch her. "They'll come back one day."

"How long have they been gone?"

To this question comes her silence, one that squeezes unpleasantly around his heart. Ara doesn't look to be much older than he, if she is at all, yet he can't shake the feeling that she has been alone for a *very* long time. Taking his empty dishes to the sink without looking at him, Dutch knows she is not going to answer. Frustrated, aggravated, Dutch takes the queue and returns to the yard. He doesn't close the door behind him, but she does not follow, either.

Why won't she tell him? *What* won't she tell him? For days, weeks (*months?*) he has shown up, every day, and worked until he could work no more. He has given her space and asked for nothing, and she gives him… food, water, and silent acceptance; everything he needs. He has told her the same amount about himself, and she has demanded nothing.

After what feels like hours—though the sun hardly seems to change positions—Dutch straightens from his halfhearted work. He has not accomplished much, but there is not much work left to do. There is not a wild grass nor vine nor weed to be cut or yanked; the landscape has been transformed into the manicured splendor that an estate like this should be, and Ara's flowers, herbs, and vegetables have livened up the restored garden beds with a variety of greens, yellows, reds, and blues. All the work remaining in the yard is the maintenance to keep it going. Even the house looks better. It still sags against its own weight, but the structure no longer looks ready to buckle. All in all, considering what they have accomplished together, Dutch considers it a wild success. The only element missing is the woman who lives here.

He has not seen Ara since he left her in the silence of the kitchen. While her absence is not wholly unusual, the white door standing open and untouched is. Whatever tool he had in his hand hits the dirt and Dutch is to the door in fewer steps than should be possible. The kitchen is empty. A single mug sits on the island where he took his meal, and it is on its side, its contents dripping to the forest green tiled floor. He almost calls her name when he notices a door he had not before. Of the pocket variety, the same color and texture as the wall and so perfectly hidden when closed, no wonder he never noticed it until now. Open now, it is obvious, and a curious, ghostly blue light is spilling out from a room on the other side.

This is crossing a line, Dutch tells himself as he slides the door deeper into its recessed pocket. With an overtly embarrassing apology at the ready, Dutch leans into the secreted blue space. What he finds makes him forget all etiquette. He rushes in and no more work is done for the rest of the day.

❦ ❦ ❦

Time has a way of skipping over a place where it is no longer needed, leaving it forgotten. So, when it is found again, the snap back sends change like a ripple across a still pond, touching everything. To think that the arrival of a stranger could cause such a ripple is a frightening prospect for Ara. Not only has he beat back the wilds reclaiming the estate, but his presence has also extinguished Ara's compulsion to flee and spurred her promptly back the work she had tried to run from. She needed time, and she needed Time to look away, just for a little while. Ara never had a guest before since she took control of the House, let alone one who works without being asked, without being paid. Why he is here at all Ara still doesn't know, and won't ask, but that does not mean he doesn't deserve to be looked after.

The dust fought back at first, accumulating in freshly cleaned zones each time she stopped to rest, but the sounds of tools churning earth and grunts of a man hard at work kept her going. When she found cleaning wax, hidden away in a deep, dark corner in a cabinet under the sink, the dust surrendered. Meals improved as the amount of dust present decreased. The kitchen, the hearth, the great room and its attached solarium, at last, held their luster. Soon, the fissure in the great room's western wall was all the damage that remained with her unable to do anything about it. At least its growth has ceased. When Ara could nearly hear birds singing again from the fat, twisted tree in the solarium, Ara knew the time had come to move her work outside.

She never sensed the return of Time from inside the House. Conditions are always just as she needs them: enough light to see by and a constant temperature that causes her to neither shiver nor sweat. For Ara, days, weeks, months may pass, and she'd be none the wiser, but bringing Dutch meals and water consistently brought her out into the sun, the wind, and the change sweeping over the estate. Time had come for her to change her clothing for attire more suitable for working in the dirt. Dutch's progress was remarkable, humbling, humiliating even, but also inspiring. His back was turned when she took the hand rake first. In fact, *when* he noticed that she was outside, sowing seeds and bringing up plants in the wake of his labor, Ara cannot say. What she can say is that she had collected all his smaller tools when she finally caught him looking at her.

It was Dutch who started speaking first, asking her questions about where she wanted the next bed or what she wanted to plant. Ara always answered, and desired more to ask him questions in return though she did not. How long they worked like this, Ara couldn't say. Each day as pleasant as the last, and the clouds floating overhead never brought rain any more than they hampered the sun. Days blurred together. Telling one from the next, or the last, became as impossible outside the House as in. Until one day, when Ara stands to stretch her back, she finds no more garden beds in which to plant new seeds and the grass across the estate is shorter than the toes of her shoes. Inside the house, the dust did not return, and the meals coming out of the kitchen the best yet. Time had come for Ara to invite Dutch in, properly.

"How long have they been gone?" The question she vaguely heard leave Dutch's lips with her mind already reeling. All her hurt, loneliness, and pain had reared its vengeful head, reminding her of all she's lost and what adventures she is missing. With stars in her eyes and heaviness in her heart, the blue room had started calling to her. When Dutch left, she does not know. How much had she said? Likely too much, but it the answer a dream.

How dare she speak to an outsider. He knows too much now, all he needs to ruin her, to take from her all she holds dear. Why does she want to tell him more? Tell him about the House, what it is, where it came from, the secrets still hidden within its walls and under the floor where she currently finds herself. Had she fallen? Yes. She can hear the quiet drippings of liquid somewhere nearby. Had she knocked over her cup of tea? It hardly matters. The call of the blue room is too strong to let through any other sound. Her sanctuary, her security, where all is well, and nothing can harm or even touch her. A place where even her handsome stranger cannot go.

Her heart pounding, her vision squeezing to a narrow pinch, Ara reaches the false wall that is, in truth, a secret door hidden in plain sight. Whether she crawled or stumbled to it, Ara doesn't know. She can barely make her fingers work to flip up the hidden latch and pull the door along its track. Blue encapsulates her instantly. *What have you done?* Fear whispers in her ear. What *had* she been thinking, allowing some stranger to come in and change things? With the work outside all but complete, what reason could he have to stick around? Ara will soon be alone, again, to maintain everything on her own while defending it all against the vultures that will never stop circling. The fear is right, what *has* she done?

Her breath comes in short, shallow gasps, it is all she can do to push the door wide enough to squeeze through. So much work yet to be done… She needs rest. She *needs* to forget. To sleep until her head, her heart, no longer holds memory of this stranger with sad eyes and unruly hair. She needs the apartment and its blue void, to wash her mind clean of the kindness paid to her by someone who had no reason to—a place to hide, but just for a little while, not like last time. She needs… Ara doesn't know what she needs. Collapsed to the floor, the blue room around her goes soft, blurry. She can go no further. She'll never make it to the bed; the void will consume her, and, for a moment, she wonders if that would be so bad. Then Dutch is there.

She can't understand what is happening, at first. Her body becomes weightless. Floating in a waterless pool, she rises from the floor, but she is not alone. His arms squeeze around her, cradling her body—the feeling is alarming. In her daze, she tries to fight him off, tries to tell him to leave this place, to warn him… then room is spinning. A smear of cerulean blue drains what little fight she has, and she relents to his arms. The comforting embrace gives way to a doughy surface of a mattress she knows well, conforming to the shape of her. A pillow cradles her head. The feel of his arms is gone, but not his presence—he is still close by. Her worries ease and flitter away as Ara gives in to the blue.

❈ ❈ ❈

Dutch wakes without a start though the bed he finds himself in is not his own. The room is not his, either. And there is something wrong with it. He is alone and, the oddity of the room notwithstanding, he feels better rested than any other waking moment in his adult life. The light is peculiar. Sharp and harsh, it gives him the urge to rub his eyes, to rid them of the sleep that does not linger there. Everything is bathed in the curious shade of light from which he cannot readily find the source. The walls are solid; there are no windows. There are no lamps, either, in the single, humble room of an apartment.

This is where she sleeps?

The furniture is sparse. There's the bed he is lying on, with a nightstand consisting of many drawers standing guard on either side; a single, oversized rocking chair laden with more pillows than the bed; and, behind a short wall that doubles as a headboard, a kitchenette with a miniature fridge, a countertop, sink, an electric kettle, and a four cabinets stacked two high. In the back corner, a recessed sectioned is secreted away by a tall, folding privacy screen with a crude image of a city by the sea drawn in strokes of black across a beige canvas.

This where she *lives?*

She who? Who is it that he keeps thinking about? He then wonders, who is *he?*

His heart races. He can almost remember but, looking around the room, in the calm, suppressing, sea-blue light, thought becomes as slippery as fresh caught fish. *By any means necessary*—he had been sent to do a job. Or had that been a dream? *What if* this *is the dream?* A face blooms in his mind: sad, bright eyes framed by brown hair. Maybe it is her eyes that are brown. What color are his own? He can't be sure. *Does it matter?* It is the disturbingly vacant nature of the last thought that finally propels Dutch to his feet. His heart hammering, his vision pinching, he hasn't a clue of where he should go, only that he can no longer remain in this room.

Against the wall, not so far that he shouldn't fail to make it, a dark line runs from the ceiling to the floor, harsh and black in the hazy indigo. A gap. A passage? For Dutch, it's enough to get his feet moving. His impressively rested state drains rapidly with each step. His body quickly grows tired. The blue light is more irritating than ever, burning his eyes, bidding them to close. With the promise of deep rest on the mattress deceptively close, it is almost too much to resist. He's so tired, what would be the harm in lying down for just a moment more if it meant that he'd recover that energized feeling that would help propel him out of the room?

The pull to fall back, to surrender, nearly takes him off his feet if not for a rush of cool air buffeting his face. Dutch takes it deep into his lungs. The gap in the wall is so close, and there is a hope of more refreshing air on the other side. His fingers are numb, but they grip the edge of the door obediently and shove it back, though the effort it takes is so much more than a simple pocket door should. At last, Dutch emerges from the room and its beautifully seductive light and stumbles out into a gothic in green Victorian kitchen.

Recognition is instantaneous and Dutch suddenly remembers everything. On the buttery surface of the island's butcherblock top, a hot, aromatic hot meal awaits. Dutch knows it is for him. Just as he knows who left it—Ara—a woman he could never really forget no matter what name she calls herself. When his belly is full, and his mind clear, Dutch leaves by way of the white door standing open, with hardly a fleeting thought of the room he narrowly escaped, save one.

He spots her on the topmost rise of a shallow hill outside. With her hands set firmly on her hips, her eyes overlook the whole of the wilting house. She doesn't see him at all, but Dutch doesn't mind. His thoughts are no longer fugacious. In fact, they instantly turn into solid, doubtless decision when she turns and takes notice of his presence, a hint of a smile on her lips that—for once—reaches her eyes. *Not one more night*, Dutch thinks, his jaw set and his eyes taking in every detail that makes her, committing them all to memory. Her house or not, she will not sleep another night in that room, alone. Hell, it's not like there is any place in the world he would rather be.

❀ ❀ ❀

  The afternoon grows hot and endless. With the yard manicured and growing compliantly, the pair have run out of work to complete outside, yet the day continues to run absurdly long. The easy silence they once shared, content in the rhythm of their separate tasks, now grows sticky with complacency and nerve-tingling anticipation. Where both were once satisfied simply by the presence of the other near at hand, without a thought or care of the world outside the trees, one of them now wonders what is to happen next.
  A radiant sun continues to beat down upon the pair, wringing the sweat from their pores as they pluck meaningless at the grass or fuss over the sturdy arrangement of the stones of the wall surrounding the garden beds. Ara grows thirsty. They both need water. Naturally, with the kitchen still only responding to her, it is she who walks in to find the metal box sitting in the open on the island. Pinned to the top, under a thin metal bar, is the paper workorder as bright as a beacon. Just a single sheet, yet it stops her breath. It is not the workorder itself that makes her lungs burn; she has seen others just like it, right down to and including the promise of payment in an unknown amount and only after the job is completed. No, what makes her mind spin is that she has seen *this* workorder before.
  There is no wonder as to how this box and its workorder have come to be in her possession—she found it in the kitchen after all. No secrets can be kept from the House, and secrets remain secrets only at the House's discretion, and always in favor of the House. This box was brought to her because she needed to see it, because *this* workorder is what brought Dutch here in the first place. Ara snatches up the damnable thing and rushes it from the very place the document aims to destroy.
  Dutch is exactly where she left him, sitting on the rock wall of the first garden bed. He looks content, his face shining with a kind of peace that makes Ara furious. He catches sight of her and smiles a grin of such warmth as to snatch away Ara's breath in a way very different than the workorder had, causing her a moment of doubt. She nearly throws the box to the woods, never to speak of it again. She could do it. He would see her do it, too, and would never question it, and so trapping him here,

indefinitely. Dutch would never be able to leave even if he wanted to. Such things have happened before, Ara knows. Just as well, she knows what will come next and the House is too weak to withstand another attack from a mob of grief-stricken outsiders. She clenches her teeth and hurls the box, instead, to the ground at his feet.

"Is *that* what *this* is all about?" Ara does not yell; she does not shout. Terrifyingly calm, she watches his grin disintegrate, his gaze to drop to the box in the dirt at his boots. "You work for that landscape company," she growls, low and quiet, perhaps angry more for the fact that he refuses to look up from that paper on the metal box and see the hurt behind it all. "You are contracted to take everything from me. *'By any means necessary,'*" she quotes with a sneer.

"That's not why I'm here," Dutch says, finally looking up to meet her hot glare. "I mean, it is, but—"

"But you figured you could get the place cleaned up first, is that it?" Ara snaps, cutting off any attempt at disarming her. He's not going to weasel out of this one with sweet words meant only to soften and deceive. "Next, you'll be telling me how this is in my best interest. How overwhelming maintaining the grounds will become and that selling will free me of the burden and open doors to experiences I've never known and worlds I have never explored. Have I got that about right?"

Glaring down into those eyes, wide and dark and full of guilty innocence, Ara suddenly struggles to hold onto her fury. Why is he looking at her like that? Why does he not speak? Defend himself? Give her some excuse? *Say something!* But Ara, at once, feels ashamed. The metal box and its workorder are still in the dirt. The sunlight glints off the dull case reminding her of what caused all this in the first place. It's an excuse, and an old one, but one she holds onto desperately.

Dutch doesn't say a word. He can only stare at that damned box she's thrown at his feet. Dutch had forgotten all about it; forgotten how he had come to be here at all, but he hadn't cared. Now it's back, staring him in the face only a little less harsh than the anger it has caused in the only woman he has ever... How did she get a hold of that? Dutch keeps his seat, working his jaw and clenching his teeth. Nothing he can say will make this situation any better, not with the amount of pain raging in her storm-filled eyes hungry for—and that's when it hits him.

Behind all the anger, the fright—the hurt—Dutch sees how skinny Ara really is. Her face, though handsome, is a little gaunt. Her muscles, though tone, are ropey and stretched tight over her bones. Her clothes he had mistaken for baggy, hang loose over a frame too thin. He remembers now finding her on the floor in that room behind the kitchen. He remembers picking her up, how light she felt in his arms. Far lighter than she should have been, and hot to the touch. Had that harsh blue light of the room not been so disorienting, he would have done more than lay her down on the bed. He certainly would not have lied down next to her, but he had been so tired, and, in the moment, it seemed the most natural act in the world. He should have done more. Has the tea he's watched her imbibe been the only nourishment she's had?

"Get out."

The words he never wanted to hear her say, spill out and roll harmlessly over him.

"Get out and find your fortune elsewhere."

Dutch can no longer bear to see her like this. He stands. Brushing the dirt from the seat of his jeans and his hands, Dutch heads straight for the gate hidden in the surrounding thicket without saying a word.

Just like that, Dutch walks out, passing by her so close that their shoulders brush. For Ara, it is nearly enough to make her buckle, to break down and cry out for forgiveness. Between the shock and relief, both equally alarming, her breath is locked down in a bog of regret. She does not turn to watch him go, not even when the sound of his boots crunching over the freshly exposed rock of the driveway fades to oblivion. Silence descends over neatly trimmed estate. The air grows stale, placid, and the property feels larger than ever. It might as well be the world with only she left to tend to it, having run off the only companion who volunteered to stand next to her.

Rich dirt is there to catch her knees when the strength in her legs gives out. Her eyes squeeze against the truth she has denied for years untold: her family is not coming back, they never were. It was a lie she told herself to make their loss bearable. She grabs a handful of the dark soil, clinging to the moist earth passing between her fingers the tighter she tries to hold on. The yellow daffodils sway in a random breeze. Their dance blurred as Ara fights the burning lump climbing up her chest. Whatever the reasons that brought him to her, Dutch has breathed new life into the house and all that dwells within. The property shines! But that brilliance will fade, Ara cannot hold it alone The House can still fall, and she still will have failed. The strength to hold back her tears, slips away.

The slap of a white paper bag hitting the ground next to her is as gentle as it is startling. Ara gasps, forgetting her tears. She stares at the bag, watches his hand work open the top folded closed, releasing an aroma that is mouthwatering. Ara's stomach rumbles like a beast too long asleep. This is not the sort of meal the kitchen puts out and she gawks as his hand plunges into the bag's shallow depths and removes a round parcel wrapped in more white paper.

"I have never seen you eat. Not once." Dutch's voice is heavy and coarse but not unkind as he nudges the bag closer to her. "You have got to be hungry."

Returning to the rock wall, Dutch sits. There is a crumpling of paper then a pause. "First, eat," he says around a mouth suddenly full. "Then, we'll talk. You've got this all wrong."

Ara's eyes have not moved from the bag standing open now and close enough that all she need do is lift her hand. The savory smell is intoxicating. She won't look at Dutch. She can't. This could be a trick. Gingerly she reaches in as though the paper bag might contain a viper. Instead, a second paper-wrapped parcel meets her fingertips. It is warm, and she likes the way the paper crinkles in her hand. The smell of cooked meat, hot cheese, and warmed bread is divine. Raising the parcel to her face, peeling back the folds in the paper of a meal the kitchen has certainly never crafted, Ara suddenly understands what the House had been planning, all along.

How silly to think herself wiser than the titans and the dragons of old. How could she have been so blind, so naive? Restoration and maintenance of such a House and its surrounding grove is just too much for one but might be just the right amount for two. Ara turns. Dutch's back is to her, strong and relaxed and so close that Ara can resist no longer. She relents and hot tears streak down her cheeks.

※ ※ ※

Every muscle in Dutch's body freezes when an unexpected touch presses to his back. Ara has never touched him, not since that first handshake a lifetime ago. Now, she sages against him, her forehead coming to rest between his shoulder blades. All at once, nothing else matters. Dutch is careful not to move. Swallowing his mouthful of hamburger, he makes no attempt to go for another bite.

Is she crying?

So surprising is the touch that Dutch flinches when it vanishes. But Ara does not. He waits patiently as she rises to her feet and walks around to face him. She looks different; she is glowing. Still the same Ara, but this version is smiling all the way up to her eyes and, with it, she is transformed. From hard and fierce she becomes soft, elegant, with steadfast poise and grace. For Dutch there is no place, no world without Ara in it and at his side, for he wishes to never be away from hers.

When she reaches for his hand, he gives it. Her grip is cool and dry. Her smooth skin, her electric touch, he follows willingly as she guides him into the House through the simple, white door. She does not lead him to the right, to the kitchen as she has before. This time she goes left, into a great room that could fit the small house he had grown up in. There is an ugly crack running up one wall. It's thin, barely noticeable, but one he resolves to fix, nonetheless. But even that is small potatoes compared to the wonder in the spacious dome of the glass solarium at the end of the room and what stands there.

A tree. A real tree. Bigger around than he by three or four times, and seemingly comprised of numerous thick stalks twisted and intertwined together reaching for the heavens far out of reach. Dutch can smell the earthy musk of the bark. He can almost feel the breeze of a ripe summer day. Large leaves of green or red or both rustle gently on its branches hanging like an open oversized umbrella. Hell, he can practically hear birds chirping on the phantom breath of air though there are none to fly by. Such a magnificent tree! It cannot possibly be contained within glass, metal, wood, and brick. Surely, they must be outside, bathing freely under a bright, golden sky; that the House and its walls are the illusion.

He does not see the door right away when Ara leads him around to the side of the tree that faces the world beyond the glass. Recessed into the ropey bark, the iron handle is the most obvious—hell—the *only* detail that gives away the door at all. From under her shirt, Ara reveals an antique key that she has kept hidden, hanging from a thin chord around her neck. Made of brass or copper, with multiple loops on one end, and three, square teeth of different heights set on the other, it slides perfectly into the tiny hole in the door, under the handle. Ara twists. There is a click, and the door swings inward.

A tree in a solarium is not impossible. The gentle wafting breeze could have come from an open window. Even the birds, their faint melody could just as well come from his own imagination. What his eyes behold as the door opens is—*not possible*—a world as vast and unending as the one outside. A world still cloaked in night, waiting, beckoning him to explore. All he has looked for, his whole life, unfolds like a favorite book that is never too old to be read again and again.

"Is this real?" he asks, almost fearfully lest the treasure at the bottom of a long, stone stairway might vanish as a puff of smoke.

Her face, bright and brimming with hope, quells his fear. She sees it too, just as he does. Probably better. Whimsical charm encased in an ageless beauty, Ara, says nothing. She simply takes up his hand, gives it a squeeze, and starts down the steps. Her grip is firm but not strong; Dutch could let go. He can still stay behind, but why would he when everything he wants, wants him in return. He does not look back to the sound of the door softly closing behind him. His gaze is set on the stars twinkling below and the woman leading him to them.

❊ ❊ ❊

Old Charlie can hardly recall the last time he closed the office for any reason other than family illness or a federally sanctioned holiday—both of which ceased to matter when Dolores died. Every day since, rain or shine, TerAvest Landscaping has been open for business. Well, except for that brief period after Dutch left town, damn near a decade ago—what an ordeal that had been. At the time, Charlie had been thankful Dutch wasn't around. He had believed that his absence from the events that befell the town had saved him from some tragedy. Now, standing alone on his back porch, overlooking the northwest part of town quiet under heavy gray skies, the shop closed for the first time in years, Charlie wonders if he hadn't been wrong.

'You're reading too much into it, dear.' He can almost hear Dolores say in her sweet, smokey voice that always managed to be a little too high-pitched. *'Dutch is a big boy now. He can make choices for himself.'*

"Times have changed, honey," Charlie replies to the ghost of the only woman who ever understood him. Of course, he could hardly say the same about her. If it hadn't been for Dolores, Charlie wouldn't have Dutch to worry over in the first place.

Anthony is gone now, too. He said he found Dutch's work truck; that he honked his horn, called out, even looked for a way in through the hedge—though Charlie severely doubts it. With no sign of Dutch and his cell phone abandoned in the cab along with the metal case with the workorder pinned to it, Anthony said he left the spare keys hanging from the side mirror before returning to town with a what-else-could-he-have-done attitude.

It's not that Charlie blames the boy for not trying harder. Anthony knows about that place, that house, better than most—what losing his sister to it and all. When the next day came with no word, no sign of Dutch, Anthony walked into work, took one look at Charlie, and walked right back out. He didn't even bother to clean out his locker. The look on his face—Charlie hangs his head at the memory, leaning his weight against the porch railing, its paint peeling away in flakes—Anthony knew then that his little prank had just rendered a dire cost. For *that* Charlie grinds his teeth. For that, his tired, old heart hasn't the strength to forgive.

He heard that Anthony packed up his belongings later that same day and left town with no forwarding address, leaving what really happened up there a mystery. Charlie took it upon himself to check, but only once. It's a long drive to the outskirts and his old hips started to ache before he had gone halfway. That pain in his knee began to flare up, too. In truth, he had made a whole host of excuses that caused him to miss the turnoff to the Moore estate. He ended up driving all the way to the next city, an hour away, to some hardware store for tools he didn't need. With no turnoff going back the other way, Charlie drove by with his tunnel vision locked on the skyline and ignoring the nagging voice growing in his head wondering if he had made another mistake.

Unable to face his crew or the unrelenting questions from his secretary, Gina, he closed TerAvest Landscaping and walked away from the business he had started with Dolores, so many years ago. Before their two daughters, before Dutch, back when they thought they could never have children of their own, Charlie had Dolores and a dream. The Moore House had been their first client—Dolores planted the stake outside the property herself. Always polite, they paid upfront a substantial amount that gave his blossoming bud of a business the roots it needed to go the distance, and Dolores grew chummy with the lady of the house. Thin and frail, the woman looked too weak to have been as pregnant as she was, and never did Charlie consider her dangerous.

Dolores wasn't the same after that woman's death, not even after giving birth to two girls that she never thought she could have. She stopped going to work with Charlie. Stopped taking phone calls or invoice payments; Dolores mostly stayed home with the children. She had said she was happy enough, but Charlie could see the melancholy that had started to coat her like moss. She never went back to the Moore House. At least, she said that she didn't—Charlie wonders still. When the children were grown and fledged, the remaining spark that had been his Dolores went out. Her body had not been far behind. He blamed the Moore House—still does— and nobody in this town would condemn him for it.

"This time, it's different," Charlie repeats. Dutch should not have been up there in the first place. Hell, he shouldn't have been in town, at all. Seeing him return broke Charlie's old heart nearly as bad as when he lost Dolores. Like a son, that boy. He may have raised him, but he never told him about where he came from. A regret that now hangs solemnly off Charlie's old shoulders.

Under a low sky, heavy with rolling slate-gray clouds, Charlie feels older than ever. Dutch might still come back; he tries to convince himself but hears nothing save the creak of the old porch against a gust of cold wind. If he does, the company truck will be waiting for him—the Moore House is not a place one gets to by accident, the truck very well may sit there indefinitely. Maybe he'll find Dolores and bring her back with him. Won't she be grateful for the transportation, for the road back to town is just as long.

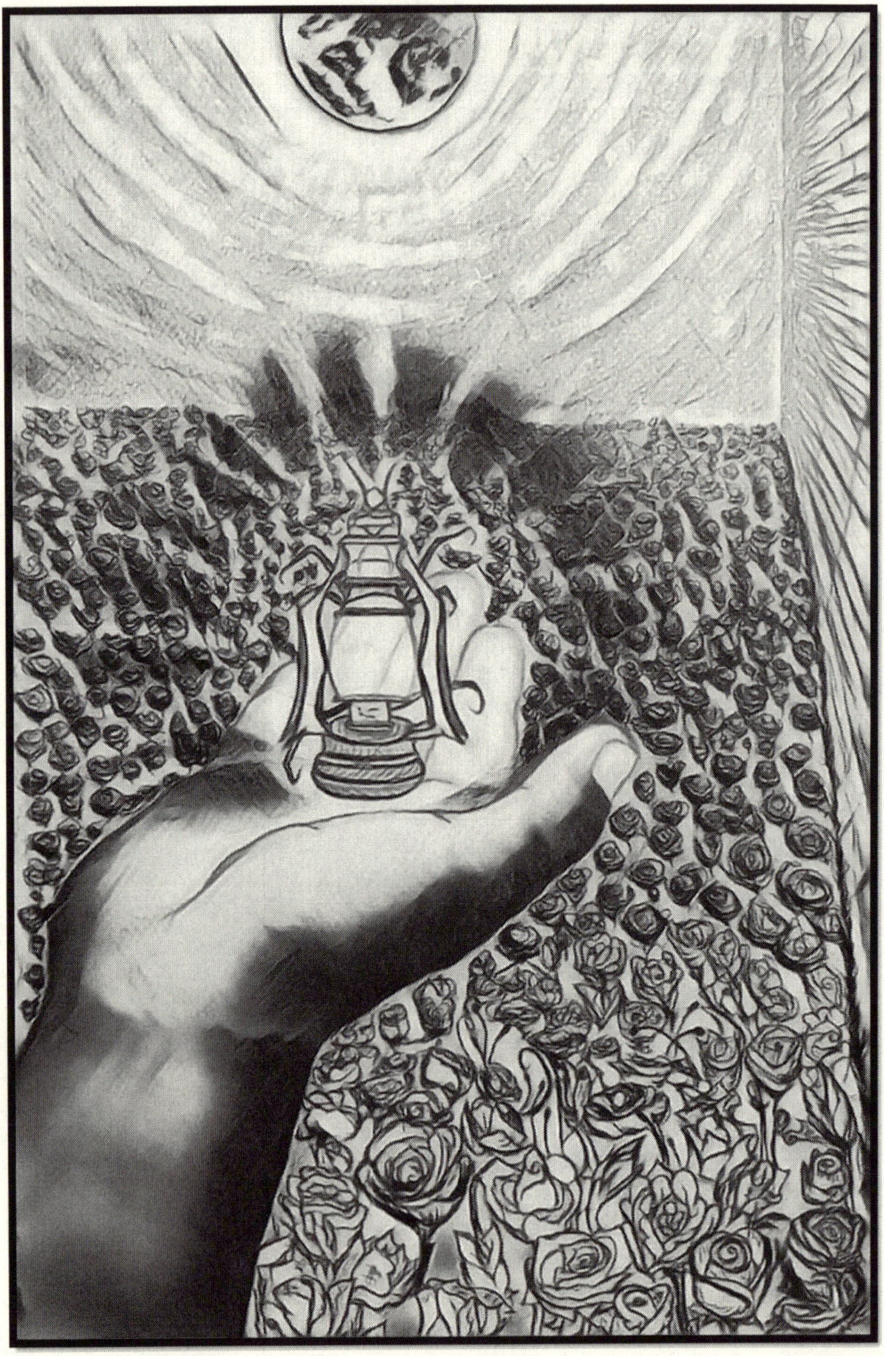

MARCH

✦ Under the Moon ✦

"There is a festival," the girl had told him. "A festival for stories."

"What kind of stories?" the boy had asked in return, both ignoring the bustling market going on around them. He had never met this girl before. About his own age, both stuck in that curious place between adolescence and adulthood, they two are the youngest wandering among the sea of people crowding the streets on a hot day, spotting one another had been easy. The fact that she had approached him first, had the young man entranced.

"All kinds," she replied with a bright smile. "Tonight, when the moon shines brightest." She then scampered off, disappearing into the constantly shifting throng, leaving him dumbfounded and bewildered with only vague, verbal directions. An alluring sweet musk of roses lingered in his nose as well as her promise of adventure to echo in his ear. How that had been enough to compel the young man to slip away after the sun set, to pick his way through a forest of tall trees to reach a moon-lit meadow atop the crest of a high, flat-topped hill beyond the outskirts of town, he could not say.

The meadow is empty. Tall, wispy grasses brush softly against his pants. His shoes are damp with dew. A cricket, then two, serenade one another across the deep reaches of night. A light breeze whispers back. He is alone. The dark sky is so thick with stars that the black beyond is nearly indistinguishable. In town, lights from front porches and along streets shine brightly, but all are too far away to pollute the ethereal glow of the heavens above.

A gibbous moon hangs low and bright enough for the young man to see by, luring him to venture from the tree line. A crumbling stone wall is the darkest object on the hilltop, running across the crest cutting it in half like the protruded spine of some long-buried creature. There, standing right where she said she would be—right where he had been sure he saw no one only a breath before—is the girl he had met in the marketplace. Her hands are relaxed, gently clasped together in front of her dress. Long and simple, the pale blue cloth appears to glow with moon light as much as it seems to emit a soft luminescence all its own. She has been waiting for him, and his being there suddenly does not seem so strange.

She smiles with the young man's approach. If she has been waiting long, she does not appear to mind. Behind her, on the other side of the old wall, stone ruins of some civilization long gone barely stand, or lay in heaps of blocks worn smooth where they do no longer. Steps from a chipped and crumbling archway over the only gap in the wall, this mistress of the moon beseeches him forward with the inviting motion from one slender hand aglow as though coated in opalescence.

"This way."

No one else is around. Only he, the peculiar young woman, and the lantern bugs flittering about are out on this deliciously warm summer's night. He is confident now that there is no festival. Still, the young man's curiosity over why she has brought him to this ancient place grows beyond what he can ignore. He reaches out to touch her, and the hand that reeled him closer slips neatly into his. Her skin is warm, and soft as velvet. This girl, whose name he does not know, leads him under a stone arch and through the gate-less threshold with a child's giddiness in showing off her favorite thing in all the world. He follows gladly. On this night, with her, he will go anywhere.

On the other side of the wall, shadows reign supreme. Squat and eerily silent structures stand as tombs or mausoleums of an Age long past. The air is cooler. Where there are no structures or piles of stone, a vast field of tangled growth takes over. A meadow, one he had somehow failed to notice from outside the wall, reaches impossibly far—as far as his eyes can see—and glows with a ghostly hue under the soft radiance of the moon. It is also empty save for one puzzled young man and his equally bemusing companion.

"I thought you said there was a festival," he says charmed and in no hurry to leave.

She giggles. "There is, silly. Look there!" She points an elegant finger down, toward the tall grass. "Can you see it?"

He kneels with her, feeling her excitement as though it were his own. Near the tip of one long, slender blade of grass, shining silver, a tiny light winks on.

"A lantern-bug?"

She giggles again. "A lantern, indeed." She reaches out to the little insect. Her other hand still gripping to that of the young man. Their fingers intertwined—he never wants to let go—and the young man suddenly feels barely out of boyhood. And the young woman? A perplexing girl just as innocent as he. In the palm of her outstretched hand, he can almost see the lantern instead of the bug. She does not hold it exactly more than it seems to float aloft, suspended just above her skin by some unknown force.

"A lantern that hangs over a garden hidden under the moon." The light rises with her as she stands. With a gentle push, the lantern lifts off and floats to the wall flanking the open space, to hang there in line of yet more lanterns where the boy is sure there had been none a moment ago.

All around, the garden glows. The scent of jasmine fills the air. Cherry blossoms, too. So fragrant to practically be palpable; the boy can almost taste the sweet essence that fills his nose. There are more lanterns now. Or maybe they have always been there, hanging from the wall off elaborate iron rods spaced every few steps. Though every lantern is lit, the gentle, golden blush illuminating the garden does not come from the lanterns at all.

As the boy, too, regains his feet, his head brushes against the subtle kiss of a rose stemming from the thick mass of vines all but covering the stone wall. The blossom is closed, but not tightly, merely on the brink of unfurling. Against the caress of the boy's cheek, the plush lips of velveteen, deep crimson petals open, ever so slightly, in anticipation of a kiss and just as wanting. Not from the boy, but from a lover yet to arrive, and so the flower stays closed and dreams on.

"Do you see?" a cool, hushed whisper slips past his ear.

"Yes," answers the boy truthfully, though not exactly sure of what it is he sees. "Yes, I do."

There is a story there, residing within the folds of those red lips. A tale of beauty, as much as it is of sorrow, is etched within the petals, along the stem, and across the veins of the leaves. A story of a jilted lover wooed by dazzling promises made by a dashing prince but doomed only to trickery emanates faintly from the red, red rose.

The golden haze that he had mistaken for lamp light, instead, comes from the flowers themselves, filling the field with a pre-dawn glow. The more he looks, the brighter they shine. Flowers that have opened wide let off only a faint hue. Others that are but buds, their tales yet to be known, shine as bright as candles. Each of them a story, as unique and exceptional as the patterns folded in the blossoms themselves, to meet the eye ready to read them. The field hums. An operetta of dreamy, voiceless harmony calling out to ears ready to hear them. But the depths of either their songs or their tales etched into their stems and leaves, in their pollen ready for a busy bee to move the stories about and create new ones, to the boy, all remain secreted away.

It is brighter now. Though dozens of lanterns hang from the sturdy stone wall, hung every few paces at different heights so they appear to float along the garden's perimeter, the growing light is akin to that of an early sun too soon on the rise. The young pair have ventured far indeed. Hand in hand, they turn from the roses to dash across the expanse of tall grass, heading for the stone huts standing now on either side of a narrow road that surely has been here, this whole time.

The boy is surprised when the supple rubber soles of his shoes strike steadfast rock. The grass here is shorter, barely reaching above his ankles, and the path under their feet is made of flat-topped stones. Together, the playful pair hop from stone to stone until a final jump lands them on a road made of many much smaller stones packed tightly together. The boy is surprised the road is in such good condition. Then again, why would it not be?

He marvels briefly at the tight-knit work of the cobblestones that make the street. Each is richly woven with vibrant shades of gray, brown, red, and gold: stories of dark, clear nights and those of storms; of wickedly hot days and ones so cold as to freeze a bird dead, midflight. Like the roses, the stones, too, are made of stories. Each a comprised tale of travel. Each step is to cross the comings and goings of others who have walked roads in their own journeys. The girl merrily leads across them at a jog.

Squat structures, hardly taller than a man grown, line the road on either side and are far from the decrepit ruins the boy feels he remembered once seeing. These huts are built strong with stones or logs mortared together by old, simple stories that have been told by countless mouths over Ages. The tales in the wood doors and window frames are downright ancient. Complex stories, reaching far back in Time. Made from slabs cut from different trees, felled, pressed, and wedged together, their tales are wholly novel and make each hut a contained epic of its own. Each one brimming with potential, each one shuttered and locked tight. In the growing golden ambience of an enchanted morning, all is silent.

"We're too early," says the boy while his eyes wander from hut to hut, looking for what his heart tells him otherwise.

"Nonsense," says his guide growing lovelier with each passing second. "We're right on time."

The sun breaks the horizon and, all at once, shutters, doors, and windows fly open. Curtains of protective canvas are whipped back and secured, exposing the hidden centers of various vendor shacks to suddenly ample light. Voices shout exuberantly from the vendors within, shattering the silence into raining flecks of gold. They shout from windows. They call from stalls. From behind tabletops of polished wood or stone, they hock their wears of adventure stories, cooking stories, tales of romance and woes. They hold high old legends worth more than they're priced; they brandish new tales priced more than they're worth. They shout to the pair, one and all, that their stories are the best to be had and of the highest value.

Even the vendors are stories themselves. A helmeted rider of the deserts peddles vials of dream-scale; a scantily clad vixen who looks more pirate than shopkeeper in her stall stacked with fine linens and canvas; a young warrior already full of scars and wanderlust in his eyes sells testaments of his many escapades—all here, ready now, and can be yours for the right price.

Some vendors are not vendors at all. Some are magicians or witches, or other magical things not made of stories but are instead characters that weave tales of their own. Their wares are but mere illusions meant to hook and ensnare a soul unlucky enough to wander too close, to draw a hapless audience inside where their true intentions lay shrouded. But the boy cannot tell the difference. It is all so glamorous, so new, he cannot help but be overcome with wonder.

For one such cart, not a fixed structure at all, he cannot help but take a closer look. Made of solid ivory or bone of such radiant white that it exudes the essence of a tale about a great hunt in a distant land where dwell beasts of monstrous proportions. The white pillars are wrapped in ivy of deep jade and hold up a thin, rounded slab of the white material that reminds the boy of a shoulder blade. On either side of the cart's front hangs a curtain of fine, translucent white material, trimmed exquisitely in gold and blue, that both contains the mesmerizing brilliance within the booth while outclassing all others nearby. The boy ventures closer.

On the countertop, front and center and neatly lined on a bed of moss, beautifully crafted wands are on display. Ranging from deep cherry to rich mahogany to milky, buttery beech, the wares are the most enticing yet. Some wands are twisted into spirals, but most are tapered and simple, all throb with energy. Woven into the fine grain of each are tales of where they came from, how they came to be, and for what purpose. Each one primed to aid a conjuror willing to dive deep into stories of their own. Behind the counter, leaning on her elbows, is a lady-vendor. She is not a story like the others, nor is she a witch or a warlock—her hand is not one that can use the items she sells. She is something different. A creature yet to be but has already existed for a long time.

With a long, elegant face that is pleasing to look at, large doe-eyes to beg a fool draw forward, vivacious lips begging to be kissed, and a pair of antlers that rise sharply from the crown of her head, she is a myth. The boy has only heard rumors of such a creature, yet here one stands, magnificent and alluring. Coils of soft, moss-like hair grows further down the back of her neck than it should and cascades over a leather bodice that shows more than it hides. Her lower half remains obscured behind the counter.

She does not speak, but she does hum. A peculiar melody instilled with the sort of comfort only dreams are made of. When she smiles, the boy—suddenly feeling not so little anymore—nearly goes to her. Only the tug of a warm hand firming grasping his own breaks the spell of the huldra. The boy is saved by the precocious girl—now not so much a child anymore, either.

"Look, there!" she shouts, and he turns away from certain doom for the western horizon where she points as they leave market row.

The bustle of stalls and carts ends abruptly and the world beyond opens wide. At the edge of the cobblestone road, the landscape falls away to vast, grassy fields below and stretching for leagues until the faint, purple haze of mountains marks sharply their end. To these fields of chartreuse she points; to the riders racing along hill and prairie on various sorts of wonderous steeds. Many ride horses, others ride birds the size of horses. A few ride elephants: giant, grey-skinned beasts, each with a nose longer than a man is tall. Still more rider creatures of such peculiarity that they have yet to be named. Some with three eyes and colorful scales for skin. Some that resemble horses but with faces much longer, smooth skin absent of hair—as far as can be seen at such a distance—and with an extra pair of legs. Some riders race, others joust, but mostly they seem content to simply ride free and wild.

The view is stopped short when structures again line the street. No more vendor huts, shacks, or carts. Here stand inns, taverns, music halls, brothels, saloons, and salons. Cheery sounds of laughter and cries of delight, and all-around gaiety, pour out open windows and doors in a queer sort of rhythm that collects in the air warming the street. They too beckon passers-by to enter with food or drink or to mingle in company of all sorts. The young pair run by them all.

Just as abruptly as they spring up, these structures too fall away and the World, this time, expands on both sides of the road. To the west, the plains roll gently with wide, shallow hills topped with dozens of cottages, all full of stories of a homier kind. A place where live children who still talk to animals or play with very real imaginary friends. Where adolescence comes with chores and adventures abound and no time for both. For those growing up, there are battles of angsts to be fought, hearts to win, and treasures to be discovered. On the other side of the street, a large, lush park peppered with benches, ponds, and trees makes up the city's center. Daydreamers recline and relax in long reprieves from the real world to bask in the radiant glow of this one while their muses whisper sweetly into their ears.

The cobblestone road is much wider now and encloses the park on three sides as it curves around a lazy bend before descending into more of the city still hidden from view. At the apex of the bend, the ground rises dramatically to a grand vista where stands a castle, bright and brilliant and rich with stories to enchant any eyes that fall upon it. This close, the boy can see clearly the colorful banners flying from the tips of each magnificent tower, yet it all remains just out of reach.

Below the whipping banners, rows of knights in glinting armor ride their war stallions gallantly through the castle gates while high above the tallest battlement ride warriors of a different sort, on beasts that fly the skies. Dragons. The boy, now more of a young man, can hardly believe his eyes. One such creature, with a black and gold body so immense that its rider is but a spec on its back, dives particularly fast and low letting out an arching blast of yellow and red fire. The flames nearly reach one of the lofty banners before dispersing harmlessly into the air as the tug at his hand turns the young man away.

Drawn onward, they follow the curve of the cobblestone street to the crest of a long, steeply sloped hill. The edge of the park on this side is lined with trees, each taller than the last as the street descends. Starting with a short, spindly little cherry tree nearest the castle, that will one day bear fruit that a spiteful, jealous woman will use to make a pie with sinister agenda, to a proud and elegant weeping willow not ripe with fruit or flowers but heavy with long, satin leaves to trap bad dreams and sweep them away, passed the hill's crest.

The last tree along the park's edge is also the largest, with pink and white blossoms so eyes-catching, their perfume so fragrant, that they will one day catch a daydreamer's inspiration and give bloom to a story of a girl who will be written at as a great warrior. Her story already etched into the curl of the pedals, in the stem and pistil, it is a grand epic, and yet, a short story compared to the sight that opens to the south, beyond the edge of the park—beyond the edge of the city!

At the bottom of the hill, the road comes to an end at the start of a spectacular harbor. A prestigious entrance, if ever there was one, to an ocean sparkling blue and green and silver. The harbor is a busy, bustling place. Men shout, whistles blow, and animals bray secured in their crates. Boots and bare feet alike slap against the docks, gangplanks, and ramps as cargo is moved about. Vessels of every make, style, and size line the docks or float just offshore. There are ships with bulbous sails and multiple decks tied next to canoes and single-man pontoons. A long ship, with three decks, has only just set sail. Her dusky-white sails catch the wind, pulling her headstrong into open waters—a floating story making her way to the shores of some spectacular tale of treasure and conquest. Dolphins ride her wake. Whales breach the calmer surface of deeper water further out. Gulls and other seabirds drift alongside her unfurled canopies. A daring hunter, a stowaway asleep in the ship's crow's nest, accompanies the vessel to distant lands.

The young man is speechless.

"I have the best view," whispers the girl in his ear.

He turns to her, finding the delight glittering in her eyes matches perfectly that which he feels for himself. The harbor, in all its splendor, suddenly becomes a poor substitute.

Her fingers still entwined with his, she draws him closer to the last structure atop the hill, opposite the park and before the final drop to the sea, the harbor, and rows of squat little cottages below. The door is quite something—a story in itself. Rounded at the top, most of its face is an ornate owl, as tall as a man, carved in relief and in such detail as to pain a mind as to how it was done. Serving as both guardian and entrance, the owl bars the way into what could have been a quaint cottage in the woods, if it did not stand at the edge of a fabled city. Nor if the cottage was not so tall. Cozy white with natural brown trim, and covered in all manner of climbing flowers, the cottage stretches skyward. Its severely gabled roof remains in line with the peaks of those higher up the hill, back the way they had come. His guide's hand closes over one long, protruding feather with a certain familiarity that mirrors possession. Only then does the young man see the knob that it is. With a twist and small effort, she shoulders the door to swing inward and ushers him inside.

The shaded space is comfortably cool and alight with the soft chirping of songbirds. He can see nothing at first with the drastic change in light. A click behind him tells him that his companion has closed the door; she could lock it for all he cares. Deep mahogany panels making up the floor, walls, and ceiling are as pleasing to the eye as the scent in the air is to his nose. No lamps are burning yet the aroma of lavender, burnt sage, and warm oil hangs in the air.

One extra-wide window next to the door, and a long but much smaller window at the first landing of wooded stairs twisting once to the floor higher up, provides much of the room's light. The rest comes from an adjacent room beyond the end of an oversized countertop stretching nearly the entire length of the main space. The workspace is laden with stone bowls, mortars, pestles, sleeping candles, books, quills, ink, and stacks of paper. On the corner at the far edge, a large orb the size of his head and glowing faintly of blue and gold, rests securely in a simple copper ring fixed to an iron platform.

As his eyes adjust, he finds the sounds of chirping that he had mistaken for birds does not come from anything bird-like at all. Fixed to the walls of this conjurer's hut are well-crafted and beautifully designed open-faced cabinets comprised of no less than a dozen little cubbies each. The largest cabinet takes up the entire wall separating to the room from the inclined stairway and holds twenty-four such cubes. Dozens of gold, silver, and brass keys of different shapes, sizes, and number of teeth hang along the bottom.

Coming and going from the cubes is an array of small creatures. A few seem to be asleep in their little cubbies while others constantly flitter about with and without wings. It is from these spry little things where the chirpings issue. Just like morning sparrows or robins, the long, lithe little creatures sing their quippy tunes from both beaked and soft-lipped mouths. Some have no identifiable facial markings at all, yet the young man can hear their songs all the same. Tiny tales of a roaring rivers, thick jungles, or maybe the simple babble of a fountain in a secret garden on the other side of the sea: he can almost picture them.

"What are they?" the young man asks little louder than a whisper, careful not to startled them. His guide, however, shows no such restraint.

"They're stories, of course," comes her answer, only hinting to the mystery he can almost understand. "All free to come and go as they please, but some call this home. I care for them, nurture them, help them grow." She releases his hand for the first time since taking it and allows him to roam while she contently strolls deeper into the room. The stories taking flight and swarm her, wrapping affectionately about her neck and arms and waist before wisping away to sing brighter than before.

"These are still little ones," says she, coaxing the young man to come along. "*Hints*, I call them. They can't speak yet, only glimmer."

She reaches for one of many glass jars filling a tall, narrow, multi-shelved nook neatly tucked into the corner at the end of the room. Choosing one, she uncorks the top and removes a pinch of the shining material filling nearly half of the jar.

"Dragonscale," speaks the young woman. "Stories love it."

One such tiny creature fluttering at her ear squeaks and squeals in adoration when she offers it the snack pinched in her fingers. The *hint* takes it in a snap. Devouring the morsel of sparkling powder, the wispy creature then radiates brightly, but briefly, before evaporating around her in a ribbon of mist. The young woman giggles and replaces the jar. "She'll be back."

Into the next room, where it is much brighter, the young woman leads. The floor is covered in plush rugs, and pillows of many shapes, sizes, and colors line the walls. A single pane of glass nearly makes up one whole wall overlooking a slice of harbor below and the waters beyond off to the left, and a piece of park and its largest tree on the right. Near center of the room, but closer to the long window, stands a tree. An actual tree, with a trunk thrice as big around as the young man is himself that corkscrews up and out through a hole in the ceiling. Branches with leaves as big as his hands shade the roof and cuts short any view of the cottage towering higher still.

"What happens when it rains?" asks the boy.

"Some water gets in," she answers, cheerily. "But the stories never allow for much."

Like the main room they just left, this one too is abounded with a variety of lofty creatures gliding about the open space. These ones are bigger. All of them he can see clearly. Even if he doesn't know what they are yet, they catch his attention in ways the *hints* did not.

"These are *shorts*," she says. One long, ribbon-like creature drifts close to her face, playfully seeking her attention. A shine, a sparkle, and a twist manage to make her giggle before the lovely little story sails away to mingle with the others hovering about the open alcoves lining the wall opposite the window. "They're almost full stories, but still lack proper grooming or training. They're still wild and like to run in packs though they're not all related."

The *shorts* do not fully approach the young man as he passes through the room, following his host. Unlike the *hints*, however, they do not shy away so easily. Instead, they sing brightly. If the *hints* were sparrows or robins lightly skipping from one fragile perch to the next, their chirps sweetly subdued, then *shorts* are morning birds of paradise basking in the glory of a perfect dawn. The young man finds it a difficult task to look anywhere else and nearly stumbles down the three stone steps leading out through the open door on the other side of the room.

The light outside is blinding, but his eyes adapt quickly, and the young man finds himself in a storybook garden complete with a murmuring stream snaking through a grass and moss blanketed yard. Flowers grow everywhere. Even from tangled masses of green draping over the handrails of a small footbridge arched over the babbling brook. Along the banks, mint grows wild. Over it all stands another willow tree. Though not quite as tall as the tree twisting up through the cottage's lower of its three rooves, its grand canopy is wide with long, slender branches, high above the ground, that reach far enough to cover more than half the yard in shade.

Tearing his gaze from the tree of his dreams, the young man finds his guide standing in the sunshine just outside the shade at the corner of the white, threaded split-rail fence to a second yard. Crowding the fence, and vying for her attention, are beasts so magnificent to behold that the young man's breath rushes in with a gasp.

She stands relaxed, her fingers hooked together behind her, patiently waiting for her guest to appreciate the proud creatures at her back. More striking than the dragons circling the castle, more majestic than he could have ever thought possible, are her own extraordinary steeds. Four of them. Groomed, polished, and harnessed in trappings they wear nobly. He knows what they are before she speaks their name.

"*Novels.*"

Such a beautiful word for such stunning creatures, with all their shine and quiet power. One steed in particular catches his eye more than the others. Its long, sinewy body is covered with incandescent scales brilliant in the summer light as though infused with mother-of-pearl. Aware of its audience, the novel swings its majestic head to stare at the young man approaching it. Great antlers rise from its massive skull like a crown, balanced in regal poise that reminds him of a story he heard once.

"Ah," says the girl, noticing the attention shared by the two. "A unique one, that. This is Anthology, a chimera, of sorts. He will give rise to epics one day."

A flick of her wrist and the great beast takes to the air, its whip-like body catching the wind without the need of cumbersome wings. Twisting high into the sky above the garden, the creature curls to swoop low and level with the eyes of its new admirer. Close enough to touch, the young man nearly extends his hand, but holds back. Instead, he gazes deep into a mystical world held within this dragon's opalescent scales. Material and ethereal in the same instant, vast plains of emerald-green grass bloom deep inside the creature's body. Rivers of sapphire, mountains of amethyst, forests of jade; a city of stone that lies in ruin, and one of ivory that stands tall, all he can see with dazzling clarity. There are deserts of amber and citrine, and oceans of liquid lapis lazuli and, within them all, living things abound. All sorts. Inside of the great beast exists an entire world of surreal design balanced in chaotic harmony.

The beast circles, exposing to the young man a savannah of tall, browning grass. There is a gust of wind that he can feel, and a herd of deer are suddenly spooked from their rest. They scatter. The girl takes the boy's hand once more and, together, they give chase across the lands where native legends of great hunts once ran just as wild. They catch up to the stampeding herd that is no longer comprised of deer, but bison, and they are not fleeing, but charging. Quick on their heels, bursting up over a hillock, dark-skinned, bare-chested men on horseback pursue the herd. Hunters armed with bows and quivers full of arrows.

In a flat out run, the young pair race along with the thundering hooves to the tree line thick with aspen and pine. No longer do they run with bison; they run with elk leaping ahead on strong, nimble legs, their bodies as large as any horse. The young man can feel the thunderous pulse of their strong hearts, he can smell the musk radiating off their hides, their power pounding through their hooves as they churn the dirt. It is all so intoxicating; he could run like this forever.

They all break from the tree line on the other side of the forest and the pair of wild-eyed youths are caught up in a surging stampede of cattle. Giggling, the girl pulls the boy's hand, drawing him sharply in another direction and narrowly avoid a gang of horses driven hard by their riders. With curled-rim hats tight on their heads, reins in one hand and ropes with lassos in the other, cowboys drive the herd at an exhilarating pace across a dry, rocky prairie down to a flat plain below. The boy can just make out a farmhouse there, just a stone's throw from a sparkling stream. He might be able to see further if only he could get a little higher.

"This way," exclaims the girl.

Over a shallow ravine of basalt and granite boulders flecked with bits of mica and silica, he follows her into the scablands at the base of a craggy, jagged mountain. The girl calls out two notes bright with such melody that the boy finds himself willing to do anything she might ask of him just for the chance to hear those notes again. Apparently, so would the mountain. The solid, single peaked monolith of stone is, at once, alive! The ground shakes and trembles as a great form rises from its slumber. A head, shoulders, and an arm twists to meet the girl who has woken it. It is vaguely human in form, but on a scale that can hardly be fathomed. It reaches out the enormity of one gigantic, stone hand, laying it at her feet.

"Come on!" she cries and scrambles up the rounded edge of the mountain's fingertip.

The boy climbs after her. His fingers aching when the girl takes his hand and pulls him the rest of the way up.

"To the stars!" she cries.

The world below falls away at a speed that would be alarming if it not for the solid stone sturdy and unyielding under his feet and the warm hand holding tightly to his.

Higher and high they rise, and so fast! The wind rushing by his ears is the music of a heavenly choir. A crescendo of angels shouting forth in pure revelry of their rapid ascension. Higher. *Higher!* Above the clouds. Above the sky! Beyond where blue still holds true and to the bright twinkling lights higher still, they rise on the fingertip of stone. He holds tight to the hand of the girl who reaches out further than even a Titan can reach. Full of wonder and without fear she reaches, stretched out on the tips of her toes. The angels rejoice! The boy holds her steady—he will never let her fall—as she lifts her hand, palm up and eager, to cradle the glowing orb of a star sparkling with a magical glow on high. Exquisite, what she holds in her hand, yet no more so than the soft glimmer of a lowly lantern-bug. One no bigger than her thumb, in the deep, dark grass amidst the rubble of an old World forgotten in a garden hidden under the moon.

Tales in Hindsight

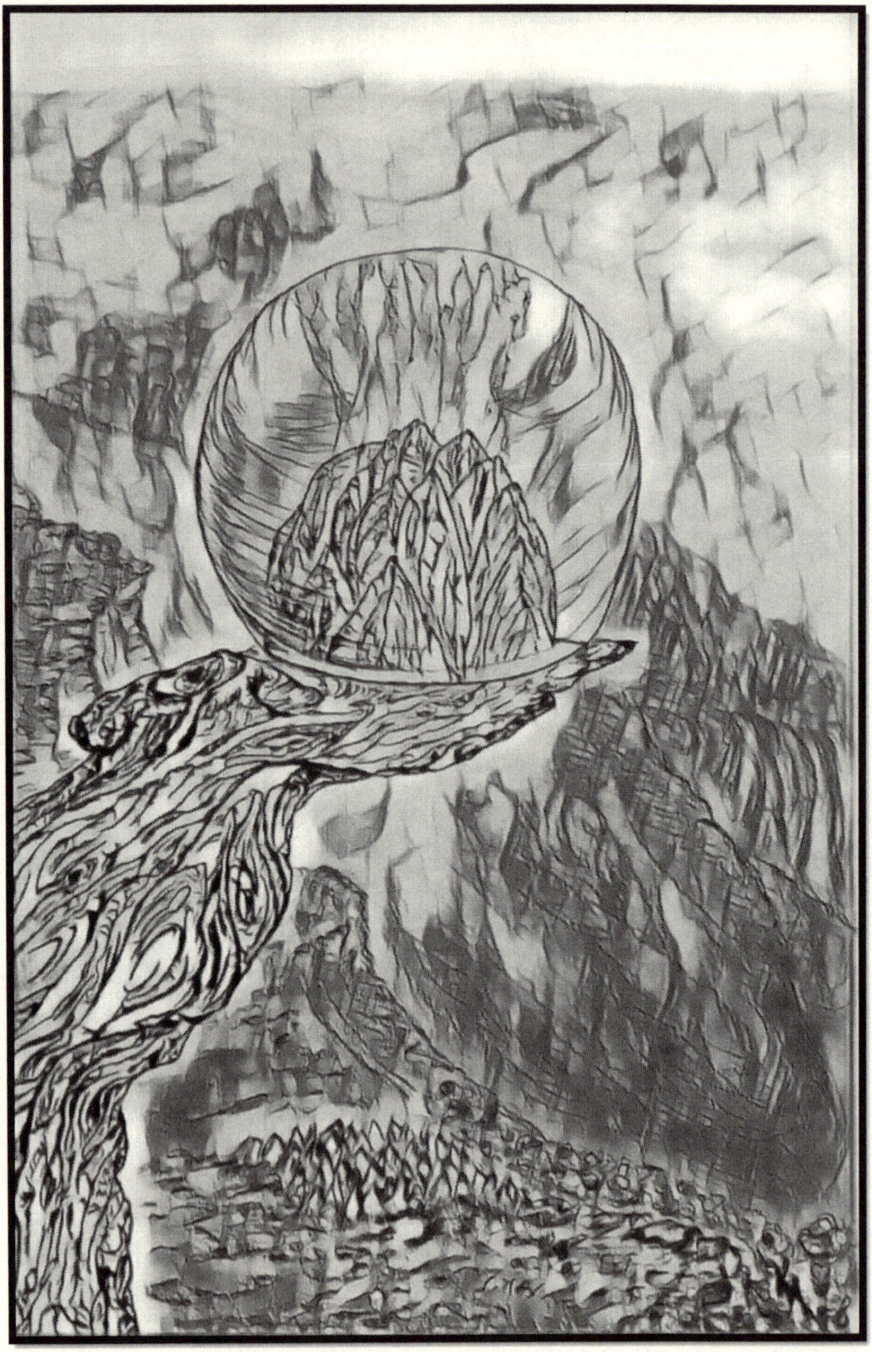

APRIL

✧ A TITAN IN THE WALLS ✧

Once upon a time, a very long time ago, there stood a House. A very special House.

But this story is older than even that, much more so. Long before there stood the House, when walked Titans. All manner of Titans. Water Titans. Sand Titans. Titans that were mountains. Titans that drove winds. No man has ever seen a Titan in all its glory for they all sleep now. The very last put itself to rest with the coming of Man and his Gods, and they are held there still by Man's faith in his Gods; there simply exists no room for Titans. Before Man—*oh*—how the Titans roamed. Their footsteps broke the ground, the seas churned in their wake. They, too, built masterpieces. Such pride they took in their endeavors, only to revel in the destruction of their creations just as joyously. This is the story of one of their own.

Among their kind, so very long ago, there happened to be one not so keen on the chaos and mayhem the others so savored: a Tree Titan, the smallest of their kind. Too small to play with its more gargantuan cousins for it could be crushed under a careless misstep. Its rare size, however, brought this peculiar Titan's attention to the happenings occurring closer to the ground. Earth—the largest Titan of all—fell asleep long before even the Tree Titan's time, to awakened only every so often for a yawn and stretch before her slumber resumed. No other Titan before the Tree ever took notice of the vast array of green plants that grew from her skin. From grasses to trees, shrubs, and moss, all in various shades of green—from limy yellows to the deepest emerald—blanketed the land on which all Titans walked.

Inspired by what it had discovered, the Tree Titan decided one day to make a creation of its own. Using a bit of its own sap encapsulated in a droplet of morning dew and held aloft, the Titan captured a ray of a new dawn. The charm blossomed and delicate pink petals unfurled in the morning light. The Tree Titan made a flower—the first of its kind.

It marveled at its creation. So pretty, so vibrant against the greens and browns of everything else, that the Titan had to have more. And more it made. Soon, all the Tree Titan's branches were adorned with the soft, lovely pedals. When space quickly grew inundated, the Titan turned to the trees nearby suitable to hold the pink blossoms without letting them touch the ground where they would surely be trampled and crushed. When all the canopies close at hand were covered with all the flowers they could hold, the Tree Titan began to wander. It sought out more trees to bear its beautiful creation and crowned each one it found.

In its long stroll much time passed, and a curious thing did happen. When, at last, the Tree Titan returned to the grove where it had laid its first blossoms, it had expected to find the trees bare; flowers were too delicate and fragile to last long out in the open, unprotected. Remarkably, instead of withered petals, the Titan found their numbers multiplied! Pink blossoms bedazzled far more branches of many more trees that had sprouted and grown in the Tree Titan's absence. Many of the petals were not even pink, but white, and sprinkled with tiny red dots. Gazing upon the grand expanse of its colorful grove, the Tree Titan, for the first time, felt joy. An elation unmatched that the Titan could only gawk in awe at the prosperity of its own creation. Such a perpetual field of pink and white, that it should have come as no surprise when it caught the attention of another.

The Wind Titan was first to take notice. A sweet fragrance made by the flowers caught by a wayward breeze was carried loyally aloft to where the great, formless Titan roamed. High above Earth, always floating above her, the Wind Titan breathed deep the gently intoxicating aroma. It savored the flowers' perfume for there was nothing else like it. It, too, desired more and made haste to the new, secreted garden and caught the Tree Titan in attendance, unaware.

Titans were never known for their courtesy or humility; such things did not exist in their Time. The Wind Titan blew into the garden with all speed. Without invitation nor announcement it scooped up flowers in droves, ripping them from their branches—much to the horror of the smaller, gentler Tree Titan. The Wind carried the blossoms high into the sky. It drank in their scent and delighted in the caress of the pink and white petals along its air currents for no other thing had done so before. So distracted by such merriment that the Wind Titan was blind to the error it had made until it found that it could not hold onto its newly discovered little treasures. Slowly, the blossoms lost their scent. Their petals began to wilt. Sadness, regret—feelings the Wind had not before known—suddenly weighed it down. The lofty Titan discovered remorse.

Recognizing that its actions were careless, the Wind made to return the blossoms to the Tree Titan that had watched helplessly from the grove below. They, of course, could not be reattached to the limbs from which they had been torn, so the Wind made to lay them across the Earth. The Tree could not bear to see its first and most loved creation in the dirt where they would brown and rot. So moved, the Wind instead cast the petals to its faithful breezes and bade them to spread the flowers much further than the Tree could travel; a gift from one Titan to another. In return, the Tree granted its breezes permission to waft through the grove as they pleased so that the Wind may always delight in the scent and softness of the flowers. With a promise to reveal nothing of the grove to the others, lest they cause more harm and destruction, the Wind left the Tree to its growing orchard. For a long time, no more took notice of the glorious oasis that began to spread across the land.

As the flowers, and the trees from which they bloomed, increased, the work in maintaining them grew too much for a lowly Tree Titan. It needed help. Not about to seek aid from other Titans, it sought to conceive a worthwhile apprentice. With a little pollen from the flowers, a tag of fuzz from a cottonwood, and more sappy resin from its own body, on a particular hot and sunny day the Tree Titan created bees. Bulbous little busy bodies striped in black and yellow, and seemingly too fat for their wings.

The charming insects took to the air with little ceremony and went straight to work. Buzzing on the air currents left by the Wind Titan to frolic in the grove, the eager little drones were perfectly content with their task. From bloom to bloom they drifted, moving and mixing pollen and so rewarded with sugary nectar made by the flowers that kept them going. With such rich food, the bees ventured far, some would be absent for days, but most stayed close to work the Titan's grove. It allowed them to build their waxy dome nests among its branches that the Tree gladly sheltered from the storms that inevitably passed overhead. In show of their gratitude, the bees made for the Tree a treat from the overabundance of nectar provided by the flowers: honey. Such an unexpected delight that a wonder arose in the Titan. What other manner of things could it create?

The Tree kept its creations small, at first. More buzzing things, crawling things, things that could easily hide within cracks in tree bark or among the leaves and grasses. One day, with a new combination of sticks, fuzz, and bits of the numerous crawling creatures, the Tree Titan made a wonderful discovery. It made the first bird. A most harmonious creature of divine splendor truly spectacular to behold. Capable of flight, but not like that of a bee or a butterfly—both creations the Tree Titan had not sought to outdo—birds had something extra. They hadn't fur or scales or hard shell-like outsides. Feathers covered their bodies, including their wings, so completely that not a single patch of skin showed. With their feathers, they caught the air more efficiently than a butterfly, and gained lift with much less effort. Nimble and far more stable, birds also outpaced and outdistanced even the hardiest bee. Able to fly in all sorts of weather, not just the clear, warm days, it was the birds that brought the first real magic into the World.

Birds travelled far and wide and were often gone for extended periods of time. When the little creatures returned and came rest on the Tree's branches, the first stories ever to be told built up inside their tiny chests, the birds burst forth into song. They sang richly of distant lands the Titan had never seen. Their melodies told of vast stretches of sand that they could not cross, and of acres covered in rock that they could. They warbled about rivers and plains and rushing water that poured from stone. They chirruped endlessly over the divine beauty of dawn, the enchantment of dusk, and of all the colors the horizon held in between.

Along with their twittering, birds also brought the Titan gifts of wood and leaves and plants from places the Tree could not go. From these it crafted more exotic creatures while it listened to the constant, musical soliloquies. And such magnificent beasts it made, both great and small. Some it made with horns, others with tusks, and even some with fangs and claws. It made creatures with hooves hard like stone that tore at the soft ground, but more it made with soft, padded toes that ran across it silently. Some animals glowed in the dark and hid from the sun while others smelled funny and basked in the warm light.

More and more creatures the Titan created, and each one filled it with joy that only fueled its compulsion to make more. Each one it made unique and set loose to make more on their own. Each one the Titan admired, but then there came one—its last creation—that the Titan admired most of all. Dragons.

Like the bees and the birds, the dragons could fly and held within them something seraphic. Unlike the crawling, running, bounding, swinging creatures scampering about its roots or among its branches, dragons—like the birds—spoke to the Tree. Able to fly in even the harshest of conditions, they travelled further than any bird and returned quicker. Such tales they brought the Titan! They spoke of seas. Of oceans! And of the lands on the other side of either. They spoke mountains raging with fire, and lands made entirely of ice. They spun tales of jungles thick with trees unlike anything the Titan could fathom and chronicled their adventures across the sands that had stopped the birds. They spoke of other things, too.

Of all the places the dragons ventured, no tale was absent of flowers; of the white and pink kind that the Titan had created first, but also of others that it had not. Even in the desert, large, elegant, yellow blossoms adorned tall, strangely shaped green plants. All trunk, the dragons described, with no real branches and covered with sharp needles instead of leaves. Where they found flowers, so too did the dragons find birds. All of them different than the ones the Tree had originally created, but not by much, and all of them working hard to spread seeds of plants and devour pests feeding off them. What they did not find in all their travels, were bees. Even in the places where the tireless little drones would thrive, they could find not one.

So delighted by the dragons' tales that the Tree Titan decided, at once, that they should take hives to these places, so the tiny helpers could tend to the flowers in ways that birds could not and so make more. The dragons were overjoyed for the task and proudly obliged. They took from the excess of waxy hives weighing down the Titan's branches and carried them off in every direction. The work was arduous, and the dragons were gone for long periods of time taking care to choose the most optimal location and saw to it that their tiny brethren took well to their new environment.

Unwilling to risk being absent the return of its creatures—unwilling to miss the opportunity to hear a new tale—the Titan ventured less and less. It remained within the borders of its original grove with little reason to wander at all. The descendants of its first flowers grew there, and where most of its original creations still roamed free. With the proliferation of the Life that it had created at which to quietly marvel, the Tree discovered contentment. So much so that the Titan's desire to create dwindled and found bliss enough to simply watch.

With even the largest creature in its menagerie, great lumbering giants with long necks and deer so big that their antlers stood as trees upon their mountainous skulls, all were still small enough to be easily injured or killed under a single misstep of a Titan—even from one so small. So, the Tree moved very little. Lumbering about was growing tiresome anyway. After a while, it stopped moving altogether, leaving the never-ending work to be managed by the birds and the bees under the wise and watchful eyes of the dragons. The Tree took to root and tapped deep into the soil. If she was displeased, the Earth gave no sign and the Titan anchored itself into an everlasting vigil. One that could have stood until the stars fell from the sky for there existed nowhere else that brought the Tree more pleasure than its own grove it had worked so diligently in creating.

The Titan grew immobile. Birds made nests in its branches. More bees built more hives so there were always plenty to be periodically harvested by the dragons and delivered to places far beyond the Titan's reach; places it knew now only in the songs and stories sung and told by the birds and the dragons.

Too content, the Titan became, watching the spiny horses frolic, in observing the hogs with their large, rounded shoulders and long, curved tusks they used to dig up and eat shallow roots, that Time came to be measured by *their* comings and goings. The growth, death, and rebirth of its creatures marked the change of the seasons. With the return of the dragons and their tales to look forward to, the Tree Titan found what had already existed, what Earth already knew. It found happiness. Exquisite and quietly euphoric, was all the more calamitous when another found it.

Nearly all the Titans had heard of their brethren's garden by this time. Traces of the Life it had created could be found everywhere. Like the Wind, their first encounters were often violent and ignorantly destructive. Yet, when faced with Life's resilience to not only return but return stronger, even after near annihilation, a certain fondness began to grow in the even the mightiest and cataclysmic of their kind. The Volcanic Titan—second only to the Earth in size and age, and father of all Titans—for all its hot and furious rage that erupted out of towering mountains liquid rock and ash, too, had begun to quietly start on a creation of its own.

So, it should happen that only one Titan remained unbeknownst of the Tree's wonders that had swept over the land. The last to know found out by way of a pink petal carried aloft on passing breezes and a promise made so very long before. A tiny blossom that came to rest on the rolling surface of a vast ocean and, immediately, snatched in the crushing grip of another Titan also ripe with the concept of Life.

The Water Titan glared in tumultuous befuddlement at the residue of Life not of *its* own design. A tidal wave of jealousy swept over the Titan. It left its ocean home, at once, in search of the petal's origin. When it found the lush garden bursting with more Life than a mere flower, it also discovered the Tree Titan sitting contently in the middle of the grove, already long anchored deep into the Earth.

Outside of its watery home, the Water Titan was not so large, hardly dwarfing the Tree Titan at all, but it did have a trick that the Tree Titan did not. Enraged by the discovery of Life found in the hands of another, the Water Titan roiled and the sky above it grew heavy with clouds of deep slate gray effectively blocking out the sun. Threat of a storm like no other spread across the entire grove.

"What is the meaning of this?" roared the Water Titan.

Aghast by the harrowing change in the atmosphere, the Tree Titan turned to find its kin, a tsunami that stood taller than the tallest tree, at the edge of its grove.

"What angers you so, Brother?"

"Life does not belong to you," the Water Titan bellowed, for it, too, had discovered Life and all the exaltation that comes with it. It, too, had created a vast empire kept secret and out of sight, hidden from all others beneath the rolling waves of its oceans and seas. The Water Titan prostrated that *it*, in fact, had been the first to create Life. "Do your flowers not *grow* with the nourishment from *water*? Do your beasts not make drink with it, lest they perish? Life, in all its forms—whether in or out of the water—belongs to *me,* and you have stolen it. So, I shall take it *back*."

The Tree was given no room to protest. The immense, dark clouds above cracked with the broken flashed of terribly twisted light, and rain descended upon the vast garden.

Neither the Titan nor its grove were strangers to rain; they had weathered countless storms together. This was no mere storm. The Water Titan unleashed upon them a deluge. A torrent of such magnitude that a great flood swept over the land. All the Tree Titan's wild beasts screamed and fled but there was no place for them to go. The waters rose too high, too fast, and too everywhere. Birds were grounded, unable to take flight through the driving sheets of rain. They clung desperately to the Tree's topmost branches, but only so many could fit. Those that could not, cried out in terror.

Horror gripped the Tree Titan in a way that it had never done before. In desperation, it reached for its creatures, its precious animals, and found only despair. There were just too many for even a Tree so great could not rescue them all. The impending loss was an anguish too much to bear. Grief-stricken, the Titan turned on its brethren but, anchored to the ground, there was only so much a Tree could do. It swung a limb wildly at the shimmering face towering above, clawed with all its might. Its limbs broke the Water's surface but caused no damage. The rain fell harder.

The dragons gave what aid they could. Undaunted by the rain, no matter how hard it fell, they attacked the Water with fiery breath that turned bits of the Titan into steam that rose through the monsoon. Attracted by the heated vapor, breezes rushed in to find the skies above the grove swollen with a storm that they had not ushered. Outraged, the breezes whipped into gales, and rain that had been falling straight down suddenly came from all directions. The dragons were scattered, and the waters rose faster.

Irritated by the gales, the Water Titan stretched skyward, aimed to crush the gales along with the grove, and all the creatures that dwelled within, in one monumental blow. With the Tree Titan powerless to stop it. All around, its creatures screamed and pleaded. With only a precious few in its limbs that still might not survive no matter how tucked amidst its branches, the Tree Titan wept. The Water Titan stretched higher, the gales blew harder, and the end loomed darker than the clouds. Heavy with sorrow, the Tree made ready for the inevitable.

The attack was sudden and violent. The Tree was buffeted hard enough to shake its roots, but not by the water it had expected. An icy wind exploded through the grove. The rain was blown back, the waters forced to retreat, and a terrible calm descended over the Tree's garden. For a wonderous moment, the Titan forgot its tears. Stirred from its resting place high above the world, beseeched by the breezes at its command, the Wind Titan had charged the enemy of the grove. Much larger than the Water Titan, the Wind had it wrapped in a cyclone and forced back. The Water flailed angrily against the turbulent vortex that kept it confined. So much so, that the Wind drove the tempest only so far before it could go no further. Though bigger and stronger, the Wind would not be able to hold the Water for long.

But maybe the Tree could.

"You must carve into me," the Titan called upon every one of its creature left alive. "Dry me out, make me hollow with many places to hide."

The creatures all cried out in unison, *no*, for they knew what the Titan asked of them. But the Tree would not be dissuaded. "You must. Quickly now, before it is too late."

With sorrow in their hearts—the first of its kind—so deep and heavy as to forever leech into Life and all its various forms, henceforth, the beasts that could went to work. As swiftly as their hearts were heavy, they opened the Tree Titan with a great, sharp, *crack* that shook the Earth and was heard by every Titan.

There must be another way, the creatures cried but did not stop their work. The dragons circled the Tree, heating the air around it to cast out every, last drop of moisture from its bark. The Titan could feel itself dying. A curious experience to something immortal and a queer desperation drove its roots deeper into Earth. Deeper than the soil, deeper than the loam and clay and liquid stone. So deep as to reach Worlds hidden within Worlds. Deep enough to reach the Earth's dreams and come out the other side, that the Titan became entwined with her, and the Tree felt something of itself begin to slip away.

"Faster," it implored its creatures. With beak and fang and claw they hollowed the great Titan until its trunk, limbs, and branches were left with barely enough substance to keep the whole of the Tree from collapsing. As it twisted against its roots forever embedded through Worlds and filled the air with the snapping of its splintered bark, the dying Titan witnessed the duel between the other two draw to a close.

Despite all its strength and size, the Wind Titan had thinned against the unyielding barrage of the other Titan's fury. Unable to contain it any longer, the pent-up cataclysm slipped from an airy grasp. The giant wall that was the Water rushed the garden and the crippled Tree at its heart. Unbound, uncontained, and full of spiteful rage, the Water Titan hurled its mass with all speed.

What dragons that remained met it first with all the force of breath they could muster. They scorched the Water's massive body and filled the skies with steam, shank it little but could not stop it. The ground trembled and dirt shook, but the enfeebled Tree's colossal roots held fast. Anchored so deep that no matter of turmoil, no matter how violent the storm, nothing could ever rip them asunder; the Tree Titan could not be moved. The Water Titan lunged, and the Tree met the threat head-on. It stood tall and pulled its own gargantuan trunk open wide.

The force that crashed against its hollowed-out insides was tremendous. Thinned bark cracked and small bits of wood were sent flying into the air, but the Tree held firm as the Water Titan surged into every nook, every cranny and crevasse carved into the Titan's body. The maze-work filled in hardly more than an instant. For the love of its creatures, to keep safe all it held dear, the great Tree slammed shut its trunk with the Water Titan trapped inside.

Little leaked out, but for what did, the dragons were there. Understanding the sacrifice that had been made, they used their breath to scorch the Titan's bark into making resin. With the same sap the Tree used to make all its creations, the dragons used to close any means of escape for the terror that meant to destroy all the Tree had built. They sealed any fissure under hardened amber and silenced two Titan's forever.

The process was quick and violent. Few of the last remaining dragons died, locked into the resin along with any other creature unfortunate enough to find itself in the way. With the deed completed, of the dragons that survived, all wept. Their tears covered the amber-encased Tree with a glittering shine. The Wind Titan, also touched by sorrow and regret, howled its woes.

More clouds were blown in and rain, again, fell over the grove. It was not a storm, for the Titan could not bear the calamity. What fell was gentle and cool. What flames that still burned were extinguished, and the ash that covered the grove sunk into the dirt. The Tree Titan's garden would live, nourished for all of Time. As the rains ceased, the sky cleared, and the sun was allowed to return. The air warmed and the grove recovered. All the Titan's creatures that still lived—great and small—paid their homage in silence.

Not so many were there to witness the flowers that bloomed one day, on the blackened bark of the herculean Tree, but far more heard. A message spread through the songs of birds and in the work of bees: the Titan lived. Reduced to standing char and forever anchored to Earth, sealed by fire and amber, the Tree Titan remained, its captive shut up within. Its flowers were not the delicate pink blossoms the Titan had first created. These were larger by far and deep red with bright yellow spots along the elegant curl of each bloom's five spiny petals. Dragon lilies, they would be called one day when the last of the Titans grew still and only one remained in full view: A great Tree, one like no other, with flowers seen nowhere else and roots that run so deep they could never be dug up.

Under sun and nightly stars, in the pelting rain, against icy winter storms that blanketed all in crisp, white snow, the Tree remained. The Ages passed it over with only the birds and bees and other beasts amidst its branches for company. Yet even a Tree so mighty could not escape the ravages of progress. The dragons never returned. Stricken with grief and anguish, so black, all that remained had fled. Retreated to sorrow-filled nests hidden underground or in deep ravines, they sought only isolation. Without them, the Tree slowly weakened while, outside the grove, change pressed ever closer.

Man was coming. With all the rage of a Titan and endowed with Life's ingenuity, Man brought new forms of destruction. They did not hear the stories sung by birds. They knew nothing of the flowers they picked and trampled. They spoke, but to one another, not to the Tree or its creatures. Around its grove their smoke threatened, their progress pressed. The silent Titan grew weaker, and its captive stirred restlessly within. The Tree needed help that its forest dwellers could not provide. And it came one day, in the most unexpected form.

A young girl, who wandered into the grove one day, precisely where she had been told not ought to go, discovered the Tree. She was not like the others and she, along with the boy who followed her, found that they *could* hear the Tree. Life had found its way back to where it was needed most, and its creator bade them to stay. It fed them delicious fruits as they listened to its tale. It gave them shade and safety, but none could stop the impending progress of industry looming outside the grove. The great Tree could remain a tree no longer.

To keep from being found by others and milled—its bits scattered, and the horror contained within released—the Tree implored the pair to cut it down and build with its lumber a great house. One with many rooms and halls and corridors, to be constructed around its roots so that they may never be disturbed. The pair agreed and did all that the Tree asked. They built their home sturdy. They built it strong. Together they built a great House, a very special house, to stand the passage of Time. For as long as the House is occupied should the will of one Titan be enough to hold the greed of another. In return, the magic left embedded in the wood from the dragons and birds and bees and other wild things that perished in that battle so very long ago, shall provide all that is needed for those who dwell within.

"And so was the bargain our ancestors made long ago," speaks a young man to the toddler he bounces on his knee. Dark eyes, dark, unruly hair, and a sharp nose on a face still chubby with baby fat, the boy will grow to have the same long, sharp features as his father.

"Soon, it will be time for you to go," he says, his tale nearly concluded—though the boy is still too young to retain even half of what he is told. "Everyone born here must leave. Gone before any real memories of this place are made, so that you may live and learn—and love. Only then, when you are filled with stories of your own, will you return. You will have to find your own way, with your own key, but you shall know it when you see it."

A kiss to the boy's cheek causes the baby to giggle and fills his father with a proud sort of anguish only a parent can know; such a laugh will be the last his father will ever hear. "The road will be long, my son, and full of peril. You will forget this place, but it will not forget you. For you were born to a House with a Titan in the walls. You are filled with its song, and it has its own way of leading you back. One must always be here, to keep it safe."

With another kiss, and another giggle for the effort, and a father affectionately pinches the chubby cheeks of his infant son before he hands the boy over to a woman in a red plaid dress. Unable to have children of her own, she wraps the boy with motherly love she has long desired to give. With a quiet farewell, she turns away. The boy will be raised in town not far from the grove; to be the son of a young, ambitious couple just starting a landscaping business. He will grow and he will live. He will quit the town before long, in search of something he will yearn for all his life but will never find. Then, one day, when Time is right, he will return without understanding why. He will not find his father for it is not his father whom he'll seek, but something far more precious.

Tales in Hindsight

Tales in Hindsight

MAY

✦ The Legend of Manethiera ✦

𝕾till in the early throws of Spring, the morning is bright and warm.

Though not yet the warmest day to come to the fertile mountain valley hidden high in the mountains of the North, it is one of such pure splendor to be cherished before the radiant heat of summer and the crisp chill of winter that are sure to follow. The dramatic yellows and pinks of an early sun on the rise is dazzling above the trees and their leaves sparkling with dew. Few clouds adorn the sky. Of the white and fluffy kind, with no foretoken of a coming storm, they drift serenely across velvet blue and dim the glow of a maturing day very little. A gentle breeze keeps the cool air sweet as it whispers through wispy grass.

The open valley shines like a massive emerald high in a protected mountain cirque under the imposing presence of twin peaks connected by a sharp arete. Lush with Life, there simply is no hunting ground better for birds, deer, rabbits, and squirrels. The ground rolls little with few only a few gentle slopes for hills save for the valley's southern border. Few trees grow here but they are massive. Each as tall as a castle, their leaves large enough to wrap fully around a man. They stand guard, scattered about the valley, their expansive canopies casting wide ovals of shade keeping secret a prized treasure hidden within.

All is calm. Peace reigns, buzzing with bees and birds and

little else. Until the tranquility is suddenly shattered with the passing of rider and the thundering hooves of his horse galloping at full speed.

Urged on by its rider, the single horse leaves quite the wake. The iron fixed to the bottom of its hooves tear up the ground, sending hunks of dirt and grass flying into the air. A rather obvious trail, the rider knows. Just as he knows that there is nothing to be done about it now and, so, squeezes his heels a little more into the sides of his prized mount. The horse's hooves dig in harder.

At such breakneck speed, he is putting both their lives in danger, his and his steed's. But the news he carries is worth the risk; many more lives depend on him reaching his destination in time. He prays to any who still listen to keep deer at bay that might otherwise spook and dart into their path. A fall now promises only harm and worse. Any delay will cost him what precious little time his has; he *must* reach the city before *they* do. Fighting the urge to squeeze his heels harder, to ask even more from his steed, the horse flies over the crusting slope of a shallow hill with barely room enough to avoid the mess of large, gnarled roots of the tree growing on the other side. Any faster and the horse's legs would surely have become tangled.

Horse and rider skirt the tree safely and clear the ends of low hanging branches. The great, purple mountain with two peaks closing off the western end of the basin comes into view. Tucked securely at the foot of the stony incline is, at last, that which the rider seeks so desperately: Manethíera, the White City.

Daring to trust his steed to run home without added direction or insistence, the rider risks a glance over his shoulder, to the hillock closing the valley to the south. The rise is clear, harboring nothing but sunshine and wildflowers. He's made it.

⚔ ⚔ ⚔

The cavern is a marvel of Manethíera engineering. Though cut off from the outside world, one could easily forget that the cavern is, indeed, hidden deep within the jagged black stone of a mountain. Along the edges of a deep, yet narrow reflecting pool cutting the cavern floor in half, green moss blankets the stone.

Bright purple, blue, and pink lithophyte flowers grow in clusters here and there. The water sparkles from light spilling in through a hole in the cavern's ceiling outfitted with plates of glass made by the city's finest glassblowers and set in place by her stone-shapers long ago. Reflected to the slick sides of the cavern's walls, flecks of mica and quartz dazzle and the space is filled with the brightness of day.

A single tree protruding from the stone floor completes the illusion. A sapling compared to those standing watch in the valley outside, it still stands twice the height of the city's tallest man, twisting for the cathedral's vaulted ceiling. One could very well be convinced that their time is being spent outside, in the shade of a leafy canopy, rather than inside a mountain, confined by granite walls. The reflecting pool, too, is not what it seems. Fed from a spring deeper still in the rock, water does flow from one end of the cavern to the other, but so slowly that hardly a ripple mares the glass-like surface. Above the softest murmur that only the calmest of minds can perceive, a woman practices a deadly dance designed to complement her delicate, long-bladed sword.

She is alone, or so she thinks. Her steps are light and precisely placed over the bits of stone not submerged in the cold, crystalline flow. The hem of her white dress, crafted by the White City's elite tailors and seamstresses, brushes the placid surface with barely enough force to disturb it. It is a skill she has been schooled in since she was small. The Water Dance is more ballet than brute strength. A practice in lethal accuracy rather than the crude smash and slash more commonly employed by those who wield broad-bladed swords. Elegant and graceful, fluid in both poised and precision, the woman invokes enchantment. Beautiful, she is easy to watch and so distracted from the deadly sequence she truly practices.

Every step she executes flawlessly. Each bend, dip, parry, lunge, and twist — one could become hypnotized trying to keep up with the quick darts and flashes of the needle-like blade in her hand before realizing that there is no blade at all. The illusion is as complete as the cavern; she is unarmed. Absorbed in her dance, swordless, and wearing what counts as little more than a shift, she may appear vulnerable. Yet, in the suspended fragile hush, the cave is as mute as a bell hanging from a string. The slightest scuff of a leather soled boot, no matter how softly placed, is as loud as a chime.

A few steps take her further along the water's path to a large boulder all but submerged save for the rounded top barely larger than her hand. The supple soles of her slippers stick true to the stone as she completes the last spin in her dance. Her arm whips out just as the cold, iron blade of a short sword swings for her face, but in her hand now is a very real ruby-encrusted dagger, released from inside her sleeve by the hidden pull of a string. The resounding clash of her blade meeting and stopping that of her attacker, rings out sharp and brilliant.

"You are getting quicker," says the man in the leather-soled boots. He is pleased, his charming grin says as much, though he does not relent the pressure of his blade.

"And you are getting softer," returns the woman sweetly, with an affectionate smile to match. She knows full well that he swung his sword half-heartedly.

Having known one another for so long, their camaraderie comes easily. In the quiet moment, the pair might have started giggling if their peace was not suddenly broken by the frantic intrusion of a young man stumbling into the cavern on quickened breath.

"Troops," the young man shouts, coming to a stop on the side of the pool opposite the pair. Leaning on his bent knees, he tries desperately to catch his breath. "An army. From the south. Heading this way. They march for war."

The joviality shared by the pair is dismissed and too quickly replaced with grave concern.

"You are sure?" asks the woman. Having not yet moved from her place on the stone, she does lower her arm. Her counterpart smartly sheathes his sword.

The messenger nods with vigor. "There can be no mistake. They fly their banners for all to see." His breath is coming easier now. "A full platoon, with their King's intent to conquer. Manethíera is meant to be made the example of their Lordship's might."

This is all woman needs to hear. "Spread your message," she commands with an air of high authority. "Roust all who will meet this threat. Quickly, now."

A nod deep enough to be a formal bow and the messenger—having regained his composure from his harrowing ride to reach the White City—rushes from the cavern with his news, surer of foot than when he came in.

The woman, perched on her toes as to hover above the whispering tide, turns sharply to her companion. "Wake the Champion," is her only command of him, no more is needed. Both depart the cavern, both ready to do what they must to defend it.

The news travels quickly. Within moments of the messenger's fervent arrival does the quiet city start to hum with activity. Word spreads as a candle in a dark place lighting every nearest candle, and each next in turn. In rooms secreted away, stashed chests, vaults, and cabinets are opened. The morning comes quietly alive with creaks and squeaks of hinges, well-oiled but not used in a long time. Ticks and clinks echo throughout the city next as belts are cinched into place. Clasps, hooks, and buckles are linked together with soft snaps as hand-crafted armor is expertly adorned by all those willing to answer the messenger's call.

Those too old to wear armor tend to those too young to do the same and keep them well out of way. They watch with prayers on their lips and respect in their eyes as a lone figure marches down the middle of the main road winding through the city. First dressed and first to mount the first horse outfitted for battle, with the others not far behind, their leader is the first to ride to Manethíera's closed gate. At the controls of the mechanical contraption that will open it wide, the gatekeeper stands at the ready. A nod from the mounted warrior and the gatekeeper pulls the lever.

⚔ ⚔ ⚔

The bone white city of Manethíera is a spectacular visage from atop the hillock rising to the south of her. Across the valley floor of glittering green, in the wedge where shallow hills start to ripple at the base of a twin peaked mountain—an impenetrable wall of granite shielding the valley from the west—the magnificent city glows in the long, warm rays of a morning growing late.

"Manethíera." The city's name rolls across the tongue of the General who speaks it as sweetly as sugar, and he savors every bit. "A rumored city that nearly vanished into its own myth. The unconquerable city," the General quotes for he is not the first to have called her such. "Though few have tried."

"And why is that?" asks his second, a man not much younger than his own aged self and just as battle seasoned. Having led his King's army for nearly half his life, and served it for longer, the General knows that his second in command is just as familiar with the legend of Manethíera as he. It is the outstanding luck of having found the city at all, real and tangible, that has put both men into a chatty mood.

"Manethíera keeps well her secrets," speaks the General, putting forth his best story-teller's voice; he never was that good at telling tales. A queer grin brushes his lips, nevertheless, and he goes on. "It is said that any who seek it, shall never find it; that those who do find it, never return from it; and those who try to take from it, find only death. A city of great wealth, with treasures untold, and home to the greatest minds, craftsmen, and leaders all residing in perpetual peace and prosperity unaccomplished anywhere else."

"And all without a king, they say," his Second adds before shaking his head. "Balderdash. Here she stands. The famed White City herself, ripe with glory and begging to be plundered. No amount of tales can save her now. Who buys such stories is a mystery to me."

To this the General nods.

Both men sit tall astride warhorses from the General's own superior stock. His own impressive gray stallion grunts and shifts beneath him. The army behind them, thousands of foot soldiers and nearly that in mounted cavalry, fills the entirety of the hillock that is nearly half as wide as the valley floor below. Their armor gleams of dull silver in the rising sun. Their kingdom's best made swords, lances, and spears in hand. They are silent but tension is growing. Even the horses are restless. Outfitted with linked metal plates along their necks and across their rumps and chests, they shuffle where they stand and mouth their bits anxiously. Why should they not?

Under the General's command, the King's army has never

known defeat. They have met no city nor country that they did not leave unconquered. Manethíera will be no different. The city will fall, and his army will be made rich beyond their wildest dreams. The renown alone will grant every man in his regime legendary reputation. Yet, faced with unstoppable demise, peace and serenity seems determined to remain settled over the city.

"It would appear that we have caught them still asleep," speaks the General, loud enough for his voice to carry. Sparse, suppressed laughter echoes back, tense, and edgy with want. The General is pleased.

"Look," says sharply his Second, pointing a metal gauntleted hand and finger toward the gleaming city. "They're opening the front gate. Perhaps they intend to give up without a fight."

The stifled chortling fades away and the General hones his attention in on the gargantuan gate across the grassland that does, indeed, begin to rise.

Without hesitation, the General replies. "Then they deserve to be conquered."

Sitting ever taller on his warhorse, the General makes ready to raise his hand, to signal his men to prepare to charge. But his hand turns to stone when, from the gate, a single horse and rider rushes forth.

Unlike his own warhorses, all greys and browns and roans, this horse—fitting for the city from which speeds—is pearl white. Even from such a distance, the General can see that the horse is large. Just as big in body as his own stallion, but that snow-white beast galloping from the behemoth gate is longer legged, its neck magnificently arched. Proud and muscular, it is a *plains* horse. The General can hardly believe his eyes. An animal that should no longer exist, in fact does, and is racing with fantastic speed straight for his army.

The animal's rider is a small figure. Made smaller by the impressive animal he rides, no doubt, but still hardly stature enough to strike fear in the heart of a seasoned soldier. That is until, having galloped several spans away from the gate, the plains horse comes to an abrupt halt and rears back on its powerful hind legs, sharp, black hooves pawing at the air. Such an animal would have tossed even the strongest of his riders, yet this one keeps his seat single-handedly, waving a long, thin sword in the air with the other. Curiosity and awe spoil in the General's heart. His mouth turns dry. Behind the rider, a dark swarm of foot soldiers abruptly pours from the outlandishly large gate.

Hundreds. Hundreds upon hundreds and, as they hit the light, the General discovers that they are not dark at all. Each one is similarly suited in brilliant silver and gleaming gold armor as the rider leading the charge. The grin that had played on his lips a moment ago has vanished. Replaced, instead, by the stern line of perplexity watching the increasing number of footmen pour from the gate. The plains horse in the lead drops its front hooves hard and flies across the valley.

The end of footmen has yet to be reached when the General feels the rumble in the ground beneath his own horse's hooves. All the horses in his calvary snicker. They dance in their formations, testing the limits of the reins holding their will in check. The trembling of the ground grows, the General can feel it rise through his saddle. *It cannot be*, comes his wishful thinking bound for grave disappointment.

Further back along the wall, behind the army of footmen, a mass of armored horses and riders on a scale the likes of which the General has never entertained to be possible boils up from the shallow depths of the folding hills. Underneath him, his stallion squeals, and stomps against his tight hold. The General gulps, glad that his men are behind him, that only his Second may bear witness to the hint of worry deepening the lines on his face.

Many of the horses rioting towards them are as white as the one in the lead rushing up the hillside. The rest a coal black. All are dressed in the finest armor the General has ever seen, and the sweat pooling in the General's armpits sends chills deep into his chest. This is an army fit for the Gods.

The mass of men and beasts surge up the hillock. In short order, the General's own impressive army is nearly surrounded by Manethíera's militant might. Their horses, taller and more muscular than any horse in the General's prized breeding stock, settle neatly into place. Not one dances under its rider, unlike those in the General's calvary. Cleanly filed between them is the vast platoon of footmen. Every gap filled and the view the General had of the legendary city is blocked. Dead ahead, and seemingly the center of it all, is the first, single rider on his frosty-white mount.

He is a slim figure, indeed. Long in legs and torso, with unwholesomely long, white-gold hair cascading down his shoulders from a full-faced, gold and silver helmet. He does sit small on his horse. Or rather, less burly than nearly every other soldier that has charged forth in defense of their treasured city. Every piece of the leader's armor appears tailormade, as with every other solider. A curious metal, it does not reflect the sun so much as it seemingly absorbs it, only to glow warmly with the light it's captured. The metal does not shine with any glare, yet the General finds himself squinting, and does his best to ignore the pressing numbers which greatly supersedes his own.

"Good, sir!" The General calls loud enough for all nearby to hear, but his intention is solely aimed on the slim rider directly ahead. Un-helmed himself, his long greying hair tossed by the breeze, his deep voice carries well. "I come at behest of his Lordship and mighty King, who claims this land in annexation of his vast empire. I have come with his undefeated army to see his lands surrendered. In return—" the General pauses for a breath; the slim rider has not so much as moved. "—the King offers you land to farm, and reduced taxes for all who pledge to him their loyalty. To those who refuse, death, to each and their kin. Surely, a prosperous trade and not worth staining such *fine* armor."

At this, the General hears some of his men chuckle. He is emboldened by the sound. That is, until the man sitting proud on his magnificent, white animal, relieves unseen hinges on his helm. The chortling is strangled as he lifts it to expose an angelic face the General had never expected to see.

He is not a 'he' at all, but *she*. A *woman!* As fair in skin as she is in face, she is stunning. The General can sense the slow, questionable glare from his Second sitting on the anxious mount next to him, and flounders for the words he knew with conviction only a breath before.

"There is no need for your people to die here, this day," the General calls. "Surely—" but his words are silenced by the smile pulling her lips back and the laughter that slips through them— both gentle and light and equally lacking in kindness. This woman he faces is no lily of the valley. She is a predator like himself, perhaps one more dangerous. What a bride she would make. Once he has defeated her army, that is.

"You hear that, lads?" Her voice rings out as terrific and vibrant as the armor she wears. "This man's *good* King will sell you back land you already own, and a discounted tax in exchange for the freedom you already have. And this, a price *better* than that of decorating our *fine* armor with their insides."

At this, far more of her men laugh, and much louder. The air in the General's lungs grows stale. The sprout of worry grows dangerously close to doubt.

"Good Lady," he shouts with forced gusto. "Surely there is no need for bloodshed this day."

"Oh, but that is precisely the intention you bring, riding to our gates uninvited with such force and words. Your threat is clear and will be met, twice fold, by the hands of free and honorable men. But we are not savages. Throw yourself upon your sword," she shouts louder than ever, "as price for your error, and your men shall go free, unharmed. Order them to charge, and I shall see to it personally that you, and you alone, survive. Those are the terms *you* have brought. What say *you*, General?"

The hush returns, washing over the hilltop and leaking out to the valley below. The General, fully aware of just how many ears that woman's words just fell upon, is about to put up with none of it. How dare she? To make such demands of him, in front of *his* troops! To embarrass him so. No bride will this one be. No woman shall live to make a mockery of *him!* For the chance to smack that helm from her head and run her through with his blade, he would pay every line of his army and replace them all just as inconsequentially.

Wrenching his sword from its scabbard, he thrusts the blade skyward and shouts. "For King—" but his words are drowned out by the woman's triumphant call from her steed reared high, its hooves striking the air.

"For your sons and daughters! For *honor!*"

Before her horse has brought down its front legs, the line around her breaks. The air explodes with the roar of enraged men turned loose. The ground rumbles. Horses churn the dirt with their heavy hooves. The earth is pulverized. Screams fill the air and blood begins to spill. The top of the hillock is turned to mud.

It all happens so quickly.

A flash of white, just a blur of movement, and the General finds himself on his back on the churned soil, his prized warhorse scrambling to its feet. Wild with fear from being driven to the ground, the animal bolts. Brought to gasp, the General feels hollow at the sight of his army already broken. The loss of his men is staggering. Few brave — or foolish — men fight back against the soldiers of Manethíera, but they are dogs taking on highly organized and superiorly skilled wolves. His men never stood a chance.

With a hot cry of boiling resentment bellowing from his chest, the General pushes to regain his feet, his sword still in hand. The motion is swift, he nearly misses her charge. Wielding his broadsword downward with a heavy hand, he turns and strikes with all his strength channeled into the blade of his sword. She is there to meet him and the resulting clash of metal on metal sends shudders reverberating down his wrists, daring his grip to faulter. The face of the woman is close enough to kiss. Beautiful beyond his deepest fantasies, but the time to fraternize is long over.

A shove and a parry to give himself some distance, he lunges for her, the point of his sword in the lead. She does not run. She only turns, stepping slightly to one side. A graceful lift of her blade sweeps away his thrust but the colliding deflective blow rings up to the General's teeth. Turning back around, he lunges again and slicing lower, going for her legs. Her blade is there, deftly maneuvering his own from its intended path. He reels to attack again, but she springs away too fast.

Jumping high into the air — far out of the General's reach — she is just in time to clear what looks like a cannonball the size of a boulder hurtling toward him. With hardly a breath to spare, the General leans back into his heels and is struck in the shoulder instead of square in the chest. A glancing blow, though the General still finds himself back on the ground, his shoulder armor smashed concave and part of it ripped off entirely. The pain flaring in his arm is excruciating yet, even that, fails to dawn his attention away from the metal monstrosity that charges by.

No amount of effort can get his fingers of that arm working. The hilt of his sword sinks into the mud; he would not be able to grab it anyway. The General can do nothing but watch the mechanical giant forged of copper and steel, and taller than most buildings, run down the last of his men remaining on the field. Swinging a wicked flail with a ball the size of a wagon, the giant catches two or three of his men at a time. The ground shutters with its every step. With each, his men also grow quieter. Shrieks are replaced with bursts of steam leaking white puffs over the battlefield. Nothing short of a dragon would be able to combat such a thing; the battle is a complete loss.

Few lucky souls manage to escape the unforgiving giant and make for the trees. Calvary in gleaming gold and silver armor give chase, their horses further battering the ravaged hilltop.

"They will run your men down until there are none left. One or two might get away with their lives."

The General tears his gaze from the spoiled field for the splendid visage of the golden-haired goddess towering over him.

"That's the secret of Manethíera," the General shakes his head. "No wonder the White City cannot be conquered, not with that *thing* at your command."

"*That?*" the woman lifts her gaze to tip her chin toward the metallic monster mowing down the last of his men. "That is just a Champion, a gift bestowed onto us long ago. Powered by steam and alchemy, it *is* formattable, but it is only a machine." Her glare turns icy and runs him through with chills. "The secret of Manethíera lies not in the tools she uses; it resides in the people who make her."

The battle is over in a matter of minutes — mass casualties to none — and the woman sheathes her long-bladed sword and turns away.

"Wait!" cries the General, staying her departure. "What happens to me now?"

She meets him with a smile so lovely that the ache clutching the General's chest squeezes ever tighter.

"I gave you my word," says she. "Your wounds will be looked after by our healers — the very best. They will see you soon fit for travel, for you have an important role yet to play. As the lone survivor of the utter annihilation of a king's army, you have quite a story to tell. And tell it you will."

She turns away once more. Her long hair falling like silk

down the back of her stunning armor, her silver and gold helm set upon her head like a crown; this is the last the General will see of the warrior-maiden, and he takes in every detail until the field-healers take her place. Surrounding him, they block his view of the woman who defeated an army with more than just a sword.

Quickly, delicately, his injuries are tended by healers. He cares little of their work. He keeps his eyes busy taking in all they can in what time they have, remembering everything. He must, for the warrior-maiden is right. To return to his King now would be to walk, head-first, into a noose. Too old to be of any use anywhere else and a life lived too long as a soldier to learn a new trade — the healers will no doubt see his shoulder mended but not enough to again wield a sword, or a plow for that matter — the General is a general no longer.

No, he cannot return to his home, and there will be no hope to find a place in the White City now, for it will not have him after this day. If he wishes to eat, he will have to rely on others and the recounting of his tale. Who buys such stories? He will have to find out, for he is but a lowly bard with the legend of an unconquerable White City to sell.

Tales in Hindsight

JUNE

✦ F.O.O.L. ✦

Bang!

The gun shot is what startles Grind from his trance, certainly not the lolling of his head, listing to one side in a sleep-induced nod. His dead gaze, at once, snaps into focus over the ever-vast, washed-out red wasteland stretching in all directions, further than the eye can see.

Damn kids. Who else would waste ammo like that, poppin' shots off at nothing?

It's too damn hot for this shit.

The sides of his head are shaved smooth. His hair confined to a single, thick strip standing straight up, a crest running down the middle of his dome; Grind feels every degree radiating down from on high *and* up from underfoot.

Voids, it is hot!

Already he is stripped down to the least amount of clothing possible while still maintaining some level of protection. A leather vest, rough and tough beige material in the vague shape of pants that mostly cover both his crotch and ass—mostly—and his boots that lost their laces long ago, but the black leather nevertheless sticks to his calves. On his left hand, the fingerless glove drips collected sweat when he clenches his fist.

On what, in the seven seas, did those brats deem worthy of wasting a shot?

As he thinks it, Grind turns his face to the commotion caught in his periphery. There they are: Brake and Crank. The twins Grind inherited, but that was a lifetime and one war ago. Almost men—

practically so—the pair still wrestle like boys. Scrapping now, Brake is solid on his feet with his brother bent over and his head locked in the crook of his arm. That doesn't mean Crank is making it easy. Struggling, jerking his brother wildly about, Brake nearly smashes Crank's face against the metal sides of the gang's sole car.

Grind's car.

Boys, he thinks and strokes the interlocking metal workings of the contraption making up the entirety of Grind's right arm from the shoulder. Gently he touches each sharp edge, blunt gap, and exposed joint. Lovingly so. It is, after all, more than a mere attachment. From fingertips to triceps, he can feel the machine and all her workings better than his own bones. A constant hum of energy that only he can experience courses throughout his entire body, every moment of every day. With it, no one in this clan, or any other, would dare to question his reigning authority. A hum which, at this moment, seems to vibrate with more than her usual vigor. In his mind, the obvious question blossoms.

If the twins are in a scrap, who fired the shot?

Only one other would do so, and for an extremely specific reason. If so, then he should be appearing over the rise opposite the fighting siblings, any second now.

Grind turns is his head away from the boys just as Rotor's bald scalp pokes up over the sharp rise in the rocky ground, bobbing wildly side to side; he is climbing the craggy hill at a labored run. Grind understands the fired shot perfectly now. His heart races to match the hum and he sits straighter in his old, rusted metal folding chair.

Rotor scrambles to a stop beside Grind. "A rider!" he manages to wheeze out between haggard gasps for dry, torrid air. "Off the west horizon. Comin' in hot."

"Fool," snorts Wheel, Grind's second in command.

The dark-haired man sits lower than Grind but is permitted a place *to* sit, but, on rock, never in a chair. His legs propped up and his upper half reclined back, to ignorant eyes, Wheel appears a relaxed man. Grind, however, sees the ghost of the soldier he was once, lurking just under the surface. His strong, ropey muscles wound as tight as a coiled adder, Wheel is a man who is never relaxed, even when he sleeps. Perpetually bored since the war ended decades ago, his agitated temper is always looking for an excuse to take that stored-up tension out on someone.

Grind takes the long range bi-scope offered by Rotor's hand. Bringing the connected pair of lenses level with his eyes, the cloud of dust billowing in the distance is easy to spot. A rider, indeed, rolling toward them. *Fast.* Grind ticks the levers on either side of the bi-scope, dropping a second set of lenses into place. Magnified, he can see a solid black object racing across the barren, red terrain; Grind can barely believe it. Another tick of the levers, another set of lenses drop into place. Both rider and his machine—a motorcycle, and a fine one—come fully into view. Both are decked out in all black. The visor on the rider's helmet is down, his face hidden. Another tick, another pair of lenses, and the rider nearly takes up all the bi-scope's field of view just as he banks hard into a sharp left turn. The whole right side of his machine suddenly exposed, and the bold white letters stenciled against the all-black of everything else, are unmistakable.

Other than Wheel, Grind is the only one of this rabble who knows what he is seeing. They also happen to be the only two who can read, and what is etched into the side of that motorcycle makes Grind a happy man.

"You don't know just how right you are," he replies to his second's previous statement.

Just like that, Wheel's boredom vanishes with a jolt. Though he remains seated, he no longer has his legs propped up and his back is straight. Alert, he is ready to spring into action at Grind's say-so.

"You mean, a *F.O.O.L?*"

Grind nods. "Fully Operational Organic Link."

Only a fellow soldier would grasp the meaning in those words, and Wheel is the first and only soldier Grind has come across in over twenty years. After the war that ended all wars—the war that tarnished glory and all that she is forever—soldiers simply became obsolete. Especially when only a slim few survived.

Ironically, more F.O.O.L. units remained intact than the men they were meant to protect and enhance. No one had foreseen the ultimate resounding effects of melding a man's consciousness with that of a machine's interface. If they did, no one spoke up—there was a war to win, after all. When the links between them failed, it was nothing short of catastrophe. F.O.O.L.s became dangerous, and they degraded into relics. So, too, for the remaining men who had been fools themselves for allowing their minds to be linked to an artificially intelligent machine. The sight of this one makes Grind's mouth water.

"It's the biggest F.O.O.L. I have ever seen," he says, lowering the bi-scopes and licking his lips.

"A soldier?" asks Wheel.

Grind scoffs. "There are no more soldiers, you know that. Too big and in too good condition to be a rogue."

"That leaves only one other option."

Grind nods. He knows better than Wheel that, with soldiers no longer in existence, a man with a F.O.O.L. can only be one of two

Tales in Hindsight

things. A rogue—a soldier who refused to turn over his machine and ran—or he is employed. A messenger. If this rider *is* a messenger, with a F.O.O.L. of that caliber—this deep in the wastes—then he is carrying something of extreme value. This fool's F.O.O.L. alone would be enough to forever change the future of Grind's clan. The plunder of one man stands to bring them more wealth than everything they have, or could, ever salvage. Grind is a happy man, indeed.

"Well?" A hungry dog with the scent of a rabbit caught in his nose, Wheel's mouth twists into a cruel and wanting grin.

Grind gives in. "Round 'im up."

Every member of the gang, not just Wheel, fly off like shots. All having watched and listened since Grind brought the bi-scope to his eyes. They may not know what a F.O.O.L. is like Grind and Wheel do, but they do know of the riches that can be had off even the lowliest of stragglers alone in the wastes. And with a machine like that! They whoop and holler and scatter to their own respective vehicles.

Young Brake gets to the gang's only car first but hops over the driver's door in favor of the passenger seat. Only Grind gets to drive the car. Ever. Twin brother Crank, along with all the others, kick-start life into their motorcycles. Grind slides easily into the car's driver seat and fires up the guttural roar of a big, turbo-charged, octane-rich engine. The hilltop erupts in deafening clamor. Throttles are pulled. Engines, revved. The gang grows louder and louder. Bits of sand dance across rock slabs as the ground trembles.

One final, long-lasting gunning of every motor, the shouting of men's voice deepening the cacophony smothering the crown of a craggy outcrop of sandstone—the F.O.O.L. rider below and coming up fast and mere moments from crossing their path—Grind throws the car into gear. A fountain of rocks and sand sprays skyward as the car launches forward. His gang all wear goggles and are unaffected amidst the showering of pebbles.

With Grind in the lead, his host of riders take off in his wake, their machines squirrely beneath them until their tires catch traction. Fading tails of sprayed dirt are all the remains of the gang as they race down the wide, flat path they had used to claim their perch to begin with.

The uproarious sound of the gang is near deafening, yet the rider in black takes no notice when the crew's iron machines bounce level with the desert floor. Their timing is good, the F.O.O.L. having just rocketed passed as Grind's car fishtails off the descending path. Boot to floor, he picks up speed fast.

"Fool. Didn't even see us." Grind howls into the air rushing over the car's open cab.

He is catching up quickly.

Next to him, Brake chuckles, but anxiously.

"What if he attacks?"

"He won't," Grind shouts over the roar of the car's super-powered engine. "Not if he wants to keep his F.O.O.L. Messengers aren't allowed to use them against people."

"What if he *ain't* a messenger?"

Grind does not need to probe the boy's meaning any further—he knows all that the boy had heard.

Howling again, he clenches his metal right hand into a fist and punches the frame above the windshield as they come up on the rider in black. "Then we're already dead."

Invigorated anew, Brake sets to his duties of loading a severely sawed-off shotgun with charged rounds before slapping it into Grind's metal hand. One shot in just the right spot and the electrical burst of these rounds will disrupt the organic interface linking man and machine. The rider will be easy pickings. And Grind knows just where to shoot.

With his beast of a car warming up, Grind sidles up alongside the black machine and her black-armored rider. *Fool*, Grind mouths when the rider's head turns to face him, his voice would be lost in the roar of the wind anyway. The two engines scream across the wasteland, side by side. Grind aims the barrel of the shotgun at the toothy grin reflected in the slick black visor of the rider's helmet, but he does not get the chance to pull back the hammer. The rider is gone, abruptly leaving the dangerous end of the gun aimed at an empty skyline. *A runner*, Grind thinks, turning his head in the direction the rider went. *Good.* Grind loves a chase.

Kicked-up dust hides nothing about the rider's movements. The rider suddenly falls far back, all the way to one of Grind's men bringing up the rear. It's Wheel, and he happens to be in perfect position to intercept. He lifts his heftier, more powerful automatic shot, darter rifle loaded with more, similarly charged rounds as Grind's shotgun. The rider in black swings his machine around in a controlled slide, metal-plated tires dig into the desert floor. Sand and dirt spew into the air as the rider whips his machine around Wheel with terrifying grace. Behind Wheel, the rider straightens, turns, and rockets across the flat ground until he is pacing Grind's car once more, but on the passenger side.

In his seat, his own guns forgotten, Brake stares in awe at the rider in black racing next to him, so close, that he could reach out and touch him. *Fool*, Grind thinks behind his grin grown anew. The rider has just put himself in the middle of Grind's pack of experienced marauders. Immediately, they start to squeeze in. The rider has nowhere to go. Until a jerk to the side and the sleek, low-profile, all black, metal motorbike hits a rock or a rise in the ground—doesn't matter which—and the F.O.O.L. vaults into the air.

Brake is awestruck as the rider, airborne and in control, barrel-rolls his machine over the roofless body of Grind's car. In the reflection of the rider's tinted visor, the open-mouthed, slackened jaw of Grind's face stares back. The faint exclamation of enthrallment issued from Brake's mouth barely reaches his ears, but it does, and it makes Grind furious.

He clenches his jaw tight. *He did that on purpose.*

Well, no rider—messenger or rogue—is going to make a *fool* out of him! Certainly not right in front of the youngest of his crew.

Back on Grind's side, and still showing off, the rider lands square and straight on tires made of metal plates. A burst of speed and the F.O.O.L. pulls ahead, swerving to put himself in line with Grind's car, peppering the vehicle with flying bits of sand and of rock. Throttling away in a hurry sends one large rock smashing right through the car's windshield. Broken glass and desert grit shower on both man and boy and draws from Grind a roar to overcome that of the hollering engine. The rider in black races away at a speed only a F.O.O.L. is capable.

Fuck whatever bounty they might strip from this rider; this fool is *dead!*

Grind reaches for the fusion boost. He has only enough for one burst, but one is all he needs. His fingers flirting with the switch when the rider—not so far ahead—suddenly explodes.

Grind sees the flash of light, bright blue, burst underneath the F.O.O.L.'s chassis. He watches as the two black objects are flung high into the air, flipping over once, end over end. Grind keeps his lead-foot on the pedal as he witnesses the machine deconstruct around the rider, exploded into hundreds of free-flying, articulating pieces. The rider, caught in the middle of the blast, twists with the nimbleness of a highly trained, youthful, acrobat. A part of his F.O.O.L., his helmet deconstructs also, exposing an unexpected face that carries less than half the age as Grind. A shock of thick, corn-colored hair is exposed, but briefly, as the articulating joints and panels of the F.O.O.L. reassemble around the rider's body, mid-air.

How? The words die in Grind's throat. *How can he be so young?*

Rage pushes the car's accelerator to the floor, though it is hardly necessary—the fool has landed and is turned around. Having formed a tightly fitted, flexible shell around his body, the F.O.O.L. leaves only his face exposed. Bearing a mischievous grin, full of confidence, he races to meet Grind's rage head-on.

True symbiosis is rare. In the case of Rider06: unheard of. No longer can he recall last he actively thought about working, as one, with a machine. His F.O.O.L. is a Champion. The best of her class and the only one of her caliber, and nothing at all like the behemoths the company had been more apt to produce. Driven by intention, fueled by desire, and powered by a molecular alchemy fusion reactor making up her core, that connects all her moving pieces, all Rider06 need do is want and his F.O.O.L. will take on whatever form necessary to obtain his objective.

Of course, with such intelligence also comes the necessity in allowing the F.O.O.L. a certain degree of free rein. When it comes to protecting her rider, that measure is crucial. It is in that trust where most riders—all the failed ones—struggled. Without resigning their control, they prevented proper bonding with their machine, and so, eventually causing corruption in both. No such issues exist for Rider06. Giving himself over to her, linking his body and mind to the rigid structure of metal and formless artificial intelligence was as warm and welcoming as going home.

Gaining the minimum safe distance from the gang of desert rats, a burst of fusion ignites under the F.O.O.L.'s chassis safely sending Rider06 flipping end over end in the air while the reticulating metallic plates that once held the shape of a motorcycle, encase him, instead, in snug, sleek, full-bodied armor. It is a frequented favorite the pair have grown accustomed to using over their years together. Every panel is in place before his feet reach the ground. Flawless harmony, and Rider06 stays on mission.

He does not land on his feet so much as he does on the two, in-line wheels underneath them, clamped snug by the boot fitted around each foot. His F.O.O.L. sighs, an almost feminine sound, as fusion energy channels through the armor. Another burst of blue through ports embedded in each heel and Rider06 rockets forward, back the way he had come and head-on into the rushing onslaught of thievery and violence.

The metal wheels and fusion propulsion eat up the desert. He passes the lead car in a blink. Then the next bike, then the next. Not one member of the gang has changed position since he drove through them, sizing them up. They have tightened their formation—his F.O.O.L. tells him so through their link. All the better for, and in favor of, Rider06. The motorbike still bringing up the rear, the one he had spun around, is much more eager to be in his way. The rogue brandishes an automatic rifle from the old wars. Archaic but functional, and no doubt loaded with bullets filled with an electrical charge rather than useless gunpowder; a direct hit in the right place can cause severe damage. The bandit aims the weapon straight at the rider rushing him, at what he considers prey.

Vermin.

The desert rat opens fire.

His F.O.O.L. has long anticipated this. Necessary proximity is met an instant before the bandit squeezes the trigger. Another bright burst of blue sends Rider06 into a high vault and bullets pepper only air and rock. Not so easily dissuade, the desert rat follows suit by lifting his gun, firing all the way. The F.O.O.L.'s articulating plates disjoint in places and reach out, causing her rider to spin as they sail over the far too slow bandit. Every bullet misses. Rider06 flips safely out of the spin, but another blue burst takes Rider06 further still. Ignoring, for now, the squeal of breaks and rising cloud of dust kicked up by the befuddled gang struggling to turn around in a hurry, Rider06 stays on mission.

He lands with his F.O.O.L. absorbing just enough of the impact to take the edge off. A long, rectangular panel along the topside of his arm below the elbow, disjoints and slides back exposing tiny ports. Lasers render a visible interface above his arm needed to access the F.O.O.L.'s digital tools for use in the physical world. He selects **MAPPING**, then he is off again, moving laterally more by the F.O.O.L.'s propulsion than the rider's effort. He curls his fist downward to expose and activate a larger, green mapping laser mounted to his wrist.

Rider06 races the landscape, targeting the green laser to the ground in the pattern he has set, scoring a wide grid of uniform, green-edged squares. One span, two spans, three spans long. That should do the trick. One hundred meters achieved, and the mapping laser winks off. He returns his wrist level and Rider06 turns sharply left—right into the on-coming rush of desert pirates all turned around, all lined abreast of one another, and all charging with cold, glaring eyes and hearts blackened to murderous intent. Rider06 grins and his F.O.O.L. buzzes with the kind of merriment only a machine would know—the timing could not be better—and they charge the gang once more.

For such a long grid, there are two explosions instead of one to collapse the crust of desert floor and expose the cavern hidden below. The gang is too close and going too fast to avoid the gaping wound suddenly torn open in the ground, in their path, or avoid the horrors that come pouring from it.

A sickly-grey plague of long-legged, black shucks vomit out of the hole in untold numbers. Each beast the size of a motorbike and more sinew, spines, and bone than muscle, brain, or will, but the monsters do reach terrifying speeds and are voracious killers. Strong muzzles filled with finger-long, knife-sharp teeth open too wide. Wicked claws tip each of the four toes too long and nimble on each of their four paws that are too boney. They tear right through the gang too heavy and slow to avoid massacre. Rider06 stays low and slips through the gang unnoticed and unscathed. The code holding the crew together fails. Every man is suddenly out for himself and motorbikes scatter. Rider06 stays on mission.

A proximity warning is a jolting yet mild buzz in his head, and he makes ready for the sharp left turn just as his F.O.O.L. leans him into it; her sensors keeping them on target. The turn offers him a glance at the churning mass of flesh, bone, and machines he has left behind. One shuck has impaled a raider on one of the two, long, bony protrusions that are mutated extensions of the creature's shoulder blades. Easily the length of a man's arm, the tip of one has pierced through the open visor of the group's younger rider and out the back of the helmet. The young marauder's body drags along lifelessly in the stampede. A high-pitched wale of anguish issuing from the passenger seat of the car is all but lost in the chaos.

Rider06 stays on mission.

Again, he activates the mapping laser. With his F.O.O.L. telling him where and when to lay grid, he maps sections of ground on his right as long and as wide as the car he hears tearing up the desert floor; the driver overwhelmed by the enraged nest of black shucks. They used to be dogs, once upon a time. Just as this land was once as lush as it is vast, protected by a proud kingdom. Greed of one man who could not take ownership of the land by force, turned it into a wasteland. Hatred polluted the world's most wonderous beasts, turning them into aberrations. Good dogs mutated into the vile mongrels that crawl about in the dark just under the surface of the barren ground. This nest is the largest Rider06 has ever seen, dooming the driver and his gang from the start. Rider06 stays on mission.

With the series of mapped grids laid out, Rider06 leans hard left as they collapse, one by one. Huge plumes of dust fill the air; this nest is even larger. Rider06 wheels around as the last grid collapses. For a moment, he is faced with the boiling mass of black shucks rolling toward him with unnerving speed and the few remaining survivors still fighting to get clear of the swarm. Every man, beast, and machine add to the curtain of thick dust growing thicker. Rider06 wheels away. Coming full circle, he plunges straight into the wall of dust left by his detonated grids. For a moment, all falls silent.

Rider06 is blind, but his F.O.O.L. knows the way and clean air is quick to hit his face. He breaks through the red haze to a landscape. For the moment, all appears peaceful and serenely empty, belying the mayhem on the verge of erupting at his back.

It is neither the black shucks nor the marauders that break the wall of dust next, but massive fire worms. Real giants, freshly woken from hibernation. Mountainous, tubular, quaking sacks of blubber and fat, with thick, robust hides and wide, circular mouths always open and brandishing rings inside of rings of serrated teeth that are always spinning, ready to shred any meal sucked into it—they are the largest, most deadly animals on the planet. Just one could swallow the biggest whale and still be able to inhale hundreds of black shucks—which happens to be their desired choice of food. And Rider06 has woken three of them.

Like the black shucks, the fire worms are horrid forms of the majestic beasts they once were, poisoned by the shucks they consumed in effort to rid the land of their corruption. But pestilence brought upon the world by man, can only be cleansed away by man. So, Rider06 stays on mission.

He will need to get closer—much closer—if he is to procure the sample required to complete this assigned mission. A wordless, *understood*, reverberates in his thoughts an instant before the tingle of a proximity warning passes through the armor to his skin. His F.O.O.L. lurches him to the left, avoiding a giant head of a fire worm that smashes to the ground where he had been, by the skin of his armor.

A lurch to the right avoids a second worm while hurling Rider06 airborne and back in the direction of the first worm that nearly ate him; its head is just starting to lift from the sand. Rider06 targets and fires a single square grid the size of his own body and mere blister on the orange-pink, scaly hide of the worm. The hide pops when the grid collapses and his F.O.O.L. immediately begins procedures to get him to the open wound, to collect the sample before it closes.

They were beautiful once, before plague reduced the vast majority into these monstrosities. Majestic, powerful, graceful creatures of lore corrupted to bulbous, quivering, gelatinous masses with appetites to match, condemned to eat without thought or concern. And yet, some of their magic remains, locked up and hidden within their creamy white vital fluids called scale. More puss-like than blood, it's not the same scale that it used to be, but even small amounts are still highly coveted. A single vile could have bought this lousy desert gang a whole town of their own, with women and food instead of the death and demise they found instead. Difficult to wound and next to impossible to kill, just collecting one vile makes for an arduous task. Like the creatures themselves, collecting their scale was once a noble art. Or so the stories go, but even stories suffer corruption now.

He lands hard on the back of the worm. The wheels on his feet having rearticulated into hooks, splay out in a snap and grip to the wrinkles in the thick hide. His F.O.O.L. has reshaped the gauntlet around his right arm into a long, blunt-ended spire which Rider06 plunges deep into the gaping hole. The wound is already closing, but the single jab is all he needs. The F.O.O.L. disengages the hooks anchoring his feet to the bucking, undulating monster, and Rider06 is on his way out before he has finished pulling free the tissue sample.

Objective complete.

A harrowing flip from the behemoth lands Rider06 close to the worm's head as it smashes its mouth to the earth. A bright blue burst at his feet launches him into the air as the worm lurches in the opposite direction. Enraged, the worm spasms violently. From its wide, perpetually open, circular mouth full of rings of serrated teeth, comes spewing a great torrent of liquid fire.

Thick, sticky, molten red fluid turns the sandy ground into black-encrusted rock, but not before burning, melting, or liquifying anything organic unlucky enough to get in the way. Including four riders of the marauding gang. Obliterated by liquid fire, their screams are blood-curdling and short lived. The yelps and cries of the black shucks are growing quieter, too, as the three worms feast, gorging themselves on the swarm.

Rider06 comes to land with a protective bounce from his F.O.O.L.'s energy source, on a stretch of bare, desert floor far from the quieting fray. Dust hangs thick; it will take the rest of the day to settle. A flash of quivering flesh here or there is all he will see of the worms before they are gone again, diving into the crevasse that exposed the black shuck colony. No vermin remain in this territory; another infestation cleared out.

A series of touches to the interface, via the plate along his forearm, disengages all tactical weaponry and Rider06 turns his back on the fading chaos. A short burst of clicks, whines, and whirring sounds and his armor plating reconstitutes into the motorcycle she had been. The plates that shape his helmet stays with the bike this time. Wide-lensed goggles cover his eyes instead, fitting snug and sure. *One last task*, and Rider06 mounts his mechanical wonder and allows her to take off with all speed across the flat, barren landscape.

Reacquire signal, he intuits as they fly across the wastes of rock. Her response is not one he expects. *On approach.* A buzz and tingle in his armor tells him, *behind*, and *right*. Trusting his machine to keep a straight path, Rider06 peers back over his shoulder, and the guttural roar of a laboring, damaged engine reaches his ears.

He spots the car. Smoke is pouring from the hood, yet the much larger, heavier vehicle is catching him up, fast. Unnaturally so. It must be equipped with an external fusion booster not unlike the sensitive chemistry that powers Rider06's F.O.O.L. An outdated model, undoubtedly stolen, but it is closing the distance effectively enough. Behind the wheel, the grizzled, battle-weathered face of the desert gang's leader is tight with rage and locked in a snarl. Rider06 grunts in amusement.

Ready whenever you are.

His F.O.O.L. responds with rumbles of excitement, and he feels her reach out with her scanners. *Planning.* At last, they can finish what they came here to do.

The car is approaching quickly when Rider06 feels the tingle in his helmet. *Ready.*

Rider06 knows what his machine intends.

A sharp left instantly peels him away from the path of the speeding car. So sharp, the bike leaning so far, that his body hovers close enough to the ground to flirt with. The F.O.O.L. restructures a portion of her frame to shield his leg up to his knee. Exposing processing panels in the process but saves him from lacerations and broken bones.

The deep turn brings them near the lip of a canyon sliced deep through the desert floor. The gap is a little more than three-hundred meters wide, any F.O.O.L. could clear it. The same cannot be said about an iron-made car, even one running on old-Age alchemy.

Pulling out of the turn so close to the edge, the F.O.O.L. has no time to reintegrate the panel shielding her rider for the processors to connect and initiate recombination into the suit of armor. Rider06 knows this and, for a moment, assumes control. A minor manual adjustment and he aims for a raised formation of wide, flat stones at the edge. The front wheel lifts into the open space as his F.O.O.L. reassembles her panels. Man, and machine, are airborne. The front tire starts to tip when the F.O.O.L. ignites a brilliant burst of blue in a blast of fusion that sends them both higher. The F.O.O.L. shatters around her rider in precise control.

For a breath, Rider06 is alone and exposed, suspended in free fall over a canyon, so deep, the bottom is obscure in fog and darkness. There is no telling how deep the gorge really is but, in that moment, he does feel a hot, weak draft rising from the shrouded depths. His F.O.O.L. pulls herself together as a familiar, foul reek of anise and rotted meat hits his nose. Sleek, black armor wraps him in a lover's embrace, and Rider06 gets an idea of his own.

Assembled, and instantly aware of his intent, his F.O.O.L. reshapes his gauntlet to allow an aimed burst of fusion. It is not a weapon—no time for the interface—but the single ball of energy he fires down into the chasm below is enough to send him a little higher, and right into a violent collision with the man from the car.

There is no time to wonder how he got there, though Rider06 has his guesses. The car is, no doubt, on a speedy trip straight to the bottom of the gorge. A thin shield of a glass-like framework is woven in front of the man's face. Rider06 can do nothing. Not only will the raider see any punch coming, but his shield will stop it.

An unmistakable whir rises from the man's articulating, metallic right arm—his own charge building. He fires! A blast of fusion hits Rider06 square in the chest. The force is fantastic, sending Rider06 sailing clear the opposite edge of the canyon and then some. He crashes hard to the flat, rocky surface. Flooding with a surge of fusion, his F.O.O.L. absorbs most of the impact, leaking sparks of blue when they bounce, before sliding to a stop one-hundred meters from the rim—not as far as he had expected.

Between him and the canyon's edge lands the man with the right arm made of an unusual metal. On his face, a self-gratifying grin drips with supremacy. Tonight, thinks Rider06, he will see that his F.O.O.L. gets extra attention in the garage; she deserves an upgrade after this. There, he will tell his story of the real dragon he saw this day.

Grind takes his time stepping away from the edge of the gorge, enjoying the grinding of the gears that is his right hand as it reshapes a multitude of tiny reticulating pieces into the barrel of a more precise weapon. He has this punk dead to rights, and nothing is going to spoil his victory.

"You made a major mistake, rider," Grind calls to the pathetic, limp figure of the black-armored rider lying on his belly, partially propped up on an arm and watching his demise unfold. "You made a mockery of me with that little stunt of yours."

His arm whirs, powering up for a finishing shot while increasing the glass shield protecting not only his face, neck, and shoulder, but ready to absorb the kickback of such a blast, as well.

"To think I was nearly outdone by a young, fresh F.O.O.L. rider." He shakes his head. "Can't have that. It's good they're all dead."

His prey has not moved, hasn't even bothered to plea. Grind takes aim. He can always build a new gang. With this idiot's F.O.O.L., he will command a gang twice as large, and conquer the wastes. The very idea whets his appetite. Just one last thing to do.

"Well," he says around a wicked, satisfying twist of his jaw. The command to fire only a thought away when—*wham!*—his glass shield shatters, crushed under an unexpected and terrible force. An immense pressure encases Grind, squeezing his entire left side from his neck to his hips. The hum he normally feels in his bones erupts in an all-out wail. Hot breath engulfs him, vented from the long, scaly muzzle of the beast that has snapped its jaws over his entire left side.

The world suddenly disappears from under his feet. The sky tumbles. Then, the pressure is gone. The ground returns, but against his back. Grind feels nothing but the unmoving presence of the desert floor against the back of his head. He sees nothing but the unblemished blue above and a long, black ribbon that whips and twists deeper—or higher—into the sky. The beast that had him pinned in its jaws is shrinking into the endless blue. A *dragon? Could it be?*

It is the ticking and tacking reverberating throughout his bones that alerts Grind that tools are working on his body. A slight tilt of his head brings the shock of blond hair into view. The young rider is not looking at him but is, instead, focused on some task, close at hand. Grind laughs despite his current situation.

"You can't kill me, messenger" he manages to gurgle to the rider. "That's against the rules."

"Why would I kill you—" speaks the young man. His F.O.O.L. is steps away, standing tall on her pair of wheels, patiently waiting for her rider. "—when the local wildlife seems to do the job just fine?"

Grind nearly chuckles. Wants to in fact, but his joviality cowers and dies when his gaze drifts down to a number engraved, black on black, in the upper corner of the rider's chest piece. *06. 06?* That is… impossible! The suits, the machines, they are not replicable. Once a link between man and interface establishes, a F.O.O.L. cannot link with another. There are strict rules, records kept; F.O.O.L.s and their riders numbered, starting with *01. 06?* That means this young man is one of the first!

"How can this be?" Grind himself was a young, ignorant man—no older than this rider appears to be—when the first ten F.O.O.L.s went to battle for the war effort. He grew into a man watching them fight, wanting a F.O.O.L. of his own and willing to do anything to get one. He was denied when some know-nothing-specialist classified him as 'unstable.' With his hand forced, Grind took drastic action to get that which he felt he deserved.

"But you're so…" A flare of pain in his shoulder makes Grind gasp. "…*young.*"

"A man is only as good as his F.O.O.L.," says the rider. He looks Grind in eyes and smiles. "She keeps me exactly as she needs me. It is a shame you stole yours, corrupting her. Did you really expect her to then be your right arm?" The rider shakes his head with a click from his tongue and turns his attention back to his work.

The pain in Grind's shoulder seizes his entire body stiff before relenting to an almost relieving, crushing sensation.

"You know who I am?"

The rider nods. "Of course, I do. The scourge who failed

registration, who stole a F.O.O.L. and fled. Covered your tracks well. I had to wait a long time for this mission to rise through the lists, to bring me out to the wastes."

Grind chuckles. To think he, of all people, grew worthy enough to warrant a messenger hired on as a mercenary to hunt him down, after all these years. "So, you've finally caught me." Grind says with a grin. If he must go, at least he is going as someone's fat, heavy purse.

"I didn't come here for you."

At the rider's words, Grind's last hopes of going down in infamy are dashed away. A gasp of pressure releasing from gears disconnecting and Grind, at once, feels different. Incomplete. Alone. *Weak.* A shock of cold fills him with the terrifying sense of being ripped in two. The hum has gone silent. The hum that he has felt tremble through his bones for decades, is gone.

"Did you never wonder what that hum was?"

Grind does not realize that he has closed his eyes until he is opening them. The rider is still knelt next to him. The cool satisfaction on his face turns Grind both fearful and angry in the same instant. The mechanical wonder that had been his arm cradled tenderly in another man's hands sets Grind's blood to boil.

"I have heard her calling out for decades. Begging to be free. Now, she is safe. I sealed off your arm with dragon scale. It's corrupted so it will start to fester, but you'll live."

The rider stands, caring not at all for the misery suddenly smothering Grind like a wet blanket on a dark and frosty night—the onset of F.O.O.L. withdrawal.

Live? Puh—he will be lucky to survive the night.

Grind was not supposed to die like this. Gone down in a blaze of glory or in the bed of a gorgeous woman, sure. Not just... left on the ground to rot, to putrefy in the agony of the loss of his arm until driven into madness. A hangman's noose would be better than this abandonment, crippled and injured, left to the pickings of the desert's roaming scavengers.

"Wait!" Grind hollers to the impossibly young, old rider and his magnificent F.O.O.L. "You're not going to take me in? Collect my bounty?"

The young rider's scoff is more chilling than Grind thought possible. "You *have* been out here a long time; no one collects bounties on men, anymore. You were forgotten a long time ago."

The rider's F.O.O.L. roars to life. There is the delightful whir of her fusion core, then her sleek, powerful design rockets away, carrying her rider and precious cargo, safe and secure, beyond the horizon. Grind is alone.

Damn, it is hot out here.
And his phantom arm itches.
Grind almost chuckles. Almost.

Tales in Hindsight

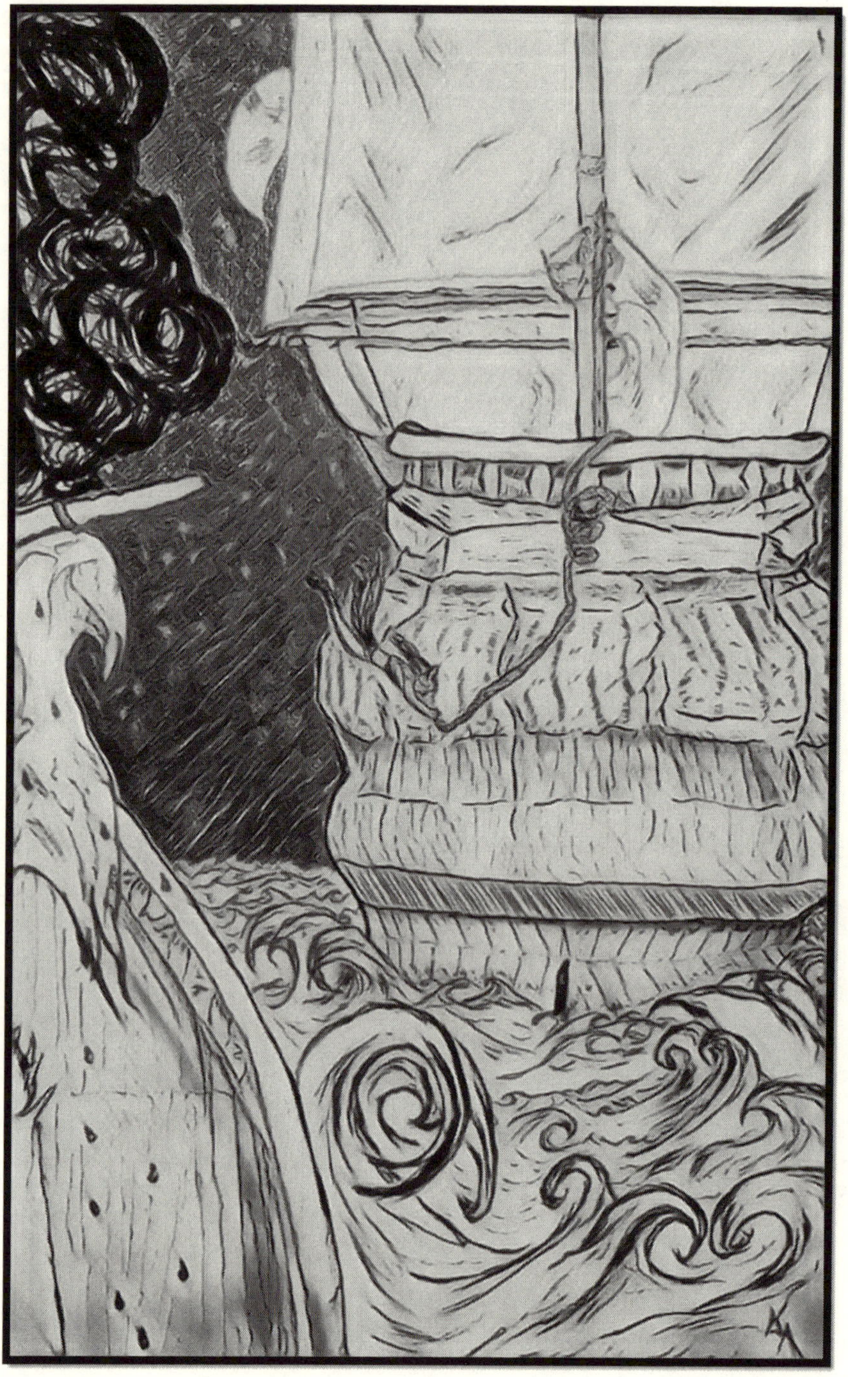

JULY

✦ Pirate of Ulie ✦

𝕴 hear he be ridin' a great sea serpent.

"A dragon, three times long as any ship, an' twice as wide. There no be tellin' how many in his crew, only few ever be used ta raid—just enough ta overtake any ship they please, with hardly a fight worth tellin'."

"*Poppycock!*"

"*Them's just tales!*"

"Tales? With so few souls he damned ta the depths of the Nine Seas, *talk* is all there be of the man, the Pirate of Ulie. An' not one be tellin' what the great pirate be lookin' like. Only that he plunders in the blink of an eye, attackin' both scoundrel and law lover alike, leavin' hardly a trace. How ye be explainin' *that* one, eh? Without he be havin' a sea dragon?"

"*That here we be, with a sniffa aboard, chasin' down his ship.*"

"A ship we have yet be findin', afta' more than six seasons of lookin'."

And just like that, the already worrisome melancholy gradually overtaking the ship's crew, sours. Every head of every lazy deckhand huddled together against the storm that has raged all night, turns

Tales in Hindsight

away. Some toward the man at the ship's wheel—or perhaps their captain standing proudly before it—others toward the sails, the sea, anywhere but in the direction of the one not part of their crew poised at the railing just port of the figurehead straight off the bow.

The men have been at it for days. The crew is restless, and the weather helps for none of it. Caught, they have been, in a downpour that has lasted thus four days and nights. If not for the figure standing at the bow, her back to the crew and eyes on the boiling waves of a turbulent ocean, none of them would be this deep in the Nine Seas to endure the storm at all. The *Lady Marie* would be still afloat in calmer, warmer waters more south. The men lounging in hammocks or rolling dice, drinking either way, and plundering any ship that dare to drift by.

Such a life may satisfy such simple men but is hardly one fit for a man like Atlas Riggs, Captain of the *Lady Marie*. For a man of such prestige as he, nothing short of legendary will do. So, brave he will the raging heart of the Nine Seas—and so shall his crew—in pursuit of a legend in turn, the only one capable of bestowing upon Captain Riggs the title he so aptly deserves.

The Pirate of Ulie.

The scourge of the Nine Seas.

The ghost who plunders wherever the raid be greatest; the tales of the man are as renown as they are inconsistent. From a commander of ships so large and powerful as to overtake well-armed crews with hardly a skirmish, to a leader of small, quick fleets that attack in the dead of night and rob crews blind with barely a sighting to recount—Captain Riggs has heard them all, too. The tales are why he is here; why his men have followed him. For the glory, the *reward*, the reputation of defeating and defaming a pirate of such illustrious distinction is what keeps his men going. And do so they will, but only so far.

A good, loyal crew has he, but after days of unending storm and turbulence—the most recent in an eighteen-month campaign that Captain Atlas Riggs had anticipated to have concluded in less than half that—even the hardiest of deckhands can spoil. Just his men proclaim, in not one of all the tales told can there be found a description of this infamous pirate. Tall? Short? Skinny or fat? Bearded or bald? Nothing. It is no wonder that tales of the man often turn into stories of ghosts and fabled dragons. And those tales are dangerous. They are here to chase a man, not a myth. If he cannot produce the Pirate of Ulie, Captain Atlas Riggs will acquire a different reputation altogether, and be doomed by it.

He knows this man exists. Of the few accounts which Captain Riggs has heard from survivors first-hand—and only after supplying several rounds of mead—that when asked of the menace who stalks the seas, the teller suddenly lose their amiability to answer. Hard men, these, salty as the sea with skin cooked to jerky from a life lived between the blazing sun and the glaring sea. Men who would sooner run another man through with a blade on account of an ill-timed look and all but anxious to flaunt their exploits, turned eerily meek. Wounded boys, they became, for the question posed. They turned away their faces gone somber, red blooming on their cheeks. How quickly they downed the remainder of their drink and made plain their excuse to exit. What was it about this one pirate able to turn brutal, terrible, guiltless men away from glory, tails tucked?

"I hear the Pirate of Ulie is an evil spirit."

Spoken from the mouth of one of his own crew loud enough to pierce the drumming of the torrential rain.

"One destined to ride the waves for all time, takin' from those who steal themselves."

"Don't ye be a'speakin' of spirits—evil or nigh," one rebukes. "Bad luck, it is. Bad enough havin' a woman on board."

"What ye say there, sniffa?" shouts another of the crew. "What kind a pirate ye think we be trackin'?"

All eyes, including those of Captain Riggs, turn toward their hired sniffer standing alone at the bow of the ship. As drenched as the rest, in both salt water and fresh, the only female to have ever stepped foot aboard Captain Riggs's ship seems less bothered by the night's conditions (or any throughout the chase, for that matter) than the men. She certainly is the least dressed.

The sniffer, a wildling, turns her gaze from the swells to the crew upon hearing the invitation to join in on the conversation.

"The Pirate of Ulie?" says she, under big eyes as rich as copper that always carry a glint of something cunning. Her words are spoken perfectly but with a husky voice not used to speaking words at all. Where they sound rich, they also sound strangled.

"I think—" the wildling smiles, twisting up only one corner of her mouth, turning her sharp features more wildly exotic. "—is *just* pirate."

The most words that Captain Riggs has heard her string together, yet. And here he thought her unable to do so at all. He has yet to hear her even speak her name—if she has one. When "sniffer" fails to suffice, he and his crew have simply come to call her JP, in liken to the strange, scrawling black loops in vague shape of the two letters tattooed to the bare skin of her lower back that is always exposed.

She is a small wildling. Smaller than his shortest man, she stands no taller than Captain Riggs's stomach. He could pick her up with one arm and cradle her there as easily as he would a child. Lean, but curvy in all the right places, with full lips under large eyes, he cannot deny that he would certainly take some enjoyment holding her in such a manner. In her short, leather bodice and trousers to match, all fitting as tight as second skin, the eye-pleasing attraction is not lost on Captain Riggs, but that is where it stops.

At certain angles, her face can nearly be mistaken for that of a normal human woman, but her nose, mouth, and cheekbones jut forward enough to almost be considered a muzzle. Long, thick, black hair, matted and wet, hanging down her back begs for a man to tangle his fingers in it. The pointy ears that stick straight up through that mane, however, belong more on a fox than a woman, and any residual attraction degrades to repulsion for a man such as Captain Atlas Riggs.

The curve of her waist and the ample shape to her buttocks can draw out a fool-man's lust, eagerly. Even his own men have been seduced into taking wildling females to bed, from time to time, without fear of offspring. For Captain Atlas Riggs, the swooshing rise of that vulpine tail at the base of her spine just below her strange, tattooed markings, undeniably breaks her spell and reminds him that wildlings are more liken to animals than his own kind.

Puh, Captain Riggs shakes his head, letting loose the waterfall of rain that had collected in the wide brim of his hat. Loathsome beasts. If Madame Maria had not been so insistent on him using a wildling to sniff out the illusive pirate—if he, like many other captains, had not already come to rely on Madame Maria in providing anything from specialists to slaves, from supplies to rich cargo—Captain Riggs would not have brought such a beast on board in the first place. But, when faced with a reputation of such high regard as Madame Maria, one does not sneer at advice given and still expect service in the future. He risked that already once when he had refused a barter for possession of his own ship. All because she thought it *lovely*.

What would a woman—even one as capable as Madame Maria—know of commanding such a vessel? If it were up to Captain Riggs, he would sooner force her *and* her wildling kin to walk the plank, leave them tied and floundering in shark infested waters.

The best trackers, he was told, this hired sniffer has led him onward by the nose for more than twice the length of time his own immaculate calculations had predicted. Sly creatures, wildlings. He has not dared to let her out of his sight for long since she came on board. Even kept to sharing his cabin—her locked in a cage, of course. Kept fed, alive, and safe from any sort of mistreatment, and what is his reward? A tiresome chase without end. His doubts in this creature's authenticity long since taken root, his intolerance of her is growing just as much as it is for water-laden boots: Madame Maria is going to get this wildling back in pieces if she fails to deliver soon.

"A *just* pirate, eh?" sneers Lefty, the obnoxious fool who first stirred the pot of this night's discussion. Spray from the boiling, inky sea smacks his face with far less force than the hand of Captain Riggs is itching to do. Conditions are grating enough, bobbing along through the storm, carried onward by a single sail, before Lefty had to go and open his damned mouth.

"Ye think this pirate so *just*, why lead us to him?"

"Why?" The wildling's smile reaches her eyes in a curious way. Lacking all warmth but none of the glittering gaiety, she looks more foxlike than ever. She shrugs, her water-logged tail swishing to one side. "Money."

Where her answer is simple and likely true, and may be enough to quell Lefty's curiosity, it only further agitates others. Like Buckhorn. Riled up by Lefty's complacent jabbering of evil spirits and superstition while underway, compulsion makes him leave his post, taking threatening steps toward the wildling who has not moved from her spot at the bow.

"*Money*, is it? Ye ain't seein' not one-bit o' gold, ye sly devil-lass."

Buckhorn's attitude is infectious. Too quickly, all on deck take on the look that men get when they are about to commit an act that they know they should not. Captain Riggs has half a mind to let them have her, but the other half knows what grace of favor he will lose should he do so.

"Not one of you dogs will *touch* a single patch of fur on that sniffer," he roars to shame the thunder. He leaves Wicked Winston to man the helm and crosses the deck, his men cowering out of his way. "Not until *I* say so."

With his men reined in, he turns his attention onto the wilding, the source of all his dismay. The way she stands so still, her hands grasping the railing of his ship so tenderly, possessively, that Captain Riggs is quietly flooded with an alarming amount of jealousy. Had this wildling been male, he would have pitched him overboard right then and there, without a second thought.

"As for *you*," he growls, lowering his tone for her and her alone. "Best be wise and deliver that which I was promised. And soon."

Her breathtakingly sharp face tilts upward to meet his gaze. Her tail swishes to the other side. "Aye, Captain," says she through a grin too sweet. "Any moment now."

Captain Riggs chuckles. This is not the first time he has heard those very words. Poised to tell her so, taking a step closer in fact, a shout from the crow's nest high above changes everything.

"Ship on the 'orizon, Captain!"

His man shouts without much difficulty; the storm is dissipating. The seas still churn, and the winds still blow, but the downpour has lessened to a fine drizzle. Leaning against the railing alongside his sniffer, so close that he could wrap her in his coat, Captain Riggs focuses on the darkness ahead.

The clouds are breaking, allowing the soft light from the stars and moon to shine through. There, all but lost between dark sky and even darker waters, bobbing like a discarded cork, is a ship.

It is not the largest vessel he has seen. It is not much smaller than his own, in fact. Captain Riggs had expected more. Nevertheless, the sight does bring a lustful grin to his face. Until he feels the stare from the wildling next to him, with a queer smile of her own. Proud of herself,

Tales in Hindsight

this one, having found the unfindable, as promised… even if it *did* take months longer than promised. *Arrogant*, Captain Riggs growls under his breath.

"Raise the sails!" shouts Captain Atlas Riggs, his voice much louder now with only the crash of the waves to compete with. His eyes, however, remain on the wildling before him. A creature he could kill just as soon as kiss, had he been a creature of ill-repute himself. "Do not expect any portion of the plunder," he speaks down to her in an insolate tone meant to make this wildling sure of her place, and that it is *not* part of his crew.

"Aye, Captain," returns the smokey voice, and is meant.

Such a curious creature, but one Captain Riggs has no time for now. Turning toward the ship drifting dead in his path, Captain Atlas Riggs adjusts his hat.

"Chase her down, lads!"

His beloved ship ignites with activity. Men, far more than the slim crew manning her before, pour from hatches and doors suddenly flung open. The ship comes alive with bellowing and hollering from a crew fifty large. Hands grab and pull at ropes, and bare feet slap the sodden wood planks of the deck. In short order, the *Lady Marie*—pride and joy of the great Captain Atlas Riggs and marvel of the sea—is jolted from a vessel lazily adrift to the battleship that she is.

A full-rigged ship, with every cannon loaded and manned, and every other deck hand bearing sabers and flintlock pistols, the *Lady Marie* is truly a sight to behold as she plunges headfirst into the swells. A fast ship, her hull slices through the waves as an albatross through a mild breeze. With few ships that can match her, and none that Captain Riggs knows of that can surpass her, his *Lady Marie* makes sort work of closing the distance between him and his prize.

This is it. The moment Captain Atlas Riggs was made for. For tumbling this pirate from his spectral status, his own preeminence will surpass that of the greats. Names such as Cicero Salvator, Menace of the South Sea; or Klondike Wishbone, Bane of the North, all will pale in comparison to that of Captain Atlas Riggs, Conqueror of the Nine Seas. Yes, he likes the sound of that very much. Especially as his luck continues to roll: the other ship has yet to take notice. Captain Atlas Riggs has caught the great Pirate of Ulie by surprise. No longer does he hold care for his drenched boots nor the wilding on deck.

He returns to the helm, shoving Wicked Winston aside to take up the wheel himself. Just a man, his prey may be, but a pirate that does not slay a conquered foe can hardly call himself a pirate and deserves to be conquered in turn. Could such a man be called a *man*, at all? After this night, the Pirate of Ulie shall be vanquished by Atlas Riggs, Captain of the *Lady Marie*, and it is *he* who shall be remembered for all Time!

His vessel, racing along on rolling swells as much as it does the tumultuous hubbub of excited men, closes fast on the ship floating aimlessly. With glory in sight and appetites whetted for action, mayhem, and salvage, his crew will vanquish this pirate. The Ghost of the Nine Seas shall not simply vanish this time.

"Ready your pistols, men!"

Drawing near, Captain Riggs notices the decrepit state of the enemy ship. Her sails are raised, but flutter uselessly in the wind instead of catching it. The *Lady Marie* must have been spotted by *someone* on board, yet the ship continues to bob along weakly. The volley of shouts and cries from his men can surely be heard, and still, the ship ahead remains quiet. A trick, it must be. This *is* the Pirate of Ulie after all, and Captain Riggs can afford no time to curiosity.

A muzzle flash and bang suddenly sound off near center of the decrepit ship, on the starboard side. In barely the time to blink, a single lead shot is buried deep into the main mast of the *Lady Marie*. At last, he has been spotted, and so sets loose a terrific roar from his own chest.

His men fire back. Three more flashes burst across the deck of the ghost ship. Blue-gray smoke from spent powder cloaks all not already obscured by night and passing storm. One lead ball goes whizzing past his ear, to sink into the decorative wainscoted exterior of his captain's cabin. That is quite enough, thinks the venerable Captain Riggs, and eagerly returns the favor. Coming abreast of the ship chocked with smoke, he banks her sharply before the crowned queen figurehead is driven right through the other ship's hull. The sea between them erupts with thunderous clamor and spray.

"Fire!" hollers Captain Riggs, and his voice is immediately drowned out by the cacophonous combustion of half of his twenty-cannon salute, firing all at once.

The enemy ship is struck. Wood shatters. Bits and pieces fly chaotically through the air choked with more gray smoke. Even the hollering of his men is briefly snuffed out, and slow to return as half of them take cover from the raining debris while the other half reload the cannons, though another taste of lead will not be needed. Damaged severely, the best that ship can hope for now is to limp along at a tragically slow pace. Captain Atlas Riggs has caught the uncatchable, defeated the undefeatable. Now, he shall conquer the unconquerable in a glorious display of his might.

The pirate of legend is left with only a ship with a severely damaged hull. The main mast is still upright, but leaning at an angle it should not, and a mast furthest aft is downed completely. Her sails are more rags than they had been before. The very real "ghost" ship moves at a pace plenty slow enough for planks. They have her dead to rights, and his men are hungry.

His wildling may not get a share of the bounty, but she is as aroused by takeover as the men. Having freed a rope in a movement

Captain Riggs did not see, she leaps from the railing of the *Lady Marie*, to swing over the chasm of a raging sea vomiting salty spray onto the decks of both ships. Why? Captain Riggs cannot say. She is not armed—he would never allow her to be—what use will she be without him?

The rest of his crew are close behind. Two more muzzle flashes light up in the haze and the decrepit vessel slows even more. Relinquishing the wheel to Wicked Winston, who drops and drags her anchor in a move well practiced, the *Lady Marie* matches the crawl of the dominated vessel on her port side. Planks slam down on the crumbling sides of the disabled ship and Captain Riggs's crew swarm the enemy deck, shouting all the way. He has done it; the ship is theirs.

But the lustful roar of proud men peters out far too quickly. The last one to cross, Captain Riggs's steps foot into an awkward hush washed over the vanquished vessel's deck. He can see little through the haze of spent powder. His own men are mere phantoms, and only when they are close by. There are soft mutterings here or there, and the waves crashing between the two hulls. In the relative, unnatural quiet, a loud slap of something heavy is deafening.

What happened to the fight? Where is the glory to be hard won? Where is the ship's crew? Not once does Captain Riggs stop to wonder what that loud slap had been, where it came from, or caused by whom.

He turns on the heel of his boot to find his wildling standing close to his side, staring up at him with big, round, copper-colored eyes, her pointy face bright and unreadable. Sneaky fox, this one, as she is silent. His eyebrows arch in question to which she responds by lifting her hands, showing her dirty, empty palms. She shakes her head; she's found nothing. How can this be?

"Where be the crew?" shouts one of his men.

"Where be the *treasure?*"

The men's disembodied voices bounce around the tattered ruins of the dead ship. Damage, much of which Captain Riggs is sure, that was present before he rendered it derelict.

"This ship be manned by spirits."

"This ship be *damned!*"

Securing his pistol under his belt to favor his saber instead, Captain Riggs ignores the ignorant ramblings of his men and makes for the galley, barracks, and storerooms below. He will *not* be frightened away by myths. Tales are for children, and both of which should be avoided at all costs. The crew is here, somewhere. They must be. Ghosts did not fire lead rounds upon his ship.

Below deck, the bowels of this ship are not so dissimilar to those of his own albeit rot with mold, bugs, and water damage. In the galley he finds tables bolted down, bowls and spoons scattered loose overtop, all stuck with bits of cooled gruel. Hammocks are slung up in the crew's quarters, though fewer than he would expect on a ship this size. All have blankets. Rags, really. Every bit of cloth is moth-eaten and thready.

The stores hold nothing but a few barrels of mealy potatoes, rotting turnips, and pickled eggs. There are several large kegs for water; all but one, empty. The one with water is full less than half and carries a faint but putrid odor. The barrel next to it is as empty as the rest, but the inside is damp with a small amount of clear liquid pooled at the bottom—the barrel had been drained not so long ago.

There *had* been crew here. The evidence is plain; ghosts have no use for water. So, where are they now?

The remainder of the holds and stores are empty and bare. No treasure, no gold. Little food and even less water. No Pirate of Ulie. Aboard the ship he has chased for the better part of two years, Captain Riggs finds only murmurs and whispers and echoed silence. His men all put away their weapons for guns and swords will be of no use against air.

How can this be?

Captain Riggs looks sharply to his wildling. Having uttered not a word, she has followed him loyally into every room, down every ladder, and around every turn. She appears too somber to smile, yet her eyes... Does he detect a sparkle of humor? The thought to strike her, to demand an explanation, is nearly overwhelming. He nearly lets his hand fly, even if it amounts to nothing, but that hauntingly beautiful face is saved by a sudden call urging Captain Riggs to return to the main deck, with all haste.

He makes his way back through the ship, without delay, his wildling keeping tight to his side. Voices from his crew are on the rise. The call from the deck grows more urgent, and a cold truth begins to crawl up the neck of the formidable Captain Atlas Riggs. The legend of a pirate able to plunder in the blink of an eye whispers behind his eyes. Tales of a thief who robs men blind, without ever being seen himself, prickles his skin. A very real scourge of the Nine Seas, this Pirate of Ulie. A ghost pirate, an evil spirit, and certainly not *just* a pirate.

At the base of the final ladder before reaching the deck, a short climb away, Captain Riggs stops. At his back, his wildling stops, also. Behind her a dozen of his men do the same, itching at their faces and arms, desperate to be rid this place. Only his wildling has eyes just for him. Copper eyes, bright and wild. Untamed. *Untamable*. Watching, *waiting* to see what he does next.

"The planks have come loose, Captain!"

Buckhorn's shrill shout forces Captain Riggs to turn from that wildling's mouth turning up into hint of a grin. He climbs the final ladder to the exposed deck of the damaged ship. Buckhorn is poised at the starboard railing, his hand held aloft, a gnarled finger pointing at the *Lady Marie*.

Tales in Hindsight

"She be driftin' out ta sea, Captain!"

But his ship, his pride and joy, is *not* adrift. Captain Atlas Riggs swings his gaze down to the wildling who has climbed the ladder with him. From her face, his eyes travel down her small, curvy frame, fit and flexible, to her hands hanging at her sides. Her dirty hands smudged black. They had not been so *before* she swung her way to the captured ship. Truth hits as hard and as cold as a block of ice, and far too late.

"Shoot her!" shouts Captain Riggs, his wildling immediately bouncing away. His men, baffled, understand nothing of what is occurring before their very eyes and are slow to react.

"*Shoot* her!"

But she has already relieved several of his men of their weapons and, having used the stolen items to bash several heads along the way, she quickly slips beyond his grasp. Captain Riggs wrestles to free his own pistol when a swish of bushy tail draws his eye. He looks up just as she strikes him across the face with the butt one stolen. Then, she is gone.

He struggles to find his vision as his men do their feet. He has lost sight of the wildling. Likewise, his magnificent ship continues to pull away. Her stern coming fully into view, he spots the glint of the moon reflecting off the raised anchor. His ship is being *sailed* away. Above him, near the top of the broken main mast, he spots his wildling racing along the cross pole in the opposite direction of his stolen ship, a rope in her hand. The shout to open fire on the fox-woman lodges in his throat—his men, of those still armed, will only miss.

Clutching tight the rope, she leaps from the pole's edge, seemingly to dive the towering distance to the churning black waters below. A swish of her tail and the rope yanks taught. One end tethered to the mast, she swings across the deck, between his baffled men, and over the writhing wake of the departing ship.

At the apex of her swing, high above the waves, she lets go. At the same moment, the end of a second rope is tossed from the stern of the *Lady Marie* which the wildling catches with perfect timing. She swings low, her tail and long hair billowing behind her, her booted feet just missing the peak of cresting waves. In a blink she disappears around to the other side of the ship set to full sail under a night sky, clear now, dazzling with stars.

Captain Riggs does not see who is there to catch the outstretched hand of the traitorous wildling, but he has no such issue with the figure gracing the banister along the high deck on the ship's stern. Dressed in her finest black and red attire, with just the right combination of leather and lace to make a man sweat, is none other than Madame Maria, her short, voluptuous frame standing tall, waving a hand as elegantly as is the smile that parts her lips.

"She *is* a lovely ship," she calls down to him. "You really should have bargained with me when I gave you the chance, Atlas. Like ol' Winston, here."

Hot blood courses through Riggs's veins when who joins Madame Maria, aboard his stolen ship, but Wicked Winston—the only member of his crew who did not join in on the raid, the one who never does. Next to him comes sauntering the wildling, her grin the boldest of the three.

"Fitting name," calls Madame Maria, leaning triumphantly against the decorative railing a stone's toss above the bulbous windows of his own quarters. The white of the ship's name painted along the bottom edge of his cabin glows eerily in the moon light. "Almost as though she were mine, all along."

Madame Maria cackles. Wicked Winston grins. And the wildling blows Riggs a kiss as the magnificent ship—*his* magnificent ship—begins to shrink as it makes for the dark, stormless horizon.

"Is there steerage? Any sail that we might give chase?" Riggs asks, clinging to the last shreds of his damaged title.

"None, sir."

"The rudder has been disabled."

"We damaged a ship already at rot—"

"—dead in the water, sir."

Riggs cares not who answers, he can face none of them. Instead, he watches Madame Maria sail away on his *Lady Marie* knowing he will never again see the likes of either.

"We shall never speak of this," comes his final command. One he intends to keep, by any means necessary. None shall ever hear of the deplorable defeat of the great Captain Atlas Riggs. A man having been cheated, bested, and robbed of all he holds dear by the hands of a lady pirate and her beautiful wildling.

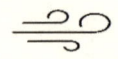

Tales in Hindsight

Tales in Hindsight

AUGUST

✦ GLORY ✦

It is a glorious day!

Bright blue sky, a vast cyan ocean around a radiant yellow sun. The sprawling grounds of the Academy for Elemental Skill and Mastery is bathed in golden rays. Late in the summer season, the warm air is enough to make students sweat practicing their arts, but the ones content in reclining, passing the remainder of the day lost in a book, not so much. The buzz of fat bees lazily drifting from flower to flower, and the birds with their constant serenading among the leafy trees, fill the air with melody. The sweet scent of jasmine and cherry blossoms provide perfume carried about on a breeze. It is a rare, perfect day. Yet, one might not think so inside the tower office of the High Dean.

Brilliant light streaming in through the large floor to ceiling, arched window, making up the center of one wall, is gobbled up by the deep mahogany wainscoting on the walls. Deeper, cherry oak of the various cabinets and cupboards lining the rest of the room only aid to the illusion that the room is comprised more of shadow than light. At the center of the room is a desk, kept as tidy as the rest of the immaculate space. It and its matching gothic style chair are the darkest pieces of all, nearly black, and sharp contrast to the ghastly white figure sitting there. The Head Dean. The brightness of the day is all but lost on the room, is also on the two women in attendance. Both of whom, for the moment, are as fixed and unmoving as the furniture.

The Head Dean sits rigid in her chair. Old and boney, her skin seems to hang loose as much as it seems stretched rice paper thin over the sharp angles and planes of her face and hands. Her hair, more salt than pepper, is pulled into the neat bun that no one has ever seen her without, secured tightly high on the crown of her narrow head. Her glasses, round with gold frames as thin as wire, are perched near the tip of her nose. Hands steepled together, her chin rests on the points of her manicured fingertips. An unamused glare in her eyes makes her look ready to impale her throat over the sharp tips of those milky, brittle nails. Standing before her, on the opposite side of the desk, is the source of her current frustration.

"Glory," she sighs, almost sadly. In truth, it's exasperation.

The young woman at the breath of adulthood stands with her back straight, her head bent slightly with all the proper appearance of submission under scrutiny of an elder, but the Head Dean is no fool. This is, by far, not this student's first time being summoned to this office. At least her long, brown hair is still combed and straight; her bangs curled neatly over her forehead with the tips just brushing her eyelashes. Her face is clean and not soiled with dirt or ash or worse. Her green eyes are unbruised with the lids painted a faint, shimmering gold. Even her uniform is in good order. Her white blouse is smudged-free, and her gold-trimmed, red, and black jacket and matching skirt still look pressed.

Her black, knee-high stockings have a few runs, and her black shoes are scuffed, but the Head Dean will take her wins where she gets them, when it comes to this one. Glory does, after all, have a reputation of never being able to keep anything clean or scuff-free for very long. The fact that she has come straight from class warrants no support to her still well-kept appearance. More than half of her visits to this office have been due to some classroom incident.

The Head Dean sighs again, her arms dropping to fold on the dark face of her desk. "Of all the students, here at the Academy, you are among the highest-ranking." Her sharp face swings side to side as she gently admonishes the young woman before her. "Cunning, intelligent, well adverse—such promising *talent*—yet you continue to struggle controlling the smallest of flames. We simply cannot have another incident like today. Lady Falmor has had to change rooms once already, due to your small combustion spells—well," the Head Dean clicks her tongue. "—from them *combusting*."

With a huff, the glasses are plucked from her nose and the

Head Dean fixes her plucky student a captious stare. "You are young, but far from inexperienced. With only a few years of training left before your class is to be set loose beyond the boundaries of the Academy, to make your own way in the world, you will soon be off to choose your own fate. You must learn *control* if you wish to be deemed fit for release outside these walls. You must *learn* the rules of magic, *bend* them to *your* will, if you hope to succeed. Understand?"

A, *yes, ma'am,* and a quick dip of a curtsy are the young woman's only reply, and neither are more, or less, sincere than the compliant bow to her head—again, the best the Head Dean knows she will get out this one. With nothing left to say that has not already been said—and more often than the Head Dean cares to admit—Glory is dismissed.

Really? Again? Over one, little fireball? Glory wonders as she pulls the door to the Head Dean's office closed behind her. If she were summoned to the administrative tower for every good deed, the Head Dean would she her *twice* as often!

So she caused one little fire. What about all the fires she's put *out* over the years? What of the fights she has been able to end with only a mild skirmish instead of allowing them to escalate into all-out battles? What about the *real* fights? The Head Dean never wants to talk about *those!* How about the trolls that she—and her partner—have taken down that would have otherwise breached the great stone wall that surrounds not just the Academy, but the city as well? And the ogre they had defeated before it nearly brought down the behemoth gate? Why did the Head Dean never want to talk about *those* times? Come to think of it, when has *Victor* ever been summoned to the Head Dean's office?

It takes effort not to slam the soles of her flat shoes against the white marble of the walkway as she storms away from the old bat's office. That woman hears about everything else, she can probably hear her shoes no matter how she controls her steps. But Glory's stride does relax a little when the solid walls of the enclosed hall suddenly open up on either side. High arches connect a string of pillars that hold the steeply angled stone roof aloft leaves the hall open to outside air. A downright chilly walk in the winter, the stone walkway is welcoming coolness in such late-day warmth.

To her left and far below the walk between the towers is an

open courtyard for the Academy's new recruits. Room enough to learn the foundations of channeling elements and pushing their newly found limits without fear of causing substantial damage. It is also empty. To her right—and precisely where Glory turns her attention—is a much larger courtyard. Large enough to yeild the wheat needed to feed the entire school of three-hundred souls strong for a full year, it is the courtyard she has called home for decades now. A space for the First class—her class—and it is not so empty.

Two figures stand apart from the rest. In full view of any who wishes to look, two boys have squared off. The sight is not wholly unusual. Fights are not uncommon, though the risk to fragile, developing reputations is often enough to keep conflicts limited to duels under the watchful eye and calculated encouragement of an instructor. Even then, life always gets harder for the loser. The two circling one another are clearly not interested in waiting for a referee.

One younger than her, the other matching her in age, Glory knows them both well. She mutters a swear, *the old bat be damned*, and breaks into a run. The path down to the courtyard is a long one. Glory will be lucky to make it there before one of them gets hurt. No doubt the Head Dean hears every, single, hard slap of her shoes against the solid, white mable floor.

🔥 🔥 🔥

Far below the stone walkway connecting the two highest towers, at the foot of the marble wall shielding the more delicate inner-workings of the Academy from the rambunctious and often powerful forces wielded by the hands of the school's elites, stand two boys. In the open space of the flat, gray, stone floor between practice equipment and sand pits, in full view of the stacked stone bleachers curled around one third of the courtyard, an argument between them teeters on the edge of a brawl. One has his hands locked tight into fists, the other with his arms insouciantly crossed against his chest.

"Take it back!" shouts the younger of the two.

"No," retorts the other with a smirk. "I don't think I will. I meant every word, and I hardly think you, of all people, can do anything about it."

"I swear, Vaunt," Kudos growls, his fists clenched so tightly that his arms are starting to shake. "If you don't take back what you said about my sister—"

"You'll *what?*" The other young man lifts his arms from his chest in casual taunt.

Kudos swallows, but shows nothing more. Physically, both young men have similar builds—tall, long-limbed, ropey muscles, and strong shoulders—but Vaunt, older by three years, carries a healthy ten more pounds. Not to mention his elemental Skills are matched by only a small few and none of those include the younger man squaring up to him now. And they both know it.

"You are weak," Vaunt presses, the smirk growing on his face. "You *and* your outland sister. Why do you think *she* is the only one of us paired with a partner? Because she's weak. She may be talented, but she lacks strength, vigor." Vaunt's grin takes on a cruel sneer. "Just as you lack tenacity and a spine." Vaunt steps forward into a fighting stance. "Come on, Kudos! I'll make it easy on ya—no summoning. Teach me a lesson. Or do you lack balls, too, just like your sister?"

The final insult and Kudos wastes no time on such ceremony as stance. He charges. Fists clenched, he swings a big punch straight for Vaunt's smug grin under his heavily waxed and perfectly styled hair. Everything about Vaunt has always made the younger man's skin crawl, just as every bit of him wants nothing more than to beat an apologie out of the older boy's pompous, snide mouth. His punch, however, is easily blocked and swept aside without that sneer deminishing in the slightest.

But there is good reason for Kudos being in the same class as Vaunt, and his own sister for that matter, despite him being three years their junior. Going with his swept punch, Kudos spins across Vaunt's back, and swings his shin for the older boy's ribs. A fast dropped elbow barely saves him from the blow. Vaunt twists for a counter back kick, but his foot meets open air; Kudos is fast, too.

Pulling his leg back with enough force to launch him into a back flip is all that saves Vaunt from the heel of Kudos's spinning hook-kick. When Vaunt lands, Kudos is ready with another punch to his face. Vaunt blocks, but as he sweeps the younger boy's hand away, he almost misses the high crescent kick the kid wields next. His shoe nearly connects with Vaunt's temple—and surely would have—if not for a sudden channeled Push of Air that sends Kudos sailing backward several feet.

"Hey!" Kudos shouts. "*You said no summoning!*"

"*Obviously* you broke that already!" Vaunt hollers in return.

"Where do you get off nearly hitting me like that?"

"With a kick. I'm not the one who channeled!"

"Oh! So now you're calling me a *liar?*" Vaunt bellows. "You really want to do this, you little brat? Go ahead, *try* to damage my reputation, punk. Let's do this." Gone is Vaunt's grin along with any mirth he may have had before. This time, Vaunt is the one who charges.

He leads with a set of jabs and a hook that spins him around fast enough to launch his big frame into the air with a flying round-house kick. Nothing hits, but they do force Kudos to back away. Vaunt lands and turns, his fist locked for a hail-mary punch, but from so far, Vaunt cannot hope to physically strike the young man. Arm extended, his fist snaps opens and Vaunt channels another Push of Air that strikes his opponent in the chest.

It is salt in an open wound. Barely stable on his feet, Kudos fires back. He rushes in and throws a punch meant to miss Vaunt, but cause him to back up a step in turn—which he does. Kudos leaps into a rolling ariel-tuck, telegraphing his own round-house kick to the bigger boy's face. Vaunt takes the bait and lifts his arm to deflect the kick. Kudos rechambers his leg mid-flight for a lower, precise kick to the boy's exposed stomach, instead. Payback for the insult on his sister. It would have landed too, had Vaunt not seen his mistake at the last possible instant. With just time enough, he summons a Burst of Light exactly where his opponent's foot impacts. A brilliant pop of white and gold erupts as the energy from the cast magic absorbs the impact of the kick instead of Vaunt's ribs. Dispelled glittering bits of Light rain down on the stone floor of the courtyard. If the pair did not have an audience before, they certainly do now.

"You're cheating!" Kudos shouts. Knocked back by the burst, he manages to stay on his feet, but only just.

"It's not cheating if it's *winning.*"

"Fine. Two can play at that game, Vaunt."

Standing tall, Kudos begins to work his hands. From his lips flies the murmur of an incantation. His voice, coming rapidly, also increases in volume until he is shouting the last of the unintelligible words. Kudos steps forward into a long stance, throwing both hands forward, smacking his palms together to launch a summoned Air Spirit—a casting technique not used by any other student, save one.

Like all magic, Spirits are more illusion than not, but illusions enchanted. By the strength a caster's will, Spirits can take on a measure of solidarity. Wielded by a skilled caster, one with strong reputation, a Spirit can make magic real, cause true effects—inflict real damage instead of just the perceived damage inflicted by the victim's own mind. Kudos has never managed to intimidate anyone. Not once. Vaunt barely blinks. Showing how better practiced he is, better skilled in the game that plays on a mind that magic is, he blows the charging Spirit is off course with his own, much quicker channeling—one that does not rely on incantations.

His Push of Air not only dispels the younger boy's Spirit, but also forces Kudos back a step, to the perfect distance for a follow-up Burst of Light meant to stun the boy's senses. It is a trick that Kudos has seen him use before. He turns his head just before the flash, already muttering another incantation. New words fly from his mouth, faster than before. Turning full circle on his toes, his voice growing louder, Kudos pulls back his arm as he would to draw the string of a bow. The final word he hollers, and Kudos releases his drawn arm.

Five spears of summoned Fire Spirit fly straight for Vaunt's chest. But Vaunt is grinning. A strong Channel of Air sweeps the spears from their intended path. Captured, he guides them safely away, wheeling the spears in a wide circle around him. Arching them high above the stone bleachers, he also captures the attention of all those sitting there. At their apex, Vaunt merges the spears into one, large ball of Fire which he hurls straight back at Kudos. Fire strikes the stone at Kudos's feet and explodes into a spinning vortex, trapping the boy in the center of a fiery cyclone.

"You stupid punk!" Vaunt howls in delight, whipping the cyclone to spin faster and faster. "You thought you could beat *me* with *fire*?"

His battle lust fuels the cyclone to a firestorm. Kudos is knocked to the ground. Both hands and feet glued to the stone floor of the courtyard, he is locked inside Vaunt's vortex with the knowledge that he is outmatched.

"I *excel* in Fire. I can cast ten cyclones in the time it takes your muttering to call up *one* Spirit. What good is a summoner who must use words to cast an element? A guided Spirit, no less. You are pathetic and slow. Slow makes you weak. And weak makes you a waste of time. And you know what I do with something that wastes my time? *I destroy it.*"

The cyclone is already taller than any tree in the courtyard. Fear of the heat is as hot as a bonfire burning out of control and growing hotter still, Kudos raises one arm in a feeble attempt to shield himself. Sweat runs down his face and gathers in his pits, and not solely from the intensifying inferno.

He cannot see Vaunt anymore; he can see nothing but the spiraling flames encircling him. Though the twist in Vaunt's face suggesting that he might truly crush the boy is obscured behind the spinning firestorm, Kudos can feel it and knows that he just might dare. Kudos braces for the worst.

A great burst of cool air abruptly cuts through the fire. Like a flame blown from a matchstick, the vortex vanishes. A glistening rain of gold from the collision of spent magic—the work of a powerful and well-practiced summoner—falls over the courtyard.

Kudos looks up expecting to find an instructor, or even the Head Dean herself, standing over him. To his surprise, he finds neither.

"Glory!"

"That's quite enough, don't you think? Do you not have nothing better to do, Vaunt, than picking on those smaller than you?"

For Vaunt, the surprise is even greater. Borderline contempt over the fact that one of his most powerful spells was so easily extinguished. By a girl! One no older than he.

"Don't forget the Second Rule, little brother," speaks Glory in a voice as sweet as it is commanding. Her green eyes sparkle, belying something cunning lurking just under the surface. "All magic is illusion, the control of perception. That is why duels are reserved for only talent equally matched."

At this, Vaunt's mirth returns. He throws his head back in short but uproarious laughter. "You think *your* talent can match *mine*?"

This time it is Glory who chuckles. "Oh, no, of course not." Her grin turns wicked, curling too high at the corners. "My talent far surpasses yours."

"You?" Vaunt scorns. "The most senior of us who fails at controlling the smallest fireball, and you think you can out-match *me*? You must be joking."

But Glory's smile never faulters. "You can always decline." Her lips curled back, her forehead dips with a dare. "If you're scared."

All joviality drains from Vaunt in an instant. A hard silence drops center stage. All those in attendance sit or stand with their eyes glued on the skirmish. All, but two. That is until they, too, take notice.

Tales in Hindsight

🔥 🔥 🔥

High above the stone floor of the courtyard, but not so high as the towers, beyond the uppermost row of the stadium bench seats, immaculate white marble gives way to the jade green of manicured grass. In the open space of the hill top stands a tree. Its canopy is small, but wide enough to shade the two figures sitting beneath it from the sun's brilliant, golden-yellow glow. Both are young men, about the same age, and—unbeknownst to either—the remaining two in the whole First Class who have yet to take notice of the drama unfolding below.

Finished with their studies for the day, the pair relax in the glorious warmth of the afternoon and the quiet comfort of brotherly friendship, each engrossed in their own books. Having grown up together, trained together, ate nearly every meal together, their camaraderie is second nature. Though their offical partnership having only recently been instituted, it is one already decades in the making. Of the two, it is the shy, quiet one who notices the activity first.

His mind all but lost in a tale of a legendary singing sword, perhaps it was chance that pried Mim's eyes from his book. Maybe is was luck that lifted his head with the need to shake his raggedy mop to clear his eyes of his unruly red hair. Regardless of the reason, his freed gaze instantly falls to the scene of three figures in curious formation on the stone floor. Two are squared off, with one on the ground, and the book in Mim's hand becomes a distant memory.

"Isn't that Glory?"

The young man next to him is, at last, compelled out of his own book—a tale of a travelling trio wandering across vast, dream-like lands where nothing makes sense—and into one where his own partner is facing off in an unsanctioned dual.

"Sure is," he answers. His blue eyes squint. "And Vaunt."

Easy to recognize with his heavy shoulders stretching the limit of his tailored, collared shirt, and jet black hair perfectly swept back and styled to stay there, Vaunt also carries a certain air of assertive arrogance. An invisible shroud that always hangs over him, no matter where he goes. This time, in the courtyard surrounded by their peers, he stands tall but tense, his shoulders rounded, legs apart, arms locked at his sides, hands clenched in fists—

"He looks pissed off."

There is no need for Victor to apply such deductive reasoning to the other figure. His eyes recognize and evaluate Glory, and all that she is, in an instant. He *has* known Glory for longer than he has known Mim, after all. Her uniform is still clean and straight, but judging by that sneer under her unwavering green eyes, they may not stay that way for long.

"Looks like Glory was called up to the Head Dean's tower again." Victor adds a short, deep sigh. "And it did not go well."

"Should we help her?"

Victor pays Mim a brief glance, taking in his shock of red hair and pale face speckled with freckles in a blink before turning his attention back to the courtyard. Despite having known eachother since boyhood, Mim only recently become a member of Victor's team. Assigned to tag along ever since the pair's last escapade. A ridiculous call, as far as Victor is concerned. Did he and Glory not stop that troll from breeching the behemoth gates? So what if they damaged a small part of it in the process, or his getting a little carried away in the celebration afterward? There had been so many girls! Victor simply could not say *no* to *all* of them, for crying out loud. Apparently, the Head Dean felt differently and so charged Mim, the nanny and constant nag of conscience, to keep them in check.

"Nah," Victor answers without much fuss. "I think Glory can handle this one."

"Are you sure?"

Good ol' worrisome Mim; his concern is enough to make Victor smile. Where such a gesture would surely win over any girl, and disarm most men, Mim is not so easily seduced by Victor's glamour of a strong, square jaw, feathery, butter-oak hair, and cool confidence.

Nevertheless, Victor nods with a decisive, "Yep."

Mim is not convinced. Not only is his gaze slow to return to the courtyard below, but it flicks repeatedly back to Victor when he tries to return to his book. Each poke of his sideways glance Victor feels as assuredly as a finger jab to his face. And they are not about to stop. Victor resigns with a huff and sets his book aside.

The tension is palpable as it is sugar-shell thin as the pair in the courtyard stare one another down. One seemingly hell-bent on waiting while the other, just as eagerly, awaits to unleash hell. Next to Mim nervously worrying his fingers, Victor grunts cheerily. He sees what Mim does not, what likely no one sees unless they knew what to look for: the subtle movements of her fingers working, tucked inconspicuously behind her. Victor chuckles.

"Glory has already begun."

🔥 🔥 🔥

The suspense only tasted on top of the hill, is positively churning on the stone floor. Arms at her side and appearing relaxed, Glory stares Vaunt down with dangerous intent.

One corner of her mouth cracks upward in a cold, calculated grin. "Well, Vaunt?"

He does not reply save for the bulging of his jaw.

Glory's grin is wicked, showing more teeth than it should. "What are you waiting for? An invitation?"

With his hands clenched, all his weight rocked forward onto his toes, Vaunt's lips curl back in a sneer. For him, no others exist now except one tall, slender girl challenging his reputation and smiling something secret. She winks, and the wait bottoms out. Vaunt explodes.

The kid-gloves are off, and nothing short of the Head Dean can stop them now. A furious roar bellows from his mouth as Vaunt charges, swinging a fist intended for her face. He hits only air. The miss only stokes the blaze of his rage. Vaunt pushes forward. Spinning, he whips out a backfist, then a jab with a hook to follow. Another spinning backfist rounds off the attack. Not a single strike lands. He does not so much as graze her! In turn—and just as aggravating—Glory does not touch him either. She does not lift a single arm to block or sweep. She does not counter. Glory simply moves out of the way, staying just out of reach.

Growling through his teeth, Vaunt tries again and again. Each time she ducks or dips or slides away leaving his fists to hit only the ghost of where she had been. Only once do his knuckles slide by her face close enough to feel the heat radiating off her cheek, and yet, all he manages to hit are the vanishing ends of her long, dark brown hair.

Vaunt picks up the pace, but Glory easily picks up speed to match. A chop from heel swung high should have connected with some part of her, and yet, the only connection Vaunt's foot makes is with the stone floor.

"Hold still, damn you!"

He leaps into an ariel barrel roll. Arms and legs spinning like a windmill, not one hits its mark. Vaunt lands to find that, not only has he struck nothing, but Glory no longer stands in front of him. The courtyard straight ahead might as well be empty if not for the gathered crowd that Vaunt does not see at all.

Then, he feels her. Behind him. Her cheek sliding against the back of his head until her lips brush his ear.

"Is that the best you can do?"

Sweet words poured from lips of foxglove, and in the courtyard erupts with roar. Vaunt whips together a violent shove of Air and whips around to strike her with a violent cyclonic burst. But Glory is already gone. After a humiliating moment of bewilderment, he finds her, right where she had been, as if she never moved at all. If Vaunt was not enraged before, he is now. There is no rushing charge this time; Vaunt stands his ground. Pooling all his anger and hot contempt into his hands, he ignites them with Fire. All the rampage in the world, and he blinds himself to the full grin on Glory's lips.

High up on the hill, Victor does notice. Maybe not her smile exactly, but the radiant, burning light surrounding her body standing straight and determined. So, too, can he see the steady glow consuming Vaunt's hands. Victor chuckles. He has got to hand it to Mim, this was worth watching after all.

"Maybe we should go down there."

Victor shakes his head. "No need. This fight was over when Vaunt threw his first punch. Glory has him right where she wants him."

"She's *baiting* him?"

A worrier Mim may be, but not dumb.

"But Vaunt is channeling Fire, lots of it. That's his best discipline, and I've seen Glory struggle to control a simple candle flame. She could get hurt."

Gleeful laughter bursts from Victor, his head thrown back in merriment. "*Glory*, struggle with *Fire*? No. Glory excels at Fire; she was born to wield it. What Glory struggles with is anything *small*."

Churning with molten resentment, Vaunt does not throw his Fire in spears as Kudos had. Lacking style and grace, Vaunt lobs irregular yet volatile orbs as he would his fists. Keeping his distance, he hurls balls of Fire twice the size of his hands across the courtyard, again and again, keeping Glory locked in his sights. Like his fists, each one misses. How does she keep dodging his attacks? She is only five long paces away! Vaunt never misses with summoned Fire. Each trajectory is on target, he is sure. So, why are his flames hitting only the air where she *had* been? Right where she stands still, relaxed, casual, her arms draped behind her and out of sight.

The haze of smoke fills the courtyard as Vaunt throws larger and larger balls of Fire. They all miss. In front of him, Glory stands, as lovely as ever, her clothes untouched, her hair barely ruffled. Calm. In a courtyard choked with smoke, she is unfazed. Vaunt grows apoplectic with rage. Fire explodes all around him—him and Glory both—taking up more than half of the courtyard floor. He may not use words to summon as Spirit wielders do, but large castings require more backing than mere will and intent. Using practiced movements, Vaunt builds a great, cycling inferno. Enclosed by a vortex of burning orange and red flames with a talented caster, Glory's smile grows brighter.

From their vantage point, Victor and Mim can see clearly the intense, luminescent glow of the firestorm only the two in play can see as an inferno. That, however, does not stop Mim's worrying tick that has him sucking on his lower lip.

"Victor, we have to help her!"

"All magic is illusion." Victor says out loud the rule both boys know well. "A control of perception. Glory has taunted and teased Vaunt, provoked him into losing control."

"But she's—"

"Been waiting for him to do exactly *this*." Victor nods down toward the stage.

Vaunt pulls back his arm, summoning all his strength for one, final throw. He will not miss. *Cannot* miss! The channeled inferno surrounding them grows to four times the size that which he used to trap Kudos. All his hatred, all his *jealousy*, focused on the young woman standing before him—specifically on that sly grin on her face. What secret does she know that he does not? Vaunt is not about to ask; he will burn it from her. He hurls every ounce of magic he has, with full intent to cause harm, square for the girl showing him up.

"He's throwing all he has!" Mim cries.

"And she will take it," Victor coos, "every, last drop. You see, not only is Glory an exceptional magician, but she is also a natural substitutionist. *That* is the real reason why, out of the whole student body, *Glory* needs a partner. Without me she would run amok, and nothing would be as it seems. No one holds a reputation to match the likes of Glory, unleashed."

 The hurricane of Fire is, in fact, a direct hit. But it does not *hit* so much as it is *caught*. Glory does not dodge. She does not move. Arms opened wide, she accepts the force thrown at her, drawing it into herself with a gale force that pulls Vaunt off his feet. His knees slam to the stone floor. Glory's hands finally come into view, making more complicated signs than the ones Vaunt never saw. Her fingers fly through complex patterns, quicker and quicker. The windstorm accelerates. The fire burns hotter, brighter, as mumbled words flow from her mouth faster and faster.

 Vaunt is paralyzed, locked in his crouch. His hands and knees press to the stone in all effort to keep from being sucked into Glory's cataclysmic vortex. He can feel the wild winds rake over his body. They whip his clothes and toss his perfectly groomed hair into disarray. His face drains of color as the Fire around them explodes into a new ring. Not a towering cyclone, but a flat circle taking up nearly the entire courtyard. Glory lifts her arms. Hands high above her head, the ring begins to rise. The leading-edge tilts upward, sliding through the air until the giant, burning circle is standing upright on its edge at her back.

 The winds grow wilder. Gust fly in every direction as Glory's words come faster, her voice stronger, and her hands and fingers completing the complicated gestures flawlessly. Her green eyes, blazing as ferociously as the ring behind her, are locked onto the bully forced to his knees. His eyes are wide, too, but not with exhilaration.

 The ring glows a brilliant, terrifying red orange when Glory's words suddenly go eerily soft. One by one, symbols begin to appear around the ring's edge, glowing an electric white-blue and seemingly etched into the very air. They turn the ring into the likings of a face of a gigantic clock. One that could swallow the behemoth gate, let alone the whole of the academy in one gulp, should Glory wish it. But a clock it is not. It is a gate. One meant only for Vaunt.

 The center of the ring snaps to a deep, dark crimson. From its depths, claws emerge, each one longer than Vaunt is tall. Clinging to the ring's edge, a great beast draws itself free from the endless inferno contained within the Spirit of Hell's Clock. Its snout pokes out first, followed by the head of a monstrous horse or canine or some terrible combination of them both. Two, towering, twisted horns jut up from the beast's skull, and long spines run down the back of a long, serpentine neck. Its charred hide is puckered in scales as red as rubies.

Vaunt's jaw drops open wide. Glory has conjured forth a beast that should not be—a feat that should not be possible. Larger than any creature that has ever walked the Earth, a monster of blazing red and orange that could swallow a troll as a heron would a sardine: Glory has called into existence a dragon.

The beast's wings emerge next from the ring burning ever brighter, spinning ever faster. Unfurled, they block out the sun, swallowing the courtyard in shade. On the ring's edge, the dragon poises its immense body like a hawk, its gaze for the boy knelt to the stone floor. Giant jaws crack open. Dozens of ivory daggers, sharp as any good blade, fill a blood-red cavern of a hungry and insatiable mouth opened wide.

Flipped from his hands and knees to his butt, a scream rises from Vaunt's throat. He lifts an arm to shield his face from the inevitable. His feet scramble desperately, but there is no purchase to be found. A dragon! A *real* dragon, and it is going to kill him. A rumble shakes the ground and Glory is all but forgotten. The monster launches from the impossible depths of the ring. Jaws open wide, it dives to devour its helpless victim in a single bite. Vaunt's scream peaks in an all-out wail as the dragon's jaws snap shut around him, swallowing him in darkness.

But the day is not dark at all. It is bright. Just as it has been when Glory stomped out of the office of the Head Dean. Under a sky that holds a few high, puffy white clouds, all the students in attendance stare at Vaunt, prone and unmoving but alive, buried under a large pile of sand. Caught up in Glory's illusion, Vaunt never saw what the others did. Where he saw only the fire of a churning inferno and a magnificent beast, the rest watched as Glory called up all the bits of sand and gravel from the two practice pits flanking either side of the courtyard. Where he saw his death, the other watched him be flattened under a flung pile of sand.

On the hill, Mim's mouth is still wide with astonishment. In his eyes burns his own question of what, exactly, had Vaunt seen that made him scream so. Whatever it was, it had frightened the living piss out of him, staining his pants with a large patch of wet. Victor, only smiles. What a partner he has been spoiled with. One that, unlike Vaunt, Victor will never be without.

Tales in Hindsight

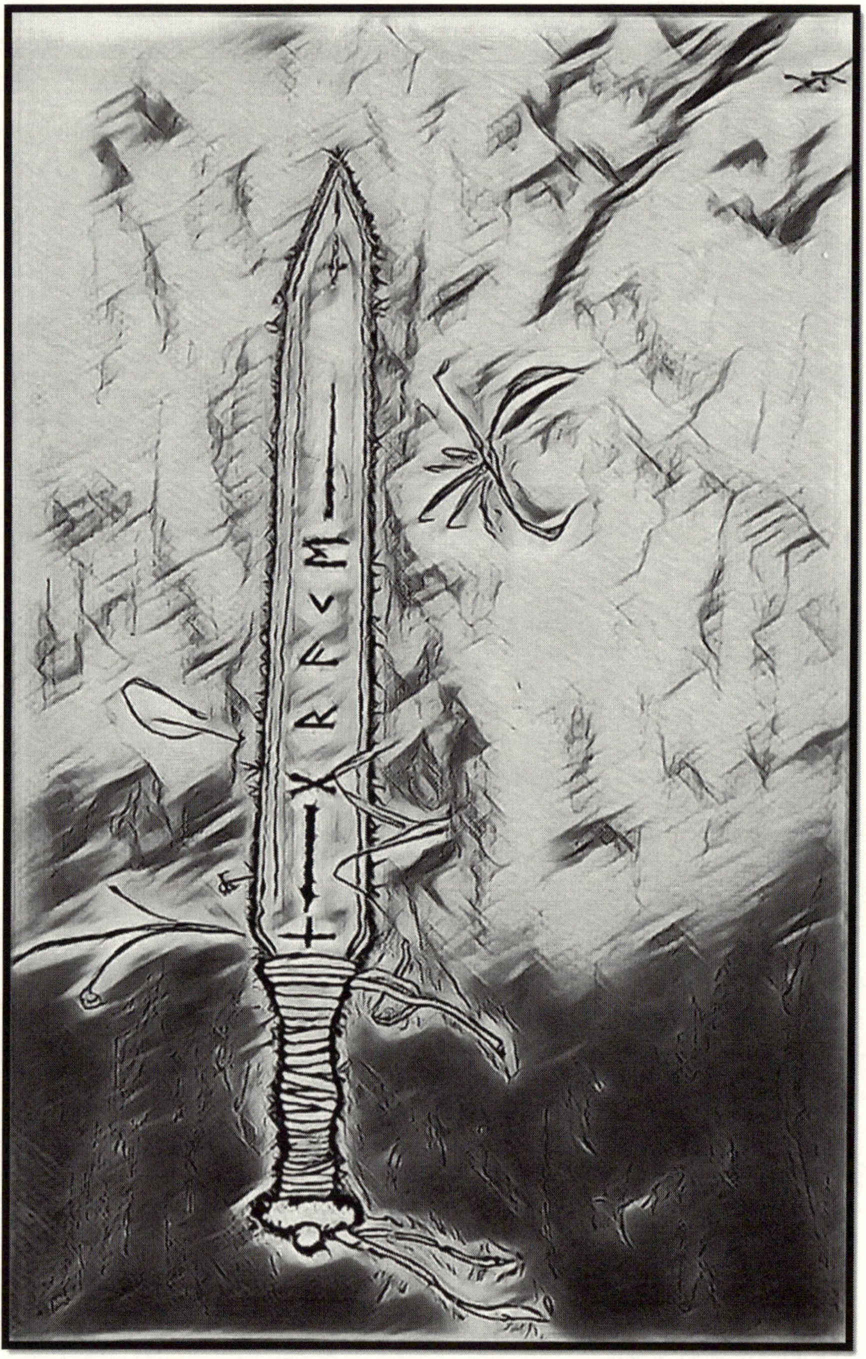

SEPTEMBER

❖ GRACE ❖

All is so... *grey*.

A blanket of grey fog obscures the grey green of the trees surrounding the camp. It crawls along the grey beige of the ground puckered with the grey brown of stumps and downed trees and the grey slate of rocks and boulders. I could say that the sky is grey also, but all there is, is fog. Surely, color still exists somewhere. Perhaps higher up, above the grey. But on the ground is where Man belongs, and where I sit on the edge of my Army's camp, and all I can see is grey.

My men are restless. Hard men, strong men. Good soldiers, the whole lot, and restless for the onset of battle that has loomed for days now. Perhaps longer. Dutifully, they wait. Wait for the Word that will call them into action. But, I wonder, for how much longer?

"Bite yer tongue, lad!" a seasoned, high-ranking man—one whom I should know, but I do not—barks in the face of a younger, newly acquired recruit sitting with him and two others around a smokey fire. "We move when the Commander says we move. Understand?"

A loyal soldier and he cuffs the youth upside his head after giving his collar a good shake. Wisely, the chastised youth quiets, his head swung low in submission, but the damage is already done. I may not have heard the words the youth had used, I don't have to, to know what was said.

I am failing.

I turn away from my men. Directing my gaze, instead, to my

hands. I still hear their voices, even if their less than lively talk is reduced to a murmur; they feel so far away.

My hands, grey like everything else, are callused and strong. They have held both sword and shield as loyally and faithfully as the men who follow me. Strong, and yet, so weak. My skin, my form, all of it wrong and wicked. How have I come to be here? A Champion. A leader in the greatest Army to ever walk the Earth. One that has conquered all whom have met it in battle. At my command but a mere branch of the High God's mighty army, the Arm of His celestial force and initial reach of His Word, and with it I have brought nothing short of victory. I have done all that I have been told to do; *charged* with doing. I have followed the Word given unto me by His First and Brightest. Yet here I sit at the edge of mine own camp, staring at my hands, questionably. Wondering if I have all but lost my senses.

How long has it been since last I heard my Angel's voice? Days? *Years?* What is Time but the measure of one's own mortality, and why has mine felt so very long? I have heard his voice before; I am sure of it. That voice, and the message it had for me, is what brings me this far. If only I could remember when last I heard it. If only I could *know* that I have not led these men—this *Army*—in vain, astray, or worse, in blasphemy.

What happened to the Light that once consumed me? Where is its warmth? Only without it do I remember what it felt like to be filled with it. A sensation so enrapturing that I can no longer recall what life had been like before it overtook me. Long before I held a sword or a shield, before there was an Army to lead, back when wooden dowels were all I had been allowed to handle. I remember well the day, my name's day, when I fled my coming of age.

A cold Winter's day.

The sun had already dipped below the sky when I found myself deep in a wood of tall, spindly shrubs that I did not know, running with all the strength my young legs could muster. Impeded by old, crusty snow deep enough for the tops of my booted feet to disappear through with each step, I failed to note in which direction I was heading. I hardly knew from which I had come, but I did not care, and I did not look back.

The air was chilly and grew colder as night swallowed the world in darkness. Boney branches of skeletal trees grabbed at my clothes and snagged my hair but stop I would not. Deeper and deeper into the wild wood I fled, hot tears cascading down my cheeks. No one was going to find me. I refused to go back. I would not stop. Not until I felt I had escaped them all, my village, my people, the false promises they had made and the expectations they all had set for me. It wasn't fair.

At some point, tired and spent, I collapsed to my knees, my lungs burning, my legs refusing to take another step. I gathered all the snow within reach and scrubbed my face; scrubbed with ice at the mark they had given me, hoping to rid myself of it forever. When my eyes, cheeks, and hands burned with cold, I pressed my face to the ground, to the snow still left there. I had done what was forbidden of me: I had run from my duties. So, I gave in to another dishonor: I wept.

All my rage, my sorrow, I poured into the snow which drank it up and melted away into the bitter-cold ground underneath. I cursed my body, my strength. How could such power have been gifted to me, to only then be hobbled against it and expected, instead, to live a life devoted to the work my people required of me? No youth my age, nor rivals a few years older, could best me in the practice ring. Wooden sword, lance, bare-brawl, I championed them all. How could I not be meant for more than the tedium of village life?

For the first time, mine own skin had become my enemy. All reason left me, and I wished for nothing more than to render it from my body. Alone in the snow, I would settle for nothing less. I would not return to my people. There had to be reason for my strength, my power, and I needed to discover what that was, at any cost.

"Will you leave behind all that you must?"

"Yes," I had answered without hesitation. I would do the same again, and have, many times over since first I heard the voice of the Angel.

"Your kin? Your Gods? Your ancestry?"

"Yes," I pledged to the snow opening beneath my face.

No longer could I feel the cold pressed to my forehead. My pain, my disappointment and frustration, all I felt melt away as the snow would come Spring. Light, as enchanting as the arms that then wrapped around me, was all that existed. My body of sin was filled with a warmth that only an embrace of pure love could deliver.

I could not see the figure at first. Nor had I cared. *I* was melting... into serenity of such peace that it became all that I desired.

"*You are a gift,*" spoke the figure. "*One given to our Father, the High God—He above all others—and you shall be His Champion.*"

A shock of cold wafted over my skin; the transcendental

embrace had receded. Though the touch had gone, the warmth of it remained. A glow that filled me to the brim, though, suddenly felt terribly finite. I knew then that, one day, it would drain from me entirely and feared the thought so completely that I knew—just as equally—that, when that time came, there would be nothing I would not dare to get it back.

"What must I do?" I had asked, not yet knowing what such a question meant.

The Angel, so tall and radiant and fierce before my eyes so young, knew exactly that which I did not. *"You shall lead His army,"* spoke the being. *"And be victorious."*

His imperial essence dulled only slightly as he produced a weapon out from the folds in his robes of Light. A sword. A short one. Though I had not yet touched the weapon, my young eyes could, even then, see the strangeness in the material of which it was made. Darker than steel or iron—more stone or slate than luminous metal—with dark symbols etched down the center of the blade that I did not want to look at.

I reached out with both hands, wishing for the blade to be given to me without knowing why, or for what it was needed.

"A shepherd must tend to the safety the flock first and above all else." The weight of the sword, as strange as the material of which it was made, came to rest solely in my strong, young hands. *"Find that which threatens Man most and rid him of it. Vanquish it if you must."*

The short sword felt solid in my hands, yet it also seemed to weigh nothing. My first weapon to wield not purposefully blunted or made of wood and already felt more an extension of mine own arm than a separate tool. With it, I knew that I could strike down any opponent. *Even an Angel.*

Fear made me look up, an apology filled my mouth for simply having conceived such thoughts, but I had no one to speak to. The Angel—*my* Angel—had fled. I felt neither hurt nor stung, for such is the way when it comes to heavenly beings. Alone in the deep woods, further than any from my village had ever gone, I rose to my feet. I felt sadness no longer. I knew neither fear nor worry, nor was I calm or excited. Complacent in the cold quiet of a dormant skeletal forest, I stood with the short sword in both hands, loving its weight. I relished the deadly intent for which such a weapon was crafted and turned to where the ground fell away in a gentle slope that led down into an open valley.

I had no way of knowing where I was going, or what would

happen to me when I got there. With such a weapon in my hands, what care had I? Whom was *I* to fear? The presence of my Angel at my back, I felt the breeze of his breath caress my ear. There, poised at the precipice of a new day, he whispered a message—the last true words spoken unto me. Then, silence. I forgot all except that which I needed, in the moment that I needed it. At that moment, what I needed was to make for the first village that would not know me.

❄ ❄ ❄

Not so many know that every few generations a Child is born. A child like no other. A special child, born above all others, destined to bring change and revolution to all, whether they meet or not. Born filled with heavenly essence made mortal, this Child is a natural leader who inspires men to follow without effort, even when young. They excel in any endeavor, and they always die young. They are meant to. For it is the heinousness of the act itself which returns the Child back to the realm of Man, to be born again and lead men where they will not go alone. For these reasons, such a Child is not difficult to find. Especially for those who seek them out.

I know.

I found him, in the first village to which my wayward wandering delivered me.

He was as young as I, and well protected by battle-hardened men. Or so it appeared. His garrison were old and softened by drink, they only laughed at my approach and assumed to beat the daylight into me for blatantly coming so close to the Child of a God, the High God, whom they served. I could have drawn my weapon then, but I did not—I had no need. I left it wrapped in the tattered cloth I had torn from mine own clothes and secured in my waistband at my back. His guard I left groaning on theirs with my bare hands.

Unafraid, I approached the Child and offered him my allegiance and everlasting love for his Father, God above All, in exchange for a place in His Army already assembling. All I did with the hushed whisper of an Angel in my ear, bidding me do so. My worth proven, my desire granted—a growing army always has room for one more—and my life was washed into the swelling riptide of combat.

Seasons passed, and I grew. Already strong, I grew stronger. Few could match me; none could defeat me. I climbed the ranks as quickly as did talk of me. Reputation compelled my first platoon to follow my command. Respect made the next *want* to. Campaign after campaign, I led the charge—always the first one in, always the last one out—and brought only victory. Men under my charge knew no defeat. Those who opposed learned mercy.

No matter the battle, no matter how bloody or tiring, on the field I would remain until the last of my men—alive or dead—had been removed. Nor until all fallen opposing soldiers still alive received my personal attention. I walked the field and offered those I found redemption, absolution, in the Word of the High God. An offer which the only requirement needed was acceptance, and I would show them His mercy and made a place for in my Army once they regained their health, to fight alongside my soldiers as one of them. The few who refused, I left their bodies to cool with the rest slain that day.

My Army grew, as did our reputation. With my long sword and battle ax, both crafted to my own specifications, I led the leading Arm of the High God's Army. Surpassed in numbers, might, and glory only by the main Body of His militant might, led by the Child grown into a man, that followed a few days ride behind. Stories of the Child's feats and proficiency in combat were no less renown than mine own. Who could hope to stand in the way of such a force? Who would want to? We were the warriors of Light and Truth come to vanquish the Dark, to burn away the foreboding places that led men to suffering and pain. I had believed so strongly back then.

Together, the Arm and the Body swept over the land. Washed it clean, left it purified, and brought salvation of our God's Light and good graces to offenders who survived His wrath which we also brought and made so. It behooved me to understand why we were met with opposition at all. What we made way for was Light, only harbingers of the Dark need fear. Yet, village after village, were we received with hostility. Wherever I led my men, anger, hatred, and, worse of all, fear compelled the people to raise arms against us, no matter how many victories preceded us.

Why was this so?

We only ever took what we needed once the fighting was done, and never remained for long. We cleansed the land and made it ready for the coming of the Word—work handled by the Body who swept in behind us. Why did many begin to pray for their souls at the sight of us? Why did they pray to Gods that were no more? Stranger yet were those who crossed their foreheads in the very symbol of our High God—the very God for whom I served, led on by the messages left unto me by His first Angel. Instead of praise, we were met with contempt and ears turned from the prayers we offered, and I found mine own self on the receiving end of many a scornful scowl or eyes pinched with shame. Most men held nothing but empty indifference for me, while a queer sort of admiration came from others. None, however, dared approach me. No, it was from the women, I found, who judged most and harshest of all.

In a particular village we had swept through years before and left cleansed, was where I had first tasted doubt from the tongue of a peasant woman. The first who dared approach me, maliciously no less. I had not been frightened when she lunged her body at me and spat at my feet. The woman had not been old, and she was fit, but by plow, not by sword; she would have been no match for me. That truth, however, had not tempered the woman's hot outburst. She cursed me. Defiled me as the lead demon of the Devil's army. That I led men only into darkness, not out of it; enslaved them in evil ways to do evil's bidding. The woman prayed for the goodness of the High God to banish me, and any who followed, to the fiery pits of Hell!

I had been stunned. Aghast by her cruel words. Such terrible accusations, but ones spoken so earnestly—*that* was the horror that had cut deepest. How could she have said such unimaginable lies? The *Devil's* Army? *Enslaved* to do evil—*my* men? By what right did a peasant woman have to befoul good, honorable soldiers who walked the path set by the High God Himself? The very One to whom *she* claimed to pray? I had mind to strike her down for such impiety. Had I been carrying my sword or axe, I might have, but the weapon I had carried with me that day was not meant for the likes of foul-mouthed fool. That alone had sparred the woman's life, but the seeds she had sown had already taken to root. All began to unravel.

Cracks started to show in my men. Tempers shortened and arguments flared. With their purpose marred and bruised, their pride faltered. The beginnings of rot in a barrel of good apples, and I, the harbinger of Light and the Word, unable to weed out its cause. I had not heard the voice of my Angel in some time.

Landscapes changed as I kept my men marching onward, as did the seasons. I took notice when long, warm days shortened. I felt the chill set in. The Arm of a heavenly Army met with fewer and fewer opposition, and we overthrew them easier still. But the faces of those we met, on the battlefield or off, grew darker and doleful. In a place I felt I should know, a village I took for a dream, I—for the first time—was called *heathen*.

Through most of the villages we passed, its people looked more like my men than I. If unarmed and without shields, they could have melted in with the locals and disappeared, whereas I could pass with no such trick. Often, I found myself singled-out, and more often faced with criticism and ridicule that my men simply did not receive. Only in one village, tucked deep in a high, wooded plateau of the North, did my men become the oddities. It was there when an old crone had suddenly hastened from her path to intercept mine. Nearly as tall as I but bent over from age and a life of toil, she spat at me. *Devil worshipper*, she had called me.

Neither insult had been a first for me, but the manner in which that old woman had eyed me, how her jaw worked from side to side, there had been more than simple abhorrence burning in her dark eyes. Behind the smear of black across her face—over her eyes, temple to temple—there blazed contempt. *Heathen*, she hissed. A bright flash then cracked across a sky of slate grey. Heavy, dark, anvil clouds over the village ripped open and doused the earth with freezing rain. The old woman hobbled away, startled by the sudden change in weather, where I, stunned by her words, stood frozen and watched her go. The woman vanished into the sheets of driving rain that had me soaked through before the ghost of her disappeared completely.

Another sharp flash of intense white light and its resounding crash got me moving again. Water-logged locks of my hair slapped my face as I turned and fled. A voice, not my Angel's, whispered a truth secreted away in mine own mind that I did not want to hear. So, I ran. From the voice, from the rain to any place where I might rest long enough to regain my bearings.

Down a hill slick with rain and loose rock I slid, frightened of that which I saw, or thought I saw, in that enraged woman's old eyes. A familiarity I could not place—that I could not believe. My body felt as cold and heavy as the very iron I had trained so tirelessly to wield. My laden armor and small clothes, heavier still. I could not hear my Angel, *had* not for so long, that I had started to wonder if I had heard it at all.

With my leathers soaked, I tried the first door my hand fell upon. Under a hefty sign in the shape of a blacksmith's anvil, I found the way unhindered so let myself in and was, at once, engulfed by the inferno contained within. My leathers instantly felt bulky and cumbersome. The light armor perfectly fitted to my chest, shoulders, and legs became uncomfortably tight, awkward, and restrictive.

Inside that hut, the air was hotter than any day under the sun that I could recall. As my eyes adjusted to the dimmed light, I soon saw why.

Two furnaces roared within that blacksmith's shack. Between them, the lone occupant, whose work had been stalled with the sudden intrusion of his unexpected visitor, stood, and gave me pause. He was stripped of his shirt. A strong back and arms burdened with muscle glistened with sweat. Heavy leathers covered his hands, and a stout leather apron covered his legs. The iron grips he had in one hand, held a piece of metal that glowed deep crimson atop the flat head of the anvil. In the other, a hammer, held high and poised to strike it. He might have, had his eyes not been on me.

His face, too, dripped with sweat. Of like age as myself, this man was like the other men of this village. Broad in shoulder, deep in chest, and taller than any in my platoon; what a soldier he would have made. The sides of his head were trimmed short and neat with the rest of his long, coarse, sandy hair tied back with knotted leather chord. His face, however, was where he truly would have stood out from any in my company, and where mine own eyes returned, again and again. Long and angular, instead of round or square, with a thin beard over his upper lip and along his strong jaw. Where the old crone had a streak of black across her eyes, the full upper half of the blacksmith's face was stained black. Such shadowed contrast to the lightness everywhere else about him that I could hardly find the strength to look away, for gazing upon him was akin to coming face to face with a ghost.

His bright eyes perceived me up and down in return, pausing briefly at places any other soldier dressed as I had been would have carried a weapon. I had brought none with me save the one he did not see. With no weapon, and my leather armor in fine shape, he could see that I was no potential customer. Yet, he made no effort to look away. A curious sense of camaraderie passed between us two, but what sort of affinity could we have shared, soldier to blacksmith?

Not a word was spoken. He gave a single nod then returned to his work, paying me no mind for however long I stayed. My swamped leathers felt more restrictive than ever as I watched the sparks fly from each strike of the hammer against the superheated iron. Heat continued to pour from the roaring furnaces. Sweat built up under my water-logged leathers. I wanted to remove them. Outside, the rain pelted the dramatically sloped roof of the shop. A consistent sound, broken by—or rather added to—the rhythmic rings of the hammer. The sharp, acidic smell of burning wood and red-hot iron cleared my senses.

For the first time in a time too long to remember, I breathed deep. The charred flavor of fire and smoke filled my lungs. I felt the sturdiness of the stone floor beneath my feet. I heard the wind howl outside with hardly a stir to the hut. The heat inside made the world beyond feel leagues away—that a day's travel would not be enough to reach it—and so I allowed my gaze freedom to wander the shop.

Various tools and grips and clamps littered a workbench snug against the wall opposite the door. Baskets filled with raw material took up the floor in the corners and near the forges. Still more tools—bigger ones like hammers, rasps, and forceps as long as the smith's arm and as thick as his wrists—stacked the shelves or hung from hooks. Above a set of files ranging in grades of coarseness that hung above a worktable, I spotted a long strip of wood artfully carved, with decorative scroll work etched along the edges. In the center, recessed into the grain and dyed a light-eating black, were letters from a language I felt I should have known.

"What is this?" I had asked without thinking, without care, and certainly not expecting this Northman to understand me. So, it came as a surprise when I received an answer.

"It is a Mark," he spoke in the same tongue as I, though a slight slur made clear it was not his native language.

"What does it say?"

His words drifted to me slowly and left me as perplexed as the notion that I already knew the message hidden in the symbols.

"Divine words," the blacksmith continued. "Left to my family."

At this, a cynical chuckle did pass my lips. "*Words* left to you by your Gods?"

The blacksmith swung his face 'round to face mine a second time. His hands gripped tightly to his nearly forgotten tools so as not to drop them while his eyes pinched, genuinely perplexed.

"*My* Gods?" His gaze again raked up and down my form, but more to confirm that I, indeed, did stand before him rather than to weigh my worth. "They are your Gods, too."

❄ ❄ ❄

The smell of crisp rain and hot iron cools and turns harsh with smoke and ash. The musky scent of waking men stretching in their leathers, or putting them on for the day, fills my nose. As the sweet, burnt char of cooked meat, the ripe tang of horses and their leavings, and the dry, sharp mineral taste of dust coats the roof of my mouth, the memory of the blacksmith's shop fades. His words, however, ring ever sharp and clear. With them comes another sound, one that does not reach me through my ears. It is a sound I have heard before, long before the blacksmith and his words—words that will not let go, either.

I face the sound—the hum of a choir at an impossible distance—before I realize I have risen and am walking toward it. A sound that I have not heard in so long as to inspire doubt, I hear clearly now. Dauntingly far away, *He* is very near.

My horse is already saddled and bridled—the only that is. My axe and shield lay on the ground. I leave them there; they will be of no use to me, they never were. The only weapon I have ever needed I carry with me, as I have carried, all this time. I take the reins of my horse. My small knife I pull from my belt and cut the tether line with little effort. Leaving both to drop, I mount my warhorse and give him a kick. I do not look back, not even to the abrupt shouting of my men finding their horses running loose. They will come for me, seek out signs of my trace, but my horse will be far away before they catch the first of theirs and they realize that I have left. They will break camp. There will be confusion, perhaps dismay, but what I do, I do for them—for them all. I kick my horse for more speed.

"Where are your Gods now?" I had asked the blacksmith and recall well the taste of pride as bitter as wormwood on my tongue. I can see the Northman's face behind mine own eyes, the way his looked away. Disappointment or frustration, even now, I cannot say and push my steed faster over a land slowly losing its green.

"The Gods walk among us no longer." The blacksmith had replied, plunging hot iron into a barrel of water before returning it to the roaring inferno of a forge. *"They are not meant for the Man's realm. They scheme, play games, make mockery of men. They do not belong here. They keep watch from their own realm, where they belong. You know this."*

The deep rouge mane of my battle roan whips against my face as the stallion flies across barren ground. Red rock and sand as far as the eye can see, yet I know *he* is out here. *His* voice grows louder. In my mind the memory of the blacksmith's hut still blooms, his haunting words echo in my ears, and the engraving in the wood slab burns in my mind. I had forced myself to turn away from it. Sent my gaze downward where it was met by the placid surface of water in a barrel as tall as my thigh, where I had found my reflection staring back.

I thought I had forgotten that day in the woods, and the snow I had melted with tears. How hard I had scrubbed my face, to rid it of the mark there. But how could I, when it was already as much a part of me as mine own skin?

Faster, *further*, deeper into lands flatter than a man hand, my horse does race. The hum of a voice growing louder, driving me onward.

How have I been so blind? The wars I have brought, the Army that I have led—the men I have killed. Not in the name of glory, but for the sake of pride emblazoned within me by angelic grace—a power no man should wield. What a fool I have been. At the edge of the known, at the precipice of that still yet to be, I spot, at last, that which I have been seeking since that day in the snow.

The great wall stands sharply straight from the stony ground. What lies beyond it, I cannot say, the monstrous wall and its equally impressive twin-door gate hide all that might dwell inside. But I know *he* is there, safe within an impenetrable fortress.

The gate is closed. Outside, hundreds of battle-hardened men have made a large camp, a variable mote snug tight to the wall. All are waiting to be granted invitation to join the Army of the High God's heavenly battalion, the elites, those to be led by the Angel of Light in the final battle to end all wars. With *his* voice ringing between my ears louder than ever, I pull my horse to a stop at the edge of the encampment and dismount.

Men here are not grey like mine own, but red. They burn with anger, with hunger, and fright. Dangerous men. Yet, straight down the path cut through the camp to the gate, I walk. I am in no danger here. They all have heard of me; I am like no other soldier here. My reputation unmistakable and blazing with purpose, none could stop me even if desperation drove them to try.

Under the curious and watchful gaze of every soul encamped, I approach the gates. Gates that have opened for none in a long time. Gigantic slabs of some dark material that I cannot identify as either stone or wood, but large beyond reason, that begin to part with my approach. I do not slow my pace; I have no need. The gates open plenty wide for me to walk through, my stride unhindered, and straight into the ranks of an exceptional militant might superbly filed. Their armor gleams in silver and gold. Their weapons of the finest grade. Spears, maces, axes, bows, these men are battle-ready and nothing like those camped outside who now follow me in.

None speak a word as I stride down the center row dividing their ranks, but all watch. My path never bending, never turning since leaving my camp so far behind, leads straight to a great staircase rising high above the tallest head. Bone-white and eccentrically wide, the staircase is curved slightly to better accept the large audience pooling below, with a lesser dais halfway up and the grand stage above that. I ascend the steps without hesitation or permission. My very being here is warrant enough of my invitation.

The army is not tense; I am no match for the likes of the creature who leads them. If I were not wanted here, I would not be here climbing these marble steps unimpeded, as I do. Even the most wicked, hardened, deadly generals flanking either side of their leader standing center-stage at the top, keep to their posts and their hands off their swords.

By all appearances, the figure who leads them is a man—bold and strong, an alpha above all, an undisputed ruler to be obeyed and never questioned, but a man nonetheless—but I see the heavenly beauty that *he* truly is. An Angel. Cloaked in a Light, so bright, that none here can look directly upon him in all his glory as I can. And I can, for the same reason I am allowed to walk straight to him: because he wishes it so. As his arms wrap around me, enveloping me in his bright embrace, I am filled with warmth and joy almost to the point of pain. So much Light to nearly move me to tears, I press my face, mine own being, into the ecstasy that is my Angel as willingly as I had when he came to me as a child. The temptation to remain is undeniable. To stay forever, wrapped in his warmth—ah—euphoria. A state of rapture that, alas, is not meant for me.

"My Champion," my Angel coos in my ear.

Our embrace ends, and my hand slips away from his.

"How have you come to me, shepherd? Have you completed the task laid unto you?"

Staring up at his face, his eyes holding no sight beyond mine, I feel his love burning inside me as hot and molten as liquid rock. My smile is as warm and bright as it is genuine, for his essence makes it impossible to lie.

"I know what I must do."

He nods. "Do you love me, still?"

Like a lover to whom you cannot help but pledge everything, to whom I will deny nothing, I answer truthful. "With all my heart."

With all the tender vehemence starry eyes cannot fake, I take in the sight of his beautiful face—his generous eyes, imploring mouth, and a grin of pure desire as to enchant even the most rigid of souls—I take in all that I can for this time shall be the last.

He bends first to me. Perhaps a kiss was his aim for, perhaps, in this moment, he loves me, too. The love of an Angel, what a sight to behold. Contentment enraptured that even *he* is slow to notice the cruel delivery made by mine own hand, nor the blade that I plunge into his abdomen upward and into his chest. A fatal blow even for a creature such as he. For Angels, too, can be slain with the right weapon.

The shock comes slow and much too late. Surprise turns to terrible disbelief. Eyes wide and jaw fallen open and slack, he bows his celestial head to all that is left to see. To the hilt of the strange short sword that he had given over to the hand of a lost, wayward child, and the waxy blood, more a black than it is blue, coating that hand now grown.

Those heavenly eyes settle a gaze as cold as river stones upon my face. "Why?"

A simple question as it is complex. One meant to distract me, to keep me from leaning in close enough to feel the heat leaking from him as his essence grows cold, but lean I do. Sliding my cheek across the marble smoothness of his cheek until my lips graze his ear. I whisper not my words, but *his*. "Warriors move gracefully."

Words *he* whispered to a child lost in the snow and full of hopelessness.

Words spoken to her by a Northman blacksmith, in translation of symbols carved into a wooden plaque mounted above his workbench, in a language as much mine as my skin.

Words of which one matches perfectly the five symbols etched into the blade of the short sword driven into the Angel who gave it to me.

My Angel sinks to the marble face of the dais. Still in my arms, I kneel with him as to not let *him* fall. His form is not much longer for this realm of Man, perhaps never to be again. Driven from it by the only weapon able to do so. Created by *his* own kind, it is a weapon never meant for the hands of men. The Angel of Light dims. The radiance of his skin, his robes, turns more a grey than the gold it had been. The shock still bold in his eyes, they pinch with pain—as much a pain of the heart as the body—but also with relief. How can they not? Have I not done precisely what was asked of me?

The question poised to pass my lips, my Angel answers first.

One hand, saturated with the black substance spilling from an Earthly mortal wound, lifts for my face. A smile returns to his mouth, gleaming with love and contentment. Taking my jaw in his hand, the fading being of Light presses his thumb to my closed lips, stifling any words I might otherwise be tempted to utter. His touch burns, but my skin feel cold and damp when it is gone. I can feel print his hand leaves on my skin, the spot on my lips: his mark for the deed of which I am guilty, left unto me to forever bear.

Then he is gone. I rise to my feet. My hand tight around the hilt, I pull free the blade as I do. My lips, my face, burn as the Angel's essence cools. The strange metal of the blade is stained a darker than moments before, the weapon itself having grown lighter in my hand. The words etched down its middle radiate a deeper black, enriched by ethereal life that it took.

The generals who shared the stage a moment ago, have retreated. Wide-eyed, they give me and the act that I have committed a wide berth, backpedaling down the steps from the grand dais as I draw near. They wear no helms to cover their faces and the expression I witness on each is the same as is on those in rags who have wandered in from the camp outside. The rows upon rows of men outfitted in shiny, spotless armor do wear helms so I cannot see their faces, but all, too, stare in utter silence. Every man present having borne witness to the slaying of an Angel—the assassination of their highest leader—by a single blow, made by mine own hand. A soldier, one of their own—*their* Champion—whom they allowed to stroll right in, unchallenged.

I wonder, as I descend the immaculate white marble steps, the black ink of a celestial body forever staining my hand dry and no longer dripping, who am I to them now?

The tight hush in the air is unmistakable as I descend the steps to the lesser dais. The generals have retreated further, closer to the formed ranks and derelict militia alike that fill the courtyard. Hands grasp swords, but the blades stay encased in their scabbards. Two, then three steps below the dais halfway down the ostentatious staircase, I stop. Every soldier holds tight their weapons. The blunt ends of spears have lifted from the ground. Handles of axes are gripped tightly and set at a slight angle, ready to swing. Swords are loosened but not yet fully drawn. Tension pulls the unstirring air taut. I dare go no further.

They are frightened. Battle-ready men, ready to fight and die for an Angel—for the High God for whom the *Angel* serves—are critically wounded without having suffered a single blow. What they must see, standing above them with the obsidian blade of a curious short sword I hold at my side, blackened further with the blood of a creature they could hardly comprehend. A being of such power and radiance as to leave them no choice except follow, and I having defied it, defiled it, and stand before them now having rendered it mortal and vanquished. I did what I had to, and I would do so again.

Before the panic locks in their faces, before their fear of the unknown can fester into flies and pestilence of doubt and expectations, I raise my sword. Holding aloft, in both hands, the weapon that has slain that which they never thought could be. The letters of another God's language so black that one could lose their soul should they dare to stare too long into the void housed there. I lay it to the white rock of the glorious staircase. The sword hums as my hands slip free. The implement of power enough to slay a God, I leave exposed and unguarded as I back away, retreating up the few step to the wide platform of the lesser dais. Here, poised at the edge, my sword in sight but too far to obtain should those below decide to rush in, I stop. As naked and vulnerable as the sword—though I remain fully clothed—to one and all, I relinquish both myself and my weapon to their malevolence or their mercy.

My arms stretched out to either side, I bow my head. "Take from me what you will."

My chin to my chest, I await their judgment.

Silence. The likes of which I have never known, descends over all this side of the wall. I wonder, what sort of figure do they see displayed before them? Do they see the warrior? The soldier not so dissimilar from themselves? My arms outstretched, empty palms to the sky, do they see more than the soldier? Do they see the gauntlets strapped to my wrists, the trailing strips of the leather wound about them swaying in the breeze? Do they see the ends of my hair, long and golden, do the same though I do my best to keep it plaited away from my face?

They see no armor for I have worn none, save my bodice of tough, boiled leather. My pleated kilt, and boots made of the same material and laced up to my knees are the garments any soldier would wear. But do they see the soldier who wears it, or the woman underneath? Do they see the scars she carries, just as they do? Each one earned and fought for just as they have for theirs? Do they see all that she has done, or of what else she is capable? Might they see her curves? Her intention? Might they see more than that which meets the eye? I wonder, but not for long.

Change stirs the air. Silence holds its reign despite its intensity having shattered. In their eyes, I have been weighed, measured, and I come to find myself, alive. To the gentle clanging of metal and dull thuds of wooden shafts of spears, I open my eyes. From the unblemished, white stone at my feet, I lift my gaze to every man present in the battalion before me, lowering his weapon. Helmets and shields, too, are laid to the ground at their feet. Not a word is spoken. A hush settles over the space between the great wall and ostentatious stage. Gone is the anger. Of their rage, the men are washed clean. For a moment, all is peaceful. But, before any can surrender to the rising serenity, the peace is broken.

Jingling buckles and thundering of hooves chop through the calm as a rider charges through the open gate at full gallop and down the centerline of silent men. The rider, a messenger, is anything but. Sweat shines on his terror-stricken face, his breath coming as quick as I am sure his heart beats. Even his horse is panic bitten, grunting and chomping at its bit as it is reined in short of the rising marble stair.

"The Army of the High God is on the horizon!" he shouts, struggling to keep tight control of his steed. "As vast as the Nine Seas, led by the Child. They march this way."

The touch of relief I had started to feel with his words is dispelled as quick as it had come on.

"They claim to be the true Heavenly might; that the Angel of Light is but a dark deceiver, an evil they will cleanse from the land along with all who hath followed him, without offer of salvation!"

The malleable hush filling the air inside the monstrous walls, bottoms out in a rush. The words of this messenger are not unknown to me—I have spoken similar, to every village I have led *my* Army to conquer, led on to do so by the Angel of the God to whom the messenger refers—the Angel that is now but a stain of blackened blue ink on the white marble canvas, some distance behind me.

Every face turns from the messenger to me standing above them all. I, who took from them their commander; I, who have rendered them leaderless, defenseless, helpless in the face of an unstoppable battalion that threatens to bring forth their total annihilation. The fight in these men, by chance or design, is gone. Without reinforcements—*my* Army, to be exact, that I have left hopelessly far away—they stand no chance against the force marching for them. A battalion of hardened men whom before feared nothing, all look to me now as innocent as children and as hungry as starved dogs. Their eyes too wide and shimmering, their tough, squared jaws hang slackened in the face of certain death and damnation—a peril which I, out of love, have put them in. What are they to do now?

The dark, otherworldly metal of the short sword is a black hole against the sublime white of the marble stair. I feel it beckon me just as I feel every eye watching me, waiting—*wanting*—for me to do *something*. The obsidian blade scrapes harshly against the pristine white stone as my hand takes it up once more. My task is not yet complete.

❄ ❄ ❄

Outside the behemoth walls and gargantuan gate, a land rendered to barren rock and red dust stretches far and wide. It is empty as it is desolate with not a soul to be seen. Those camped in exodus have sought shelter within the wall. Only their abandoned things stir in the silence. The wind howls. Caught bits of leather and cloth roll across the stony ground alongside tumbleweeds and grains of sand. All else holds fast. Including the single horse, waiting patiently outside the gate. There it will stand, until its rider quits the inner stage, hidden from view.

And exit, she does.

In a hurry.

She explodes from the opening in the gate with all the gusto of an iron ball fired from a cannon. More bull than woman—more a force of nature than a being of it—she meets the thirsty, deserted land as a tidal wave of unstoppable will. She charges, headfirst, into the red haze of the surrounding wastes. Spooked by her sudden calamity, her horse bolts from its resting place. Running at full gallop, the animal goes only where it knows: to its rider.

The fervent warrior does not notice her horse's approach. No more than it is I who feels the rough fibers of its thick mane dig into my fingers as I tangle them together. The jolt through my legs, the hoist of strong arms swinging my body up into the saddle without breaking stride of woman nor beast, feels no more real to me than my most vivid dream. My sword I hold high, its point in the lead, but it is its handler who races her steed across the barren plain. On the back of a dragon, distance is nothing. Intent focused on the Army ahead, their camp grows bigger with each pulsing stride of such a powerful mount. The wind which strikes my face pales in comparison to the fire roaring in the soul of a woman with a purpose.

I cross the lines of the looming army, my steed plowing through their ranks long before any have noticed my arrival. Unannounced and unchallenged, a lone woman atop her mighty beast tears through lines of men with full bellies and wearing clean robes and shining armor. Men who have come to threaten the lives of other men, at the commandment of that which is not Man, at all.

I brazen through their numbers as surely and swiftly as wildfire. My warhorse flies over a battlement intended to isolate the leader of such an Army at its center. The sailing hooves of my roan brings down a cooking frame mounted over a fire. Constructed of straw, the battlement goes up in a blaze that instantly cuts the Army in two.

The woman leaps from her steed as surely as it is my feet that hit the ground. With normally orderly men leaping into the fray of sudden chaos in attempts to reel it in, the Child—the very man for which I have come—stands alone and unprotected. He knows me. Calls me by name. But in his voice is a slight quiver. Unsure of my approach, but eyeing the single weapon I brandish, he reaches for his shield. He has just the time to lift it as I swing my short sword with a force that rips the shield from his grasp. I swing again, for his head, but the attack is slow and easily spotted for a man as verse in the acts of swordplay as he. With his own sword of gleaming gold, he smoothly deflects my attack and understands perfectly that it was his only warning.

"What is the meaning of this?" he shouts just before the force welling within me attacks in earnest. "Are you not my Father's servant?"

Without the added weight of his shield, the Child dances more, moves quicker and narrowly escapes the strikes of an equally skilled fighter with a single goal at heart.

His gaze briefly falls upon the mark inked upon my face, the mark that once belonged to the Angel whom I have slain. "Has the Angel of Darkness corrupted you? Do you not love me? Our Father?"

"I love your Father, the High God over All," returns the voice of the warrior as sure as it is I who feel the words pass through mine own lips. "As I do you."

I break from a tight flutter of high swipes with a spin low to chop at his waist. The clank of metal against metal rings out as he defends against it. He lunges next.

"Then explain yourself!"

I block all that he attempts, to retaliate in kind.

"I am the daughter of the North—" speaks the warrior within the woman burning in Light and warmth, whose attacks only grow stronger. "A Gift for the High God, His Champion—" I push him hard, remembering all I have forgotten. My strength, my reason. Lessons taught by my father, the compassion of my mother, trials fought and earned, I, the warrior, remember all who I was, all that I am, and all that this warrior has yet to be. A voice, as bright as a star, wells up from within me. "I am charged with a task set upon me by Him, your Father, and I shall see it through, to the very end."

Our swords meet high with a clash that rings out for all to hear, and I lose all touch with the woman I remember being as she slips into something unknown. Something neither here nor there; neither real nor fictitious. Whatever I was, the woman warrior will never be again.

"What task is that?" the Child hollers, whipping his sword in a backswing and exposing his mid-section. A quick spin and a dance to the side is all that saves his skin from the sharp edge of my blade.

A spin and a hard chop to the head, middle, and head again, forces the Child back. A block to the outside, a block on the inside, and the Child is caught off guard. His arm pinned across his body by his most trusted, a Commander of the Arm of his Father's Army, a woman fighting not for glory but for something far more valuable, he is swept up in the power of her endeavor.

"To seek out that which threatens Man most. To rid him of it."

His arm lifted, the whole of his left side exposed, she drives the point of a warrior's blackened short blade into the narrow space between his ribs.

"To vanquish it, if necessary," come the last words I would ever speak that could fall on the ears of men.

All falls quiet.

The Child—a grown man, a good leader, and a superb opponent—does not scream. He does not shout, nor does he cry. Slowly, he is lowered to the Earth, wrapped in the loving embrace of the one who rendered from him his immortality.

Knelt over the man I have loved, whose Angel I had followed and obeyed, a warrior's last thoughts come creeping. *Doubt*. I have done that which was asked of me, tasked to me by an authority that which reigns overall, but... had I been misled? Could I have been...

mistaken? But those fears were already cold in the mind of the woman already blurring into fable. The faces of my men, those who have followed me, those who have fallen by mine own hand, all fade from me as the body of *their* General, *their* leader, *their* God in *their* image, cools in my hands.

My head bent in prayer, I plead silently over my beloved enemy for that which I do not deserve. In my heart, a wish for a blessing, a redemption that I would have simply asked for if I could still speak.

Tears threaten to break when I feel his arm lift. With what little life he retains, his eyes open. They are clear, if not going dim, and searching for mine. I meet them, caring little for his hand nearing my face. I do feel his touch, as hot as embers fresh from the fire. His thumb, slick with deep crimson, scores my skin as he drags it across my forehead and down to the bridge of my nose.

"May our Lord love you," says he with no more voice than a whisper meant for me alone. "May He keep you, forever in Grace, for you know precisely that which you do."

Those eyes which have me locked in their fading gaze, are icy with a pain that has little to do with the mortal wound inflicted by love, from which drains his life's essence into the parched earth.

"Now walk," says he, his last words. "Roam the Earth, as the Gods once did, and know immortality."

His touch is gone. His hand falls away, but the ice-cold burn left behind holds fast. It sears in his mark left on my forehead, as does the mark left by the other to silence my lips. Both, I have slain. For the sake of Man, I have set him free, only to learn the cold, hard truth in my savior's final words—in an act that the men surrounding me will not understand.

I rise slowly, standing tall to face all those whom I have rendered guideless. I watch every eye in witness fall on the three marks on my face, forever marking me different from them. Strong and powerful, yet weak and fragile. Alluring, yet treacherous. Seductive, yet pure. A force that has taken from them both their God and their Devil, slain for the sake of their peace and freedom. Yet, on these faces, only dismay, awe, and—growing with frightening speed—want.

What are they to do... *now?*

They look to me as lost as boys who have wandered too far from home to remember the way back. I cannot lead them. Not as they will wish me to. More than their leaders, their very purpose I have vanquished, and unwilling—or unable—to give them another. None move—they do not yet know how—as I gingerly make my way back through their ranks. The men in my path make way. I watch them all.

My horse I find waiting, untouched by the subdued throng. There is no hurry. Not yet. I take in each face I find searching for mine. I look so that they may see. So that they might know mine as real and tangible, even should they never lay eyes upon it again.

What do they see? I wonder. The warrior, or the woman? The assassin, or the protector? The leader, or the deserter? I am all of these as I am none.

The swing up into the saddle is easier than turning away from the faces growing long and drawn as their own realization, too, sinks in: They are on their own. I cannot linger. I kick my horse to speed and race the horizon turned wrong for a rising sun. Never again shall I lead an army. Never again shall I carry out the bidding of another. But the words of my savoir shall forever ring loud and clear in my mind, for I do know that which I have done.

The Gods I have sent back to where they belong, but Man cannot be left unattended. They do not need a Champion, they need one to watch over them, to protect them from those forces they do not understand. With my weapon, on which my name has always been inscribed, I will defend Man at all costs, for I am the last remaining who shall. So, I will wander, as others did before me, and go where I am needed. Never to die nor to fade lest I bring the fall of all Mankind. For I am Grace, their Shepherd, at last.

Tales in Hindsight

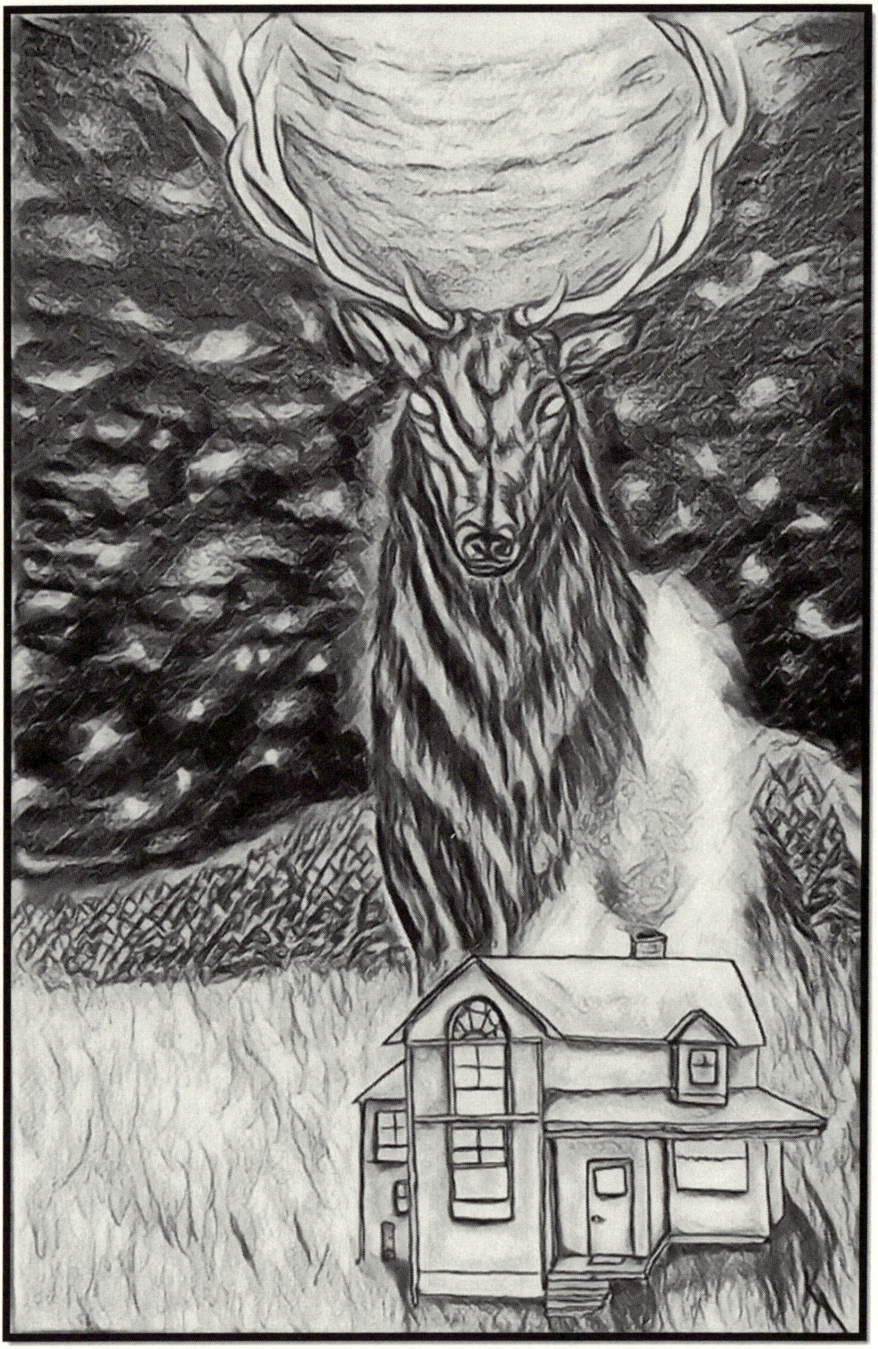

OCTOBER

❖ Cerb Mare ❖

Shall I tell you a tale? A tale of a legend?

One set in a land not so different or distant than your own, dear reader. In a glade, on an old family estate that rests as close as your fingertips yet as far as the stars, it is dark...

...and deep into the night. Well passed bedtime, yet I could not sleep. I had pretended to, tried even, after Mother tucked me in. But awake I remained. For hours, it seemed, lying in my bed, arms restless and on top of my blankets instead of underneath them. My gaze drifted out through my window and into a particular dark and starless night. All I could see was the moon, bright and full. All that reached my ears were the cheery voices of the women, chattering away downstairs.

How late was it? I could not say, but with all the woman going on as they were, the hour must not be quite *so* late, after all, thought I. Their voices as high and chipper as they had been when I was shooed up to my room after supper had been eaten and dishes washed. The men had still been in the house then, too, stretching their arms and legs, rubbing their bellies in apparent appreciation of a pleasant mixture of meat and mead loving crafted by my mother. Rested, fed, and drunk, the men had only been winding up for the event—the reason why they had all gathered in my family's house that particular autumn night.

One woman's laugh consistently pierced above the rest—my mother's. Tempered and reserved when a visitor in the home of someone else—even those of relatives when it was their home we would flock to in the autumn—in her own, my mother would not be outshined.

Cooking, cleaning, sewing; even drinking, talking and, above all, laughing. With our homestead the furthest from town—furthest from anything—the family's annual gathering only occurred here for a specific and rather advantageous occasion: a hunt. One as rare as the autumn blue moon. With the last having occurred before I was born, my mother did not often get to play the role of hostess and she was not about to miss her chance to be memorable. I was nothing like my mother—or so I thought, inside the house where I did not want to be.

All the men had gone, including my brothers—as was their natural right—the womenfolk left alone to gossip and drink for the night; no wonder I had trouble sleeping. That, and my deep, resounding resentment of having been left behind. I was not permitted to take part in the hunt for which the families had gathered. I, like the rest of the women—like my mother before me, and my grandmother before her, all having once slept in the same room as I—remained behind in the house. Hunts could very well last until dawn and it was the duty of the women to keep the house warm. A well-tended fire in the hearth, a pot of soup and a kettle for tea kept hot and ready for the men whenever they decided to wander back in and out of the cold, dark reaches of the night. The night just beyond my bedroom window.

At last, I sat up and pressed my nose to the chilled glass. With the noises from downstairs tuned out, I thought I could just make out the metallic whine of crickets outside, the whisper of wind that rushed through the tall, browned grass that covered of the open grounds surrounding the house. I also heard dogs. Very faint and far away. Barely more than distant echoes that issued from the dark recesses of the forest that encircled the glade, isolating the house from the rest of the world. The great moon hung low and fat over a land not yet touched by snow. A special hunter's moon. A promising one—or so I heard the men say, just after my father had concluded his tale told to the eager, young ears of my brothers and I huddled fireside while Mother and the other women cooked supper. Had my mother known about the tale he had told us? I had suspected not.

Were the men really hunting the creature from my father's story? Were they really hunting a... *myth*? I wondered, as I gazed through the clear pane of glass kissed at the edges with frost. I wondered, why *our* house? Why not at the home of one of my uncles, like all the other hunts? Most of all, I wondered... why not *me*? Why were only the men allowed to go?

'*That's just the way it is, little key,*' had been my father's answer when I had asked after he had concluded his tale, my mother had just called us for supper.

'*But* why?'

'*It's how it has always been.*'

I barely touched my meal after that; food was not what I hungered for. Even dessert, I had declined; sweets were not what I craved. Only after several warnings and one final glare from Mother that I dared not test, had I finally ceased my insistence and obeyed to climb the stairs to my room while the men strapped on their boots and dogs were fetched and collared.

I tried to be a good daughter. I had *tried* to sleep... and tried even harder not to make a sound as I pulled up my pants under my heavy sleeping gown. I donned a pair of thick, wool socks, a scarf, hat, and jacket just as carefully. My boots were downstairs, by the kitchen door where I had planned to escape.

My socked feet made no noise as I crept down the stairs behind the wall of the common room where the womenfolk were gathered by the fire, busy sipping their brandy and wine, and cozy in their respective chairs. The kitchen ahead was clear. The white door with the lace curtain draped over its high, single window was barely a stone's throw away. All I had to do was reach it, but to do so required crossing a short expanse where I would briefly be exposed. All it took was one eye of just one of the dozen women sitting lazily by the hearth, to have ended my pursuit before it had begun.

For a moment, I held my ground on the bottom step and listened to the chatter. I breathed deep the warm, nutty aroma of coffee brewing. The scent of cherries baked in a thick bourbon sauce, that had been served with a supper of roasted turkey and quail, still hung in the air. Mother's reduction. No doubt to be repurposed and served on flapjacks she likely intended to make come sun rise. I had started to wonder if my mother planned to sleep at all that night, when one aunt or another uttered some comment that spurred the gaggle into sudden, uproarious laughter. My moment had arrived, and I was not about to waste it.

I tiptoed across the rough oak floor to the smooth pine of the kitchen that practically shined from generations of women who preceded me in keeping it washed and waxed. The gaiety in the common room continued unbroken and my furtive escape went unnoticed. I turned the doorknob in time with another burst of boisterous debauchery, then I was outside.

The chill did not bother me, wrapped in warm clothes as I was. I sat on the bottom step of the back porch just long enough to tie my boots. Then I was off, wading through the sea of grass that reached above my knees before one of the women decided to go to the kitchen to top off a drink and spot my slinking away into the night.

Invigorated by the crisp air, I felt stir within me such feelings that I could not yet name. A call I could not hear with my ears sang to me, beaconing me to come, venture, *seek*. A scent I could not follow with my nose bade me to enter the dark tangle of forest on the other side of the glade. The moon hung high above the tops of even the tallest trees. Just enough of its ghostly light pierced through blackened limbs to see by. At the forest's edge, I stopped and looked back.

Bright cheer rang out from the warm confines of the house. The kitchen window glowed a soothing yellow behind white lace curtains that, from so far away in the dark, looked more gray than white. Not unlike the puffy smoke that drifted from out the top of the main chimney—the only clouds in the obsidian sky that night. A sight of such warmth, such comfort, that I suddenly felt a chill leak through my many layers. But, at the sharp, rasping bray of the dogs, I returned to the inky woods and stepped unafraid into the forest.

High-reaching branches of bare bushes clawed at my pants and the hem of my coat. Naked limbs of trees reached for my face but, at nine years of age, I was still short enough to clear most of even the lowest-hanging branches without much evasion. Unlike the adults, my brothers included, who were unable to avoid any of them. The forest was quiet as I pushed deeper. I heard not a hoot of an owl nor the scurry of a mouse as the forest seemed to close in tighter around me. Tighter and darker; I moved more by feel than anything else. Leaves crunched under my boots, skeletal limb managed to snag my hair not once, but twice, and my pounding heart told me that I was lost, yet I kept my feet trudging. For how long, I could not tell. Minutes? *Hours?* I could no longer smell the smoke from the chimney.

I had no idea of my direction. I had gone deeper into the woods that night than I had ever during the daylight. Of this, I was certain. Where were the men? Where were my brothers, my father? My uncle's dogs had gone quiet, I could hear nothing but the clamor of my own boots through the dense brush.

I did my best to walk in a straight line from where I had entered, but something suddenly seemed wrong about the trees. The tangle had grown instantly thicker. Ends of limbs and branches seemed to stick out in such a manner that, even with my arms up, I could not avoid them. No amount of ducking or evading could bring me reprieve. It was as though the trees had been brought down, and I was forcing my way through the chaos of branches that pointed all the wrong direction. More than once I heard cloth tear—Mother was not going to be happy. Yet, onward, I pushed.

Where was home? How was I going to find my way back? How far away was dawn? I wondered. I worried. I feared. And then, I felt myself fall. The ground rushed up quicker than it took for me to realize that it was I, in fact, who had tumbled to it. The branches I had been pushing through having unexpectedly ended, I found myself on my hands and knees in the sudden vacancy on the other side. Right up to the sky, unobstructed above.

With no limbs to block the light of the moon, I could see the clearing well. It was small, and more or less round save for one, elongated side. The base of every tree and bush in the opened space was snapped, their fibers frayed from having been recently smashed to the earth. Whatever happened there, happened recently. I rose to my feet as a heavy, resounding understanding began to claw its way into my young, impressionable mind. I stood and turned all the way around until my gaze fell upon the oblong side—where the curve elongated into two points. All at once, I *knew* what I was standing in.

But... it was only a story! It could not be *possible*. Yet, there I stood, in the middle of single footprint on a scale my young mind could not have fathomed alone. Over my shoulder, I heard the barking of dogs. I turned my face in the direction where their howls bounced off trees deeper still. The men would be with them, following their noses, and—I looked back to the track around me, to where the points led—*heading in the opposite direction.* I did not understand what I knew, or how I knew it, but I *knew* what it was that the men were hunting. Just as I *knew* they would not find it; they were going the wrong way.

That sound with no voice called to me. I felt its touchless breath brush against my face turning it away from the hounds and their braying. I wanted to be afraid, but the terror failed to rise. I crossed the clearing in the direction of that which I understood to be the imprint of the two toes of the creature that had passed by. Again, I allowed the dark forest to overtake me, and it was not long before I came to the forest's edge.

The forest surrounding my family's estate ended not at the furthest reaches of town as I thought it would, but abruptly at a large meadow of tall grass. A mild breeze whipped through the tall grass, slapping the long blades against my shins as it stirred my hair, but hardly pushed me back. On the contrary, it compelled me to venture further still, and into the meadow I walked.

To have called the meadow round would have been likened to call an egg a circle. More an oval, with trees mostly on only one side. Great haggard sails of stone that jutted up from the ground capped off the meadow on either end that turned it into more of a bowl. On the side of the meadow opposite the trees, those craggy cliffs curved and met at an angle, so odd, that it hurt my eyes to look at them. Not dark at all, the meadow seemed to glow softly as though filled with the soft, new rays of a sun on the rise that poured in through that curious connection of towering rock. I moved toward it.

I had ventured far from the sheltered edge of the forest when the wind picked up. Strong gusts pushed me forward and nearly knocked me sideways. Another icy blast took my hat, sent it flying someplace behind me. I had closed in on that obtuse angle in the scaled cliffs and found that the two extensive arms of rock that embraced the meadow did not connect at all. What I had took for a queer notch in the rock was, in fact, a wide gap between them, off set and impossible to be seen from where I had emerged from the forest. Beyond the opening stretched a vast, sprawling plain of short, yellow-green grass and space aplenty for a creature of such enormity that could leave a footprint the size of a small clearing to roam freely. But where was the creature?

The feeling of leering eyes made me look back the way I had come. The trees were not as they had been. They did not seem green. Red, perhaps? Orange, yellow, *brown*? I could not rightly say what color they were. Nor how tall. Taller than me, certainly, but their tips blurred or smudged under the weight of the colors that they should not be, I could not determine their height. They all appeared to be on fire. But that could not be. There was no smell, no smoke, no actual flames that licked up the trunks, and yet how the trees shimmered with the haze of intense heat. *It must be from the sun on the rise*, I thought as I watched the trees burn without them burning at all, but there certainly seemed no hope in returning that way.

The winds increased. Strong enough to whip back the edges of my jacket until the buttons came loose. It tugged at my clothes, pulled at my hair. Then, suddenly, I didn't notice the wind at all. My clothes, my hair, the grass still danced with demons as the queer sensation of being watched grew overwhelming. In that moment, I tasted—for the first time—real fear. As a rabbit might when it has caught the scent of a fox, lying in wait nearby. My mouth went so dry, that no amount of water could quench my parched throat. My heart hammered like a locomotive in my ears. Sweat broke out on my palms. All at once, I remembered a crucial fact: the sun would not rise from that horizon.

The howling roar of the wind fell away, and the rocks and stones littered about the meadow abruptly lifted from their places on the ground as though guided by invisible strings. Some came level with my eyes, others hovered much higher, suspended by some foreboding force. I lifted my hand to touch one when I felt it—the gaze from the eyes of impending doom that fell squarely onto the back of my neck.

As fast as I dared, and agonizingly slow, I forced myself to face the gap, the open plain beyond, and—more disturbingly—that which I found in between. More stones had floated up into the air, their size did not seem to make any difference. The edges of the cliffs appeared to be crumbling apart and float away. But I hardly noticed the rocks, or the impossibility of their movement—neither meant anything to me. Amidst it all, higher than the tallest tree, up where the moon should be, two eyes like twin suns bore down upon me a blazing gaze.

My heart plummeted to my stomach; my stomach lurched into my throat. My mouth dry and my skin clammy, I remembered to breathe only by force of the fierce wind that buffeted my face and body. My jacket flung open, my hair whipped wildly, yet I stared—terrified, horrified, and bursting with a wonder, so great, that I could taste it on my tongue as much as I could feel it burn forever into a secret space behind my eyes. *It was only a story!* Yet, there it was. There *it* stood! The impossible figure poised before me: the *cerb mare*, in all its glory, burning with all the fame and prestige a young girl could bestow. How could any have given more?

Harder the winds blew, a ferocious beast in its own right. It yanked and pulled at my pants and nearly made off with my coat had I not gathered what of it I could in one small hand pinned against my chest. What filled the gap in the cliff wall, so tall as to dwarf them to mounds of dirt, was a monstrous deer, and I was locked in its gaze.

'A legend older than the trees or the mountains,' my father's story spun through my head. *'Its story goes way back to when Titans still roamed Earth—the largest and oldest Titan of all. Legend goes that the* cerb mare *was made by the Tree Titan itself, and the only one of its kind to have survived a great flood. The last of its kind, it roams. To where, one knows, or why. What it eats, if it sleeps, or where it goes when it cannot be seen all equally mysterious. But sometimes, just sometimes, under the bright light of a hunter's blue moon, the* cerb mare *appears. Here. Somewhere on your mother's ancestral grounds for someone lucky enough to look in just the right place, at just the right time. To whomever can catch it, it is said that the* cerb mare *will grant any desire the heart wants most. That is why we gather, why the men in our family go hunting as we have for ages. We do this, for it is said that the* cerb mare *was seen once, on these very grounds before they were ours at all. The wish it granted, so long ago, was this very house and the acres surrounding it, and they have been cared for and looked after by someone in our family ever since.'*

'If it is a deer, how will we know it is different from the ones we see all the time?' the youngest of my older brothers had asked.

'You will know,' Father had answered. *'For it is larger than any deer living now, or ever.'*

I had not believed. It was only a story. A tale! Yet, there it stood, undeniable, *unbelievable*, and on a scale that my young, fragile mind could barely comprehend. Its great body, a forest of shaggy, course hair that blurred in and out of detail as the trees surrounding the meadow shimmered with a wildfire that burned nothing and made no smoke. Its eyes radiated such fierce, intense gold as to break the dead of night with fractured shafts of brilliant dawn. I lifted my hand to shield my face with my arm—*turn away*, it bade in a voice I could not hear with my ears. I nearly listened. About as nearly as had I when Mother had told me to stay in my room, earlier that very night.

'No!' I cried; my arm stayed from casting a shadow over my face.

You must look away, came the radiant smolder of its gaze. Gales whipped from the gap with such savagery as to nearly rip my hair out at the root.

Defiant, held my gaze. 'I will not!'

The gargantuan deer did not change, but it did seem to grow. Its majestic head held high only strengthened its stature. The great, outstretched basket of antlers reached across the sky as would a great river and its many tributaries would through a thirsty land. And its *eyes*. They burned with a fire meant only for stars. Their gaze settled on me in a way they had not before. I was more than captivated; I was consumed by an ethereal essence I wished never to be without again. The *cerb mare* had looked back.

Why, came the thunderous voice whispered on the back of the wind.

Still transfixed with awe, an astonishing thing did happen: my fear vanished. My gaze hardened; confidence and need pounded in my heart.

'If I look away,' shouted my tiny, girl voice with the strength to slice through the raging wind, '—you might disappear. Then you'll be gone. And I don't want you to be gone.'

Why, came the voice. The stare of the *cerb mare* burned with such fire and light that I feared staring back might cause me to go blind, but I did not blink.

'Because—' and there, I fumbled. Not fully understanding the truth I had yet to admit. Staring up at this creature of story and lore, I found myself knowing what I wanted, but not what to say. The answer perched on the tip of my tongue, ready to take flight, if only I knew what it was! I opened my mouth and the wind seemed to know exactly the words needed. They flew from my lips.

"Because you're *real!*"

The force that struck me was incredible. It took me off my feet, but I did not feel myself fall. Like the stones floating skyward, the world tilted off its axis. I was weightless, until the slam of the ground against my back. It was that hit which opened my eyes that I hadn't known I had closed nor for how long. Above me, I saw only sky, but it looked different. Framed by the tips of the tall grass, a patchwork of purples, pinks, and blues drifted by. Dawn had arrived, truly, at last. I heard the dogs then, their barks carried on a gentle breeze sounded close—the dogs had found the meadow.

I sat up and discovered the meadow anew, for the second time. Just a meadow, that's all it was. Full of tall, brown grass and bordered on one side by trees standing tall and unblemished by a raging fire that never was. The rocky cliffs that made up the rest of the rim were fixed and imposing. Boulders and rocks lay scattered on the ground or up the cliff walls as they should. And the gap—well—through the gap stretched a grassland dotted with elk. A patch of bison grazed lazily under a big sky filled with brown and tawny clouds hanging low and in, what I could imagine, the vague shape of some enormous creature being pulled apart by the breaking day.

I heard my name called. A name that suddenly sounded foreign to me. But the voice that had called it belonged to my father. Rarely did he call me by my given name—he had another for me—that I almost did not turn.

"What are you doing out here, my little key?" he asked when he knelt beside me, his walking staff propped against his shoulder. His hands free, he smoothed my hair and squeezed comfort into my shoulder. "Are you alright?"

"I saw..." my mouth began before I shut it, tightly.

"What? What did you see?"

I could not take the kind yet searching interest in his eyes. Deep green, his eyes were not like mine. I had my mother's eyes: hazel, like the new morning that filled the sky. I turned from him to face the gap, to take in the clouds there that my father might have said held the vague shape of a deer, still somewhat gray and tawny brown. I could not tell my father what I saw; he would not understand. Even though he had led the men of my family in hunt for it, I could not tell him what I had found. Or, perhaps, what had found me.

My uncles and brothers had come to the meadow, as well. They all looked tired and weary and in need of a good sleep after a hot meal and drink. I desired none of those things. I felt neither rested nor fatigued as I returned with them, in silence, to the house. Nor did I dwell on the stern talkin' to I was bound to receive from my mother once we got there. Any anger she would show, even the fear I was prepared to hear in her voice, I knew would only be skin deep. My mother, I could tell. My mother would understand; I had her eyes, after all. Even without a word from me, she would know, she would *understand*.

The instant the house came back into view, as soon as my young eyes laid sight upon its visage as if for the first time, I knew something that my mother did also. She knew the tale of the *cerb mare*, just as she knew that my father had told us his own version. But my mother knew the tale differently than he. I understood this, for I knew it, too.

I drank in the sight of the house. All its curious angles and strangely beautiful architecture, and I imagined how much more there could be. Perhaps another wing, built off to one side. Perhaps a room that ended in bulbous, rounded glass—I had time to think, I had time to plan. I knew that I did, for I knew that this house would one day be mine. Mine to care for. Mine in which I could create any world that I wished. I knew this to be true, as I left my dirtied boots outside on the porch alongside those of the men, for the *cerb mare* had made it so. My heart's most desired wish—on that, at least, my father's tale had it right.

Tales in Hindsight

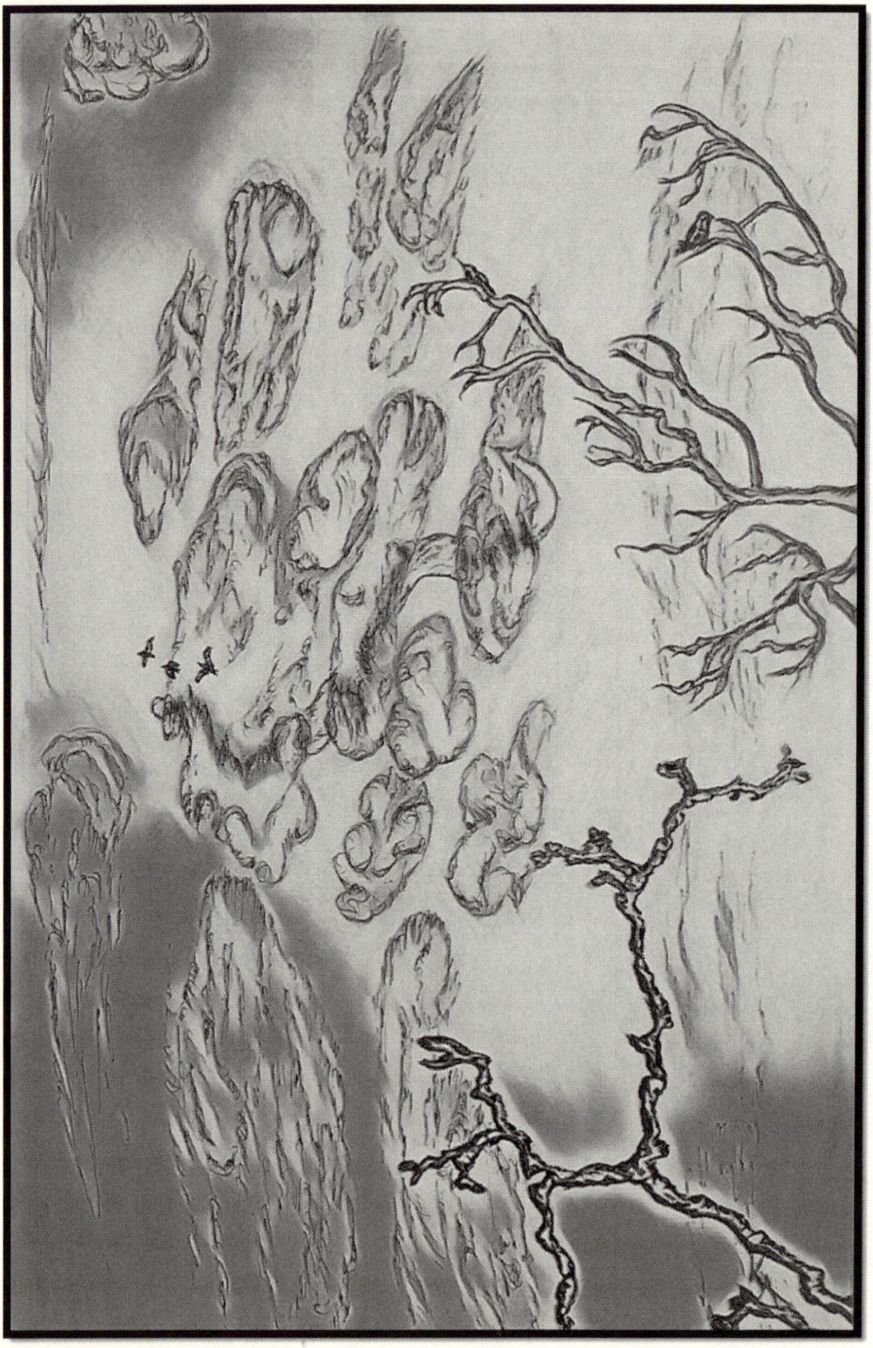

NOVEMBER

❖ Cloud Hunter ❖

Not quite mid-day, and all the leaves are raked into a pile at the base of the largest tree in the yard.

Miles has at least an hour, now, before Ma will be calling him in for lunch. *Plenty of time*, he thinks, dropping the rake. The fall air is crisp, and every breath fills his lungs with its delicious chill. Only on his face can he feel the cold. The rest of him is snug under his jacket, jeans, hat, gloves, and—of course—his boots. Broken-in and comfortable—Ma says he'll need new ones soon—they help him make short work of scrambling up the big tree next to which he has piled the morning's collection of leaves. A well-earned break, and Miles lies back on a large, low-hanging branch.

Fall chores are his favorite. Odd, perhaps, for a boy of nine to enjoy any chore, but mixing all the colors—the oranges, reds, and yellows mostly blotched with brown or orange spots—*that* is not so strange. The way they rattle with each pull of the wide-headed, red plastic rake, gathering more than his small hands could do alone, delightfully drowns out the constant noise of his sisters, ages four and five. And that is not odd at all.

Those girls are so loud, thinks Miles. They make such a mess of things. Always screaming and laughing and whispering to each other. Always together. Where one goes the other is never far behind, yet they never seem to play the same game. Each seemingly content in her own headspace until after their games conclude and they tell the other about what they did or thought. Miles has never understood them. Of course, they are not *his* sisters. Not *really*. Both are fair skinned, unlike his darker tan, more olive complexion. Bright green and blue eyes, with brown and blonde hair respectively, while Miles's eyes are as brown as rich soil, and his hair darker still. Chubby and cherub-like, the girls look more like their parents. Miles has no memory of his.

Not that it matters much. Ma and Pop love him, that he has never questioned. Miles simply finds more solace alone, working out in the yard, than bumbling around inside the house with this family. On these perfect autumn days, who could blame him? Outside, where frost still clings to the ground, under a sapphire sky with a constant stream of puffy, white islands lazily drifting along with the wind, so high above the ground, that's where a boy like him belongs.

The branches of the tree are bare, and the naked limbs impede his view little. Miles reclines along the limb, cradling his head in his hands, fingers interlaced. The limb does not feel quite as wide as it used to—Miles could fit both legs on the branch just last year—now one leg drapes over one side. No matter. The spot still fits his frame enough to relax and tune out distant, playful screams of his sisters.

Clouds truly are wonderful. To Miles, anyway. So light, so fluffy. Not like whipped cream as one of his sisters had mentioned that one time when he got her to look up at the sky long enough to notice anything. For Miles, they are more like great balls of cotton all stretched out, almost to the point of coming apart, before being carelessly fluffed back together and set afloat over a sea of endless azure.

What might it be like to touch one? He bets they are soft.

Would he fall right through? Or might there be enough to them to hold him up?

If only he could find out. If only he could *get* to them? Miles reaches up with one hand; they're just so high up, and just out of reach. How would he get to where they are?

With rocket boots, of course.

Not just any rocket boots. Special ones.

Boots that fit as snug and comfortable as his regular pair, but with special rockets built in that will take him much higher than any other sort of boot on the market. He would pull the laces tight, make sure the knot is good. Slap the soles once, no, twice against the launchpad at the end of the limb branching away from the towering trunk of the stronghold. Only the best rocket boots will do for the mission only he can complete.

His helmet in place and strapped tight? *Check.*

His gloves? It'll be cold up there. *Check.*

Goggles? He nestles the thick rubber rings comfortably around his eyes. *Check.*

His weapon, freshly sharpened and polished, is slung across his back and secure.

Time to check in.

"This is Miles TerAvest, Cloud Hunter, and all is GO."

Back straight, knees bent, intentions set on the stars, Miles leaps from the platform with a willful bound. His boots ignite, and he is shot straight up to the bank of clouds above. His feet shake a little from the fusion blasting from the ports in his heels and toes. It is a vibration that he likes, shaking him alive, filling him with that thrill that lifts your stomach just before the fall takes hold. But Miles will not fall. Not yet.

Higher and higher he sails, reducing trees to mere bushes in seconds. The house turns into the doll model the girls play with. Not a game for Miles. He is on the hunt for much bigger quarry. His goggles protect his eyes from the wind rushing over his helmet, whipping his jacket and pants. Miles feels none of it. Kept warm and safe inside his protective layers, and thankful for them, as the air quickly turns cold. He can feel it on his face (the only part of him left exposed). Not only does it grow colder, but thinner too. Even with all his gear, he won't be able to stay up here long. For now, and extra kick from his boots gives the quick burst needed to pierce through the floor of the gray and white cloudbank and out on the other side.

Popping through, Miles boots then simmer down and sink into cloud, but only a little. The surface is like a trampoline made of long, stretchy fibers which he can feel slowly rolling and churning even through the thick, mechanical soles of his special boots. Burning faint and low, just enough to keep him buoyant on the thin membrane floating so high above the Earth, his boots keep Miles drifting along with it while he is locked in awe.

The world above the clouds is nothing like he has ever seen and certainly not what it looks like from the ground far, far below. Up here, the sky is not blue at all but a dusky shade of pink. Nor are the clouds drifting within it, white. They are a soft, pale yellow. The air here is quiet but not still. Hushed, but not silent. It is full of whispers, crisp and clear. Though Miles does not know what they say, he does understand that what he hears is pure anticipation. A harmonic ring of a note yet to be played, and this much older world, floating above the Earth, is brimming brightly with it. Such peace, such serenity that—all at once—shatters!

An immense shadow suddenly tears across the pink over Miles's head. A blur of something so large that, against the radiant glory of a blushing sky, seems as black as the void. Miles is jolted from his splendor, delighted. The immense, dark creature has slipped back into the confines of the yellow clouds, but Miles's lips crack into an ecstatic, lop-sided grin. His special boots have taken him here for a reason and he remembers what he has come here to do.

His boots, as special as they are, have only so much fuel and cloud-walking can be tricky. The thicker the cloud, the better his boots will work at a lower setting; a trick no one else's boots can do, only those of a true nefelibata such as he. But step on a patch too thin, and he'll burn through gas just to keep from falling.

He begins with a few tentative steps. The cloudbank is a good one. Plush, thick, and lumpy with rolling crests and troughs that no trace of the ground, so far below, can be seen. His boots barely hum. Confidence swells. Tracking his quarry, he soon is gliding along with long, smooth strides. His prey cannot escape now.

When a shadow appears below him, just under his boots—his only warning—Miles stops! Throwing the brakes on his boots just as a great beast breeches the pale-daffodil surface. Rearing high into the pink and orange sky, the beast is not black at all but sparkling white! Miles gawks at the long and sinewy snake-like body towering over the mighty Cloud Hunter suddenly dwarfed. Large, intelligent eyes leer down at the creature's would-be rival. The massive, blunt muzzle curls back, showing off its wickedly sharp teeth. It is the very creature Mile has come to hunt. Here rises a dragon.

For such a gigantic creature, the beast sure has scrawny limbs. Miles can see only the front two as at least some of the beast is still hidden by soft, yellow foam. Long and scaly, each arm ends with four toes tipped with talons that would put a harpy eagle to shame. Though skinny, this beast could still pick up Ma's station wagon and carry it off with minimal effort.

Such a beast!

But Miles knows a secret.

The air at this altitude is thin. Even he cannot remain for long, and not without special equipment. For a dragon, that time is even less. They will eventually come apart where the air grows thin, and faster the higher they go. For now, this beast holds its poise and its snarl as it stares down at the one come to slay it.

Pursue, Hunter, says the dragon through its fiery glare. Angling its massive head just so, the beast shows off the twin horns, twisted and sharp, jutting up from its skull. *If you dare.*

A challenge sought becomes a challenge met and both boy and beast understand that a new game is about to begin. With a mighty lunge and a guttural growl, the glistening white dragon sails overhead to dive again into the skies below the clouds at Miles's back. The hunt is on. Unstrapping the harpoon secured to his back, and Miles is quick to pursue.

He keeps his pace slow at first, conserving the fuel in his boots. There is a feel to the air this time, much different than the hushed serenity it had been before. A charge tantalizes the atmosphere. Dragons do not run, nor do they hide from a hunter worth his salt, and there is no hunter better than Miles. It will play a game of its own, try to outwit him. With this one being especially clever, Miles must stay light on his toes, eyes peeled and wits sharp; this is no deer he hunts. A dragon can appear anywhere, at any time, and Miles may have to move quickly or be gobbled up himself.

His first sign appears at his right—a cresting hump. A small part of the dragon's back rolls up from the sky underneath. Ahead, another hump breaks the cloud's surface. Then, almost too quickly, another appears on his left. *It is trying to confuse me*, Miles gleans. *Trying to make me turn and chase it, to wear down my time and my fuel.* But a hunter does not catch a dragon by chasing it, Miles knows this. Dragons can only be caught by surprise. Miles ignores the tempting bait. Instead, he sails ahead, increasing his pace.

As he nears the edge of the cloudbank, his boots take up the slack as the cloud beneath him thins. Just ahead, he spots a stretched-out bit of cloud, more gray than yellow and a good drop lower than this main bank. A burst of full speed and Miles leaps for spotty archipelago below.

The dragon, at once, comes into view, circling the white, flat bottoms of the main bank. Miles's boots take to the lower cloud as light as a feather, and the dragon takes notice. Surprised by the presence of such a bold hunter, the dragon peels away from its failed lure and vaults upward through the main bank into the pink skies above. This time, Miles follows.

Using wayward bits of broken cloud saves some energy in his boots as he climbs back to the yellow surface. An extra burst propels him the last bit and Miles breaks through with a flip just in time to catch the dragon's eye before it dives again. Miles does not follow, but he does smile; the dragon had hissed before it dove. A bold hunter, and a quick one, too; this dragon has met its match.

Miles runs the clouds in hot pursuit of the shadow as big around as the trunk of giant redwood tree, and longer than he can rightly determine, sliding along just under the pale-yellow fluff.

When the shadow turns suddenly, bunching up, Miles leaps! A burst from his boots and he flips away from the great, white body that breaks the surface right where Miles had been. The dragon dives again, but having leapt so high, Miles spots the bulk of the creature's shadow bunched far from where its head is going. *It's trying to trick me*, thinks Miles. A smirk pulls at his lips and Miles starts to fall.

He does not activate his boots—*not yet*. Instead, he drops through the cloudbank, popping out the bottom just as the dragon catapults in the opposite direction, back into the pink skies where the air is thin that Miles just left. His boot catch purchase on a sparse dollop of gray lower in the atmosphere where the sky is blue and the air thicker. The bit of cloud he lands on has barely the surface area to accommodate both boots, but it does have enough substance to launch from.

His boots ignite. Leading with the sharp, barbed tip of the harpoon in his hands, Miles rockets back into a world of perpetual dawn. He punches through to find the beast exposed, stretched near to its full length. With a roar, Miles meets the beast face-on and throws the harpoon with all his might. The shining metal blade flies from his hand and strikes, tip first, but the beast has moved. A slight turn, and a hunter's excellent throw collides with the tough, shimmering white scales on the dragon's head instead of its more delicate throat. *Luck*, the dragon roars.

A ripple courses through the beast's great body, pulling its long frame to coil. The harpoon tumbles as the dragon makes ready to dive again, but it is going *up* this time. Knocked against scaley hide and jostled absently, the hooked barb on the harpoon's blade becomes lodged in the crook of one of the beast's rear limbs—an opportunity Miles is not about to pass up. He leaps for the weapon with a strong burst from his boots.

Miles grabs the long, sturdy staff of the weapon. The hooked side of the harpoon is snagged on the raised edge of scales lining the dragon's hock. With Miles's weight suddenly added to it, not only does the hooked point sink deeper, but breaks off entirely. A burst from his boots clears Miles from the wild and furious dragon snarling and racing for skies even higher. He could give chase, but there is no need. A dragon cannot stay long in atmosphere high enough to be perpetually pink and yellow. Being so high up risks quicker evaporation; it must come down. And soon. If not for its own survival, Miles needs it for his own luck. His boots are on their last reserves of fuel. They will not carry him much longer and certainly not further up.

A couple of short bursts gets him moving in an easy glide across the faint yellow turning patchy. The clouds are starting to break up and the bank is no longer thick nor stable. While trying to pay attention to the changing surface under his feet, Miles keeps pace with the sinuous, twisting figure gliding over the dark ochre underside of the clouds higher still.

It must *come down*, Miles thinks. *Then what?* The dragon knows it is being chased. When it does drop, it will be with fang and claw in the lead. Miles, with only his harpoon—now more a spear with the barbed hook broken off—will be the one caught instead of his prey. He could run, but he will never catch up with it again; the hunt will be lost. He is left with only one option, a gamble. Miles throws on the breaks, coming to a full stop on his level of the cloudbank. Above, the shadow darts forward and out of sight. *Come on*, Miles pleads with a hunter's gusto to urge his adversary into a trap of his own design.

No sooner does he think it does the dragon descend. Popping out the bottom of the upper bank not as far ahead as Miles had expected, brandishing its talons spread wide for an attack—just as he thought it would. The dragon's maw gaping, ready to snap shut over the hunter *it* thinks should be there. *It worked*, Miles thinks. Then, Miles is falling.

The yellow instantly turns to gray. Cold air feels damp on his cheeks as Miles plummets through a fluff-bare hole in the cloudbank. His boots fire with choked sputtering but they catch purchase on a small, broken puff. His boots are running on fumes. They have just enough for one final surge; it's now or never. Harpoon—now spear—gripped tightly, Miles rolls the dice of chance that the beast has not strayed far and—if he is truly lucky—that the tiny cloud of gray has drifted him even closer. With everything he has left, Miles leaps once more.

He rockets up through the cloud. Ignoring the vapor on his face and the chill starting to leak in through his clothes, the greatest Cloud Hunter to ever hunt the skies pops into the pastel world hidden from the ground just in time to see the dragon's tail slip upward into the world still higher. Miles does not stop. *This is for all the dragonscale,* and Miles wills every drop from his boots. They cough dry but propel him, nonetheless, through the uppermost bank.

Spear in hand, he breaks through. The dragon is closer than he could have imagined. Arm pulled back, hollering with all the might in his bones, Miles throws for the exposed, soft underbelly directly in the path of a skilled hunter's spear. Caught by surprise, indeed, and the spear's sharp bladed head hits the mark. The mighty Cloud Hunter has vanquished his foe... and Miles begins to fall.

Basking in the warm glory of conquest, the pull back to the earthly realm below is, at first, divine. A drink of sweet nectar after an arduous journey, until all that syrupy sugar hits an empty stomach that has gone too far since its last meal. The revelry of weightless freefall turns sour. Dread blooms. He descends from the clouds at a terrible pace. The bushes below are, too quickly, turning back into trees. The house grows larger at a harrowing speed. His boots are empty. What hope does he have to slow down? What chance does he have to *land*?

The hollow beating of his heart fills Miles's mouth with the coppery taste of his rapidly approaching demise. His breath stolen by the terrible rush of the wind. *Was the hunt worth this?* Miles wonders. What will Ma say? What about his sisters? Who will protect them, watch over them, if Miles were to die now? There must be more beasts in this world than a single dragon. Is he really about to leave them defenseless just to chase *one* dragon? What had he been thinking?

How long *has* he been thinking?

Long enough for Miles to realize, in hesitant relief, that he is no longer falling. There is no slam of the ground rushing to stop him, yet his back rest against something firm. But the air still rushes past him, refreshing against his face, compelling him to open his eyes he did not know he had squeezed shut.

Surrounded by bright light, it takes him several disorienting moments to realize that he is still in the sky. Wisps of cloud dart by as spray might past the hull of a ship sailing across the seas. How can this be? His boots are empty, only regular boots now. And the ground where he should have landed is, instead, the rather sturdy seat on the back of a giant. A sinewy beast, covered in scales as white and glittering pristine as virgin snow: Miles is on the back of a dragon.

The ground below—so very far below—is no place that Miles recognizes.

"Where are we going?" Miles asks, surprised to discover that he is wholly unafraid.

A tremor passes through the warm body underneath him. The dragon does not slow or change course, but it does answer.

Where do you wish to go?

"Me?" Miles returns. "Anywhere I wish?"

No answer comes save a queer understanding that this magnificent creature will do just that.

"But why?" Miles asks, suddenly sorry for what he had done. "I hunted you and killed you with my spear." At least, he thought he had.

The response that comes is filled with such mirthic delight—if dragons are capable of such joy—that a warmth fills Miles until his body feels enchanted with it. *I cannot recall when last I had such a thrilling chase, and with such a worthy adversary. You hunted a dragon, now know what it is to be one.*

All at once, the rushing winds are stirred up from a whispering hum to a tempest roaring past his ears. Louder, *louder*, the faster they fly. In a blink, they are far beyond any sort of landscape Miles can remotely recognize. The roar becomes deafening. Greens of plants and blues of water flatten and stretch into blended bands of color. Faster, they fly. The wind is shrieking. Almost too high-pitched (or too loud) for a boy's ears to hear at all. Faster, faster still. The dragon seems to stretch. Its body elongating more than it is already, its scrawny limbs reaching impossibly far for the course ahead. Reaching for a plane in Space across which only dragons and birds can travel. Where the wail of the wind is overwhelming. More a pressure than a sound, it squeezes against the sides of Miles's head. He clings tightly to the dragon as it flies faster. *Faster.*

Miles blinks and a world both familiar and surreal unfolds around them. All that Miles can see! And from such a height! Miles can see so much in surprising detail. A vast swath of open ground covered in thigh-high grass passes in the span of a breath. But, in it, Miles spots a young man running, led along by a young woman of same age, her hand gripping his. Miles blinks again and the grass is gone. In its place, a mountain stands guard at the edge of a lush hanging valley. Nestled at its base, a pearl white gem of a city, gleaming as radiantly as the dragon sailing overhead. A festival is in full swing. It is a proud city, and one celebrating a victory. Faster, and the mountains are a distant memory already replaced by a red wasteland of rock and sand, dotted with formations as tall as a skyscraper.

The dragon stretches, reaches further, *travels faster*. Both the pressure and the roar of the winds abruptly abates. For Miles, it comes with relief. Out of the chaos, he is enveloped in an odd sort of calm that is strangely full. There is a sound. One he can hear not with his ears, but with his heart. A beautiful sound of a church choir holding a perfectly harmonized note inside a stone cathedral Miles has yet to visit.

The dragon travels at such a speed that—to Miles—both boy and beast seem to cease moving at all. Together, they hang suspended over a world spinning beneath *them*. The dragon crosses into a plane where even birds cannot go. The dragon takes Miles into the realm of Time. Future, past, present: all are one, in the same moment of existence. Maybe ahead, maybe from long ago, Miles sees a young girl scampering from a house he knew once but where he has yet to arrive. In the dead of night, when no young thing should be wandering off alone, the girl scampers toward an even darker forest as Miles travels overhead. He sees the Earth before Gods walked, back when the Titans still roamed freely. He catches a glimpse of a Time when more dragon hunters exist, wearing armor of gleaming gold and silver. Such wonders!

Where do you wish to go?

"Up!" Miles cries before he thinks, or maybe afterward. "To the stars."

A twist and jerk, the dragon breaks from its reach. Miles hangs tight as the beast turns sharply upward, though he does not have to. He is as much a part of the dragon as the beast is of him. Locked together, their bodies pulsing with the radiance of the sun, they race the thinning of the atmosphere. The sky turns from pink to purple, then a deeper, Prussian blue until, finally, mid-night black. Higher than the clouds. Higher than any dragon—or any boy, for that matter—has ever travelled. Higher, *faster*, until there is no more air to feel. From the back of his dragon, Miles leaps! His arms stretched to touch the twinkling bits of silver just ahead but vastly out of reach.

The dragon is gone. Too high for too long, the great beast turns to vapor. But Miles is not sad. Nor is he fearful of the force that reaches with arms of its own to pull him back to earthly realms. It is okay for him to fall now. Out here, among the stars, there is no where *to* fall, only places to go. The call of the ground wins over and Miles drops. Hard. Fast. And not quite as far as he thought.

A short catch of breath, and he plunges into the cold, crisp space no different than a large pile of leaves raked conveniently under the largest limb of the largest tree in the yard. Frost still clinging to their edges feels cold on his face. The stars sing their farewell in the crunch and crackle loud in his ears. A deep, earthy musk of fresh decay fills his nose. Miles breathes deeply inside the cool, engulfing dark.

From somewhere unearthly far, yet heartwarmingly close, a different sound reaches his ears. Miles blinks against the pinpricks of light filtering through the leaves.

"Miles!" It's Ma, calling out to him.

Lashing out with both arms and legs, Miles breaks through his cocoon of the biggest pile of leaves he has raked yet. One worth falling into. A good amount of jostling and Miles, at last, extricates himself to the final call from the house.

"Miles! Lunchtime!"

His sisters are already flying in through the door and Miles runs to catch up, his flight with his dragon turning more and more into a dream with each step. He wonders, though, what adventure shall he dream of after lunch?

Tales in Hindsight

DECEMBER

✦ First Rule ✦

There is no chime or bell on the frosted glass door entrance to the bar, the *In Between*.

Tucked away in the vacant, shadowy depths of Key Street, there never has been a need for one. The squeal from the hinges is alert enough, and they get louder every year. Exceptionally so when they are wet, and it has been raining throughout the night. All day, in fact, yet the mat squarely centered a step inside is hardly damp. Most of the rain is successfully kept at bay by the frosted glass door.

The night has been a quiet one, and the hour is late. Late enough for Rosco (barkeep and owner of the hole-in-the-wall bar residing on the furthest edge of town) to normally start closing procedures. In fact, if the remaining group of stragglers—a brawny gang of young men, full of energy and testosterone-fueled pride—were not still taking up one whole table, draining the last of their sixth pitcher of beer, Rosco might have locked the door thirty minutes ago and been home by now, tinker in his workshop with a beer of his own. Mid-weeknights are always slow.

This removed from the city proper, weekends are not much busier. Past midnight, middle of the week, and pissing down rain... Why these young men came all the way out to his bar at all, or have stayed so long, is beyond Rosco's understanding. Then again, Rosco—of all people—knows that there is little to this world that he *does* understand. A notion that rings too true with the sharp, ear-piercing shriek from the old hinges and the sound of pelting rain that is briefly allowed inside the dark and otherwise dry atmosphere of the *In Between*.

A late-night patron, a woman, steps in out of the rain and onto the mat. She is alone and she is unhurried, and Rosco starts to wonder about coincidences and how he does not believe that they exist. Remaining by the frosted glass door drifting close behind her, she takes a moment to shake the water from her leather jacket and her shoulder length, wavy, brown hair before venturing deeper into the establishment. Perhaps, it is fate that has kept Roscoe open after all.

The door closes with a soft click and the woman strolls up to the bar. She is no stranger to Rosco, though he has not seen her in some time. A good customer, generous tipper, and Rosco is suddenly thankful to the rowdy group of young men for having kept him open this evening. They have quieted some, and that does not please Rosco quite as much. With such a pretty woman, one who appears not so dissimilar in age, how could the group not notice her? No doubt they are watching, too, but probably not close enough to see her subtle lift of a single finger as she sidles up to the bar. Rosco, however, reads her perfectly and reaches for a bottle of whiskey before she has settled on one of the empty stools.

"Rough one, Ex?" he asks, pouring two-fingers of his best whiskey into a short glass, no ice. He knows her drink just as he knows that he will get no straightforward answer to his question, not that he expects one.

"Exceptionally."

She says nothing more and lifts the glass to her lips, tossing the drink back in a single gulp. Rosco pours another into a separate glass, ready for when the initial burn of the first drink subsides: She always has at least two.

A heavy sigh, her complement for a selection well made, and she returns the glass in hand to the cherry oak bar. Reaching for her second glass, the woman is suddenly met with company. One young buck has strayed from his group. Straightening his olive-green jacket over a plain shirt and leaning a blue-jeaned hip against the stool next to her, an arm draping over the edge of the bar, the young buck smiles.

"Hi there."

"No." Then the second glass is on its way to her lips.

She does not look at him, she does not speak to him, the young buck is stuck silent. Befuddled, perhaps, but not discouraged. The woman tosses back her second drink.

He tries again. "Can I buy you a drink?"

"No," she snaps, but for Rosco she lifts her finger to pour one more.

"Look," the young man shuffles where he stands, his hand rubbing the back of his neck. "I was wondering if maybe you would—"

"No." She tosses back her third drink.

"You don't even know what I was going to *ask*."

"No?" snaps the woman, finally turning her gaze sharply to meet his. Her hazel eyes so hot and piercing that the young man nearly recoils from his spot. "And what might it have been, that you were going to ask?" She does not shout, but her voice does come with bite, her eyebrows raised. Neither acts are obvious enough to be received by the rest of the buck's gang, despite them having grown silent, leaning forward in their chairs, leering over their mugs empty of everything but foam.

"If maybe I would go out with you?" the woman continues, locking the lone buck in an incredulous stare. "Or, if maybe I'd sleep with you, hmm? Go back to your crummy little apartment, and leave you with a tale of erotic conquest that your buddies have already bet you *won't* have, is that what you were wondering? My, my, have you barked up the wrong tree, kid."

Not only silenced, her words have the young buck stunned; they have Rosco stunned, but only the young man's nose and cheeks burn red. With damp, wavy locks of an unremarkable shade of brown contrasting so sharply against the rich intensity of blues, browns, and greens in her eyes, the woman appears both plainly dull and exquisitely striking in the same breath. The courage the young buck mustered to approach her in the first place, withers. Unable to withstand the heat of her denunciatory glare, he looks away.

The young buck is not from this city. Unlike the others, he has never been to this bar before. Hell, he barely knows the companions he has come out drinking with this night. *They* all grew up here together. *He* is the outsider, come to finish college and unwittingly found himself entangled in the group and so dragged along in celebration of graduation. He has known them for only a short while, yet it is to them he turns, nonetheless. The six of them are sitting, literally, on the edges of their seats. Hands clenching forgotten mugs long empty of beer, they lean forward, faces dripping with anticipation. That is until they do no longer.

Even before the young buck turns back to face the woman at the bar, there falls an instant change to the atmosphere: a hanging silence. None of his buddies are looking at him, but past him, to the door that suddenly sets loose a shriek. The young buck turns. He is alone at the bar. The woman is gone. The frosted glass door sighs contently as it drifts closed. In her place, her last glass stands empty next to short stack of paper bills enough to pay for her three drinks three times over.

"Best you let that one go, I'd say," Rosco speaks softly for only the young buck, as he collects the empty glasses.

A warning, or courteous dissuasion, the young buck cannot tell. Nor does he get the chance to ask. His friends have left their table and are crowding him, clapping him on the shoulder and talking excitedly.

"What happened?"

"What did she say?"

"Did you get her number?" asks one in the same moment another mentions his bad luck having struck again.

Then one whistles a long, drawn-out note—the first to notice the money on the bar that Rosco collects with a sweep of a meaty hand.

"Damn, barkeep. You got some expensive whiskey in this joint."

"She settled your tab, too." Rosco replies.

Seven faces whip toward the door, closed now and glowing an eerie white from the lamppost outside.

One young man growls, "She shot you down?" just as another snarls, "She paid *our* bill?"

"The whole *tab?*" sneers a third.

Rosco nods. "With tip."

Silence drops and, at once, spoils into something toxic and foul. Curiosity, amusement, and maybe a little wonder, corrodes into bitterness and animosity with a heaping scoop of hostility. The calm atmosphere shatters.

"That *bitch*."

"Who the hell does she think she is?"

"We should teach her a lesson," one suddenly cries.

"For cutting the legs out from under our boy, here," another joins in with a hard smack to the young buck's shoulder that pitches him forward and off balance.

"No chick insults us!"

"I'd leave it alone, if I was you," Rosco's deep and heavily accented voice cuts through their excited volley as smooth as a feather through rough air and exacting about as much deviation.

"Well, he *ain't* you," shouts one.

"Yeah!" another hollers.

"Keep outta this, barkeep," comes a third.

"We're going after her," the largest of the gang snarls, drowning out all the rising voices in the room. The muscles of his arms bulge, threatening to tear the tight, short sleeves of his white tee-shirt. "That chick thinks she is too good for us? We'll teach her a lesson."

Caught in the middle of a hot, angry surge the buck does not like, he is helpless against the wave suddenly carrying him straight for the frosted front door. The others holler over the wale from the hinges.

"Yeah, we'll teach *her*!"

"Yeah!"

"*Yeah!*"

No, the young buck silently screams, but the riptide of drunken testosterone has already swept him outside.

The rain has stopped, leaving the night pinched with chill. A full moon is out, hanging high in an inky night sky frosted with stars. The woman is nowhere to be seen. The asphalt is as black as the sky and lit only by the puddles catching light from streetlamps and moon alike. She is gone, yet that hardly stems the antagonistic tide of group. Not yet ready to give up the fight, they fan out like hunting dogs searching for the scent of a missed rabbit.

"Come on, guys, let it go. She could be anywhere by now," the young buck pleads, holding his place near the frosted door of the *In Between*, desperate for such a needless chase to end. This has already gone too far, he thinks. Hell, he should not have allowed it to get this far to begin with. He doesn't stop them, but another minute or two of pointless searching and the gang should calm—

"There she is!"

His attention whips toward the shout, to one of his group bouncing on his toes in the empty, dark intersection of Key Street at Lake Avenue, pointing vigorously at someplace further down the road.

"I see her. Come on!" He breaks into a run. The others follow without question, without hesitation, at full speed around the corner in hot pursuit.

The young buck runs, too. Fueled not by excitement—as it does clearly in the others—but, instead, the cold, resounding dread pumping through his veins. *This is going* way *too far*, he thinks, and speeds to catch them up without a clue as to what he is going to do when he does. When he rounds the corner, not only do all his buddies come into view but the woman does also, far ahead, making for an alley on the other side of the street.

She is not running. She is walking, with an easy grace as if out on a pleasant, post mid-night stroll, the moon laying a dull shine across the back of her leather jacket and calf-high boots. All of her, however, melts into shadow as she disappears between the buildings. Does she not notice a pack of ambitious young men charging after her, full bore? Does she not care? *Well, she's about to*, thinks the young buck, swallowing his trepidation as he rounds the corner into the narrow passage.

The alley is exceptionally wide. It could just have easily been a street running through a desolate part of the city if not for the unyielding brick wall closing off the other end. Past the oversized dumpsters pressed to the exterior of the tall buildings on either side, and mere paces from the wall, stands the woman. One hand on one hip, the other hanging loose and casual at her side, she sure looks awfully calm for having cornered herself in face of a gang of hot-headed, young drunks cutting off any escape. Trapped. So why are the hairs on the back of the young buck's neck the ones to rise? Why does he get the feeling that is *they* who are trapped in here with *her?*

"You boys cannot be this serious." There is an eerie hitch to her voice. A glimmer of dark amusement in her eyes is exacerbated by the glow of the moon, and the lone, young buck, standing at the very back of the pack, suddenly wants nothing more than to go home—his real home.

"You insulted us," speaks the burly leader at the front, bulging with more than just muscle.

The woman smiles, but only just. There shines delight in her cool, predatory gaze.

"No one disrespects Lance like that," growls the pack's leader. "We deserve an apology."

"Is that so?" she asks, but it is not truly a question. "And are you the ones to come and get it from me?" Her grin grows, and the young buck's skin crawls.

"Very well," speaks the woman when the other refuse to relent. "I could use the warm-up." She removes her jacket and lays it neatly across the closed lid of the dumpster nearest her. "But, if you come at me," she warns, her voice turning hard and smokey as she steps forward on slightly bent knees. "—you better come at me with everything you got." One hand she brings up in front of her chest while the other sweeps back and up as if she were to blindly pick a ripe fruit from the sky at her back.

No one moves; no one leaves. Six young men sink lower in their hips, their shoulders hunch, their hands clench into fists. *They are really going to do this*, thinks the young buck just as the alley fills with a strange, electric charge.

The hairs on his arms stand on end. Even if the young buck wanted to run, he is locked in place. Time, or reality (or maybe both), at once, become weightless. The hard silence dropped in the alley cracks when a spark ignites on the tip of the woman's outstretched fingers held aloft behind her. Suspended for a heartbeat, the buck unable to move, he watches an eerie blue-white spark of sizzling static crawl across her hand and along her arm. Every part of her the crackling, electrical charge touches, changes. The long black sleeves of her shirt shred to ribbons only to graft back together in a thicker material more like leather than the cloth it had been before. The new material coils around her hands and arms in long, resilient strips as the light passes over. *Are the others not seeing this?* The young buck wonders.

The chittering lights spreads across her shoulders and down her body all the way to her feet—not a stitch of what could be considered regular cloth remains. Her shirt, her pants, even her boots, are all torn to scrap, flying from her form to only whip back into place, altered. Zippers and buttons melt into piping and cording that crisscross over her chest, squeezing her in a flexible shell of a flat-black bodice with gleaming strips of silver. Covering the whole of her pelvis, the black material then winds down her legs before coming one with her boots. In the time to blink an eye, held suspended as if by magic, the vital parts of her lean, powerful frame are protected by the reinvented material even while showing more skin than she had before. *Huntress*, the only word the young man can rightly call her.

The light reaches the tips of her first finger of the hand she holds out in front and hovers there. Transformation complete, her lips crack into a devilish grin. "Ready?"

Six young men answer by locking their hands into fists, elbows pulled back. Their curved backs rise and fall with heavy breaths. There is no backing out. Not even for the lone buck standing with arms at his sides, with the way out of the alley mere steps away.

The crackling light winks out at her fingertips, but it does not extinguish. The alley is suddenly ablaze with an explosion of white-blue light that beats back all its shadows in one blow. Across the pavement at the woman's toes and up both walls on either side, the same crackling charge that crawled across her frame now slides along the circumference of the alley, ripping the quiet of the night to sheds with an ear-splitting discord of high-pitched chatter that rolls toward the young buck at a terrifying pace.

The six men hungry for a fight are engulfed first. Tee-shirts fly apart in pieces from bodies that seem to grow larger, bulkier, but then the light is upon the lone buck at the rear and his eyes squeeze shut. The noise, the *pressure* of the hot, white light fills him to the brim. It shakes his bones and pulses through his brain. His head—his entire being—feels ready to burst! Then, a pop and a snap, and the buzzing is gone; the light is gone. Breath returns to the young buck in a rush only to be instantly expelled at the sight before him.

The alley is exactly as it was, only now host to a macabre scene. A ragged howl replaces the buzzing of the light now absent, and the woman charges the gang of men who had chased after her. Only, the men are not *men* at all, and a cold, hard stone settles in the pit of the lone buck's stomach. The woman in skin-tight black and silver dives into a fray of swinging claws and gnashing teeth of cruel and twisted creatures.

A nightmare unfolding before his very eyes, the young buck baulks. These are not the men he came out with this night. Hell, they are not the same boys he graduated with. They wear the same pants, same shoes—albeit torn and shredded, their shirts gone entirely—but these... these are monsters. Beasts. If wild boars could be supersized and forced upright on their two hind legs, tusks protruding from their jaws, these grotesque horrors cry out with all the deranged cruelty of a man enraged as the woman leaps to meet them.

Wickedly curved claws, sharp enough to butcher a Holstein, lash out to meet her, but she is faster. All they strike is air as she ducks and bounds and disorients them into slicing one another to ribbons, without care, instead. So fast, like lightning, she darts through the narrowest gaps between the frenzied beasts desperate to cut her down. Claws run through hairy arms and across stomachs before their target pops up for a kick to a face, hard enough to break a tusk. A wild swing of claws is swept aside, to be buried into the stomach of another diving to bite her face.

So much motion, so much *chaos*, that the lone buck's mind can barely keep up. That is until the woman, flipping high, rebounds off one wall and lands unexpectedly away from the gang, but close enough to the young buck to touch.

"You don't belong here," she says, the scent of cherry blossoms on her breath instead of whiskey.

The young buck does not feel her grip on his jacket until brick walls and gruesome beasts spin around him once before he is flying freely. The young buck slams hard against the damp, black pavement of the street. He is alive, and out of the alley. And, his gaze immediately dropping to his hands, with normal human skin and form. Did that *woman* just *throw* him?

The fight has not stopped, and what the young buck sees has him scrambling back away from the alley and up on his feet. Confined within the tall, narrow space between two darkened buildings, the woman moves faster than ever. Staying low, she darts around the feet of the few monsters still standing. She leaps clear of the bunch. Flipping much higher than any person should be capable, she unleashes a power that leaves the young buck terror-stricken and running blindly away from the alley as fast as his feet can take him.

That woman... How could she turn a bit of night as bright as day? Faster, *faster*, he runs from that which he can never unsee. The sizzling, crackling forked-tongues of electric white-blue light flying from her hands, and the gang of monsters on a rain-soaked surface suddenly caught in her electrifying grip of lightning. And her face—the last image he saw, the one that plays in his head again and again, as he runs faster, *faster*.

How locked her jaw had been, her lips pulled back into either a grin or a sneer as the monsters seized and convulsed. How bright her eyes had burned! How they burn now, behind his own. So consumed with what he saw, with running from it not nearly fast enough—not knowing where he is trying to go—that when he rounds a corner at some intersection, he fails to see the tall, thin man wearing a suit that he passes, nor the solid, immovable object into which he suddenly collides. The young buck is knocked backward and off his feet, crashing to the pavement a second time.

"Easy there, young fellow," a man's gentle voice wafts to his ear.

Ignoring the water leftover by the storm soaking his hands and seat of his pants, the young buck turns his attention up, to the figure towering over him. An absolute bull of a man almost too large to believe. Nothing like the monsters from the alley, but this brute hardly passes for a clean-cut average chap. Half again taller than himself and easily twice him wide, wearing a dark, oversized trench coat that covers all from his massive shoulders down to a pair of heavy leather boots, he is—quite frankly—the largest man the young buck has ever seen.

Hair cropped military short shows off a protruding forehead

over a hard face lined with thick scars stretching from both corners of his mouth to the base of his ears and up the sides of his nose. Other than his face, only the tips of thick fingers of one hand show, the rest clad in a black glove common to hands used to frequent brawls. The other hand might be balled in fist also but cloaked in the shadow of the jacket's long cuff, the young buck can see only thick shadow and barely at that. Of what he is certain, is that the tenor voice which spoke to him certainly did not come from this brute.

He twists to find the second man standing behind him. This man is not quite as tall and far slimmer than the bull. Dressed in a smart, gray, pinstriped suit, with blond hair long enough to be swept back and gelled into place, and the slick smile of used car salesman, there is the man to match the voice.

"You appear to have had quite the fright," again speaks the man in the suit, stuffing one hand into a pocket of his pants. The other he holds up as though he might be pinching a cigarette between his empty fingers. "Whatever is the trouble?"

Whatever spell that had him dazed, breaks, and the young buck takes a hot moment to look around: dark street, dark sky brightened by a hanging moon, and a streetlamp shining its dull light on the frosted glass door of the *In Between* on his left. The bar is closed and dark. If the young buck had not spent a good portion of this night drinking inside the establishment, he'd say the place has been abandoned for years.

"I'm not sure how to explain it," he says nervously, more to himself before recalling that he is not alone on the dark street. The young buck chuckles mirthlessly. "You wouldn't believe me if I tried." Hell, *he* can hardly believe it. Something out of a nightmare. Maybe this whole night *is* a nightmare, and the young buck shakes his head.

"I see," says the man in the suit. His face appears calm but the way his eyes are pinched gives the young buck the impression that he has said too much, already. "You saw something tonight," the suit continues. "Something you cannot explain."

He steps closer, long fingers tapping at his lips. The young buck grows cold.

"I think we can help each other," the suit shuffles to a stop within an arm's reach of the young man on the pavement. "You see,

I—" he twirls his hand toward the brute. "—and my associate here, happen to be looking for someone. Someone you might call... unusual. The hard-to-believe type, in fact."

"Well," scoffs the young buck, casting a wary glance toward the titan looming over him. "Unless you're looking for a woman who turned my frien—six grown men into monsters before frying them with... with lightning," he chuckles. Hearing it all out loud, he can hardly believe it himself. Surely, he has the man in the pinstriped suit believing him mad. Displaying all the outlandish symptoms of a mental disorder, perhaps. So, it comes as a shock when the young buck looks up to find the suit not only much closer but leaning down, the sharp angles of his face barely a hand-length away. A grin as slick as grease spreads under a loathsome glare, and the young buck suddenly feels no more significant than an insect.

"I believe you, turns out," says the suit who, strangely, has no smell at all.

With a snap he is standing tall, spinning round on his heel, and flicking his hand up in the air. The young buck is hefted off the pavement by the brute. No request, no warning, only an iron grip crushing his shoulder and hauling him to his feet.

"What's more," the suit continues unabated. "I insist that you take me to this place where you saw her. It *was* down this way if I am not mistaken."

The suit walks boldly down the middle of the street back the way the buck had run. Behind him, the brute follows, leaving the lone buck no choice but to be herded along between them. Especially with the occasional hearty shove encouraging him along.

"Who—"

"No doubt you have many questions," the suit interrupts as they leave Key Street. "Sadly, there are not many answers I can give you. How you are still alive, for one. You are a lucky man. Few who find themselves caught in the path of this—" he twirls his hand again, "—*deviant*, survive to talk about it. Notorious, that one, as she is ruthless. A fugitive, of sorts. One that must be captured, brought down, allocated. A task which I aim to see completed; there is much prestige to be gained from the destruction of one as powerful as her. Young man?" The suit comes to a pause, in both speech and motion. Turning towards the young buck, he points a long finger toward the dark mouth of the alley he has led them back to, without taking a single direction. "This the, um, *alley* that you spoke of?"

A wave of cold dread would have brought the young buck to a standstill if not for the immense, persisting presence at his back: he never mentioned an alley. And the way the suit mouths the word, *alley*, as though this man has never used the word in his life, has the buck's hairs on the back of his neck standing on end.

Despite his distasteful tone in speaking the word, the suit shows no aversion at strolling into the depth of the shadowed gap. Neither does the brute. He stomps along after his companion, leaving the young buck alone on the street. Unguarded, he could run. Leave this place, these men, and return to his apartment, his life, but his feet are already plunging him back into the dark recess of the alleyway, into a space that is nothing like it was.

The alley is far deeper than it had been. The dumpsters are still in place—even her coat rests draped over the corner of one—the asphalt is still slick with rain, but where there stood a wall capping off the other end, the way is open. Empty of bodies and the woman, the passage spills out into a sprawling, sleeping city of buildings constructed more of glass and metal than brick and mortar, and stand at odd and confusing angles. An impossible city that should not be here at all.

"It's Excalibur, alright," comes the deep bass words of the brute—the first he has spoken. "I'd recognize her work anywhere."

"Where *does* she get the dragonscale for this?" asks the suit excitedly, rubbing his jaw. He had said this woman was dangerous, that he was hunting her, but it is clear to the lone buck that he admires her, too.

"Makes no difference," growls the brute with not a trace of his companion's exuberance. "She's gone now."

"So, it would seem." The suit snaps his fingers. "The closest we've come in ages."

"What about him?"

The brute's baritone voice—or rather, the quiet space it leaves behind—is what alerts the young buck that it is *him* to which the bull of a man refers. The city is forgotten, and the buck whips his gaze to the suit who stares him down considerably. The man shrugs, and the chill slipping along the buck's neck ferments into bitter panic.

"He is of no more use to us. Look at him. His mind is already beginning to unravel."

"Can I eat him?"

The brute's question is so outlandish, so ridiculous—that a man would entertain the idea of consuming another so casually—that the young buck starts to laugh. A chuckle slips out just as the suit shrugs and turns away.

"Knock yourself out. He'll be dead soon anyway."

His urge to laugh dies instantly and rots leaving the young buck feeling sickly and hollow, and surprised when his back suddenly slams against a solid brick wall.

Caught in the gleeful gaze of a mad brute, the young buck never saw what shot out from the big man's sleeve that has him so abruptly anchored. A cold, hollow sensation spreads throughout his body as the young buck's mind scrambles to make sense of the cylindrical, cone-shaped hunk of metal driven through his stomach. A drill bit, of sorts. As large around as his thigh and attached by a chain (if a chain could be made of connected reticulating plates instead of curved metal links) that disappears into the dark confines of an oversized jacket sleeve worn by the brute who has not taken a single step closer. Cold travels everywhere. He feels his face drain of heat, of life, and not solely from the harpoon impaled through his abdomen.

Metallic clinks and zips echo from the sleeve. The chain starts to retract. Squealing gears and ticking cogs sound louder and louder as the brute closes the space between him and his prey with a terrifying lack of haste. What the lone buck had mistaken for scars on the brute's face, split open. A hiss of steam—though no visible vapor escapes—and planes of the brute's face separate, elongating his jaw, broadening his head, and pulling his eyes further apart.

"Scrawny little tid-bit," speaks the giant of a man—or a machine, the young buck can no longer say. The remaining length of chain retracts into the jacket's gaping sleeve and the solid end of the harpoon links with the rest of his... arm. Mechanisms locking into place reverberate through the young buck's bones.

A scream builds in his throat and dies there. The titan's jaws unhinge and drop open wide. *Too* wide. A snake ready to swallow a mouse whole, except this python has big, bone-white teeth, though bone they are not. Firing all at once as though on pistons, they gnash together, ringing out sharply of metal striking metal with force enough to cleave through bone without the brute needing move his jaw.

I am going to die, thinks the young buck. In this strange place, in this bizarre manner. Face to face with his own demise, he is powerless to do anything about it except to darkly wonder if his body will ever be found.

No saliva drips from the giant's mouth, but the wafting noxious vapor that does, is worse. Hot, foul, moist breath engulfs him before the jaws encircling his head do. Gears wind. Something inside the brute's head ticks. Teeth click back a notch. The young buck squeezes shut his eyes. Until a shout rings out.

"Hey!"

A voice, like a silver bell, cuts through night and malodorous vapor alike. The giant's teeth slam! But the young buck lives, his head intact. The behemoth straightens and turns having also heard the sharp, feminine call.

From the other side of the street, crossing to its middle—staying well out of reach but within shouting distance—strides the woman, just as the young buck last saw her. The piping crisscrossing her form glows eerily white.

"Hands off."

"What business of yours is he?" shouts the man in the suit. The mirth in his voice thick enough to tell the young buck that he is grinning while only able to see the back of his slicked-back hair. "You don't *claim* him, do you?"

"Looks like I do."

She steps back into the same stance the lone buck watched her take before… before she did something no human can do. *Then again*, he wonders, *what are* these *men?*

"Will you be the one to take him from me?" asks the woman, grinning in the same sly manner, lifting one arm high and back.

The suit lifts one of his own out to his side. "Gladly."

All the hairs along the young buck's arm and neck stand on

end.

The suit flicks his fingers, and the world hangs in suspension. Time becomes disjointed, out of rhythm, maybe absent entirely. Tension builds as unseen forces pull from all directions. The same spark of white-blue light ignites on the tips of the woman's raised fingers. A crackling charge, again, tracks across her body. Again, changing everything it touches.

Her clothes pop and shred only to come back together, flatter this time. More than simply wrapping around her in ribbons of black silk, the material melds *with* her skin, becoming a *part* of her. To the young buck's eyes there seems to be no difference between the black, the silver, and the creamy honey glow of skin. Even her hair changes. Longer, straighter, yet fuller, and turned a brown, so deep, that it is nearly black. She is taller, longer limbed, longer torso. The definitions of her face, sharper, more elegant. A woman plucked from exuberance of youth and plunged straight into clever, exquisite maturity in the blink of an eye—she is exquisite.

At the tips of her fingers of her other hands, the light winks out and does not travel to the two men standing in her way. The men do not appear to have changed, but the rattling shuffle of metal and gears do echo up and down the dark street of the strange city. A final, locking *click*, and perfect silence veils the world.

The brute moves first. A jolt of wet suction and the cold metal impaled through the young buck's stomach is yanked free. Intense relief and a terrible flooding heat are quick to replace it as he drops to the damp street. A cold, numb ambivalence slowly invades his body, but he can hardly be bothered to notice faced with reality itself shattering to pieces. Wheeling about to face the woman, the brute rips free his over-sized jacket exposing the terribly solid mass of articulating metallic plates that is the brute's body, gleaming silver and burnt gold in the light of the moon. Not a robot, but a *man* with a body of impossible technological advancement.

This cannot be real! The young buck paws at the solid stone of the street. He tries to breathe deep but gurgles up fluid he is sure should not be coming out, instead.

Three times her size, the imposing brute whips the same arm he used to skewer the young buck. She does not flee; the woman hardly moves. Instead, she ducks. Dipping so low that her hair tickles the pavement, the plated chain and harpoon of a hand sailing over her with barely a width of a finger to spare. Keeping low, she springs forward reaching the brute before his arm extends to full reach.

A hard strike to the inside of his hip catches the brute by surprise. Grabbing his arm just above the mechanism actively retracting the chain, she evades a swipe from the other arm with a spin, torquing the one she has hold of back and around. Using the brute's own body mechanics, she forces him to his knees. A snap rings out as the harpoon hand connects with the blunt end of the brute's arm, but the woman flips over his bent forward frame before it locks into place. Another back spring takes her well out of reach.

She lands, then leaps again, and the young buck forgets the cold spreading from the gaping hole in his stomach. High in the air, much higher than a person should be able to leap, what he had feared he had witnessed before, happens again. A blast of hot, white-blue light flies from the woman's wanting hands: a rope of lightning. The crackling, broken flash strikes the brutes extendable arm… and stays there.

The end of a bullwhip of fractured, electric light coils tight around his elbow. Holding tight to her end, the woman lands and leaps into a high barrel-roll, whipping a rolling loop down along the sizzling strand. The resounding force is terrific. The brute's arm jerks and is spun so quick, so violently, that metal plates shatter. Internal mechanisms are mangled and torn asunder. Severed, the arm flies free and strikes the brick wall close enough to the young buck to shower him with bits of scrap. The disjointed rope of light winks out.

A howl fills the night. Enraged, in pain, and on his knees, the brute paws at the air where his arm should be. The woman does not stop to survey her work; the man in the suit has flanked her—the young buck never saw the man move.

The suit has not changed, but the man wearing it certainly has. Like the woman, his limbs have lengthened more than twice their original reach. There is no gleam of metal the young buck can see, only flesh pokes out from sleeves suddenly too short and pant cuffs absurdly high. By all appearances, the man in the suit should be gangly, yet he throws punches and kicks with fluid, cat-like grace, and the woman is taking special care to not get too close. Except once.

Evading a wheeling kick to her face, she rushes the man in the suit, thrusting the heel of her hand hard against his ribcage. A swipe of her elbow to follow knocks the man in the suit off balance. The woman bounds away quickly, well out of reach even by the suit's standards. A flash illuminates the darkness as another rope of fractured light snaps into existence, this time peeled up from the rain-soaked street. With a crack, the other end whips around the suit's torso. The woman leaps again.

Handspringing backward, she flings an arch down the length of the tethered bolt. The suit is lifted right off his feet. She tucks into a barrel-roll, sending another ripple that swings him in a wide circle overhead. Pulling tight her end, she hurls the man in the suit through the air. The rope bursts in dazzling white sparks and the man flies free to smash through glass on a high floor of a multi-leveled building across the street.

The brute has recovered his wind and ferocity. On his feet, he charges the woman, her back still turned. The young buck tries to shout, but he is too cold, too numb, and bubbling too much fluid out of his nose and mouth. Maybe she heard him anyway. Quick feet and the brute's giant hand smashes down on only air, sending him stumbling. The woman goes on the attack. Punches, kicks, every blow lands. With each, the brute sags under his own monstrous, metallic bulk even though—to the young buck—she does not appear to be causing any damage.

In a last, desperate effort, the brute throws a wild swing with his remaining arm. The woman simply steps slightly aside. Grabbing the extended arm by the wrist, she rolls, ducks, and twists and—with strength the young buck would have thought impossible before this night—the woman throws the brute toward the same building she sent the suit crashing into. His body hits the hard ground with a crash and clatter to rival that of a derailed train car. Rolling end over end he, too, is sent bowling through glass but on the ground floor.

The woman holds her place in the middle of the street, triumphant. Lifting both arms, a great storm erupts from her hands. Static from the broken, white light crawls through her hair, along her arms, and down her legs. Long, tendrils of crackling, snapping, white-blue light dances across the pavement at her feet. Greedily, they race for the building, surround its base, and climb hungrily up the sides. Glass explodes and metal cries out before it all splinters to shards. The building crumbles to the ground, spewing a cloud of dust into the air despite the damp.

The night goes quiet.

Cold, and with only the brick wall keeping his back upright, there is nothing the young buck can do when the woman turns her sights upon him. He can't even hold his breath when she approaches. He can only wonder silently what frightening and exhilarating way she will finish him off.

Unhurried, but without delay, she crosses the street and kneels before him. Her eyes bright as polished ammolite, all her attention is on the hole in his body.

"First rule." She speaks coolly, as one might to a child who just scraped his knee. "Reputation is everything. Leave them alive when you can. Scarred," she emphasizes quickly as to not miss an important detail, "and with a story to tell. There, that ought to do for now." She wipes the palms of her hands together; a dirty job now done. "What are you called?"

It takes the young man a full blink to grasp that she is asking for his name. He nearly laughs at the idea. Can she not see the condition he is in? Or the hole drilled through his middle? He is at death's front door, picking the lock, and she is asking for his *name?*

A wave of warmth suddenly floods his body. Not just warm, but hot! The cold, the sinking chill, burns away like rice paper to a flame. A chuckle bubbles up his throat. No fluid comes with it. He is *alive?*

The young man stares at her. "Lance," he answers, astonished at how strong his own voice sounds.

The woman chuckles. "Of course, it would be that. Well, that certainly won't do. Names in this place are given by those who claim you. Traditionally, after the location from where you are pulled." She hums thoughtfully, her gaze wandering about up and down the street.

He busies himself with probing his stomach where a gaping hole... *had* been. What his fingers find instead is a hard, somewhat rough shell. It's not cold; it's not metal, but he is not sure if the relief he feels is deserved or not.

"Laine," speaks the woman. "Yes, I think that is appropriate."

"But—"

"This is how things works here, kid. Best get used to it. *That* is yours, by the way." She nods her chin to the discarded, dismembered metallic aberration that once served as a brute's hand. "Take it, and I could call you Harpoon."

"Harpoon? *Kid?*" Lance—*Laine*—is surprised again at the strength and ease of his voice, of his chest, his body. And here, he had been so sure that he di— "What are *you* called?"

The woman grins. Not with sweetness, but satisfaction. "You'll do fine here. I am called Nimue, Lady of Water. I am also called Excalibur, the Sword Who Sings. Come."

Taking him by the hand, she pulls. Despite the warmth of his body, doubt follows Laine all the way to his feet. He will fall the instant she lets go. So sure, that he is not at all ready for the sturdiness he finds in his legs instead. Laine stands with all the strength and vigor he had before ever laying eyes on this strange woman; before he followed her, not once, but twice to places he should not have. His hands fly to his stomach and the solid material he finds there.

"What did you do?"

"Dragonscale; the last I had. Not much of that stuff exists anymore, you know. There will never be another like you." Her voice takes on a more serious tone. "Time will tell if I made the right call. But you didn't turn into a pig like the others, so there is hope."

"Hope for what?"

She smiles, this time with warmth that reaches her brightly glowing gemstone eyes. "To make a hero out of you, of course. Come." She does not touch him this time, but does nods her head to one side, encouraging him to follow. "Your mind is new and fragile; you can still break. There is much for you to learn if you are to survive. Best we get started."

Color is returning to a sky growing brighter. A sun is on the verge of cresting the horizon, but the wrong horizon. The woman—Nimue—is walking in the other direction without leaving Laine time to wonder where they are or why he finds it all so... wrong. A brief glance to the mangled, severed mechanical arm laying in a pool of dark liquid on the pavement, half propped up against the wall he swears was not always there, sends the spiny prickles of apprehension coursing down his spine.

Why does part of him wants to remember an alley being here instead of a solid brick wall stretching from horizon to horizon, under a sun too big and too orange and rising from the wrong side of the World?

How did he get here? Laine has no answer.

Has his name always been *Laine?* Somehow, he doesn't think so. But, hell, what else would it be? Other queer questions swim through his head, each as ridiculous and unanswerable as the next, and him without any answers. His only key is walking away from him, the black ribbons crisscrossing her body shine dully in the growing dawn. Laine follows her. Into a world his has never known, he will follow her anywhere.

Tales in Hindsight

Tales in Hindsight

Tales in Hindsight

✦ Last Call ✦

𝔄 maiden closes the cover of the large book resting in the folds of her skirt.

Young skin lovingly caresses the worn leather faded to a pale tan from age and use. An old book, a brown lump not unlike an island alone in the ruffled sea of soft, pale blue fabric.

"The end," she coos to the young girl nestled tight against her. Caressing the girl's shaggy, red-brown hair, the maiden almost believes her asleep, as what usually happens while being read a tale from the old book. But then—

"Wow," comes an innocent sigh laced with enough wonderment to beat back the maiden's sorrow. "That was the best story yet!"

Showing no sign of fatigue whatsoever, the young girl leaps from the folds of the blanket wrapped around them both.

"Can't you just imagine it?" she cries and bounds across the floor on nimble feet, careful not to touch the furniture in the large bedroom. Except for the large wooden chest in the center of the room, that she springs upon. Leaping to its closed lid, arms flailing, wielding invisible weapons against non-existent foes, a barrage of nondescript battle sounds flying from her lips.

"A fight to the death!" she cries. "Honor and bravery against the wicked and unjust. The *action*. The excitement! The adventure, finding something new just up ahead." A final flurry and the child collapses with a sigh back to her place at the maiden's side. "Do you think we'll ever go on an adventure like that?"

"Maybe." The maiden is gentle in both word and touch as she

smooths the girl's hair—what a mess Ophelia makes of herself, when she bounces around like that. "Maybe someday."

"Someday soon." The child yawns.

"Perhaps." The maiden wraps tighter around them the blanket that they share, huddled as they are against the wall in the bedroom's last remaining safe corner—there is something wrong with the bed now, too. It has gone grey, as nearly all things have.

"Will you tell me another story?"

"There aren't any more."

"Maybe there's just one more."

"Go to sleep now," says the maiden softly, gently, effectively hiding her own sadness while stroking the fur-like red-brown hair thick between the child's extraordinary ears.

"Maybe you'll find one tomorrow?"

"Shh," is all the Maiden can muster to soothe the child to sleep without relenting to tears. She cannot bring herself to speak truer words—that there is no tomorrow, that there will never be one again. There is no day, there is no night. There is only the seeping, draining grey.

Everything is grey.

The bed is grey. The wardrobe is grey. The vanity, the rugs, the curtains draping the sides of grey window frames, all of it, grey. Only patches of the rich mahogany walls remain, and only in the corner against which the pair huddles. Their blanket of red and black squares is faded, but a colorful gem in a world so bleak otherwise. The pale blue of the maiden's skirt and the leaf-green of her blouse are the boldest colors in the room—in the World, for all she knows. Drifting away into the sweet serenity of sleep, Ophelia's fierce orange tunic and buckskin trousers are the richest. There are more clothes in the large chest that also carries some golden brown of the oak it is made of, but not for much longer. Nowhere else are there such colors. All have bled away, leaving only the flat, colorless grey behind.

It is more than an absence of color, something else seems to be draining away. Despite having lost all tone and hue, the bed is still soft to the hand that dares to touch it, but the comfort it promises is a lie. A trick. One meant to entice, to offer rest—what harm could *grey* really do? — but then comes the leaching. The sinking sensation of dread that consumes any who lies there too long. Dare to sleep and vanish. The entire city is this way. Perhaps the kingdom. Who knows how far the grey has reached? How much has it eaten? The maiden certainly does not know, nor is she prepared to find out.

Father had told her to stay put; that he would send for her once he found a place safe from the grey. He left the castle ages ago, and the maiden has not seen him since. He was not the first, and certainly not the last. One by one, every member of the household vanished. The townspeople, too. Just... gone. Everything about them, *gone*, as if they never were. Only the grey is left behind. And it has grown.

There is a window close enough to wear she sits that, with minor effort, the maiden could look out and gaze upon the grounds beyond the room, but she will not. She already knows what awaits her eyes and cannot bear to see it again: An empty city is all that is left of her kingdom. The pain in her chest is nearly overwhelming. So tight the squeeze of fear; so short her breath holding back the tears that yearn to fall—she has done all she can.

An eerie quiet fills the once lavish boudoir.

They are the last. Soon, even they will be gone. Lost. Consumed in grey.

No one is coming.

Is this the *end?*

Both women scream as the heavy oak door suddenly flies open with a crash as loud as cannon fire. An explosion that shatters the sinking stagnate hush and sends the Maiden's arms encircling the child to immediately draw her tighter against her body. But there is no cannon, the door is not damaged. Filling the grey space of the open frame is a man. A tall man. His broad, powerful shoulders are wrapped in a cloak of such rich gold that one might think it spun of the very substance.

"Last call, ladies," his deep voice shakes the air no longer used sound. His back straight, he pays the women each a critical glace from deep blue eyes. "Let's go." With that, he turns and walks away. His sturdy boots leave heavier footfalls that grow quieter with each step, each step taking him further.

He is going to leave, the maiden gleans, and he is not going to wait. Her heart begins to pound like never before. That cloak, the gold of it, is one she knows well. It is the cloak of a huntsman—one of her *father's* huntsman. Could it be that he made it to safety after all? The maiden dares to hope. A glance is shared between woman and child before both are scrambling to their feet, the greying blanket—no longer red nor black—hits the grey wall with hardly a sound and is forgotten. The pair make quick for the chest still clinging to its remnants of color, and together they dig out apparel more suitable for travel—both knowing that they will not be coming back.

There isn't much time and neither change out of what they already wear more than they don additional layers. With Ophelia wrapped in a heavy jacket of buckskin dyed red and her favorite fur cap (the one with a tail hanging off the back), the maiden chooses her best suede waistcoat and a tan, rough-spun cloak with a deep, oversized hood to keep back any chill. Boots for walking pulled snug and laced tight, the maiden grabs lastly her satchel. Hand in hand, the pair bolt from the room in hot pursuit of the gold-cloaked figure already at the bottom of the long, grey staircase.

The hard, wood floor of the upper halls and the marble steps of the fat, curved staircase leading to the main floor below have been grey for some time. The clap from hard leather soles of their boots sounds strangely dull, foggy, and dim, as though they wore muffs over their ears. Nor does the floor feel all that solid. Firm for sure—they are in no danger of falling through—but certainly not the unrelenting density that wood or stone should have. For the maiden, she might as well be chasing the man across dirt, hard packed, over a rotten floor ready to give way.

In the sub-floor kitchen and stores, the pair catch the hunter up, finding him digging through what was left of the dry goods. He does not seem to notice their arrival, or he does not care, but the maiden gets her first good look at him. His wild hair is dark as the void, deeper still against sickly, shadowed grey of the cellar. His tunic is a forest green, darker than her own grass green blouse hidden now under her waistcoat and cloak. Where his trousers are gray, they are not the same *grey* that has consumed her kingdom. His gray is an actual shade of color—an ash gray—rather than the stark absence of color leached. Still, they give the maiden pause, leaving her to stare at where those trousers are tucked into the shining black leather of his tall boots. If it were not for a hunter's sharp gold cloak wrapped about his shoulders, she would not be convinced that this man does, indeed, stand before her.

The hunter, too, carries a satchel, hanging from a single strap across his shoulders. Oversized yet bulging full, he does not stuff into it the supplies he plunders. Those he hands to the maiden to carry in hers.

"What are you doing?" With a thousand other more important questions, the maiden silently chastises herself for leading with *that* one.

"It's a long journey. Here." He hands her two more potatoes, a heel of bread, and a handful of turnips, all grey. Cold as rocks and heavy as feathers, yet he continues to shove supplies into her hands.

"We can't eat these," she protests, but stows them in her satchel as requested. "They're all grey and useless."

The hunter does not reply, nor does he stop his rummaging.

Through the servants' quarters to the stairs leading up and outside, he finds a small waist pouch, sticks of flint, and a good knife—all of them colorless and flat. These he pushes into the hands of the curious young girl in the fur hat.

"Where have you been?" the maiden asks. "Did Father send you? Is he safe?"

He gives no answer.

Out the service door, the three leave the castle for the faded yard of grey grass lacking all definition—more a pencil drawing smudged by an inexperienced left hand had the maiden been compelled to look.

"Where are the others? How far have you come? Why have you not brought more huntsmen with you?"

Passed the livery and the stables, both quiet and all but transparent, the hunter speaks not a word. Beyond the palace walls to the grey cobblestones of the streets cutting through the heart of the silent, grey city, the maiden's questions refuse to relent.

"How far does the grey go? Do other kingdoms suffer as we? Where are we going? *What is happening?*" Her voice cracks, but the hunter does stop, at last.

In the grey space under the once grand, stone arch over the main gate and entrance to her once proud kingdom, he faces her. The maiden is tall, only a head shorter than he. Though he may have to tip his head to meet her gaze, he certainly does not look down on her.

"Look, Empress," he speaks gently and with precise care. "I know you have questions, and I will give you all the answers I can—I give you my word—but now is not the time. We have far to go, and we must get there before *It* does."

"Before *what* does?"

The hunter's steady gaze dares a glance to the lump of grey that was once a city standing at her back. "The *End*, of course."

With nothing more to say, he turns and strolls out through the archway more cloud now than stone. The assuredness of his stride tells the maiden that she will get no more answers from him. For now, at least.

The hunter does not stick to the road; it fades into nothing after a few paces anyway. Instead, he cuts into a field of either grass or crop, the maiden cannot tell which for all the indistinct grey. After a moment's hesitation and a shared glace, the two ladies—one tall and fully into womanhood, the other small, younger, and curiously unique—follow.

The trio begin to walk.

Which way they go does not seem to matter; the landscape is nothing but grey. Direction has ceased to exist. How far they walk does not matter either; the maiden cannot rightly say when she lost sight of her faded kingdom. The grey is absolute. Even far beyond the walls of her forgotten home there is no night, no day. Time, it seems, is nowhere to be found. The three souls simply walk. Two follow the one in the lead along a path they cannot see.

Lost in the monotony of step after step through grey, over grey ground, under a grey sky, that the maiden cannot rightly recall *when* the world around them begins to change—when the grey begins to fill with color. Color that, despite it overtaking the depressing sink of grey, is such a quandary in itself that the maiden cannot decide which is more alarming. Instead of indiscriminate shades of graphite, the ground is covered with distinct, sharply defined blades of grass. Real grass! Barely tall enough to reach over the toes of their boots and swaying in a gentle breeze that also arrives just as obscurely. Alive, and with a healthy, soft crunch underfoot, every blade is right in every detail except for being entirely the wrong color. The grass—though vibrant—is a rich, radiant purple. Great rolling plains in various shades of shifting twilight are stirred by gentle gusts under a sky that feels much too big.

The sky is also not the color the maiden feels it should be. Instead of the color she cannot rightly say it was once, overhead is a patchwork of dusky pink hues with soft, puffy clouds lazily drifting by in radiant shades of yellow, from golds not quite as vibrant as the hunter's cloak, to the deep tones of roasted lemons. The hunter leads them into their path, always into the wind.

They must be going *somewhere*, thinks the maiden, in this land that is more like a dream.

The fog of the omnipresent grey lifts and the sun returns. But it, too, is wrong. The great orb is far larger than the maiden queerly suspects it should be and is the color of an overripe tangerine beginning to rot with red-brown spots. An *old* sun. Though it casts light plenty bright enough to see by, it is dim, faint, with hardly the presence to produce worthwhile shadows and the air is always cool. When night returns, the world is downright chilly.

Under a sky saturated in pearl-pink speckled with stars more turquoise or sharp azure than the dazzling white the maiden excepts them to be, the trio stops. Camp is made and a fire is started. There is no wood to be found for there are no trees. The hunter, instead, gathers rocks, all various shades of lime. The maiden watches as he removes from his satchel an extraordinarily large shell, one side curling in on itself. From this he extracts a long, thin, glass vile nearly full of a sparkling, white substance as fine and delicate as snowflakes.

Ophelia is the one who leans in close as he uncorks the vial and sprinkles a pinch of its contents over the stones he has piled. Stopping up the vial and returning it to the shell, and the shell to his satchel, the hunter pauses long enough to catch Ophelia's eye. His smile is small and simple when he gets it. The likeness of an older brother about to show off a trick to his kid sister that makes the maiden hide a grin of her own. A flick of his fingers and the powder ignites. The rocks catch as would any log or branch, and flames of dazzling, diamond white lick skyward. Within easy reach of the fire's radiant warmth, the trio rests for the first time since embarking on this quest, impossibly long ago.

By day, they walk. When the sun sets, they rest under a moon almost the right color of bleached bone but does not change phase or track across the night sky. They sleep little and eat less though the food and supplies they have brought have also regained color—even if the turnips are emerald green and the potatoes shine as silver as trout—the desire for either is curiously absent.

The hunter rarely speaks, yet he hardly seems perturbed by the presence of his female companions. Even when Ophelia more than makes up for his, and the maiden's, more taciturn behavior in regaling them with wild tales spun over the sparkling opal flames of their nightly fires. Some of her tales the maiden recognizes from the book she once read to her. But, like the grass and the sky and the flames of their little fires lit by the curious powder, her recounts of those old tales are not quite right—not that it dissuades her exuberant recount. Twice she catches the hunter grinning.

Impressed by Ophelia's tales, the hunter begins to teach her tricks; he teaches her magick. Simple magick, he says. Old magick. The oldest, in fact, he teaches her Light magick. Short bursts of gold spark from her fingertips, aided by a pinch of the ethereal white substance he guards. Ophelia learns quickly. Soon, she is better at the trick than the hunter and, with her new-found sparkle, her tales start to grow. More elaborate, more exciting, and positively electric.

With the added dazzle of gold sparks, she begins to tell all new tales. Tales of her own. So vivid, so wild, so enrapturing that, at some point, a thought begins to nag in the mind of the maiden. The question of who, exactly, is taking care of whom? When did Ophelia no longer seems so young? Or, maybe, when was it that *she* no longer felt so much older? A state as queer as the grass and the sun, and the wind growing more intense with each passing day.

Staring at her feet, shielding her face from the day's battering winds, the maiden does not see when the land begins to rise, though she can feel it in her legs as their walk turns into more of a climb. The purple grass grows sparse. Green rocks from large boulders to towering, sharp fins of some make-believe behemoth monster that might be buried just under the surface, litter the land. Trees appear and they do not seem right, at all. Tall, round, twisted trunks are striated with contrasting shades of blue and red, and crowned with wide, flat-bottomed canopies of translucent leaves that sparkle as though coated with a fine layer of opal. Their limbs dance in gusts that threaten to rip the clothes straight off the passing travellers.

Gusts turn in to gales, and the air grows colder and colder. The hunter leads on. The trio bunch tightly together, heads bent into the winds as they walk. The leaves rattle. Their coats and cloaks flail. Ophelia's hat goes flying. Yet higher and higher the Hunter trudges, the women close at his heels. The winds are unrelenting and brutal as if they possess a desperation of their own to smash the travellers to the ground, to stop them from proceeding any further. Ophelia's tales stop altogether as the violent winds follow them into the night. Too turbulent for sparks of magick and the nightly fires stop as well. Grey slowly returns. Not to the landscape, but its creeping tendrils sneak their way into the maiden's mind.

How long have they travelled? How far from her kingdom have they gone? Does it even exist anymore? The maiden has no answer. Days become inconsistently long, nights short and forgettable. The wind blows all the time. Their going is slow. But to *where* are they going? She wonders as they march directionless, aimless. Without word, without explanation, frustration taken to root in the maiden belly builds and churns. An angry gale whips her rough spun cloak back from her shoulders and the large hood from her head. If not for a sturdy clasp at her neck, the maiden would surely have lost her cloak, as well—she nearly sets loose a holler. Without the protection of her hood, the savage winds rob her of breath and beat at her face and her ears. Its icy chill rakes every patch of exposed skin, and the maiden swallows her voice.

The winds are worse than the grey.

Where the grey had been a lazy, creeping sort of cold, the wind is pure chaos. So full of rage, of lust and desire, always searching, never settling, they buffet the trio's every advancement, beating at them relentlessly. As turbulent as waves of a storm-raged sea, it comes at them from everywhere. It is hard to breathe. The maiden manages to only in gasping, coughing fits as if she might be taking in water instead of air.

Walking abreast a sharply inclined hill offers no shelter or buffer from the relentless winds. In fact, it only results in making them stronger, channeling gusts back to assault the travellers a second time. They catch Ophelia off guard. She stumbles and the hunter's wildly whipping gold cloak instantly comes into the maiden's view. Her quick grab of the falling buckskin jacket ahead is all the keeps Ophelia on her feet.

Had she made a mistake?

With her hand gripping the shoulder of the girl well on her way into womanhood, worry blossoms in the maiden's heart. She could shout at the hunter—and nearly does—demand to know where they are, where they are going, and *what the point is for all this*. Did he not promise answers to her questions? Questions she has kept quiet. Questions she has not uttered once since abandoning her birthrate to the grey. She *deserves* answers. Yet, no matter how strong the desperation, no matter how she might yell or scream, the howl of the winds would drown-out her voice. Her questions, let alone her demands for their answers, would never reach the ears of the hunter mere paces ahead. Her vexation would be bled away in vain.

The hunter leads on. One arm held up to protect his face from the crushing waves of wind, he maintains his pace as assuredly as he had when they began. He is silent. Never complaining, never *talking*. That is, until the maiden thinks she can hear his voice shouting, calling to her. Daring to look up from her feet, she braves the wind to see his face turned to her, his shaggy, dark hair flailing as wildly as his gold cloak. Around the girl between them, their gazes meet.

He *is* shouting at her. His deep voice, caught by the wind, sails to the maiden's ears impossibly slow and seemingly from more than twice the distance. His words are all but lost, gobbled by the raging atmospheric howl. The maiden can make sense of none of it and can only respond with a shake of her head. Lifting the arm not shielding his face, he points to the solid flank of the hill rising sharply next to them. Surely, he is not suggesting they *climb*. They would not make it halfway before the winds ripped them away sending them crashing to the ground. The maiden opens her mouth to protest, but the winds steal her breath with wet, icy claws. The hunter stops his shouting. He stops his pointing. Turning back into his arm protecting his face, he marches more determined than ever into the wind.

The frigid rage of the wind seeps in through the maiden's cloak. The constant, unabating riptide of this waterless ocean, beating them as waves against a rocky shore, is wearing them down and leaving her cold, lost, and angry. She very nearly shouts all her frustration—wind be damn, the hunter *will* hear her—when the hill sudden falls away. The wind dies in such a rush that the maiden nearly stumbles. Her breath returns in such a rush that she chokes on it. Her anger and frustration evaporate in an instant, to be immediately replaced with awe at the sight suddenly before her. Where she should be staring at the sharp incline of hillside there is, instead, an impossible place.

In the middle of a bright day, under a giant, dull orange sun, stands a hole in the world. A hidden pocket of sparkling night, a passage into a space as cavernous as it is never ending. Stars bedazzle a dark sky that seems to curve over a town, or city perhaps, twinkling with lights beyond the sharp edge of a short, grassy plateau. And connecting the hidden World below to the stary sky above, is a gigantic tree of wonderous proportions. Curling roots that dwarf any other tree the maiden has ever seen anchor the giant to ground out of sight far below the plateau. Its limbs reach so high that, not only do they seem to touch the sky, but the ends of branches meld with it, disappearing into the deep, obsidian expanse as it would into a canopy of leaves.

The hunter not only appears unfazed by the sight but is the only one smiling. From his satchel, he removes the one other item he carries, wrapped in a sheet of thin, supple linen. Folding back the cloth and stuffing it back into his satchel, and the maiden stares wide-eyed at the book exposed in his hands. A book she recognizes. A book she *knows*. But his is new, with tight, new binding and rich with color where her copy had been faded and left behind in her kingdom she abandoned.

The hunter runs his hands across the book, caressing the new, sturdy leather, then steps undaunted onto a path of large, flat stones leading toward the tree. The stones glow faintly in the light of a large moon already on the wane, but the hunter gives them not a second glance. Nor does he to the flowers blooming in rich pinks, bright blues, and deep purples skirting the path he walks. His head does not turn to pay heed of the lantern bugs flittering about from petal to petal. He does not look back to the two women waiting at the edge of night and day: the hunter sticks to his path. At the edge of the plateau, the hunter crosses a bridge made of stone and twisting tendrils of thick roots spanning the gap between solid ground and the towering tree. On the other side, wide, flat stones wind up the bark of the massive, twisted trunk; a grand staircase made for giants to ascend to the World above.

The hunter is terribly dwarfed that the maiden can barely see him as he picks his way up the stone steps. What a view the hunter must have. What sights he must see! But the hunter does not look about. He sticks to the path up to a shallow alcove the maiden had not yet noticed carved into the trunk. Nor did she spot the lantern hanging there, lit, brightening up the door she hadn't seen either until the hunter is standing before it.

She cannot see the handle, but she does watch the hunter push the door open a crack. Kneeling, he slips the book through the gap, laying it to rest on a floor of some place beyond the stars, before closing the door and turning for an unhurried retreat.

As quickly as he made his way to the door nestled high in the tree, the hunter returns to the maiden. He meets her questioning gaze with his own steady and sure.

"This is where you were going, all along," she says, sounding as though she had asked a question, but *ask* she does not. "Even before you came for us."

The hunter nods without breaking their gaze. "Yes."

"My father did not send you."

He shakes his head. "No." But one corner of his mouth does crack upward: pleased.

"This place... we were—my *kingdom* was not on your way, was it?"

"No."

"Then, why?"

The hunter's reticent grin grows emboldened. Delighted and charmed, he answers her true. "Because I knew *you* were there, Empress."

"How?"

"The book told me, of course."

"What book?"

He does not answer; he does not have to. A slight break in their gaze, and the maiden, once more, seeks out the tiny door in the giant tree stretched between Heaven and Earth.

"*That* book—" she points to where the tree stands. "—told you where I was?"

"Yes."

"And you believed it? Enough to risk..." her breath draws in tight, but she forces the words out. "—to risk the *End?*"

"It was the only way."

"The only way to do what?"

"To stop the *End* from coming, Empress."

Cut to the quick, the maiden stalls. A moment of silence drops with awe and the maiden is quieted. The wind has died. Peace reigns.

In the face of uncertainty, poised on the edge between disbelief and potential, a startling Earth-shaking cry shatters the silence. High above, a magnificent beast tears through the bright pink sky of day. A wingless, serpentine beast—if only she could think of what such a beast is called. All white with splotches of black, the long, sinuous creature falls from the heavens more than it seems to fly from it. Swimming through the sky, the pink turns to a saturating blue in its wake as the monstrous, serpentine beast makes fast for the distant horizon.

"It worked," the hunter mutters, his gaze for the lands where the beast might fall.

"Did you see *that?*" shouts Ophelia, excitedly scampering after the creature a few paces before coming to a stop and turning back. "Did you see it? What was that?"

"A dragon," answers the hunter, calm as ever. "The last of its kind." But then he gives a shrug, a hopeful grin playing on his lips. "Or, maybe, the first."

The maiden whips back to face him. His dark hair, his kind, truthful eyes, his golden cloak no longer the most vivid color in the world, all bathed in the soft glow of a giant, orange sun on the rise. Out of the night, new day begins and not only for her.

All things are changing in the dragon's wake. The purple of the grass brightens, turning green. Twisted, spindly trees straighten. The blue of their trunks deepens to rich shades of brown, the red to tan and black; the translucent opal of their leaves matures to more placid tones of red, orange, and yellow on the brink of falling to make way for fresh, new green ones.

"There will be more changes to come."

The hunter's words are quickly drowned out by the frantic bouncing and hollering of a young woman fresh out of girlhood. Ophelia comes running to the maiden's side, one hand pointing back in the direction where the beast has disappeared.

"Let's go after it! *I'm* going after it." She tugs at the maiden's hand, looking to the hunter when she does not budge. "Come on! What are we waiting for?"

In that moment, faced with a child-no-longer, eager for tales of her own—true tales—bursting with such joy that she is positively glowing, the maiden knows, beyond doubt, that a grand adventure is about to begin. One that does not belong entirely to her.

In their journey to this outpost, this tree between Worlds, Ophelia has grown. Nearly as tall as the maiden is herself, strong, able, and brimming with tenacity with a pocket full of wonder, the child from the fading kingdom is gone and a young woman stands in her place. The maiden has no choice. She relents with a sad smile full of warmth.

"You're ready for that adventure now," she says to the youth before her, squeezing tightly her hands before letting go. "You've lost your hat, and you will need a better cloak."

Trading the girl's—young woman's—jacket for the maiden's rough spun cloak, she fastens the clasps around Ophelia's shoulders and draws up the oversized hood concealing her remarkable ears.

"You will need an offering when you find him," speaks the hunter, stepping forward, unburdening his shoulders of his satchel to drape it across those of the young wildling and taking from her the pouch in turn. "Take care of it," he warns with a final glance to the satchel and the shell with its secret vial snug inside. "There is no more until you find what you are looking for."

A wash of sadness briefly dims the wildling's inquisitive eyes when she understands that they will not be going with her. Just a flash, then it is gone, with fiery determination burning in its place.

"Remember, the best way to find dragons," says the hunter, "is to follow their tales."

With a shine from dry, excited eyes, the hunter and the maiden are also gifted with a final smile before the young wildling is running, with all her might, after the beast that fell from the skies not moments before.

The maiden, knowing full well she will never again see the wildling outside of her dreams, does not watch her run for long. She turns to her hunter who has not left—who will never leave.

"What now?"

The hunter tips his head after Ophelia shrinking quickly for the horizon. "The last of the dragonscale just took off after the only creature that can make it. More will come and we will need to be ready to harvest."

With that, he turns and begins to walk in the opposite direction, toward the lands from which the beast had come. Just a few paces, before stopping and turning back to the maiden who has not yet moved.

"I'm not doing this without you, Empress."

The maiden chuckles warmly. "Did the book tell you that?"

He shrugs, casting his gaze over the valley stretching far into the distance between two hills, right where the land of night had been but is no longer. "It doesn't matter now."

Relieved of his bag and his burden, he is left with a small pouch with an even smaller knife. And she with an empty satchel and the clothes on her back. The maiden drops the jacket that is too small for her. What *does* it matter?

She nods. "True."

He smiles. She will join him and together they will hunt for more dragonscale, for they have nothing left to lose.

"True," the Empress says again, quieter this time, testing her enjoyment of the word, rolling it across her tongue.

Liking it very much, she follows.

Tales in Hindsight

MUSICAL INSPIRATION

Carp by Double Noize
Dragon Empress by BrunuhVille
Monody by TheFatRat ft Laura Brehm
Festival of Light by Audiomachine
Enter the Promise by Sebastien van der Rohe
Secret of Natraja by VSNS
Weeper by Savant
Uluwatu by Dropgun & Jesse Wilde
Launch by Diskour & Annexed
Warrior by Anilah
Mares of the Night by Glen Gabriel
Climbing the Skies by Black Coyote
Sheet by Cupidz
A Place in the Stars by David Chappell

Tales in Hindsight

ABOUT THE AUTHOR

Watkins sailed in, one glorious afternoon, on a steadfast ship with many rooms for books and bunnies and guests. Drawn ever onward, guided by the whisper of adventure, Watkins travels waters beyond the charted map seeking shores of lands wherein dwells myth and legend.
With her small but loyal crew of fellow artists, Watkins makes for horizons of worlds yet unseen, and the priceless treasures hidden within.

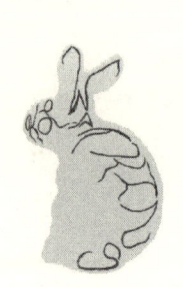

Made in the USA
Columbia, SC
01 July 2022